The VARSITY DAD Dilemma

USA TODAY BESTSELLING AUTHOR
LEX MARTIN

The Varsity Dad Dilemma Copyright © 2021 Lex Martin

All rights reserved. This book may not be reproduced or transmitted in any capacity without written permission by the publisher, except by a reviewer who may quote brief passages for review purposes.

This is a work of fiction. Names, characters, businesses, places, events and incidents are either the products of the author's imagination or used in a fictitious manner. Any resemblance to actual persons, living or dead, or actual events is purely coincidental.

This adult contemporary romance is recommended for readers 18+ due to mature content.

Copy editing by RJ Locksley

Proofreading by Julia Griffis, The Romance Bibliophile

Cover by Najla Qamber Designs

Model Photograph by Perrywinkle Photography

First Print Edition

ISBN 978-1-950554-02-7

ABOUT THE NOVEL

What's worse than having Rider Kingston, the star quarterback, give you the big brush-off because he doesn't want to get serious? You'd probably think living across the street from him where you get a firsthand view of his hookups, right?

That's what I thought. Until someone drops off a baby with a note pinned to her blanket that says one of those jocks—either Rider or one of his roommates—is the father. The problem? Baby mama doesn't mention which of these numbskulls is the sperm donor.

I wouldn't care about their paternity problems—not the slightest bit—except my brother lives there too. Which means that adorable squawking bundle might be my niece, and there's no way I'm leaving her unattended with those bumbling football players.

They need my help, even if they don't know it yet. Once we solve this dilemma and figure out who's the daddy, I'm out.

I'll just ignore Rider and those soul-searing looks he gives me every time I reach for the baby. He broke my heart three years ago. He won't get a second chance.

As always, to Matt & my girls

"We must be willing to let go of the life we have planned, so as to have the life that is waiting for us."
— E.M. Forster

1

GABBY

WITH A FEW TAPS on my iPad, I pull up the interview questions I prepped over the weekend.

A quick glance at my roommate Ramona tells me she thinks this is a waste of time, but she just needs to trust the process.

I smile at Ramona, who doesn't smile back. But that's her style. She's Wednesday Addams in adult form, complete with black clothes, a love of heavy eye makeup, and an undying affection for The Cure. Basically the opposite of the girl sitting across from us.

Our potential new roommate gives us the basics: Her name is Sienna Cruz, from California, non-smoker, a junior.

"So, Sienna, on a scale of one to ten, how messy are you? Because Ramona and I try to keep this place as organized as possible."

Sienna pops her gum and nods with a smile. "I'm totally neat. No worries there."

I wonder what she's doing in Charming, Texas, but don't ask the question. Our rental isn't very big, and there's nothing I hate more than stumbling over someone's shoes when I'm racing out of the house in the morning. A potential broken ankle takes precedence over what brought her to the Hill Country.

Not many West Coasters venture this deep into Texas just to attend Lone Star State, especially when UT has the advantage of being nestled in Austin while Charming boasts of nut festivals and weiner warmers. As in, for weiner dogs. Although I've heard sometimes students order extra-small warmers for *personal* use. Like the meatheads across the street.

With an internal eye roll, I concede football is likely a draw too.

Don't get me wrong, Charming is small-town quaint with a side of quirk. I love it, in fact, but it's not for everyone.

I check the box and scroll down to the next question. "What about noise level and parties?" My eye twitches at the thought, and I surreptitiously rub it beneath my glasses. "Ramona and I are seniors and really need to concentrate sometimes. Are you okay if we don't let things get too rowdy?"

Like, ever.

Because I could go a lifetime without another kegger breaking out on my front lawn.

I'm not trying to be condescending, but I've seen completely sane students lose their minds, not to mention clothing, when faced with the party scene on this campus. But who knows? Sienna is a junior, so she might appreciate peace and quiet at night.

She waves her hand at me. "Not a prob. I don't drink much."

Excellent.

Not that I have a problem with a glass of wine once in a while or a beer on a Friday night, but I'm not a fan of people indulging until they're blackout drunk and puking in my bushes.

For the first time, Ramona pipes up. She holds up a finger.

"Now, for the most important question. How do you feel about football?"

My lips tug up. She loathes football almost as much as I do.

"Not a fan." Sienna shakes her head. "I prefer surfing and hiking."

Glee. That's the only way to describe this feeling.

At this school where the football player is king and the entire town pays homage, this girl is a rarity. A gem, in my opinion.

"Sounds like we're going to get along great!" I reach for the rental agreement.

Too many students around here become roommates without any legal parameters, and before you know it, one person bails and everyone else has to scramble to pay the rent. I can't afford to make that kind of mistake right now.

Sienna skims the agreement. I'm about to ask if she wants to take more time to consider the contract when she signs at the bottom. A few minutes later, I have her rent check and I'm handing over a set of keys.

And Ramona thought my interview questions were a waste of time. Ha!

As I walk Sienna to her car, she squeals. "Holy crap, is that Rider Kingston?"

Without my permission, my gaze slides across the street to the oversized man-child, who has the gall to be moving furniture shirtless while flexing his stupid abs. Judging by the other sweaty minions pouring out of the two-story, Rider's getting new roommates too.

My eye twitches again, and my focus snaps back to Sienna. "I thought you said you weren't a fan of football."

"Oh, I'm not. I can't sit through an entire game. But I *am* a fan of football players." Her gaze turns ravenous as she scans my neighbor's front lawn. Or, likely, the glistening eight-pack Rider's put on display. "All that testosterone. Those bulging muscles. That deep, masculine grunting. Oh, yeah. Get me one of those!"

She cackles, and Rider hears it.

Of course he does.

Shockingly, he deigns to speak to me.

"Hey, Gabby," he shouts. "How was your summer?"

I'm not sure when he decided to stop ignoring me, but that's better than pretending we're friends, which we'll never be.

I close my eyes because I don't need any reminders of his masculine beauty. And I definitely don't need to see that sexy smirk, the one more powerful than his cannon that took the team to the playoffs last year.

No, I'm not interested in the star quarterback. Not anymore.

Turning on my heel, I wave my middle finger and march back to my house.

Laughter is all I hear as I slam the front door shut behind me.

An hour later, I'm still feeling like an idiot, but I don't have time to wallow in the ineffectiveness of my interview questions because I have my own interview to get to.

After a jittery swipe of mascara, I lean back to find that one eye is now bigger than the other thanks to my lack of makeup skills. I wad some tissue and try to rectify the problem, but only manage to make a bigger mess.

Lord, help me!

With a groan, I remove the black smear and attempt it again.

I stare at my pale face and the lopsided topknot. At the clumpy mascara and vanilla lip gloss. At my glasses that always got me labeled a nerd when I was growing up.

With a sigh, I untie and re-knot the mass of black hair.

Having long hair in the Texas heat is a pain, but it reminds me of my mom, so I never cut it beyond a trim.

My arms shake as I finish my quick updo. I call out to Ramona. "Can you do me a favor and throw an apple in my bag?"

Which is a dumb thing to request since she'll probably ignore me, but that's okay. To each her own. I'm nothing if not a respectful roommate. I don't ask too many questions or get in anyone's business. Life has taught me to keep my nose down, work hard, and avoid distractions.

I grit my teeth when the sound of a lawn mower blares toward my side of the house.

At least he's almost done.

Because Rider can't just be the star quarterback. No, he has to go and do thoughtful things for our elderly neighbors.

I bite my bottom lip as my eyes slide to my window. It's not like he'll know if I take a peek.

Before I can stop myself, I race over to the blinds and carefully peel one up. Just a smidge. Just enough to see Rider in all his sweaty, eight-pack glory as his muscles bulge and glisten in the bright sun.

That man is too handsome for his own good.

And I'm not sure who I hate more. Him, for being so tempting, or me, for being tempted after all this time.

My hand trembles on the window pane, reminding me that I need to eat something or I might get slammed with another twelve-hundred-dollar EMT bill when I can't afford the first bill.

That's one of the reasons this job is so important.

And when my car doesn't start—again—I'm reminded of another.

Groaning, I swing my bag out of my old Honda and pray I have time to catch the bus.

Thankfully, Rider is back to his side of the street where, lo and behold, a party has broken out. Out of the corner of my eye, I see the telltale red Solo cup parade. Someone has placed the stereo speakers in the window, and AC/DC is blaring *Back in Black* for the whole neighborhood to appreciate.

I moved here before the Victorian across the street became the Stallion Station, otherwise known as the football fuck-pad and party palace.

I would've looked for a new place this summer to get away from these Neanderthals, except the rent prices in Charming have skyrocketed, while my older bungalow still has lowish rent, so I'm loathe to leave it.

As I hoof it to the bus stop and navigate the cracks in the sidewalk in my dress heels, a brand-new Range Rover pulls up beside me. The window rolls down, and I yank my purse to the other side of my body, but before I can pull out my mace—because a girl can't be too careful—Ben's serious face pops out.

"Where you going all dressed up?"

That's my brother. Never a 'hello'. Never a 'how you doing?' or 'what did you do this summer?'

But his question makes me self-conscious. "I have a job interview. Why? Is this too much?"

I'm wearing a simple black pencil skirt and a white button-up blouse. It's nothing fancy, but it seems appropriate attire for a secretary. Except thanks to the August heat, I'm already sweating.

"What happened to your job tutoring?"

I adjust my glasses. "I lost it after I got sick last spring. I told you." May, to be exact. The last time I saw Rider.

Ben frowns. "Sorry. Guess I forgot. It was a busy time of year with mid-terms and spring break."

It must be a rough life, partying it up in Cabo with his douchey friends. I bite my tongue, not wanting to add more friction to our relationship, and ignore how he's misremembering the dates.

I'm older by a year, but you'd never know it from looking at us. There's something about Ben that screams confidence. I may have a big bark from time to time, but Ben commands attention. Never mind that he's well over six feet and I come in at a whopping five foot four.

"How was camp?" I'm assuming he got here a few weeks ago for football. I ignore the spark of hurt that he never called.

"Ball-busting. As usual."

The silence grows, and I struggle to think of something to say. That's when I notice the boxes in his SUV. And is that... a bed frame sticking out the back window?

"Are you moving?" A terrible thought settles into the pit of my stomach. *Say it isn't so!* Because if I have to watch my brother's one-night stands make the walk of shame on the weekends, I'm going to hurl.

Seriously, there's no judgment on my end toward those girls. They see these beautiful men who shower them with affection. For one night or one weekend. Of course they're going to lose their minds and undergarments.

But then the party ends.

It always ends.

And those guys *always* send the girls packing.

I know because I've seen them crying on that front lawn. I've even made one or two of them breakfast while they waited for their rides. Thankfully, they were never Rider's hookups, but still. I can extrapolate what he's been doing.

Ben grins. "Yeah, just up the street, actually. With Rider—"

"—Kingston." I shake my head, disgust roiling in my stomach. "You know I live across the street from him, right?"

His brow furrows. "I knew you lived here on Pine, but I thought it was closer to the coffee shop."

"Nope. Right. Across. The. Street."

Which Ben would know if he ever bothered to visit or hang out with me. He's probably partied steps away from my house.

That desolate feeling I get whenever I think about how close we used to be as kids settles in my chest, and I step away from his SUV. "I've got to go."

If I've learned anything in this life, it's that I can't rely on anyone. Not even my own brother.

"Wait." He frowns, and that brief pause gives me a glimmer of hope. Ben never wants to talk. I hate that I'm so desperate to want a connection with him, but the hope fizzles with his next words. "You're not going to be checking up on me all the time, are you?"

My gaze hardens. "No worries there, Ben. I'll never walk into that house."

And I mean it.

Never.

2
RIDER

My unease grows as I watch Ben Rodriguez, my tight end and new housemate, talk to my neighbor.

Gabby Duran is the last person I want living across the street from me, but I didn't know she'd be sleeping a few yards away when I signed on to live with the guys last year.

But life is like that, tempting me with things I can't have, shouldn't want, and can't deal with.

Today Gabby's all dressed up, like she's ready to star in some dirty librarian fantasy.

It's a fantasy I'm familiar with.

The first time we met freshman year, she was wearing a t-shirt that said "I'm silently correcting your grammar," while I was wearing a shirt that had two atoms talking, saying something about losing an electron.

Her eyes lit up as she read my dumb shirt, and I never had the heart to tell her it was something I got from Goodwill because it was cheap, not something I picked out because I was smart.

But yeah. She got under my skin faster than I'm comfortable admitting. She's smart and focused and kinda fierce. And fuck, those long lashes and hazel eyes have always done something to me.

My former tutor is all grown up now. She was cute as hell three years ago, but she's filled out in the best ways and is downright mouthwatering now.

Not that I can go there or that she'd let me, given the fire in her eyes when I tried to say hi.

Not gonna lie. That stung.

What did you expect, you dick? You've barely spoken to her in the last few years.

Some part of me was hoping that what happened this past May might've changed the dynamics for us a bit. Broken the ice in some weird way. I mean, I never wanted the girl to hate me. But I shouldn't be surprised she gave me the finger earlier today. The last time I saw her, she slammed her front door in my face.

Women—even former flings and hookups—usually love me. Not that Gabby and I ever went there. Not exactly.

I rub my chest, wondering where she's going and why she's not taking her car. Unless it didn't start again.

I'll admit there's one advantage to living across the street from her. If she ever has another emergency, I'll be there for her. She might tell me to go fuck myself, and that's fine, but it gives me peace of mind to know she's close if she needs anything.

I wave at my other neighbor, the one who liked me even before I started mowing her lawn. "Can I bring you some barbecue or pizza, Mrs. Goode?"

She nods and smiles even though she probably has no idea what I just said if her hearing aids are off—which is great when our music is too loud because she never complains.

Mrs. Goode pays me for cutting her lawn with Super Saver coupons. I always accept them because I understand letting people have their pride.

Mentally, I prepare for that long-ass nap I'm gonna take this afternoon. After an early workout, moving furniture all afternoon, and mowing Mrs. Goode's lawn, I'm more than ready to bypass this party.

My best friend Tank marches through the chaos on our front lawn in ridiculously small swim trunks, scuba flippers, and a snorkel mask. "Cannonball contest in ten."

"Who's dumb enough to challenge you?" We bump fists.

"I know, right?" He gives me a wide grin. "I think people just want an excuse to see my beautiful Samoan ass glide gracefully through the air."

I choke on a laugh. Tank, whose real name is Tamatoa Salamasina, is six five, three hundred pounds, and the heart of my O-line. "Don't get hurt, man. I need you."

"I got you, baby! The only thing that'll be hurting my ass is Bree."

Overshare, dude.

Tank is obsessed with his girlfriend. The guy already has a wedding ring picked out and plans for a half-dozen kids. I used to wonder how he could forgo the buffet of girls who throw themselves at us, but I'm starting to get the appeal. Especially when he gets all those home-cooked meals he won't share.

These days I prefer hooking up with one woman for a few months rather than random one-nighters. As long as we're on the same page that this is just for fun. And condoms are a must *every* time. No slip-ups allowed.

So yeah, I'll pass on Tank's dream of having six kids. One would make me crap my pants. Six might put me in an insane asylum.

When I turn, I find that Ben is still talking to Gabby down the street and clench my jaw. What the hell does he want with her?

Blonde hair pops into my vision, and I barely have time to

school my expression before Miranda leaps up, wrapping all of her tanned limbs around me like a koala bear.

"Whoa." I laugh half-heartedly. Guess I won't be locking myself in my room for a nap.

Grabbing Miranda's bikini-clad ass with both of my hands, I hoist her over my shoulder, and she squeals so loudly, my ear rings.

Everyone on my yard stops to stare. The guys take a long look at this girl's rear, which wiggles against my shoulder. I don't even have it in me to glare.

Mira and I have always had fun, but we have an agreement—nothing serious. Ever. That's why it works between us. Because I have never felt that pull toward her, and she never wants more.

My eyes dart to Gabby across the street, still talking to fucking Ben.

For the briefest beat, I wonder if it would be so bad to be committed to one woman for more than just hookups. To not have to worry she's using me for my social media following or the great parties or the attention we garner on campus.

Someone who thinks I'm more than my stats or the last touchdown or the potential millions I stand to make if I'm drafted. A friend, someone I can be myself around and let my guard down with.

Would it be so bad to have a warm woman to snuggle first thing in the morning?

And then I come to my senses. *What the actual fuck, Rider?*

I almost snort with disgust.

No, this is what I signed up for. Casual is what keeps me from going down the rabbit hole and losing focus on what really matters: Football. The game. Winning. That's it.

Because without that, what's left? My father's trashed-out double-wide? The bills we can't pay? The locals who think we're dumb hicks? I'm lucky Charming is far enough away from my hometown to avoid that gossip.

No, football is my ticket out of here, and she's my only mistress. The girls who warm my bed know the deal. I'm always upfront about that. And the beautiful woman across the street already got that memo.

The look of contempt on Gabby's face this morning rushes back to me, and I cringe. I hate that she probably thinks I'm scum.

If she talked to anyone in my town, they'd agree. They'd tell her like father, like son.

I like to think I did her a favor by stepping away when I did. She knows I'm not into commitments, and I know she's a forever kind of girl.

Oil and water.

So however much I might like her, however much I might be attracted to her, she's someone I can't be tempted by again. Because she'll never be down with a hookup, and I'll never want more.

"Let's party, people!" Miranda screams over my shoulder, and the growing crowd roars in agreement.

I laugh right along with everyone else. It may sound hollow to my own ears, but no one else notices. They never do.

3

RIDER

After unloading my duffle bag into the stall, I take a deep breath of locker room air, a unique combination of mold and questionable male hygiene, and toss up a prayer I can take the team all the way this time.

We got so fucking close last year.

But close doesn't get you a championship.

Close might not get you a first-round draft pick.

And I'll do anything to take my team to the top. No sacrifice is too big. No workout too hard. No pain too great.

I didn't come this far to place second.

I must not be the only one with victory on the brain because there's an electricity in the air we haven't had in previous years.

"We're seniors! Can I get a 'woot, woot?'" The guys echo Tank's rally call as he does a round of high-fives and some hysterical dance moves that no man his size should be able to pull off. "We gonna kick some ass and get those alums to cough up the cash so we can level up and y'all baby Broncs can finally have some nice digs."

The team shouts in agreement.

I glance around, taking in the drab paint and the fading

Lone Star State logo on the back wall. Our bucking bronco Buckee has definitely seen better days.

Not only does our college name sound like a sappy country song, until a few years ago, our football team never got a lot of national recognition. The locals may love the sport, but that never brought in the dough. Hometown fame gets us free or discounted meals at local dives and back slaps at the Mini-Mart, not multi-million-dollar investments in our locker room, like the amenities at UT or A&M.

But the bells and whistles are not what brought me here.

When Coach Sullivan looked me in the eye when I was a high school player, he didn't see the kid from the wrong side of the tracks who barely got the grades to play. He didn't see my threadbare jeans or the holes in my faded t-shirts. Coach saw my potential. He said if I kept my focus on the game, he could make me one of the best college players in the country.

My answer was simple: Hell yes, I wanted to play D1 football for him.

After I got to start freshman year when our QB got injured and his backup got redshirted, Coach Sully never wavered. No, he doubled down. On a punk ass like me. I'd basically give my left nut sack for the man.

Hopefully it never comes to that. I'm kinda fond of my nuts.

One of the assistant coaches sticks his head in the locker room and yells, "Conference room in ten, gentlemen!"

Hell yeah. Let's get this started.

I'm tucking my phone into my locker, feeling like I can conquer the world one touchdown at a time, when it buzzes.

Got a few bucks to spare? Short on rent.

My father's text drops the smile right off my face.

Fuck.

I close my eyes.

He swore up and down he'd use that money to pay his landlord.

Motherfucking fuck.

Jaw clenched tight, I remind myself I need my hands. I can't put my fist through the wall if I hope to throw any touchdowns this year.

I get four disbursements from my scholarship per semester, and my father already blew through a chunk of the first one single-handedly. What the hell am I supposed to eat for the next month if I give him any more cash? At least athletes from marquee sports can grab one meal a day on campus, so I guess I won't starve, but that still requires juggling my schedule so I can get to the cafeteria before it closes.

The game begins. The one where I try to shuffle around my father's debt and my meager income so we don't both end up on the street.

He was doing better this summer when I was home, laying off the sauce long enough to do some odd jobs. I hoped and prayed he'd keep it together my senior year. Because this will all be for naught if I can't make it to the draft. And I'll be damned if I spent high school and college busting my balls to come up short on the fourth down.

Suddenly, I'm so damn tired I'm not sure how I'll tie my cleats, much less run my offense.

If my father had his way, I'd give him every last cent and be stuck selling my fucking plasma to buy ramen.

I plunk into a chair in the conference room and scrub my hand over my face.

Tank takes the seat next to me and whispers, "Coach is looking rough."

It takes a second for his words to register. I open my eyes and focus on Sully, the man who's more of a father than my biological parent. Coach is basically the antithesis of Hank Kingston.

As he heads to the small podium, Sully shucks off a long-sleeved button-up, which leaves him in a Bucking Broncos t-shirt. Why he's wearing a long-sleeved shirt in the Texas heat is beyond me.

Coach isn't a spring chicken anymore. He has to be pushing seventy, and it's starting to show. He had pneumonia the last week of training camp, but only took a few days off to recover. Maybe he needs more time to rest. We've all been worried about him since his wife died a few years ago.

"Boys, it's good to have everyone here at once." Sully's raspy voice is warm with affection. He's not like the coaches who throw clipboards at kids and browbeat them when they make mistakes.

We lean closer since he can't project his voice the way he usually does.

"Summer camp was great, but there's nothing like the first practice of a new school year, and I have a feeling this is our season to go all the way."

The guys hoot and howl and stomp their feet in agreement.

Sully reviews the plan for the day before he leans one arm on the podium. "Just want to share a few last thoughts, something to focus on for the year, which I'm sad to say will likely be my last as head coach. Retirement is in the cards for this old codger."

A collective gasp goes through the room. I'm a little heartbroken to hear the news, but also grateful as hell I'm a senior and will get to end my college career with this awesome coach.

He waves his hand. "I love going out on a high note, boys, and this room has the best talent I've ever had the honor of recruiting. And as much as I love the game, I want to remind everyone that no matter what happens in the future, I hope you carry the lessons we've learned here into your everyday lives. That you're men of honor and respect." He pauses for a second and arches his bushy eyebrow. "I hope I don't need to say this, but please stay out of trouble. No crazy pranks this year, and definitely no arrests or too many wild parties. Let's end this being the best versions of ourselves."

I think back to our impromptu pool party a few days ago, which we kept fairly tame. Nothing to get arrested over, at least.

"We promise we'll be good, Sully!" someone shouts. "Home by midnight before we turn into pumpkins!"

Coach chuckles. His tired eyes meet mine as he looks across the room. "Keep your eyes on the prize."

For a flash, my mind inexplicably goes to my neighbor. To her wide, beautiful smile. The one she never shoots my way anymore.

I shake my head, wondering where the hell that thought came from. Because thoughts of Gabby have no business in this locker room. It's why we parted ways.

Irritated with myself, I lean forward to focus on Sully.

"Commit this year to excellence, boys, not only in football, but in your personal lives. Be the gentlemen I know you to be, bright stars both on and off the field. I'll do everything in my power to take this team to the top, but I want you to know y'all are already champions in my book."

Someone sniffles.

"Coach, don't make us cry!" Tank shouts, and everyone laughs.

As our meeting wraps up and we take the field, the guys are talking about one thing and one thing alone: Winning a national championship for Sully.

And we all agree, no sacrifice is too big.

4
GABBY

With a swipe of my elbow, I attempt to get the flour off my mom's recipe card. Thank goodness for sheet protectors.

Pride fills me as I survey the pan filled with my newest creation—pumpkin and cream cheese sopapilla bars. It's a twist on the original concept, but so darn tasty.

"*Que piensas, mami?*" I ask my mom.

I think she'd love them.

My mom's cookbook—a collection of her recipe cards I've preserved in a binder—is one of the few things of hers I got after she died. The best part is that she hand-wrote so many of them.

After tucking away a few bars for my boss to try, I clean up for my shift at the Rise 'N Grind.

On the way to my barista gig, my day gets better—I get the call from Archer Academy.

I got the job!

Even though it's only an entry-level administrative assistant position and I still have to pass the background check, I know I can turn this opportunity into more down the road.

Archer is an elite private school. If I have any hope of getting a teaching position there after I graduate, I need an edge over other candidates. At least this way they'll know firsthand I'm a hard worker and a solid employee.

My mom used to tell me she hoped she'd have enough money to send me and Benny there. Now that I know what tuition costs, I realize that was a pipe dream, but it's the thought that counts. I think she'd be proud of me if I could get a job there, though.

I blend into the crowd of students and townies, bustling across Charming's quaint downtown in the mid-afternoon sun. Whiskey Row is teeming with patrons, and old-school rock echoes down the street from the breweries. I head toward the rustic brick facade of the best coffee shop in town.

Glancing around, I smile. It's hard not to. Everything in this town belongs on a postcard.

From the absurdity of Longfellow's, which sells foot-long hot dogs and those ridiculous weiner dog warmers, to the Buck 'Em Brewhouse, where all the patrons yell "Buck 'em!" at the top of their lungs at midnight, or the Crazy Horse Saloon that hosts Wild West shootout reenactments—it's hard not to be enchanted with this place. Now that I'm not brimming with animosity for the idiots across the street, I can admit the football team is a good draw for the town too.

I've been trying my best to brush off that awkward interaction with my brother all week. The fact that he lives with Rider is annoying, but it's not like Ben knows our sad little history. And when I say little, that's likely an exaggeration. More like a blip on Rider's radar. But that didn't make it hurt any less.

When I push open the door to Rise 'N Grind, the rich scent of coffee hits me.

"Hey, Fanny." I wave to my boss, who inherited this place from her father, who inherited it from his. Half-coffee house, half-book shop, its homey retro vibe makes it the perfect crash pad for students between classes.

She gives me a smile and a nod as she pours a drink. "Thanks for coming in today, doll!"

An hour ago, I got her frantic call that two of her staff had called in sick, so I booked it down here.

"Coffee or books?" I ask, waving between the two parts of the shop.

"Coffee!"

The place is packed, so I give her a thumbs up as I rush into the back where I wash my hands and grab an apron. Sixty seconds later, I hand Fanny the container of pumpkin sopapilla bars before I start ringing up customers. I don't mind being slammed. It makes the day go by quicker.

"Do ya have any of those *empanadas*?" a gravelly voice asks, his words slow and rhythmic.

I'm used to that drawl because I was born in Texas, but here in Charming, it's even stronger. As expected, I look up to see one of the locals.

"Sorry, Mr. Pearson. We usually just have those on the weekend."

"But I promised Essie." Brow furrowed, he hooks his thumb over his shoulder. I try not to laugh when I see the goat, his beloved Essie, nibbling some kid's backpack on the sidewalk.

"Maybe she'd like a scone or bagel?"

"Nah. Those are too processed. I hear you girls make them empanadas from scratch." His voice lowers to a whisper as he leans over the glass counter. "And I know for a fact that Fanny sometimes keeps one or two back there for emergencies."

No doubt his promise to Essie counts as an emergency. Deep down, I'm unreasonably flattered to know his farm animal is enchanted with my sweet bread.

Ironically, I don't cook much, but I love to bake, and after Fanny tasted one of my creations at the St. Patrick's bake sale, she hired me to make *pan dulce*, *sopapillas*, and other sweet treats on the weekends.

I hold up a finger as I dart into the kitchen where I find one apple empanada. It's probably a little stale, but maybe the goat won't care. I wrap it in a box before I return to the counter. "Let's keep this between us, okay?" I whisper conspiratorially.

Mr. Pearson closes his eyes and places his hand over his heart. "Always and forever."

I chuckle as I watch him tuck that box into his overalls like he's protecting Pentagon secrets.

As he ambles away, someone says, "No playing favorites, missy."

"Adele!" I come around the counter to hug the older woman. She reminds me of Betty White in *The Golden Girls*, an old show one of my foster mothers used to watch. "I haven't seen you in a while."

"My grandkids have been a pain in my a-s-s." She whispers that last part. "Been spending a lot of time down in Austin."

She and Fanny chat while I ring up Adele's order. I know some people hate the idea of small towns, but I love the familiarity that bonds the locals.

When the crowd dies down, I'm about to take a break and fill out Archer's employment forms when my second least favorite person strolls into the bakery.

And just like that, my great day circles the drain.

Zoe Evans rolls her eyes the minute she sees me standing at the counter. I can't paste a smile on my face, so I go for pleasantly bland. *I'm guessing Fanny will get upset if I jump over the counter and strangle this girl.*

"What can I get y—"

"Lemon scone and a double latte with organic soy milk. Three stevia, but only if you have raw."

The entire time I ring up her order, I bite my tongue to keep from asking whether her goal last spring was to get me fired from my tutoring job or if that was just a nice perk to her enormous screwup.

But judging from her evil smirk when she walks away, it doesn't matter because the end result was the same—I got canned.

I try to look on the bright side. At least I don't have to work with Zoe Evans any longer.

Moral turpitude.

I have to look up some of the terms in this employment contract, and that one gives me pause.

Not that I'm planning to "commit an act or behave in a way that gravely violates the accepted standard of the community." But jeez. Add that to the NDA I have to sign, and you'd think I was applying for a top-secret-level position with the FBI instead of wanting to answer phones and pour coffee. Although my Type A personality appreciates the thoroughness of this application process, the practical side of me wants to nail this down already.

"Those bars are delish," Fanny says when she ducks into the kitchen. "Another family recipe?"

"Some of it was."

"I might need you to add those to what you're baking for me."

I can't do a cartwheel in here, but a piece of me wants to. "Be happy to."

"How's that fancy job of yours going?"

"Hasn't started yet, but it's just for one semester. I'll be filling in for someone on maternity leave." I motion to the mountain of paperwork I have to sign. "Their hiring process is intense."

"Those snooty-snoots called me and asked a million questions about you."

"You said I was your favorite employee, right?" I bat my eyes at her, and she chuckles.

"'Course I did. Told them how you stay late during finals to help me when all the other kids bail."

Staffing at this place is really tough at the beginning and end of the semester, but I'm able to get time off in between to focus on classes.

"Aww, thanks. You're the best. I'll be honest—those discounts you give me on journals and pens help." Next to vast quantities of caffeine, working at a bookstore has its benefits.

"Still hoarding pens, huh?"

"You say that like it's a problem."

She laughs as I head back out to cover the counter.

The front door opens and the noise level rises a hundred percent.

Rider and a handful of other guys stroll in. From the back of their entourage Ben gives me a nod. Rider has his hands full with that girl Miranda, who's hanging on him like she's Kate Winslet in *Titanic* and he's the floating door keeping her from drowning.

Whatever.

Fortunately, they head toward the bookstore where I know they'll hog the tables in the back or pile on to the couches, but at least I don't have to see them. We serve food on both sides of the store, but this side is self-serve at the counter whereas the other side has waitstaff to serve customers.

Ten minutes later, I'm even more irritated when I end up being switched to the bookstore side, where I studiously ignore the football crowd in the back that's swarming with fangirls. Thankfully, they're not in my section.

I stomp over to the two guys who just sat at a small table

along the wall of books. "What can I get you?" I bring my pen up to my order pad.

"Your number if you're single."

My eyes dart up to catch this guy's huge smile. He's handsome with dark hair and eyes. He looks familiar. Maybe I've waited on him? They're both wearing dark blue uniforms. Not cops, but maybe paramedics.

I laugh. "Does that line ever work?"

"I don't know. You tell me. I've never used it before."

"Uh-huh. How about we start with drinks and we'll go from there? The list of specialty coffees is on the board." I motion to the giant chalkboard menu mounted on the wall behind me.

I feel his stare as I put in the order.

Darlene nudges me and motions to the paramedics. "He's cute, and he's obviously into you."

I shrug. I'm more gun-shy about dating than I care to admit. Besides those ill-advised few months hanging out with Rider, I've only dated one guy seriously. When Sean graduated at the end of my sophomore year, he accepted a job in New York, and we parted ways. It was all very civilized. He didn't suggest a long-distance relationship, and I didn't pine after him when he left. Rider taught me to guard my heart, and it paid off when Sean moved.

So while I might not have a ton of experience with men, I'd rather not get my hopes up about someone who'll eventually let me down or break my heart.

As Darlene settles several sandwiches on her tray for the football players, she blows the bangs out of her face. "I swear if they stiff me on a tip, I'll hunt them down."

Our sports teams are notoriously bad tippers, probably because they think they rule the earth.

"I got this." I march over to Ben's side of the table and lean down. "Hey, please be sure to tip your waitress. You guys always eat like pigs and barely leave the staff any gratuity. It's rude."

His jaw tightens, and he gives me a stiff nod. The girl practically sitting in his lap gives me a dirty look. I laugh. "Relax. He's my brother."

The whole table goes silent.

It takes me a second to realize what this means.

Even Rider looks surprised. "No shit, Rodriguez. Gabby is your sister?"

I stand there like an idiot, and my throat tightens at the realization that Ben doesn't tell anyone we're related. We have different last names since he was adopted by our uncle, but I didn't think this was some big secret.

One of the other guys—I think his name is Tank—scratches his head. "You don't look anything alike."

It's true. We're an odd mixture of our parents. While we both have black hair, Benny is a foot taller and has our mom's soulful brown eyes while I have my dad's hazel. He has our father's beautiful olive skin, but I'm pale with a smattering of freckles, like our mother.

God, this is awkward. I back up only to run into a hard body. When I spin around, I come face to face with the paramedic.

He motions toward the street. "I have a call, so we gotta jet, sweet pea, but I was serious about hanging out sometime." Lowering his voice to a whisper, he leans closer. "I don't know if you remember, but I was the one who took you to the hospital. Last spring, I think."

Another humiliating day. "Sorry, I was really out of it that afternoon, but you do look familiar."

He places a hand over his chest. "I was about to be heartbroken if you didn't remember me."

I laugh and roll my eyes.

Clearing his throat, he raises his brows. "So... can I call you sometime?"

That's when I realize the entire table behind me is still silent and listening to this conversation.

One of the dumbasses pipes up. "If she's available, I'd like to call dibs on a date with Gabby. *Ouch*. What the fuck, man?"

I turn to glare at my brother's friends and drag the nice paramedic away by the elbow, pausing when we get to the front door.

"Are those the foot—"

"Never mind them." I turn him so he's facing the opposite direction. "Look, I'm sure you're a really nice guy..."

"Jason."

"Jason. Hi."

"The nicest." He gives me an award-winning smile, one that should do something to my heart, my belly, my pulse, *something*, except it doesn't.

"But..." I pause and my attention automatically goes to Rider, which annoys me.

I'm not thinking about Sean, whom I dated for a year. No, I'm thinking about the douchebag who doesn't give a damn about me. The guy who's currently nestled against Miranda, a very buxom blonde, who, by all accounts, gives him exactly what he wants, when he wants it, with zero commitment.

While Sean never made my heart race like Rider, he didn't break it either.

My gaze connects with Rider's, and there's nothing there in those stark gray eyes. No apology or regret or longing. Just that enormous wall, the one he erected almost overnight three years ago.

This is the real Rider. The guy who pushes away anyone who gets too close.

And I am one hundred percent sure I'm a fool for still giving a shit about him.

Sometimes I forget he's a jackass, and I need a reminder so I can keep waving my middle finger at him.

"You know what?" I turn back to Jason and give the guy who actually wants to date me the biggest smile I can muster. "I would love to go out with you."

5
RIDER

A FEW OF the guys walk with me to Connor Hall to grab some breakfast, but they know the drill. I'm fun and laughs and shits and giggles until game day, and then they give me a wide berth. I need to clear my head.

The deeper into the season we go, the more imperative this becomes. Even after six wins, I can't let myself consider the playoffs or going undefeated, no matter how often reporters pose those questions. The only thing that matters is today's game against Iowa.

Faces in my path blur. When someone says my name, I nod, but I'm thinking about play completion. Following through on each release. Checking for secondary plays before I commit.

I slip on my headphones and relax into the pounding beat of the drums in my ears that provide another layer of concentration.

In a weird way, I have the shit that went down freshman year to thank for my game day routine. I had to block out all that noise until the only thing I could recognize was the steady beat of my heart.

I had to focus on what I wanted for my life. Everyone else in my family got to be selfish. Why couldn't I? I had one chance, *one*, to make my mark, to show Sully I could do my part, and I decided then and there that nothing—not the bullshit with my parents, not the antics of my friends, and definitely not the drama of a woman—would threaten that goal.

By the time we're at the stadium, my breathing is slow and my hands are steady. Someone could probably slap me, and I'd barely blink. But this is how I know we'll win. Because my head's on right, and when the whistle blows on the field a few hours later, I can read the Iowa defense.

One touchdown. Two. A long throw to my wide receiver, who runs it in for another.

Like curtains rising on a stage, the sound of our roaring crowd finally breaks through to me, and I crack a smile and smack Tank on the ass after he plows through the defense, giving me plenty of time to release the ball. "You're the fucking man. Keep it up."

"All day and all night, baby!"

By halftime, the nerves are long gone, but I know better than to let up. We need to keep our winning streak going, and the worst thing you can do is relax before the final buzzer sounds.

Tank points to the end zone where Buckee is humping the goal post. "Guess our mascot needs to get laid."

I laugh, taking a minute to appreciate that the stadium is filled. Everyone is decked out in our colors, and they scream like maniacs whenever we charge down the field. For a kid who was told he'd never amount to shit, this ain't too bad.

My good humor is short-lived when Iowa comes back with a vengeance, but our defense eventually finds its footing.

With two minutes left on the clock and a six-point lead, I'm itching to make this a decisive win. We played too well to take this by such a small margin.

The Varsity Dad Dilemma | 31

Just before we jog back onto the field, I elbow Ben. "B-Rod, be ready to work your magic."

He gives me a stoic nod. Even though he mostly rode the bench last year, Ben's shaping up to be a hell of a tight end. Bonus that he's a humble dude. Not everyone on this team is.

Two plays later, as I drop into the pocket, I find Ben through the defense. He catches the ball with one hand, cradles it, shakes off two defenders, and blazes into the end zone.

The crowd erupts, and I let out a roar as the clock runs out on our opponent.

That sharp rush of euphoria blasts through my veins, and I swear I could walk on water. I give my boys some high-fives and grin for the cameras. When I lock eyes with Tank, we leap up to chest-bump.

The whole team is riding the high, one that's well-deserved.

And then I make the mistake. The one I make every damn game.

I look to the stands.

I don't know why I do this, somehow expecting things to be different.

But still, I look. Isn't that the definition of insanity? Repeating something over and over, expecting a different outcome?

Just like that, I slam back down to earth because the truth is I've never had any family at a game and likely never will.

In an attempt to abide by Coach's "no shenanigans" rule this season, we've kept celebrations mostly out at bars since restaurants limit capacity, and this way I don't have to worry about people jumping off my roof into the pool and breaking their necks. It's not the same as the hedonist free-for-alls we tend to host, but at least we're staying out of trouble.

The Yellow Rose might qualify as a dive bar, but the owner loves the football team, and I like giving them our business. Besides, beer is beer.

"What can I get ya, darling?" Our waitress winks at me, and I smile. We had a class together last year.

"Hey, Sherry. Another one of these, please." I hold up my bottleneck.

Miranda squishes closer to me. "Honey, I asked for another shot *twenty minutes* ago."

"Calm down. It's busy in here." I mouth "sorry" to Sherry. "A shot for the lady when you get a chance."

I lean back. Any closer and Miranda's tits would be in my face.

Annoyance prickles my skin. Mira and I have been hanging out more socially lately, and I'm starting to think we should've kept our interactions to the bedroom.

I slide out of the booth. "I see someone I need to talk to."

The place is packed, and I get some congratulations on my way to the pool table where my roommates are taking bets on who can eat the most chicken wings.

Out of the corner of my eye, I see her.

Gabby.

She's sitting at the bar, slowly stirring her drink, looking like she'd rather be getting a root canal. Her thick black hair is down, and she's wearing this shimmery little dress that hugs her curves. When she looks up, our eyes lock, and just for a second it's hard to breathe. Damn. She's beautiful.

Despite the fact that we're neighbors, I haven't seen her much this semester. I swear, she's hotter every time I see her, which seems impossible. But despite having some damn good reasons for creating space between us, I'm tempted to cross the bar to talk to her.

Then he walks up to her, that scumbag I inadvertently introduced her to when I called for the ambulance last May.

But what was I supposed to do? Let her lie there on the concrete, pale, passed out, and bleeding, and not do anything? How was I to know Jason would show up like a fucking white knight?

Nothing that day went right. They told me I'd just missed her at the hospital when I tried to track her down and make sure she was okay, and when I went to her place, she slammed the door in my face.

She doesn't see him yet, but Jason leans in to whisper in her ear.

She arches away, clearly uncomfortable, and I realize I've made a fist. He'd better not be fucking with her. If this is what she wants, cool. I don't have to like it, but making the moves on a woman who's not interested is another thing.

It's been at least a month since I saw him ask her out. Have they been dating all this time?

"Kingston, you look ready to kill someone." Tank tosses his meaty arm over my shoulder and squints at the crowd until he finds his target. "Ah. Our lovely neighbor." He coughs dramatically. "That's Ben's *sister*. In case you need a reminder. Bro code and all."

"I'm not making a move on Gabby." I'll never make a move on her. Just being near her makes me want to toss her over my shoulder and carry her back to my place caveman-style. That's reason enough to avoid her like the plague. My reaction to her has always been too strong, and I don't need to test my control when I have too much on the line this year.

I can face three-hundred-pound linemen and not bat an eye,

but something about this woman makes me want to run before I do anything stupid. It's baffling.

Needing to change the subject, I motion to our new roommate, who's busy wooing a table of sorority girls. "Ever wonder why Ben rarely talks about Gabby? They live across the street, and I've only seen them talk once. I don't think they ever hang out. They're ten feet apart now, and I doubt they've acknowledged each other."

Ben and I have never been close, but I always thought he seemed like a good guy. When we had an opening for another roommate, Olly suggested him, and so far he's been working out, gelling with the other guys even though he tends to keep to himself when he's at the house. At the end of the day, we're clicking on the field now that he's getting more game time, and that's the only thing that matters.

"Ben's a strange cat. A damn good tight end, but he's not exactly in touch with his emotions."

"Shut the fuck up. 'In touch with his emotions...' Imma start calling you Dr. Phil." I chuckle. "Kinda afraid what you'd say about me."

"Nothing I wouldn't say about myself. We all got daddy issues, brother."

Guess I asked for that. Tank knows me better than anyone at this school. We were roommates our first year, and while we never really talk about my home life, he always seemed to understand I had crap I couldn't deal with.

"You'd be a damn good shrink." I pretend to cry. "Please help me with my daddy issues."

"Fuck off."

We laugh and drink our beer.

I try to relax, but it's pointless. My awareness of Gabby persists. Everything else feels like noise. It's annoying as hell.

Why now? Why is this girl in my head all the fucking time now years after we stopped hanging out?

After a minute, he nods toward the bar. "Bree says she's cool as fuck. Gabby helped her with some essay the other day. I think they have a class together."

"Bree hates everyone."

"Bree loves Gabby."

"I thought you were trying to talk me *out* of being interested," I say. "Not that I am." He gives me a look. "What? I'm not."

"I'm conflicted." He sighs. "Bree is an excellent judge of character. And as we both know, she does, in fact, hate Miranda. It adds a kind of drama you and I both dislike."

"Miranda and I aren't an item. We pass the time together."

Although lately, I've been wondering if we've reached our expiration date.

"Naked time. Yeah, I get that. We all need our outlets. I'm just wondering if you might benefit from someone who's interested in more than your signing bonus."

I tsk. "That seems awfully judgy."

"Miranda's a party girl, and there's nothing wrong with that, but I've *definitely* heard her asking around about what kind of dough we'd get for signing at the draft. And she's *definitely* eyeballing the WAGs club."

I lurch back like someone slugged me. "She does *not* want to get married."

"So she claims. But like I said, nothing wrong with her game play. To each her own. Except what happens if you got her pregnant?"

"What the fuck?" I swear my balls shrink and crawl up my sack.

"Hear me out. What if you got her pregnant? Then you're stuck with her *and* a baby. *For life.* Or at least eighteen years. I'm just saying that scenario is less frightening if you're dating a woman who has your back."

I follow his line of sight and see Miranda flirting with some guy in a polo.

"She's free to do her thing. There's no exclusivity clause in our situation." Hell, we're not even dating, technically. Not that I go around fucking other girls while she and I are doing... whatever this is.

"But you and Miranda have gone a few rounds, no? Freshman year and then again last year, and now. I'm just saying she gave Sherry some evil looks a little while ago when she was serving drinks."

I rub the back of my neck and turn just in time to watch Jason escort Gabby out to the little dance floor in the back. He pulls her close, aligning their bodies together, and I swear to God, I want to knock him the fuck out.

Tilting his drink, Tank clinks it with mine. "Don't shoot the messenger." He glances at the dance floor. "Or anyone else, for that matter."

Easier said than done.

6

GABBY

THIS IS A BAD IDEA.

"Sienna, we're not even close to the same size." I motion to my boobs and butt. 'Nuff said.

"I know. I'm so jealous of your bodacious bod."

I wouldn't describe myself as having a "bodacious bod." More like someone who enjoys tacos with extra guac. Even though I forget to eat sometimes, the weight never seems to come off my hood or trunk.

I'm not sure when this happened, but Sienna has taken it upon herself to be my fairy godmother of makeovers. And while I can always use help with my makeup, this getup seems a little extreme.

It started when I had that date with Jason, which was a waste of good mascara and a nice dress, if you ask me. All he did was take me to the bar so he could talk football with his bros. I mean, I liked the one or two slow dances we did in the back, but he wanted to talk about the game the entire evening. Not that I expected some fancy restaurant or anything expensive, but trying to avoid getting beer spilled on me all night was not my idea of fun.

Of course we went to the same bar where the players were hanging out. *Of course* Rider was there. My first date in ages, and the very last person on the planet I wanted to see was a few feet away, which made my mood worse.

Miranda looked like she wanted to maul him right there on the table. It'd be funny if it didn't still hurt to watch him date other women.

Rider and I will never happen. I wonder when my heart will get the memo.

Smoothing a hand over the silky baby-pink fabric, I sigh. The costume would be lovely... if there was more of it. "I don't have a bra I can wear with this."

"You don't need a bra. This puppy will hold you up."

Straps crisscross everywhere, so I'm not sure how to verify her claims, but it's getting down to the wire. If I want a different costume, I need to figure that out in the next half-hour before Jason comes for our second date.

I groan.

She holds up a finger. "To quote Herodotus—except I'm changing pronouns—'If a woman insisted always on being serious, and never allowed herself a bit of fun and relaxation, she would go mad or become unstable without knowing it.'"

I tilt my head. "What's your major again?"

"A little of this and that." She waves my question away. "But really, don't you need a break?"

Do I want to go out and relax? Of course. Do I want to do it with Jason? That's the question. I keep waiting for the butterflies to take flight, but so far, I only have nerves from hanging out with someone I barely know.

"What if I get arrested for public indecency? There's a very good chance I might poke out someone's eye with my nipples if it gets cold tonight."

She cackles. "My old roommate used Band-Aids over her

nipples for extra coverage." With one arm, she holds it up to me. "You've been working your ass off since I moved in. I barely see you. What's a few hours of letting your hair down?"

Ugh, she's saying everything I want to hear. Where the hell's Ramona? I need someone to talk some sense into me, and I can usually trust Ramona to give it to me straight. There's nothing she loves more than raining on someone's parade. But Sienna, the annoying little ray of sunshine that she is, seems convinced I'll enjoy myself tonight. "Screw it. You only live once, right?"

"That's what I'm talking about!" She does a weird dance in her Poison Ivy costume that makes her strategically placed vines shake.

I have to admit that after my initial annoyance with her for lusting after football players—which is totally hypocritical, I know—she's worn down my resistance to being friends. I have, like, two, and honestly I wasn't looking for more. But she's so damn nice. Always doing things for me for no apparent reason. I should be suspicious. Except I get the feeling she's genuinely a good person who—get this—likes doing nice things for people just for the hell of it.

By the time she gets me strapped into the costume, I'm having major second thoughts. "I'm supposed to be Marie Antoinette, right? And not a French prostitute?"

"Gah! You're gorgeous! You look like a Victoria's Secret model."

"You know they wear underwear, right? Typically worn *under* clothes." I attempt to yank the skirt down, but there's so little of it. "For the record, there's a very strong draft shooting up my rear."

The doorbell rings, and my heart pounds, and not in a good way.

"I know!" I wave my hand to prevent her from answering. "I

can go as a schoolteacher. I can toss on a turtleneck and a pencil skirt and call it a day."

Sienna shakes her head as she charges out of the bathroom, presumably for the door. "It's not a costume if you wear it to work!"

I stare at the stranger in the mirror, a little awed I don't even look like myself. I guess that's my answer. No one will even recognize me, so what's the harm?

∼

If I had to guess what most people thought I was tonight, I'd definitely have to go with French prostitute.

I ignore the catcalls I get as I pump gas for Jason, who's inside paying.

It's freaking freezing, and this sad excuse for a shawl does nothing to help me stay warm. We've been hopping from one Halloween party to the next where I don't know anyone. Jason's having a great time, though. At least one of us is. My feet are killing me, my nipples are so cold I could carve my name in the windshield, and I have a headache from hell.

"Ooof."

"Dude, why'd you stop?"

"Oh. *Damnnn*."

I turn around and stare at five zombie football players. Who are actually football players.

See, Sienna. I totally could've been a teacher tonight!

I squint at the guy in the back whose familiar scowl I recognize. "Ben?"

He does that thing with his chin that's supposed to pass for a greeting.

I'm really tired of how my brother's turned into a raging

asshole. Our parents would be so disappointed by his lack of manners.

"How's it going, Gabs?"

My heart drops at the sound of that voice.

Rider Kingston. Of fucking course.

Because being on a second date means I have to run into this man.

My attention goes straight to those criminally beautiful gray eyes fringed with dark lashes. Even with zombie makeup, the man is ridiculously handsome.

I want to punch him in his pretty face.

Before I can say anything, a gaggle of women swarm around them because these guys travel in an entourage like they're the Kardashians.

Some girl—a new one this time—wraps her arms around Rider and giggles into his ear.

If this is the universe's idea of a joke, it sucks.

I roll my eyes and open the door to Jason's SUV.

One of the other zombie football players coughs. "Since none of us *knew* Gabby was your sister, Ben, we should totally be able to call dibs. Fuck! Stop hitting me."

I'm not sure who smacked him, because some of my Marie Antoinette extensions get in my eyes, but by the time I peel them off my face, Jason is back and draping his arm—the one not holding a tray of gas station nachos—over my shoulders.

"Hey, guys! Great game today!"

Irritation crawls over my skin, but he doesn't notice my lack of enthusiasm. He just keeps rolling with the ass-kissing extravaganza.

"That forty-yard pass you drilled into the end zone in the fourth? What a play, Kingston. I'm still freaking out about that."

"Thanks, man."

A deep sigh escapes me.

Rider *was* amazing today. I can't even pretend I didn't catch part of the game, but I'm not about to gush over him and let his head get any bigger.

"I'm going to let you guys chat, but I'm freezing." I yank the door open again and crawl in, trying my best to not flash my ass to the football team.

A full ten minutes later, Jason joins me. "We're in luck. The next party is across the street from you."

Jason's only twenty-three, but that qualifies as a full-grown man, right? Why does he still want to party with college kids?

"I'm going to pass. I have a terrible headache." One hundred percent true. "And I have an early morning." I have to get to Rise 'N Grind by six to make a boatload of *empanadas*.

"Aww, babe. Really?"

Something about this "babe" nickname makes me cringe, and now that I'm facing the prospect of him dropping me off, I can't help but wonder if he's going to try to kiss me goodnight. He didn't last time, thank God.

And shouldn't I want to kiss a guy I'm interested in?

The fact that I don't tells me everything I need to know.

There was a time I lived for the *possibility* of kissing Rider. Sad as that sounds.

Thankfully, Jason's so psyched to hang out with the football team, he barely gives me a second glance when we pull up to my house and I mention he doesn't need to walk me in. He has to find parking anyway, and there are ten million cars on our street with a stream of people headed toward the Stallion Station.

It's still early, only eleven, so I'm not surprised when I find my house empty. Ramona hasn't been around lately, and Sienna was hanging out with friends.

I'm suddenly exhausted, probably from shivering for the last several hours, so I don't bother taking off my costume before I pull on my fluffy white robe and toss back two Advil. I'm in bed sixty seconds later, ready to cleanse myself of this day.

Except there's a steady beat of music coming from across the street that seems to get louder when I close my eyes. My room is in the front of the house, unfortunately, and I hear all of the noise on the street.

An hour goes by.

Two.

Three.

The revelers traipse through my yard. Puke in the bushes. Pee in the street. I know this because there's always a drunk sidekick who yells out a play-by-play. Like, "Dude, are you really peeing against the fire hydrant?" Insert loud hiccup. Or, "Don't yak through your nose next time. It'll hurt less."

My head is throbbing so hard, I wanna stay curled in this ball and cry.

At four in the morning, I snap.

"This is fucking bullshit!" I slip my feet into my fluffy slippers, pull my robe closed, and march across the street.

As I bang on the front door, it flings open. There are at least a half-dozen naked women traipsing across the room, gyrating on beefy athletes and doing God knows what.

My eyes dart to the sound system, and since I've given into my inner psycho, I head straight to it and yank the plug out of the wall.

The silence makes everyone look up, and I realize I'm staring at my brother, who looks horrified to see me. And then I realize why and turn away before I hurl. Because the girl down on her knees in front of him is obviously not praying.

Jesus, I'm gonna need so much therapy one day.

I clear my throat and address the crowd at large. "Some people have to work tomorrow, assholes. Can you keep it the fuck down? Stop terrorizing this neighborhood. The world *does not* revolve around you and your dumb football games!"

I'm screeching. I can't help it. I'm half-asleep and so hungry I'm nauseous. My eyelids flutter.

God, I feel woozy.

It's almost like...

Almost like... that time I passed out.

Oh, shit. Am I going to pass out again?

I can't remember the last time I ate. Jason and I were supposed to get dinner, which turned into soggy nachos from the gas station, which I passed on.

I blink. And blink again.

Everything feels fuzzy, like it's wrapped in film. I don't even care that Jason is here, and he's missing clothes.

"Shit, Gabby. This isn't what it looks like."

Ignoring him, I stumble to what I think is the front door, lean against it, and close my eyes.

I want to tell Jason to leave me alone, except I'm afraid I'm going to drop to the floor if I let go of the doorframe.

Then I hear the little cry.

It sounds like a baby.

And that's when I know I must be losing my mind.

7

RIDER

Bang, bang, bang!

I crack open my eyes, surprised to hear anything with these noise-cancelling headphones on. They really are amazing.

My door rattles with another series of knocks.

"Hold on, fucker. I'm coming."

My bed is blissfully empty.

I'm starting to wonder if something's wrong with me. We have a roaring party, and the last thing I'm interested in is getting laid.

Truth be told, watching my friends get shitfaced tonight just made me feel like an old man with my one beer and early bedtime. But no one wins a national championship guzzling booze and staying up all night. The guys on the team know to keep their intake to one or two beers.

After dragging my sore ass out of bed and pulling on some sweatpants, I yank open the door. "This better be good."

Michael Oliver, who we call Olly, holds up his hands. "We got a problem, chief."

I scrub my face with both palms. "Is the house on fire? Did a tornado blow through? Is there a plague of locusts raining down on our yard?"

He cringes. "No, but it's pretty bad."

Fuck. "Please tell me nobody was dumb enough to jump in the pool."

I'd insisted we cover it before anyone came over. The guys had wanted a "small get-together." And after kicking ass today for a major win, how could I veto? They said they'd keep it to a dull roar.

But I wasn't really taking into consideration that it was Halloween, and half the school showed up with kegs.

Olly makes a face. "I wouldn't get in the hot tub anytime soon after what I saw go down there tonight, but no, there are no water emergencies."

Thank God for small mercies.

I check the clock by the bed. Ten after four. Damn, I need to get up in a few hours. "What's going on?"

"You really need to see this for yourself."

Reluctantly, I follow him down the stairs and slowly take in the scene. A few of the guys are sprawled on the couch. Girls in varying state of undress. Solo cups everywhere.

Nothing new, basically. I yawn.

So far, the only thing that's weird is the music is off. I blink into the brightness.

And the lights are on.

Olly's eyes widen, and he tilts his head toward the kitchen, where a very pissed Marie Antoinette is chugging juice and... and...

"Is that Gabby?" It's taking me a hot second to process what I'm seeing because it doesn't match our typical debauched Saturday night activities. *Why is she here?* Not that she couldn't stop by if she wanted, but partying at the Stallion Station isn't her typical M.O. And... *What the hell?* "Why is she bouncing a baby?"

"That's what I'm saying," Olly huffs.

Gabby's wearing a little white robe that hangs open over her disheveled costume and some fluffy pink slippers, looking cute as hell. Hotter now that she looks freshly fucked.

I freeze.

Did she sleep with that tool Jason?

For a minute, I feel like I might get sick. I have no reason to be jealous about who she dates, but for some reason, the thought of him getting his hands all over her makes me want to put my fist through the wall.

Olly whispers out of the side of his mouth, "I think her boyfriend hooked up with someone else tonight. She totally caught him. Not that he was being very stealthy. She told him off, and he slunk outta here."

What an idiot. He's going out with this gorgeous, smart woman, and he tosses it all away for cheap beer and some rando.

You broke things off with her. If he's an idiot, what does that make you?

I shrug off that uncomfortable thought. "What's with the baby?"

"Um." Olly hops up and down on his toes. "You should go check that out."

For some reason, those words give me chills. What's that saying? Like someone walked over your grave? Or maybe I'm cold because I'm not wearing a shirt.

Scrubbing one hand over my face again, I sigh and decide to get this over with. I need my beauty sleep.

"Gabby. What's going on?"

When she turns toward me, she wobbles, and I grab her

shoulders and steady her. She's pale, but not from makeup, and her eyes are wild.

The hair on my arms stands up, and I can't figure out if I'm more freaked out by the baby in her arms or the crazy look in her eyes.

The last time I saw her like this, she passed out cold.

Is she upset over that dick?

"Sit." I ignore the dirty look she gives me and usher her to the table where I pull out a chair. After she sits, I grab the one next to her.

We stare at each other over the head of the baby.

"Wanna tell me why you're carting a child around our house in the middle of a party? I won't mention how inappropriate it is to bring it here."

"It? *It?*" She blinks. "Has anyone told you lately that you're an ass? For your information, your excellence, I didn't *bring* the baby here."

Someone chuckles, and I turn and give my roommate Johnny Johnson a dirty look.

That's really his name. Johnny Johnson. But he likes to go by Johnson because he says it makes women think he has a big dick.

Gabby reaches into her pocket, pulls out a crumpled note, and slams it on the table. "This is for you." She glances around the kitchen. "Or for one of your miscreant roommates."

I glance at the paper. "You wrote this?"

She rolls her eyes. "No, I found it in that basket over there." She points to the corner where a small wicker basket sits. "Along with the baby."

The baby snuggles closer to the beautiful French aristocrat who's barking orders at me in my house. I almost smile. Gabby's a lot bossier than she used to be. I kinda like this take-charge vibe she has going on.

She taps her finger on the paper, and I realize I'm staring at her like a dumbass.

I clear my throat and focus on the note. The paper is smudged but still legible.

This is Poppy, you're daugter.

What the fuck? It doesn't matter how many times I read it because it doesn't make any sense.

I glance around the room. I read the words again. "Whose letter is this?"

For once, everyone's quiet. My eyes return to the slip of paper I'm gripping.

"Seriously, who's this for?" Because the only thing jumping out at me right now is the fact there is no name at the top.

Olly shrugs. "Doesn't say."

I read the words again.

This is Poppy, you're daugter. Sory I can't take care of her anymor. I tried. I really did. She loves her blankie. I'll call you when I get their.

Whose daughter? Get where? What the fuck is this person talking about?

"Whoever wrote this can't spell," Olly mumbles. "Either that or she was blitzed."

I flip over the paper, but it's blank. "Where's the rest of the note?" There has to be more.

Olly shrugs. "That's it. Just the baby, her blanket, her beanie, and the letter." He roots around in the basket. "Wait. There's a bottle and a couple of diapers."

Gabby snuggles the baby closer. "So there's no formula?"

Olly just stares at her.

"So we can feed her more once the bottle runs out." Gabby runs a hand over the tuft of blonde hair at the top of Poppy's head.

"No, that's it. Just the one bottle." He hands it to her.

She offers it to the baby, who sniffles before she starts to drink.

Olly peeks over and pats her back. "Poor girl. She was crying when we found her."

Gabby shoots me a dirty look. "No one could hear her, though, because the music was so damn loud."

Olly chuckles. "Until you got here and yanked the sound system out of the wall."

It hits me like a Mac truck on I-10.

"If this is someone's idea of a joke, I'm gonna bust your balls when I figure out who did this." I look around the room, but no one pipes up. And what really troubles me is the rest of the guys look just as perplexed as I feel. "Where's Tank?" He's good at sniffing out pranksters and liars.

I turn to Olly since he always knows everyone's business.

"He's at Bree's tonight. You know he doesn't stay here when we party."

Tank says he doesn't want to put himself in a situation where he might drink too much and do something stupid that would fuck up his relationship. Seems kinda extreme in my opinion, but no one asked me.

"Call him. Tell him we need to have a household meeting."

"Chief, it's four-thirty in the morning."

"Olly, I'm well aware of the time. And unless you're offering to accept paternity of our little visitor, I highly suggest you call Tank. In fact, tell him to bring Bree."

She has her shit together. If we all put our heads together, maybe we can figure this out.

8
RIDER

SEVERAL HOURS LATER, and we're definitely not any closer to figuring this out. We got rid of the rest of the people at the party.

Someone made coffee. My roommates and I are sitting around the living room, bleary-eyed and annoyed. I called off my study session, and the guys cancelled their immediate plans. Gabby had to call in to her job at the coffee house.

If this is a joke, someone has a sick sense of humor.

I tip back my cup of coffee, wishing I had gone to bed earlier last night.

After insisting that the couch be covered with a blanket because she questioned our hygiene, Gabby and Poppy eventually settled there, where they both fell asleep.

"They're pretty sweet, all snuggled up," Tank whispers.

I stare at the baby, who's drooling all over my neighbor. They are pretty cute.

Bree pokes me in my shoulder. "This is going on too long for it to be a prank. No one with any sense would leave a baby at the football house."

"So we're just supposed to accept what was in the note? That she belongs to one of us?" I don't state the obvious—that it's fucking insane.

Could one of the guys have knocked up some girl? Sure. But did this happen and none of us have a clue? Only for this mystery woman to leave her on our doorstep like a damn Amazon package? Doubtful.

Gabby stretches with a quiet groan while still somehow keeping Poppy cuddled comfortably. She peeks through tiny slits, like it's painful to open her eyes. "I think you guys should take the note seriously."

Her brother laughs dryly. "There's *no way* that kid is mine."

"How do you know?" Gabby sits up straighter. Her voice is raspy with sleep. She sounds sexy as hell. If this weren't a totally fucked-up situation, I'd spend this morning appreciating her smoking-hot cleavage in that getup. "Pretty sure you don't remember the name of the girl you were hooking up with a few hours ago when I walked in here. How do you know *for sure* who you banged, what, a year and a half ago?"

I'm almost afraid to ask what she saw when she stormed into our house last night.

Ben scowls but doesn't respond.

She makes a good point. Unfortunately.

Damn. Who was I with back then?

The idea that this kid could be mine is scary as hell. They scream all the time. They take big shits. They never sleep. That's about the extent of my knowledge on the subject.

In fact, I've never considered having any. Although this one seems nice enough, it's just... Fuck. How the hell am I or any of the guys supposed to juggle a baby, classes, and our grueling football schedule? It's impossible.

Gabby pats Poppy's butt gently. "The baby is maybe six or seven months old. Add in the gestational period, thirty-seven to forty-two weeks. Someone please calculate that. My head is too foggy to figure this out."

Olly hums for a second. "By that math, conception would've been mid-June, July, maybe early August. Not last summer, obviously, but the summer before."

"Okay, so who'd you hook up with the summer before last?" Gabby glances around the room slowly, and my heart hammers hard in my chest for some reason, but when she gets to me, she stops and looks away.

I exhale. *Christ.* I do not want to sit around with Gabby and discuss my hookups. My chest hurts thinking about it.

"How do you know her age?" Tank waves a finger at the kid. "The note didn't say."

Gabby shrugs. "I've done a lot of babysitting, so I've been around babies. Plus, I want to be a teacher and had to take child development."

"You want to be a teacher?" Ben asks.

How is her brother so clueless? Judging by the glare Gabby sends his way, I'm not alone in thinking this.

She ignores his question and turns back to Tank. "Poppy can hold up her head, and when I asked her if she wanted her bottle before she fell asleep, she said, 'Baba.' Which could just be baby babble or indicate she's really smart. And, I'm no expert, but really young babies aren't this sturdy. You have to hold their heads and give them more support."

"Huh." Tank pulls out his phone, and after a minute nods. "Google agrees with your assessment."

"So what are we supposed to do?" Ben mumbles. "Make a list or something?"

Trevor gets up and motions to himself. "Sorry, chief. I'm out. One, she looks nothing like me." He lifts an eyebrow dramatically. Trevor likes to brag he's a younger and even better-looking version of Idris Elba. The ladies seem to agree. "Two, I was dating that Brazilian model back then, and there's no way the two of us together could've popped out a blonde baby. Though she's cute as hell."

Bree nods and looks to her boyfriend. "I have to agree."

Tank shrugs. "Before we finish out this game of Clue, can we all vow to take tonight to our graves? No way can this shit get out. It's bad enough people were at the party when we discovered Poppy."

Fuck. "Coach will kill us if he hears a baby got left on our doorstep and we can't figure out who's the father."

I swallow. *No way. No way this kid is mine. Relax.*

Taking a deep breath, I realize I just need to help the guys troubleshoot until we get to the bottom of this, and then I can take a gargantuan nap.

By this time tomorrow, we'll be back to normal and laughing at how ridiculous this was. It'll be fine.

9

RIDER

I TEXT my study group because this is obviously going to take longer than I thought. Maybe we can meet up this evening.

Olly breaks out a notebook. "By process of elimination, Trevor is out, and so is Tank because Bree would cut off his testicles if he had a baby with another lady."

Everyone laughs, and Bree grabs her boyfriend's face in a fierce hold before she peppers him with kisses. "That's right, boo. You'd be dead, but you know better, don't you?"

"I certainly do, my little honeybee."

We all make puking sounds, and I turn away from the love fest. "Fine. That leaves Ben, Noxious, Johnson, and Olly."

Olly squawks, but I level him with a look. He might be a big nerd, but I know he got major ass last year, so there's no way he's wiggling out of this. Knox looks like he wants to puke.

Ben's eyes narrow. "What about you?"

I shrug. "She's not mine."

"How do you know?"

My eyes dart to Gabby, and once again, she avoids my gaze. I turn back to Ben, who's officially on my shit list.

"Because I do." God, why am I sweating? "I never..." I lower my voice. "I never fuck without a condom, okay?"

"Neither do I."

The peanut gallery chimes in.

"Me neither."

"Ditto."

"Never ever."

I run my hands through my hair, wishing I could be back in my bed and blissfully unaware of this situation. "Fine. Assuming one of our Titan-sized swimmers got through the latex"—*please, God, let it not be mine*—"how do we test for paternity without walking up to the hospital and declaring ourselves major fuckups and sparking a scandal that will probably give Sully a heart attack? This is a small town. Yesterday, everyone was talking about our win. You want that to shift away from the game? Because if this gets out, everyone will be gossiping about how one of us knocked up some girl and we're too fucking stupid to realize it."

No one responds.

If anyone gets how small towns work, it's me, and I'll be damned before I let my reputation get smeared to hell. Charming has been good to me. It'll kill me if that changes.

"This is crazy, Kingston." Ben tosses up his hands. "A baby gets dropped off on our doorstep, and we're actually wondering if she belongs to one of us? What we should do is call children's services or social services or whatever."

A gasp has us all turning to Gabby, who's turned her body as though she's shielding the baby from us. "You'd really call Family and Protective Services, Ben? After..." Her voice drops to a whisper. "After what happened to me, you'd call DFPS?"

The look on her face sends a pang of regret through me so strong, I have to fold my arms to prevent myself from crossing the room and sweeping her into a hug. I hate that I haven't been there for her all this time. That I was so wrapped up in my own shit, I didn't stop to think about what she must be going through with barely any family to rely on.

We all look from Gabby to her brother and back again.

"This is not the same thing, *Gabriela*."

"The hell it's not the same thing, *Benjamín*."

After a long silence where they stare each other down, Tank coughs. "Sorry, Gabby, I hate to ask this, but can you tell us what happened? The guys need to make an informed decision."

She looks to Bree, whose eyes soften. "Sorry, girl. I think he's right. If you know something that could shed light on this for everyone, it might be helpful."

Gabby's jaw clenches, and I hate that she has to relive this. "Our dad died when we were really little, but our mom died in a car crash when I was eight, and Ben was seven. He got adopted right away by our uncle, who did not want another daughter. So I went into social services until a family member finally got around to picking me up. Almost four years later."

Fuck. She told me some of this during our long talks that fall we hung out, but hearing it now, it makes more sense.

Back then, she made it sound like it wasn't a big deal that she'd gone into foster care, but judging by the pain glittering in her eyes right now, I realize maybe she was just trying to be strong.

What the fuck, Rider? Of course being a foster kid sucked.

Ben starts to pace. "That's not fair, Gabby. *Tío Julio* couldn't afford another child. It wasn't that he didn't want you."

She laughs, but blinks rapidly, obviously trying not to cry. "Sure. Tell yourself what you need to sleep at night, Ben."

Her brother pales but says nothing.

Bree scoots over to Gabby and wraps her and the baby in a hug. "That sucks, honey. I'm so sorry. That must've been horrible."

When Bree lets her go, Gabby shakes her head. "Ben, if this is your daughter, you can't let her go into social services. Never mind my experience—I've heard so many horror stories from other foster kids. Don't do it. You have no control over who could get her. She might get a nice, normal family or some sick fucks who are just fostering kids for the paycheck or worse. Trust me when I say you don't want the latter."

All the hair on my neck sticks straight up at the warning in her voice.

After an awkward silence, Gabby puts a trembling hand to her chest. "Ben, if she's yours, I'll help you, okay? I will. I know you have football and... everything else. But I'll help. I'll literally do anything you want to keep her from going into foster care."

Damn. This girl is breaking my heart.

A few of the guys wipe their eyes, and I can't deny that I'm choked up too.

Ben shakes his head, but his tone is soft. "And if she's not mine? If she's not ours?" He motions to the rest of us. "What then? You can't keep some random kid."

She nods slowly and takes a shuddering breath. "I agree we should call the authorities if she doesn't belong to one of you."

Tank and I make eye contact, and he nods.

I pray this doesn't come back to bite me in the ass, but Gabby has a good point. "Do we all agree we don't want Poppy to go into foster care if she is one of ours?" I'd hate to send her away even if she isn't ours, but it's not like the football house could take on that kind of responsibility.

Everyone nods. Even Ben, eventually.

Bree rubs Gabby's back. "How can we figure this out without going to the hospital for a paternity test?"

"Doesn't the pharmacy carry those?"

Olly scratches his head. "Even if it does, I don't think we

should go to any stores in Charming. Someone will notice us buying five. It'll be on social media before we pay for them."

I nod. "He's right. We have to go out of town for that."

"I'm on it." Tank is Googling as fast as his giant fingers will let him. "Walgreen's has a test that's affordable and will give us results in two days. We'll just take a quick drive down to Austin. No problemo."

Thank fucking God. That's two days longer than I want this to drag out, but at least there's a finish line in sight. "Great. Tank, can you handle that for us?"

"You got it, chief."

"Wait. I didn't pork anyone that summer!" Johnson jumps up and humps the air like he's doing a victory dance in the end zone. "I've never been so grateful for a dry spell in my entire life. She's not mine."

"It took you all that time to figure that out?" Ben snarks. "Speaking of which, maybe we should make a list of chicks we hooked up with, like on the whiteboard or something."

We all cringe, and Bree snaps her fingers. "That's gross, bro, and you don't want someone taking a pic of that board and slut-shaming the women on it. Do it in your head or phone or somewhere *private*."

His eyebrows pinch together. "Yeah, I guess you're right. I wasn't thinking."

The baby lifts an arm and drops her hand right over Gabby's perky tit. My neighbor turns an adorable shade of pink and moves it. "Fine. By tonight, can you all think back to that summer so we can consider who the mother might be? We'll need everyone to check in and swab or whatever the test calls for."

The guys agree.

"And who's going to take me to get supplies for Poppy? I'm thinking Target."

Bree claps. "I wanna come. I love Target."

Both girls look at me.

"What?" I ask.

Bree smirks. "You're the captain."

"Of the *football team*." I motion to her. "I don't see your uniform."

"You're so cute when you try to be funny." She laughs. "But really. Why don't you collect money from the guys, and then you can drive us to the store?"

"Why do you need me to go? I have a test to study for and a paper to write."

"Like we don't have shit to do? Besides, who's going to carry all the boxes?"

I don't even know what she's talking about. "How much does *one* six-month-old kid need for a few days?"

The guys mumble in agreement.

Bree smirks at her cohort. "They're so adorably clueless, aren't they?"

Gabby laughs and then starts counting on her hand even while she somehow keeps her arms around the kid. "Diapers, formula, clothes, blankets, a car seat, some pacis, a pack-and-play, a few toys. Minimum."

What the fuck is a paci?

"Minimum." Bree nods and crosses her arms.

"And how are we supposed to go to Target without a car seat?"

"Easy. One of your roommates has to watch her."

Well, hell. I'd rather go to Target than babysit.

But her comment sends all of the guys scrambling out of their seats like their jock straps catch on fire.

I hold up my hand. "Get back here, assholes. Number one, I need some cash. Let's assume if one of us is the sperm donor, that person will pay everyone back for these expenses." I say another prayer it's not me, because how the hell am I supposed to support my drunk-ass father, myself, *and* a baby? "Number two, you can watch Poppy in pairs. And when I say watch her, I mean one set of eyes need to be on her at all times. We don't know if the kid will do somersaults off the beds when she wakes up or chew on cords or whatever."

"She's not a puppy." Gabby snorts. "But I agree redundancy is needed in this case."

Ignoring her, I continue. "And three, if there's an emergency, call one of the girls."

Gabby and Bree give out their numbers, and the guys dutifully program them into their phones.

I look up from my screen and smirk at Gabby. "Does this mean you'll unblock me?"

She taps her chin with her index finger like she's deep in thought. "I'm not sure. Has hell frozen over yet?"

I'm laughing when I realize the room has gone quiet. "What?"

Ben's holding his fists at his side. "Why would my sister need to *unblock* you?"

I want to tell him to mind his own fucking business when Gabby stands and holds the baby up to her brother until he reluctantly takes her.

"Here's the thing, Ben. If you had been in my life *in any way at all* since college started, you'd probably know the answer to that question. But since you weren't, not even when I tried, you don't deserve to ask."

And with that, the beautiful Marie Antoinette stalks away.

10

GABBY

Rider is tight-lipped as he follows Bree and me through the aisles of Target.

Thankfully, I changed out of my Halloween costume before we came, and I can breathe again now that I'm wearing yoga pants and a hoodie.

"Oooh, this is pretty," Bree coos at a pink bodysuit.

I don't know Bree that well, but she and her boyfriend seem pretty devoted to each other. "Are you and Tank planning a big family?"

"Huge. Like five kids."

"That's sweet. Terrifying, but sweet."

She laughs and tosses the outfit in the cart. "What about you? Do you want a big family someday?"

I can't bring myself to care that Rider is within hearing range. He's the one who thought we wanted different things in life. I guess he was right. "Assuming I can find someone to date who isn't an idiot? I guess I'd like a big family."

"I heard about the paramedic. That he was hooking up at the party behind your back. You want me to spike his drink with a strong laxative?"

A smile almost makes its way to my face. "No, but thank you for the offer." I sigh. "It wasn't working out between us anyway. It's okay. He wasn't *the one*. I'm not all broken up about it, honestly. I just thought I should go out with him since it's been a while since..."

"Since you got any bow-chicka-bow-wow?"

We both laugh. "Yeah. That. Plus, the last boyfriend I had was sophomore year. I thought it was time to venture out there again."

"Are you telling me you haven't dated anyone since sophomore year?" Her eyes bug out.

"What can I say? I'm picky." The back of my neck heats, letting me know that Rider is *right behind me now*. And it makes me want to clarify something. "I dated this great guy Sean sophomore year. He was my first. *Some guys* are afraid to date a virgin. Afraid they'll get too clingy or make too many demands. But we had fun together."

It was a relief to break the seal. Guys get weird about the virgin thing, and I was starting to get a complex. I used to think I wanted to have sex with someone I loved the first time, but now I'm grateful I wasn't too gone for Sean. He was leaving anyway. This way, no one got hurt.

"Where is he now?"

"New York. He got offered a job after graduation, so we parted as friends." I pick up a baby blanket and run my finger over the ladybug stitched in the corner. "But back to your kid question, if I did find *the guy*, I'd want more than one kid if I had any at all. Because bad things happen to people all the time, and at least this way I could be assured the kids would have each other."

My brother obviously doesn't realize we're supposed to support one another and be a team.

This whole semester has been a painful realization of where

I stand with Ben. When we lived on opposite sides of campus, it was easy to rationalize the distance since we didn't grow up together after our parents died, but now that he lives across the street, I can see he's not interested in having a relationship with me.

She squeezes my arm.

"I'm okay. I usually try to forget all of that stuff, but with Poppy being in this situation, I felt I had to speak up, you know?"

"You did the right thing," Bree says. "Those dumbasses will thank you someday." Rider coughs dramatically, and Bree smirks. "Yeah, you heard me right back there."

I glance behind me and see Rider's lips tugging up.

Bree nudges me. "How'd you end up doing so well in school given everything you went through? Going through foster care? Not having parents?"

"I kept to myself mostly." I shrug. "School and studying were always safe. Books don't level you with a backhand to the face or a kick to the ribs."

When I see the horrified look on her face, I cringe. "Bree, I survived. A lot of other kids have it worse. Which is why I'm really glad we're protecting Poppy."

She stops to hug me, and I smile. I've had so few hugs in my life, I forgot how good they feel. She sniffles and waves her hand at me. "Ignore me. I'm not crying."

Over her shoulder, I catch Rider's fierce expression, but I don't want his sympathy. I don't need *anybody's* sympathy.

I resume our trek down the aisle and change the subject before this gets any more awkward. "So how freaked out are the guys who are babysitting right now?"

Bree snickers. "They're prolly shitting their briefs."

When Rider picks up a random box off the shelf, Bree cackles. "Chief, we don't need that unless you're planning to breastfeed."

"Oh, shit." He puts the manual breast pump back so fast, we crack up.

But his laughter is long gone once we're at the checkout, and he gets the bill. "How can one small child cost this much?"

Remembering back to when my mom struggled to afford stuff for Ben and me as a single mom, I almost sympathize, but then I remember this is Rider, the golden boy. Everything always works out for him. He doesn't need my concern.

∼

Bree has to make a phone call, so after loading up Rider's old Jeep, I find myself alone with this man for the first time in three years.

It's more unsettling than I anticipated.

Sitting in the back seat, I try to appear absorbed in people-watching out the window and ignore the sense of déjà vu that almost overwhelms me.

The soft scent of his cologne threatens to whisk me back three years ago to that time we rolled down the windows and drove around through winding back roads in the Hill Country.

I remember it clearly, that night he finally kissed me, and I made the mistake of thinking he meant it.

"Gabs, can we talk a second?" He clears his throat.

Nothing good ever follows that statement. I brace myself for what's sure to be an awkward conversation.

"I just want to apologize for our... misunderstanding freshman year."

I'm silent for a moment, but the rush of anger that spikes my pulse has me responding before I think better of it. "You'd call it a misunderstanding, huh?" I roll my eyes. "Funny, I didn't think I misunderstood anything, but if you want to mansplain it to me now, go for it."

Why make this easy for him?

It's always been difficult for me to make friends, but for some reason, Rider slipped through my defenses.

I was assigned to tutor him in English. I remember meeting him in the library, and the shy smile he gave me. He was embarrassed to need help. It was the most endearing thing I'd ever seen, and I swear when he leveled me with those big gray eyes, the ground fell out beneath me.

I'm a practical girl, but foster care made me cynical, and ending up with my aunt did nothing to help my outlook on life. But Rider was funny and sweet, not to mention ridiculously good-looking, and I went over faster than a felled log in a forest.

This was before he was the golden boy of the football team. When he was just this guy Rider from some speck-of-dust small Texas town like me.

Even though he rode the bench, I went to all of his games, and we'd grab pizza afterward and talk until late in the night. Although he didn't outright say it, I knew he had a rough home life. He mentioned that his father was an ass. I wanted to wrap my arms around him and make it better.

And I thought I meant something to him. That what we had was special.

Until he became the starting quarterback.

He runs his hand through his hair. "It's just that I needed to focus on football. I had all this pressure, and—"

"And you wanted to sleep around and fuck all the pretty girls while you weren't playing. I totally get it. And I was just some little virgin who couldn't possibly comprehend your need to sow your wild oats. See? No misunderstanding at all."

"Jesus, Gabby, it wasn't like that."

I'll admit he gave me one awkward-as-hell conversation

where he cancelled our tutoring session and mumbled something about needing to focus on football. How he couldn't get too serious about anything.

I thought he meant partying and socializing. I didn't realize he meant me.

My teeth bite into my bottom lip as I think back to that weekend.

It was the first time I'd gotten a little drunk. That night I told him about being in foster care. About losing my parents and being separated from my brother. Things I didn't tell anyone. Ever.

He kissed me. Held me in those big strong arms. For the first time in years, I felt safe.

And then the asshole ghosted me.

I catch his searing gaze in the rearview mirror. Even now, years later, those intense gray eyes hit me squarely in the chest like a grenade. But I breathe through it and remind myself he doesn't care for me. Not one bit. I won't be fooled again by the sincerity in his expression.

It means nothing. It never did.

I shouldn't have a laundry list of offenses ready so long after our "entanglement" ended, but I do. And it erupts out of me before I can tamp it down.

"Really? Then how do you explain suddenly not returning my phone calls or texts? Or blowing off our study sessions? Or pretending I didn't exist when we ran into each other?"

The fact that he knows I blocked his number means he eventually tried to contact me, but I didn't do that for at least a month.

I vowed never to be so dumb again, and in a binge of junk food and angry music, I swore off Rider Kingston and all men like him. I decided then and there never again to be duped by a pretty smile and some bulging muscles.

Jocks like Rider can suck a dick, because I'll certainly never get down on my knees for a douchebag.

Blinking rapidly, I wish I could take back everything I just said. Because I know I shouldn't care this much three years later.

He clears his throat again. "I'm sorry. I was an ass. I'm not denying that, but what I'm trying to say is that it had everything to do with me and not you."

The old *it's not you, it's me* brush-off. Nice. What every girl wants to hear after she's been ghosted.

I shrug, desperate to wrap myself in my dispassionate armor again. "Whatever, Rider." The words are right, but I'm hot and sweaty and ready to crawl out of my skin.

I don't think I'm fooling anyone, but what am I supposed to do? Admit he broke my heart? Tell him I was devastated? Sure, when hell freezes over in South Texas.

A thick silence descends, and I'm two seconds from leaping out of the Jeep and tracking down Bree so we can get out of here when Rider turns in his seat so that we're face to face.

"Look, I don't mean to dredge up the past. I just wanted you to know I'm sorry I hurt you. That it wasn't my intention. I... I didn't think we were that serious."

I'm too incensed to respond. He didn't think we were serious? Isn't that every man's lame excuse when he's an asshole and blows off some unsuspecting girl?

I wish I were one of those aloof women who could pretend I wasn't hurt, but I'm sure he can read me. No matter how many *Glamour* and *Cosmo* articles I read about playing it cool and being detached, I have yet to master that female skill.

Before I can tell him to go fuck himself, his voice softens. "I also wanted to say I'm sorry about what happened when you were a kid. That had to be tough."

My jaw tightens, and I blink back the heat in my eyes. "Don't do that."

"Do what?"

"Don't feel sorry for me. I don't need your pity."

I've had a lifetime of pity. *That's the new girl. She's the foster kid. Just look at her clothes. Poor thing. So skinny too. Bet they don't feed her. She doesn't have parents, but her aunt finally took her. Someone had to.*

Crossing my arms over my chest, I determinedly stare out the window, grateful that dumb wetness in my eyes disappears.

I never tell people I've been in foster care because the second you do, they start giving you side-eye, like they're afraid you're going to steal the silverware.

Deep down, I always wondered if that's the real reason Rider ditched me, and he just didn't have the balls to say it.

I swallow, hating how bitter I feel. Hating that being a foster kid tainted my world view so much.

It's why I try to never think about that time. Why I've busted my ass here. Why I work as many hours as humanly possible. Because I'll never be that poor again or that dependent on another person. I can do it myself, thank you very much.

The passenger door opens, and I'm so grateful to see Bree, I could cry.

And that's the biggest problem of all. Being around Rider brings all of my emotions to the surface, but I won't let myself fall apart. Once was enough.

11

RIDER

Laden with a dozen Target bags, I open my front door and pause.

All of my roommates are on the floor of the living room, playing with Poppy.

And they're trying to get her to crawl through... an obstacle course of Amazon boxes?

"What the hell is this?" Even I know she shouldn't roll around on that dirty floor.

I drop the bags, exhausted from being woken at four this morning and that fucked-up conversation with Gabby. But it's still the early afternoon, and if I hustle, maybe I can be productive. God knows that essay isn't gonna write itself.

Knox hops up. "You should see her. She kinda scoots on her belly. It's so fucking funny."

I'm seriously not in the mood for this today. "What's that on her butt?"

"We ran out of diapers, so we wrapped her in Tank's old t-shirt, but we figured that wouldn't hold in the piss, so we fortified it by wrapping her ass in a plastic grocery bag and duct tape."

I open my mouth and close it again.

I'm so out of my element, it's not even funny, but I know Bree and Gabby would not let this shit fly, so I open the Target bags and pull out the diapers. "Please put this on her." The girls showed us how to change a diaper before we went shopping.

Surveying the room, I consider the hundred people who marched through here last night and cringe. "Let's get her off that floor."

Maybe I can keep this kid from needing to bathe in disinfectant.

I pinch the bridge of my nose and try to think through this. The girls are coming over in a little while, and I'd like to have this situation in hand before I give Gabby another reason to think I'm an idiot.

My stomach rumbles, and I glance at Poppy. I'm guessing her bottle is long gone by now.

I hand off a container of formula to Olly, who seems to understand what I want him to do without me explaining.

After I retrieve the rest of our Target haul and make sure Olly will keep an eye on things, I take a quick shower.

The moment the hot water hits my skin, I groan. I took a nasty hit in the fourth quarter of yesterday's game, and my muscles aren't letting me forget it.

Once I'm clean and dressed, I attempt to get some homework done, but all of the words run together on the page. I give in and take a nap. While it helps my aching muscles, my brain is still foggy when my alarm goes off an hour later.

I return to the living room and collapse on one of the sofas. It's quiet for once, and I'm immediately thinking of that conversation with Gabby.

I scrub my face, wishing I could take back what I said this morning. None of that shit came out right. I wanted to tell Gabby I missed our friendship, that I fucked up three years ago.

That I wanted to make amends, but every word out of my mouth was wrong somehow.

I never wanted to hurt her. I wanted to protect both of us. To put some distance there before I did something I couldn't take back.

What I said was true. What happened was one hundred percent my fault. I was stressed as hell that semester, and I was freaked out by what happened when I went home that weekend. I was desperate to get my head on straight when I got back to campus and made mistakes that I regret, but I'm guessing she's not interested in the details.

Freshman year feels like a million years ago, and I'm not sure digging up the past will help make things right, but knowing I've injured her feels like a lead weight.

What really resonates with me, what's been sounding in my head like a gong all afternoon, is the hurt expression in her eyes. She's always so confident and buttoned up. Almost closed off. Today, though, I saw it. Saw that I really wounded her.

Add that to hearing more about what happened to her as a kid, and I feel like the biggest dick on the planet. Knowing I added to her burden kills me. That woman is smart and driven and fucking tough. I respected her before, but now, she's in a league of her own.

Ben, Knox, and Tank charge in like a herd of wildebeests and settle around the living room as the front door opens and Bree and Gabby stroll in. Gabby has a clipboard in her hands and a pen behind her ear and looks so fucking cute, I wanna bite her stubborn ass.

It hasn't been long since we parted, but I'm stupidly excited to see her. Except judging by the death glare she sends my way, she hates my guts even more than she did before I tried to clear the air.

When I think of the past, I can't help but consider that

agonizing detail she shared with Bree. That she gave her virginity to some guy she dated sophomore year.

Yes, I was reluctant to go there with her, reluctant to form any kind of serious attachment with a woman. Especially when I knew what kind of damage that does when it goes south.

And it always goes south.

That doesn't mean I want to think about her fucking another man.

I slump back and wonder what she's seen living across the street. I hope she's not painting me with the same brush as the rest of the guys who live here. I'm not a saint, but I'm not half as degenerate as some of my roommates.

My eyes lift to her. She's wearing a hoodie and those leggings that make her ass look amazing. I almost swallowed my tongue last night when I spotted her in that Marie Antoinette costume. Gabby looked sexy as fuck in that getup, and I thought long and hard about that outfit in the shower this afternoon. But even now with her hair pulled up in a messy bun, zero makeup, and comfortable clothes, she's still gorgeous.

Olly comes from the kitchen with Poppy strapped to his chest. "This baby carrier is incredible. Two thumbs up."

"You look adorable." Gabby waves her pen at him. "Pretty sure that look is a huge chick magnet, so be prepared if you head outdoors with her."

"Really?" His lips pull up further. "Wait. What should we say if someone asks who she is?"

The girls confer, and Bree says, "Just say you're babysitting for a friend."

"But this raises a good point." Gabby whips out a folder and hands around copies. "This is an NDA, a nondisclosure agreement."

Knox holds up his hand, which almost makes me laugh. I

guess class is in session. When Gabby turns to him, he asks, "If the kid is ours, why do we need to sign this?"

"Good question. I figured we'd all sign. The forms will eventually go to the father once we get these results. Y'all are little celebrities around here—"

"Ain't nothing little about me." Noxious smirks.

She rolls her eyes, likely well aware the perv isn't referring to his height. "My point is these might tamp down on the gossip a bit. Since we know how fast that travels in this town, I thought the parent would appreciate a certain level of decorum. Think of long term. You might be drafted into the NFL. Who wants the story of what happened last night to end up on *SportsCenter*?"

"Damn. That's a good point," he mutters.

She takes her pencil from behind her ear and taps on her clipboard. "I figure we should have everyone who babysits sign off on the form too, just to maintain your privacy. It's no less than celebrities require their nannies to do." Then she picks up a spreadsheet. "I'll also need everyone to sign up for time slots to watch Poppy. That way we can ensure coverage while still getting everyone to class and practice. Bree and I hope to find a few people to help, but we'll take turns watching her during your games. I'll need everyone's email, and I'll send you a color-coded copy of the sign-up form."

Bree catches my eye. "Gabby is good, no?"

No, she's fucking fantastic.

Gabby ignores the compliment and scans the list on her clipboard. "Before we get to the mommy list, we'll do the paternity tests, but I have some bad news for you guys." She flips through the pamphlet tucked among Q-tip vials and instructions. "There's an additional hundred-dollar fee to process the results." She glances around the room. "Per test."

Fuck. The guys all groan, and mentally, I'm tabulating how much more of this I can handle financially. I keep telling myself we'll have the results in a few days, and one of my roommates will pay me back. Because damn, I need this money.

Tank apologizes for not realizing that detail. "I looked online, though, and this one is still the most affordable."

"It's okay, bro. Thanks for getting them." I reach over, and we fist-bump. "Did anyone give you strange looks for buying so many?"

He laughs. "I told the pharmacist I had a busy spring break. Ow!"

Bree punches him in the arm. "You even think about sticking your dick in another girl, and you're in some deep shit."

"Aww, boo. You're the only love bug for me."

After a huffy moment where Bree seems to contemplate whether forgiveness is in the cards for her boy, he pulls her to him for a kiss. Which eventually leads him to mauling her on the couch. Tongue-in-mouth, hand-on-tit mauling.

Gabby coughs. "Don't worry about us. I'll just make some popcorn."

Tank and Bree separate with big smiles on their faces, and Tank adjusts his junk. "What? My woman's hot." He waggles his eyebrows at her, and whispers, "Ten minutes. My room."

Shaking her head while trying to hide her smile, Gabby cleans the coffee table with a Clorox wipe and then organizes the paternity test kits. I can totally see her as a teacher. With her hair up in one of her buns and those skirts she likes to wear sometimes. I'm busy entertaining a full-on teacher fantasy featuring one feisty but beautiful Gabriela Duran when she claps her hands.

"Okay, guys, let's get to this."

Knox leaps up and grabs his crotch where he's rocking a massive boner. "I'm ready to go. Give me my cup."

Gabby arches an eyebrow as she points to his junk. "What *exactly* do you think you need to do for the paternity test?"

"Jerk off. Spooge it. Rock out with my cock out."

Bree chuckles, and Gabby shakes her head. "Sorry to disappoint you, stud muffin, but I just need to swab."

Knox's eyes bug out. "Swab my dick?"

"*Nooo*, your cheek."

"You need to swab my ass?"

We're all laughing at this point, and I tell him to sit down. "Get your weapon of mass destruction out of the girls' faces. Gabby means you need to swab *the inside of your mouth*, dumbass."

"Oh, shit. Guess I was off base there." He presses on his dick, likely trying to get it to settle down.

Gabby opens a box and hands him a long Q-tip. "It's okay. Why don't you swab first so you can go… deal with your problem."

As she rotates around the room, my heart jackhammers in my chest.

This situation is so out of control. If Coach hears about this before we get some answers, he'll be pissed. But worse, he'll be disappointed.

Who's the dad, you ask? Well, funny story about that…

Fuck, no. I definitely don't wanna have that convo if I can avoid it.

Jesus. I should be working on my essay and studying my ass off right now. Not lounging around the living room waiting to swab some spit. Seriously, I need a kid like I need a shiv to my kidney. I'm so fucked if this baby is mine.

My leg jiggles against the couch, and I rub my palm down my thigh to try to calm down.

When she swabs her brother, they don't say anything to each other. Seriously, what is his deal?

I understand she's upset he's standoffish, but why has he been pretending he barely knows her all this time?

When she gets to me, I stare at her unabashedly. It's a great distraction from the fact that I'm taking a fucking paternity test.

A thick strand of hair falls into her face, and my fingers itch to tuck it behind her ear. She smells warm and feminine, and everything in me aches to stick my nose against her skin and inhale.

I study the gentle slope of her neck. The graceful tilt of her head. The intense hue of her eyes.

Hazel is too simple a description to describe her eyes. They're a deep golden color with flecks of green, like the shade you'd see on some exotic animal.

She's no bird. No, more like a lioness. Fierce. Unyielding. Uncompromising. Characteristics I never thought I'd find so attractive.

How did I miss all of this freshman year? Was I always such a spectacular idiot?

I knew she was intense. Back then, I probably viewed that as a negative trait, but now, watching her take command is sexy as fuck.

If Miss Duran was my teacher, I'd never miss a day of school.

When she finally looks up, when our eyes meet, my heart kicks in my chest again.

"Thanks for doing this, Gabby," I whisper with all sincerity. This baby situation is pure insanity, but for some reason, knowing Gabby is here makes it less crazy.

And then I realize the crazy part.

I can count everyone I trust on one hand.

And yet... I trust her.

Except for this emergency, we haven't really spoken in years, but I know down to my soul that she'll do her best to help us figure out what's going on and take care of Poppy.

A pink hue heats her cheeks, but she nods.

I want to say so many other things, except now's not the time.

But maybe with all of this baby stuff going on, I'll get a chance.

Because I need to make it up to her. One way or another.

12

GABBY

TECHNICALLY, I've taken all of my English credits, but who wouldn't want to take an extra British literature class? Plus, right now it's a great distraction from worrying about Poppy.

We're supposed to get the paternity results today or tomorrow, and I keep checking the website every five seconds.

I know it's stupid to fall in love with that baby, except I can't help myself. It's not like she asked to be in this situation.

But I'm definitely worried I'm getting too attached.

If the baby isn't my brother's, he'll probably throw a block party, I think morosely.

You'd think a crisis like this would make us closer, but Ben's as distant as ever, barely bothering to make eye contact with me. I'd like to grab him by his dumb designer t-shirt and shake him silly until he tells me what's wrong.

After checking the paternity website one more time, I drop my phone into my backpack and chide myself when my thoughts drift to Rider, as they've done more times than I'd like to admit in the last few days.

I don't think about his apology, and I don't let myself revel in the long looks he's given me ever since.

Nope. I definitely don't.

Those big gray eyes got me in trouble once, and I don't plan to be a sucker a second time.

Except... he did seem sincere.

No, Gabby. Stay strong.

Our professor leans back against the windowsill and reads passages aloud from EM Forester's *A Room with a View*, one of my favorite books. Even though I was little when I first saw the film and couldn't grasp all of the nuances, I understood that at the heart was a really cool love story.

As I munch on a granola bar, Bree bumps my elbow and whispers, "I watched the movie this weekend. Did you know there was a full-frontal nude scene?"

"My foster mother covered my eyes when we got to that part. Took me ten years to finally see the dangly bits."

Her shoulders shake with laughter, and I smile.

This unexpected friendship with Bree is the most surprising part about helping the football guys. I've seen her in class before this and I helped her with an essay once, but now that I'm so involved at her boyfriend's house, it seems to have gotten me a cool new girlfriend.

I could use a few friends. It's hard for me to meet people sometimes. I spent the bulk of high school babysitting for my aunt and being an awkward nerd. The one time I really took a chance socially and put myself out there was with Rider, so when he blew me off, I withdrew even more.

By the time sophomore year rolled around and I moved off campus with Ramona, I started dating Sean, who was a bigger homebody than me. After that, it was just easier to keep to myself than to try being friends with people who would eventually disappear or move away.

My attention returns to the professor, who reads, "'If Miss

Honeychurch ever takes to live as she plays, it will be very exciting both for us and for her.'"

I pause, that line hitting me in a way it never has before in all the times I've read the book.

Lucy Honeychurch is a prim and proper young English woman who refuses to give in to the advances of the free-spirited George Emerson, a man she met while on vacation in Italy, opting instead to get engaged to the very stuffy and condescending Cecil Vyse. That quote my professor recited refers to the fact Lucy plays incredibly emotional music on the piano but lives a buttoned-up, repressed life.

I used to think I wanted a George Emerson, someone who could get me to loosen up and enjoy life and take chances, but this book fails to tell you that taking chances and putting yourself out there doesn't always work the way you think it will.

Sometimes taking chances gets you ghosted by the quarterback.

I cross my arms and whisper to Bree, "Is Cecil Vyse really so bad?"

She snorts, and we pretend to be engrossed in the lecture when our professor turns sharply our way.

"Daniel Day Lewis was pretty DILF-y in *The Crucible*," I mumble once he returns to his notes. "I watched it over the summer. We shouldn't judge him by his portrayal of Cecil. That role required him to be pompous and anemic."

"You're such a nerd."

She has no idea. I wrote up a whole unit of lessons for that play, and I don't even student-teach until next spring.

Being a nerd used to bother me. Now I view it as a badge of honor.

When class lets out, we stroll out to the courtyard. Sienna is walking by with some friends and does a double-take. "Gabby!

Hey! Oh, my God, I never see you." She rushes over and gives me a hug, almost knocking me down in the process.

No one is ever this excited to see me. *My social life has turned into* The Twilight Zone. I chuckle to myself.

She waves to her friends. "I'll call you later, Destiny!" When she turns back to me, her face lights up. "How did your date go on Saturday night?"

"How have I not seen you all week?"

"I know, right?" A giggle escapes her. "Kinda met someone over the weekend."

"And you've been hooking up ever since?" I say it as a joke, but her cheeks redden, and she nods wildly.

"Crazy, right? I mean, I eventually put my foot down and demanded we go to class, but otherwise, yeah." She sighs deeply. "It just feels karmic. Like, I've put good vibes into the universe, and it's finally coming back to me."

I swear she's speaking another language. I don't understand exactly what she means, but I'm happy for her regardless. "That's great. Is he a jock?" We've already established she loves football players.

Her eyes roll back in her head dramatically. "Yes. So many muscles!"

Laughing, I sidestep the topic of Jason and introduce Sienna to Bree. In my peripheral vision, I see Zoe walk by with a bunch of her catty friends, who all stare at me and whisper.

I want to flip them the bird and ask Zoe what the hell I ever did to her. She got *me* fired from my tutoring job, and she *still* gives me shit? For a brief, nausea-inducing moment, it's like I'm in middle school all over again, and the popular kids are making fun of my hand-me-downs and thrift-store fashions.

Annoyed, I'm about to take off before I'm late to my job at Archer, when Bree pulls up her phone and squints at the screen.

"Rider says he's been trying to get ahold of you." She glances at me, then at Sienna, then back to me. "You know, for *that assignment*."

We agreed we would limit the Poppy circle of trust as long as possible, but I feel weird not telling Sienna. Still, it's not my secret to tell.

I pull out my cell. "I don't have any messages from him."

Since I had the guys email me their daily routines last weekend so I could set up the babysitting schedule, I've only communicated with him in group emails.

I'll do anything to avoid talking to Rider right now, especially since the guys are working on their "mommy list" and trying to narrow down their possibilities. They eventually did draw up a list on a whiteboard, but I made them use anonymous monikers so some poor unsuspecting girl didn't get dragged into the drama.

If I weren't so annoyed by the whole thing, the pseudonyms would make me laugh. With names like Harley 'I'm Coming' Quinn, Doggy-Style Catwoman, and my personal favorite, Super-Tits & Ass, I wouldn't be surprised if they all had a super-hero kink.

I made a point to leave before we got to Rider. The last thing I need in my life is a list of the girls he banged.

Bree elbows me. "Rider. He needs to talk to you. He said he tried texting you."

Speak of the devil.

Flipping my phone around, I show her my messages. "I don't have anything from him."

But then I pause because...

"Wait." Oops. "I forgot to unblock him."

Sienna's eyes widen. "Are we talking about Rider Kingston? Hottie neighbor and all-star athlete? A face to die for?" She doesn't wait for my response. "Why would you block him?"

I swallow. "It was years ago."

"Is that why you gave him the finger that first day I came over? I thought you were joking." She blinks slowly. "Holy crap, were you two fuckbuddies? I've heard he has a stable of girls. That they all love him but hate each other."

I cringe, hating that I care.

That insidious question niggles at the back of my brain, and I wonder why he wouldn't go there with me. He basically screws anything with two legs, but I wasn't his type. I know I accused him of not wanting to bone a virgin, but I can't help but wonder if there was more to it.

"He and I were never like that." I'd like to tell her we were more—we were friends, and we had a blast together, and he made me feel optimistic about life again.

But what's the point? It ended before it began.

Bree loops her arm through mine. "Gabby, don't believe the gossip. Rider isn't a fuckboy."

Sienna and I give her the look, the one that says she's full of it.

"Okay, he *might* have been in the past, but he's not quite the same player he used to be."

"Whatever." I unhook my arm from hers. "Did he say what he needed? Because I have to go to work."

"I think he's just stressed about that project." Poppy.

"Tell him to email me. I'll call him tonight if it's important."

Maybe I can get away with filtering our conversations through email.

A girl can hope.

13

GABBY

This girl would be wrong.

Because Rider Kingston is *not* excited about emailing me.

To: GabbyGabs@LoneStar.edu
From: RideHim911@gmail.com

Would you please unblock me? I need to talk to you ON THE PHONE. Or I can wait on your doorstep until you get home. P.S. Did you forget how charming and persuasive I can be?

He ends the message with a winky emoji.

To: RideHim911@gmail.com
From: GabbyGabs@LoneStar.edu

Calm down. NO NEED TO YELL AT ME. I forgot to unblock you. Simple mistake. But I'm at work, so this will have to wait until I get home. If this is about the test results, I don't have them yet.

P.S. You must have me confused with another girl. I don't recall anything particularly charming about you.

Lies. All lies. I remember all too well.

Maybe that's enough to get him off my case. I'll do anything to avoid having to speak to him in person or on the phone. Keeping my distance all this time has helped me keep my priorities straight. Besides, I'm not about to drop everything to help him like every other woman in his life likely does.

But then my email dings, and I roll my eyes because of course he says he still needs to speak with me.

Annoying.

I quickly tuck away my phone and paste on a smile when Mr. Barstow, the assistant principal of Archer Academy, darts into the copy room where I'm collating a presentation for tonight's board meeting.

I'm about to ask if I can help him when he barks, "I need two hundred copies, double-sided, ASAP," slaps the form on the counter, and disappears out the door.

My smile drops. "Sure. No problem. And, hey, no thanks necessary."

Unfortunately, this has been typical of my experience here. The staff is curt, the students are demanding, and the job is tedious. If I ever had daydreams of sharing my *Crucible* unit with teachers and discussing literature over mildly burnt coffee, my shifts here have disabused me of that notion.

I'm giving myself a pep talk as I head to the administrative office to drop off the copies when a student charges around the corner and plows into me, leaving me on the floor and sending my neat stack of paper all over the hall.

"Oh, shit. Sorry, sorry." But then the little turd runs off without bothering to lend me a hand.

And I always thought I'd enjoy working in a high school.

My day gets better when I knock on Mr. Barstow's door a few minutes later and enter to find Miranda, Rider's favorite hookup, sitting on the credenza.

She's ultra-blonde with blindingly white teeth that stand out against her inordinately tan skin. But commercial enhancements notwithstanding, she's gorgeous. So attractive, in fact, it makes me reconsider why I questioned Rider's standards. Because the women he sleeps with are stunningly beautiful, and I'm not arrogant enough to put myself in that category.

No, I don't have some weird self-confidence issue. I mean, yes, I'm sensitive about the foster kid thing, but that's why I try not to think about it. And I'm in touch with my strengths, but blonde bombshell is not one of them. I'm nerd-tastic and proud. Girl-next-door with a side vibe of stern librarian. I'd rather read a book than hit up a kegger. I'm cool with all of that.

However, I'm also a firm believer in not burying my head in the sand, so I get why this girl is in Rider's bangable category and I'm not. This is a good reminder that Rider is in a different league.

Obviously, *this* is why he never tried to sleep with me.

Judging by her wide eyes, she's just as surprised to see me as I am to see her.

We've never officially met, but I'm pretty sure Rider ditched me to fool around with her freshman year.

I clear my throat. "H-hi, I'm looking for Mr. Barstow. I have his copies."

Without taking her attention off me, she yells, "Daddy!"

I flinch. Then realize what she said and hang my head.

Awesome. Just what I need. To work for her freaking father.

The assistant principal enters from the adjoining office. "Miranda, I told you not to do that." When he sees me, he points to my desk. "Drop them off there. Thanks."

Well, at least I got a thank you this time.

He leaves just as quickly, and then I'm left with Miranda, who is looking me up and down. I mentally catalogue what I'm wearing and internally cringe when I think about how I used a black sharpie to fill in the scratches on my shoes. A neat trick I picked up from *Pretty Woman*. Thank you, Julia Roberts. But based on the way Miranda is eyeballing them, I wonder if she can tell.

"You're bleeding." She points to my legs where blood trickles down my knee.

Oh. I look down and sigh.

"It's nothing. Some kid ran into me."

She makes a face. "You need to clean it up before my father notices and freaks out. Anything dealing with 'bodily fluids' requires a report."

I nod, remembering something about that from the stack of paperwork I filled out when I was hired.

Her phone pings, and I'm hoping to use that distraction to get back to the copy room when she holds up one finger.

Why does she want me to wait?

She finishes her text and pins me with a long stare. "You look familiar. How do I know you?"

Of course she has no idea who I am while I'll never forget who she is to Rider.

"I'm not sure," I say slowly, deciding to leave Rider out of this equation. I'm never in favor of raising high-drama topics while at work. "Maybe we passed each other on campus?"

"Hmm." Something about the way her eyes narrow makes me nervous.

After an awkward moment, I motion to the hallway. "Well, I have to get back to work, so—"

Before I can finish, the door opens behind me and a huge

smile spreads on Miranda's face, and she squeals, "Baby, I'm so glad you could pick me up!"

I turn to find myself face to face with the guy I've been trying to avoid all week.

And he's here for Miranda. As always.

14

RIDER

My brain short-circuits.

What is Gabby doing here?

And what's with that look in Miranda's eyes? And *why* is she calling me baby? We have never done pet names.

This can't be good.

Based on the weird vibe in here and the hard expression on Gabby's face, she knows exactly who Miranda is.

My mouth opens, to say what, I'm not sure, but then I close it because, fuck, this is awkward.

Smiling wildly, Miranda leaps off the desk and throws herself into my arms.

What the hell? Why is she so clingy? After the talk we had last week, I thought she understood what I wanted—space. Lots of it. When I didn't see her on Halloween, I thought she'd gotten the message loud and clear.

But then she called me today, begging for a ride because she got stranded at the school where her father works. I didn't want to be an asshole and blow her off, so here I am even though I have a ton of homework to do.

Hurt flashes in Gabby's eyes before that blank mask I'm so

familiar with slides into place. She mutters, "Excuse me," and scoots by me like she has no idea who I am.

Fuck. I literally beg her to forgive me over the weekend, and aside from the group convo we had at the house when we took the paternity tests, she hasn't uttered one word to me.

Not. One. Word.

I fucking saw Olly text her all morning about the number of times Poppy has taken a shit, but Gabby won't unblock me. And thanks to her efficiency with that online babysitting spreadsheet and group email updates, we haven't had much of a reason to interact. Well, besides the fuck-off email she sent me today when I asked if she'd unblock me.

The need to make things right with her has been overwhelming. I'm not sure why now, of all times, this feels so pressing, but ever since our talk in the Target parking lot, it's been weighing on me.

Blowing out a breath, I peel Miranda off me. "I'm leaving, so if you want a ride, get your stuff."

I head out without waiting for her. Predictably, Gabby is nowhere to be seen when I enter the hall, but my pea brain is starting to piece together the puzzle. This must be where she works. I heard her and Bree talking about her job at a school.

Why she'd want to work with these assholes is beyond me, but if anyone could make a go of it at snob central, Gabby could. After watching her work her magic on Poppy and a house full of dumbasses, that's one woman I'll never underestimate. She'll probably have these jerks eating out of her hand in no time.

The ride to Miranda's is tense. She's no longer smiling.

"Rider, come on," she whines. "You didn't really mean all that." She waves her hand like what I want doesn't matter.

"No, I *really* did." My grip tightens on the steering wheel. "We've had fun, Mira, but I need to focus."

She runs her finger along my neck, and I resist the urge to

slap her hand away. "You always get so grumpy during the season. How 'bout we just fuck on the weekends? We're both stressed, and we'll blow off some steam together. No other obligations required."

I don't point out how we're not supposed to have any obligations beyond using condoms when we screw, an agreement she said was "perfect" when we first started doing whatever this is.

"As tempting as that sounds," I lie, because being with Miranda right now is suffocating, but I don't wanna hurt her feelings, "I think we should just be friends and go our separate ways."

Between classes, practice, homework, games, and a damn baby at home, I really can't handle one more thing. Thank God we're supposed to get the paternity results any day now. It'll be one thing off my plate. But I'm not comfortable sharing anything about Poppy with her, so I keep that shit to myself.

An angry laugh spills out of her. "Just friends? Rider, we haven't been 'just friends' in years, and you want to start now?"

I've avoided relationships for years to avoid drama, and yet here we are.

I barely keep the growl out of my voice. "We agreed to keep things casual—your suggestion, in fact—but if I'm being honest, I'm not getting that vibe from you anymore. So I'm respectfully bowing out, okay?"

We drive in silence until we get to her place, where she slides out and slams my car door behind her.

I'm so relieved to have her gone, I almost laugh, which should tell me all I need to know about that relationship. It's a liability. And I can't afford any more of those.

When I hit the gas, I know I need to track down Gabby. Lucky for me, I know exactly where she lives.

15

RIDER

After what happened at Archer today, I'm anxious to talk to Gabby. I drop off my gym bag and books in my room and beeline for the door when Tank tells me to hold up.

"Where you headed?"

"Across the street. You need something?"

"Didn't you get Gabby's text? She's on her way here." He pauses, lifting his brows. "With the results."

The results?

Holy shit, the paternity results.

Sweat breaks out on my body as I pull out my phone. Sure enough, there's a group text to meet here in ten. I don't have time to marvel over being unblocked because Gabby might be deploying an atom bomb in my life in a few minutes.

"Did she give you any details?"

Tank motions to Bree, who's on the couch, bouncing Poppy on her knee. "She's printing everything."

My heart wants to beat out of my chest. "Is there a match?"

Bree nods slowly. "She doesn't know which one of you, though, because you're only identified by a number. She told me she isn't comfortable knowing the results before the father, so she hasn't looked to see whose name matches."

Within the next five minutes, all of my roommates are sitting in the living room, even Trevor and Johnson. They might not say it, but since they're not cracking jokes and cutting up, I'm guessing they're here to offer support. Ben's texting on his phone, being his usual closed-off self.

Someone cracks open a box of donuts, and suddenly this reminds me of that group my father meets with once a week. Well, when he goes.

I glance at Poppy, who giggles, totally unaware one of us is about to get slammed with a life-altering tidal wave tonight.

Guilt builds in my chest. I've barely spent any time with her. Bree's cousin took my babysitting shifts this week in return for some signed football swag for her brothers.

But there's a good chance she's not mine, I remind myself.

I've seen the one friend I was hooking up with roughly around that time, and I don't think she could've popped out a kid and still walked around campus looking like a Barbie doll.

Besides, Knox told us the other day he's wondering if he knocked up this chick he's been calling Supergirl Big Tits since he hasn't seen her around school in a while. She's blonde and fits the timeline.

Except...

I watch Knox shove half a donut in his mouth, and I still.

Something about my teammate shoveling chocolate in his pie hole like he hasn't eaten in a week reminds me of...

Reminds me of...

Damn.

I close my eyes and sink back on the couch and try to think back to that summer. I was pissed at my dad and came back to do some conditioning with the guys who were around.

We hung out. Ordered food. Called some friends. Went swimming. Shit got rowdy, rowdier than usual, even for us.

"Knox, remember that party we had? It was like late June. And some girl made those 'special' brownies."

He groans. "Bro, I had like a dozen and woke up passed out in some lady's garden down the street buck-ass naked with some daisies decorating my nut sack."

I nod slowly as I feel the blood drain from my face. During the season, we're pretty good about abstaining from anything illegal since we're randomly drug-tested. No one wants to get kicked off the team. Since that was the summer, though, none of us were worried.

What I told the guys last weekend was true. I never mess around without a condom.

But that assumes I'm fucking conscious.

I clear my throat. "Is it possible we ended up with one of the girls that night...?"

The room goes silent. Only Knox, Olly, and I were around that weekend.

Ben lets out a sigh. "Thank God I had to go to that wedding."

Olly's eyes bug out. "I forgot about that party."

"The shit we ate was so strong, I forgot that whole weekend," I admit as the front door slams shut and Gabby enters the room.

Guess with all of her coming and going due to Poppy, she's made herself at home.

She glances around the room. "I feel like I'm interrupting something."

Bree scoots over and makes room for her on the couch next to Olly. "I think the guys might have pinpointed the weekend of conception. Ben was out of town, so now we're potentially down to Rider, Olly, and Knox. But Ben, you should double-check your printout."

He nods, but it's clear from his expression that he thinks he's out of the woods.

Gabby gives her brother a weak smile. "Okay, well, before we look at the results, Bree and I wanted to let you all know we're happy to help out regardless of who's the father."

Olly hooks an arm around her shoulder and hugs her tightly. "You're awesome, in case we haven't told you lately. None of us would've survived this week without you and Bree."

Gabby's face flushes, and she gives him a shy smile. "Thanks."

The fuck?

I wanna peel my teammate off Gabby, one broken finger at a time. I'm also kicking myself for not complimenting her. Of course those are words *I* should've offered on my and my roommates' behalf. I'm the captain of the damn team. I'm just always thrown off balance around this woman.

And right now, she has a pen tucked into a messy bun, a skinny black skirt, heels. *Is that a Bugs Bunny Band-Aid on her knee?*

I resume my perusal of her hot little body. Her tits are pressing against those white buttons on her top. She's lithe in all the right places and deliciously curved in others. *And she's about to read paternity results, of all things.* I can't figure out if I want to fuck her on the coffee table or duck out the back door.

She clears her throat as she hands out folded pieces of paper with our names written in what must be her handwriting. "Don't kill the messenger, okay?"

Knox rips it open, jumps up, and howls, a giant grin lighting his face. Fuck. I was really hoping Poppy was his.

In my periphery, Olly gives Knox a high-five, and my stomach tilts. I tear open my sheet and scan the results.

. . .

Mother: Not tested

Alleged Father: Probability of paternity 99.99999%

Goddamn it.

I crumple the paper in my fist. It takes me several deep breaths before I can look up.

Everyone is watching me with varying degrees of concern and pity in their eyes.

Turning to Gabby, I ask, "Is there any chance these weren't labeled correctly? You did four tests that day."

"You watched me swab, place it in the container, and seal it in its individual package," she says softly, as gently as she's ever spoken to me. "Then I labeled it on my sheet so I wouldn't get the codes mixed up. I repeated those actions for each one of you. So no, I don't think I labeled them incorrectly. I can show you my notes if you want. You're also welcome to do your own paternity test, of course."

Fuck me. She's right. I remember her jotting down notes in between each of us. Gabby's always been incredibly capable, but this week we all learned she's a powerhouse of organization.

I rake my hands through my hair. "No, sorry. I don't doubt your attention to detail. I'm just trying to make sense of this."

"You actually might want to do a formal paternity test, for legal reasons."

I nod, not really hearing anything but the pounding of my heart.

The baby coos and giggles, snagging my attention. A little tuft of blonde hair sticks straight up from her head as she tries to wiggle out of Bree's arms. Someone tied a bow on it, but now it's hanging sideways.

She gives me a wide, toothless grin, and with my heart in my throat I realize, *Holy shit, I have a daughter.*

16

GABBY

Rider's hair is sticking up on end from running his hands through it for the last ten minutes. It's obvious he's shellshocked.

The guys offer words of encouragement and pat him on the back and offer to help, but I'm not sure he's processing any of this.

Bree gives me a look, and I shrug.

Am I supposed to do something? It was different when Poppy might have been my brother's, but what now? I offered to help before we read the results because the guys looked like they were ready to hurl, but does Rider actually want my help?

And what about Miranda? Surely she'll want to be a part of this. If the way she greeted him at Archer today is any indication, they're more than just hookup buddies.

It makes me feel like an idiot for thinking his apology last weekend somehow meant more.

Not that it would've changed anything, I tell myself firmly.

But that sense of disappointment I haven't been able to shake all evening since I saw them together suggests I'm not as apathetic as I'd like to be.

Ben gets up and crosses the room. "Thanks for helping this

week," he says when he reaches me. "At least now you don't have to worry about all this baby stuff." A pause. He rubs the back of his neck. "Sorry shit's been weird between us."

I nod, not expecting the apology. Even though he doesn't explain why he's been so distant, getting anything out of my brother feels like a win. He gives Rider a back smack before he disappears up the stairs.

Tank and Bree are whispering back and forth to each other and glance at Rider every few minutes. They don't seem to want to break whatever spell he's under.

Well.

He's a father now. It's not like he has a choice about it.

Unless he wants to give her up.

I shudder at the thought. He wouldn't, would he? I mean, I know a lot of people give up children for adoption, but Poppy is so dang adorable. And he might be a poor college student right now, but he's on the brink of being drafted into the freaking NFL. The world is his oyster. This baby will want for nothing in a few months. Surely he plans to keep her.

You have to convince him to keep her.

I begin to consider how to do that, but another voice in my head yells, *This is none of your business, Gabriela! None whatsoever!*

But what if helping Rider means the difference between Poppy going into foster care and ending up with complete strangers or staying here where we can all love up on her? Where I can keep an eye on her and make sure she's being cared for properly?

Bree told me Rider wiggled out of his babysitting time slots this week, so he hasn't had a chance to get to know her like the rest of us.

What did I expect, though? We're talking about the captain of the football team, the star quarterback, Mr. Popularity himself. People bend over backwards for him left and right. I heard he had a crew of girls who took notes for him last spring when he had a minor wrist sprain. Internally, my eyes roll.

Guess it's time for a wakeup call.

Before I can talk myself out of it, I take the baby from Bree and sit next to Rider. "Do you want to hold her? I promise she won't bite. Well, she doesn't have any teeth, so if she does bite, it won't hurt."

He doesn't laugh. In fact, the devastated expression on his stupidly handsome face makes me want to give him a hug.

All of my irritation with him drains away.

He may not be able to help how he feels about this at the moment, but I can lend a hand until he has a handle on things.

Until he doesn't need me.

For some reason—one I'm not interested in evaluating—that doesn't make me feel better.

I speak quietly, like I'm talking to a wounded animal. "She needs you, Rider. She doesn't have anyone else. Not one other person on the face of this planet, and I speak from experience when I say that's a terrible feeling." I give him a minute to consider that and then ask again, "Do you want to hold your daughter?"

Finally, our eyes connect, and he blinks. Clears his throat. "Ye—yeah, yeah. I do."

17

RIDER

According to what Gabby told us about gestation, this baby-making thing takes roughly thirty-seven weeks. That's nine months and change to get used to the idea of spawning another human being.

I've had about ten fucking minutes. Or less than a week if you count when she landed on our doorstep.

Neither of which provide time to come to grips with this kind of situation.

Suddenly, all I can hear are my father's warnings to wrap it up *every time*. That it would be the biggest mistake of my life if I knocked up some girl. That I'd regret having a kid so young.

But it feels wrong to say I regret my daughter. At the back of my mind, I wonder if that's how my mother felt before she took off. If she regretted having me. Judging by the fact I haven't seen her in three years, it's a strong possibility.

I shake off those old memories and try to focus on the situation in front of me. Football has taught me how to compartmentalize. How to shove shit into a box so I can keep my head in the game.

But at the thought of how I'm supposed to balance football, school, and a kid, panic sets in.

Damn. I have a child. A living and breathing little person I'm responsible for. How is this possible? Why would the universe give *me* a baby? The only pet I've ever had was a goldfish, which died after a week. I am *not* a good candidate for parenthood.

Gabby places Poppy in my lap and tells me to hold her firmly. "She can be a little wobbly. Don't assume anything about her abilities until you see it for yourself. Otherwise she'll roll off the bed or something equally terrible."

I nod. "Right. Hold on to her."

Gabby touches my arm. "Listen, I'm going to give you two a few minutes. I need to go home, but I'll be back in a bit. I figure you might want to talk about her schedule, and you can ask me any questions, like, I don't know, a refresher on how to change a diaper?" Her lips tilt up in the first smile she's directed my way in three years.

"Gabby." I grab her hand. "Olly was right. You've been amazing. I don't know how to thank you or how I'm going to pay you back for all of this."

Which reminds me how much money I owe my roommates. For all that baby crap we bought last weekend and those paternity tests. Not to mention the processing fees and express postage.

I haven't a clue where I'm supposed to get those funds. What is it up to now? A grand? At least. Jesus.

Gabby starts to say something, but hesitates, then squeezes my hand. "I adore your daughter. I'll do whatever I can to help."

When she stands, I reluctantly release her and watch her leave. I have so much I want to say to her, but right now I'm too fucked up to contemplate where to start.

I look down as Poppy tugs on my shirt. Her big green eyes

blink up at me, and I swear my heart skips a beat. Maybe two. For a moment, everything in my head quiets.

Gently, I run a finger over her chubby cheeks. Through a wisp of her curly hair. Over her perfect button nose. She's a beauty.

"Hey, Poppy. So you're mine, huh? Sorry, kid. Guess you're stuck with me now."

I bounce her on my knees a little the way I saw Bree doing earlier, and she gives me a slobbery smile.

As my coach likes to say, it's time to grow up. Fast.

18

GABBY

When I return, Rider's house is quiet for once.

Poppy is glued to her father's chest and is sucking on her fist while she watches me with solemn eyes. I swear the little muffin knows something serious happened tonight. She hasn't made a peep all evening.

Rider is barefoot, sporting a faded t-shirt that hugs his muscular shoulders and bulging biceps. His dirty blond hair is messy, like he just got out of bed, and he's so damn handsome, it hurts to look at him.

I told myself I'd go back to my side of the street and stay there if my brother wasn't Poppy's father, but then we got the paternity results, and Rider looked so freaked out. Like a virus crashing the mainframe of a computer, the minuscule piece of my heart that still had a hardcore crush on him somehow rewired the rest of me and weakened my resolve.

No, this is for Poppy. *Not* Rider.

I rub my temple, wondering when I turned into such a liar.

Fine. I'm doing this for both of them.

She snuggles closer, and he kisses her forehead.

Poof. There go my ovaries in a flash of lust.

I look around, hoping one of Rider's roommates will come stomping through the kitchen, but they're giving us a wide berth.

Mesmerized, I watch Rider rub Poppy's back as he reads her feeding and nap schedule I tweaked today.

Shifting in my seat, I motion toward the paper in his hands. "You probably don't need me to tell you this, but you can adjust anything as you see fit. I just threw something together that worked with your training and classes. She was already taking two naps, but I thought if we moved them around a bit, you can get some time with her in the evenings before she goes down for the night."

He probably doesn't want to hear my thoughts on child-rearing, but I suppose he could extrapolate that I think he needs to spend more time with her. I don't mention how he got out of his babysitting shifts last week, but judging by the overwhelmed look in his eyes, he's regretting not paying attention sooner. "You'll also find accompanying NDAs under the next tab, listed alphabetically, with people's contact information, for everyone who's already had a shift. I included blank copies in the back for when you get additional babysitters."

I wait for him to say something, but all he does is nod, so I continue.

"Her formula has directions on the can, but I included the tabulations here if you need to make bigger batches."

After twenty minutes of blabbing endlessly about diapers and rashes and burping, I take a breath because I'm getting tired of hearing my own voice.

"Rider, please stop me if you already know this."

His eyes meet mine. "I don't know anything." He pauses. "*Anything*. Before you showed us how to hold her last week, I couldn't even do that."

He looks down at the floor and his cheeks turn ruddy. Oh,

dear God, is he embarrassed? I can't handle seeing this vulnerable side of him.

"You're doing great." Tonight, he gave her a bottle and burped her afterward. Changed her diaper and her onesie. Of course, I explained everything, but he did it all without complaint. And although he's been somewhat taciturn, he's super gentle with her. "I'm sure you'll ace this just like you do football."

His face pales, and he swallows. "Gabby, how am I supposed to do it all? I'm not a great student. I'm not horrible, but I'm definitely average, which you can attest to. I have to study. A lot. When I'm not practicing or playing, I'm in class. When am I supposed to sleep?"

I don't bother to sugarcoat it. "You gut it out. You go hard or go home. All of those sports adages apply here. You're a senior, an All-American athlete, in your final season. You just have to get through, what, two more months of football, and your schedule will lighten up. Then you study your ass off, graduate, get drafted, and live happily ever after with your beautiful daughter and give her the life she's meant to have. At the end of the day, everything you sacrifice now will be worth it. I promise." I mean every single word. "Do you have any family who could lend a hand?"

He shakes his head. "I can't leave her with my father. He's a drunk, and my mom took off a few years ago. There's no one else."

Damn. I never realized he's almost as alone as I am. I knew his father was an alcoholic, but I had no idea his mother left.

Another piece of my self-protective wall crumbles.

"Okay. *Okay.*" I nod slowly. "I can put together another babysitting schedule. Ask people to pitch in? You'll probably have to take the night shifts, but maybe I can get you some coverage during the day so you don't lose your mind."

"Really? God, Gabby, that would be amazing."

I won't lie. Having Rider look at me like I'm the center of his universe is doing things to me. It's definitely time to get out of here and rebuild my defenses. Because nothing good can come from letting down my guard around this man.

"Listen, I'm going to get out of your hair because you play Clemson tomorrow, and that's a big game. They're going to be tough." I make a face. "I'm sure you have all kinds of things you need to do to prepare. Why don't I—"

His intense gray eyes narrow. "You know we play Clemson tomorrow?"

My breath catches. *Shit*.

It's my turn to blush. "I... I overheard someone talking about it today."

I stand too quickly and almost knock over my chair. I start babbling because I can't handle his scrutiny. "I can pick her up in the morning. Just text me the time. I have to take her back to my place, if that's okay. I'll need to tell my roommates what I'm doing, and I hope that's okay too. But I can get them to sign NDAs. You know, I bet I can talk them into babysitting..."

I'm yammering so much, so fast, I run out of breath.

He agrees and then calls my name. Trapping his bottom lip between his teeth, he pauses. "So does this mean you've unblocked me permanently?"

Shrugging, I pull my bag over my shoulder and try to act nonchalant. "Do I have a choice?"

His lips hook into a smile, and it's another direct hit to my heart. "Nope. No choice at all."

I take an exasperated breath and scramble for footing. "Rider, this doesn't mean we're friends." I don't know if I say it for his sake or my own.

His smile widens. "No, but it's a start."

19

RIDER

Somehow I'm still smiling after Gabby leaves. I flip through the binder she made for me that has notes on how to do everything. Okay, well, *maybe* she didn't make it for me. There's a strong possibility she made it for her brother in the event Poppy was his, but I tell myself she made it for me.

She's following my game schedule. Wasn't expecting that. Nor was I expecting how fucking happy that would make me.

Not sure what to make of it, though. People tell me this kind of thing every day, that they're following my games.

But it's never made me feel like this. Like I can conquer the universe.

Before I lose my head over a girl who might only be feeling sorry for me, I drag myself off the couch while trying not to jostle Poppy. Let sleeping babies lie and all that.

A smile tugs at my lips again when I think about how Gabby basically told me to nut up and deal.

She's right. My head was spinning, but after her little tough-love speech, I'm feeling more like myself.

Perspective. That's all I needed.

Of course.

After all, women have babies every day. Probably every minute of every day.

Really, how hard can one small baby be? I'm holding her with one arm, for fuck's sake. She's the size of a bowling ball or a large cat. Hell, we ate a pizza last week that weighed more than this kid.

I've totally got this.

While I run through plans in my head, I creep up the stairs to my room.

I'll get Poppy tucked away and get myself a good night's sleep. We'll annihilate Clemson tomorrow, I'll finish my essay on Sunday, and I'll be bright-eyed and bushy-tailed on Monday.

No. Big. Deal.

20

RIDER

An ear-piercing wail has all of my roommates rushing into my bedroom that's now packed with baby crap.

I pace the floor while I pat Poppy's ass, jiggling her gently and swaying the way Gabby showed me. "I don't understand. I fed her, burped her, changed her diaper. What else could this kid possibly need? Why won't she sleep?"

The baby glares at me, bleary-eyed and flush-faced, and lets out another wail.

"Poppy, you're killing me. I'd give anything to know what you want right now."

My roommates don't look amused either. It's two in the fucking morning, and we have a game in a few hours. I can't settle her down, and I'm starting to panic. I can't even think about running plays right now.

Like an avalanche, that's when it hits me—I have no clue who the mother of my kid is. I vaguely remember that the girl who plied us with brownies was fair-haired, but as for a name or some other identifying feature? Nada. Nothing. Zilch. Even worse? She might not even be the mother. The guys know to quietly ask around, but isn't that something I should know based on the fact she gestated my goddamn kid for nine months?

I'm truly the world's biggest piece of shit, aren't I?

Olly and Tank take turns trying to calm Poppy, but eventually hand her back to me. Out of the corner of my eye, I see Ben make a phone call, but I can't hear what he says because the cute demon spawn in my arms is trying to deafen me with her cries. It's such a sorrowful wail, that black lump of coal in my body that used to resemble a heart actually aches.

When he gets off, he smirks. "You can thank me in the morning." And stalks off.

Five minutes later, my favorite person in the whole damn world pauses in the doorway. I'm so relieved to see Gabby, I close my eyes and thank the powers that be for sending me this woman.

She juts out her lower lip in commiseration. "How long has she been like this?"

"I don't know. Hours. It's just getting worse."

"Aww, little boo." She unzips her hoodie and pulls it open to reveal a snug, thin white tank top. Despite my sleep-deprived state, my dick sits up and takes notice of her banging cleavage. One that is not sporting a bra, I note as I study her beautifully pert nipples.

My baby must approve as well, because the moment Gabby rests her on her chest, Poppy calms down. Gabby pulls the sides of the hoodie around my daughter, who snuffles and whimpers but is no longer crying.

Tank leans over and kisses Gabby on the head. "Dinner's on us tonight. You're a fucking angel."

Gabby sends him a big smile as she snuggles Poppy closer and starts humming. Not ten minutes later, the kid is sound asleep.

"How'd you do that?" I whisper.

"It's my special power." Her amused eyes tilt to mine, and she's such a vision with her messy long hair splayed over her shoulders, I could kiss her. "May I?" She points to my bed.

"Sure. Make yourself comfortable."

She sits on the edge and bounces gently, and Poppy lets out a little shudder, but within a minute, her face relaxes and she breathes deeply.

It's surreal to see Gabby on my bed, much less with a sleeping baby draped across her. When I've fantasized about this woman—and let's be honest, I've had more than a few fantasies—this isn't exactly the situation I envisioned.

"Do you want to put her down?" We both look at the square contraption Gabby calls a pack-and-play. "Fair warning, though, every time I placed her in there, she freaked out. I guess I need to get her a real bed."

Gabby considers this for a moment. "How about you lie down? Take off your shirt first."

I give her a playful look. "Why, Gabby Duran, I'm not sure that kind of activity is appropriate, given that we have a young audience."

She chuckles. "Not for me, perv. For the baby. She likes the body heat. Babies like being skin-to-skin. I'm guessing with everyone shuffling her around all week and not being with her mama, she needs some extra TLC."

Not being with her mama. Which reminds me that some chick left my baby in the middle of a damn party on Halloween. Who does that? How about giving a guy a heads up, for fuck's sake? Like, *Your kid is incoming. Make sure your friends aren't getting head in your living room when I drop her off. Oh, and by the way, my name is...*

My brain finally processes the rest of what Gabby said. Babies like skin-to-skin.

I strip off my tee. Much to my disappointment, she doesn't

look at me when I do it. I throw a few pillows against the headboard before I lie down.

Gabby comes to my side of the bed, and for some reason, the image of her all disheveled and staring down at me sends heat straight to my groin.

I yank the comforter over my hips so I don't weird her out. She's clearly not interested in me anymore.

Nice job, douche. You're getting exactly what you wanted. A part of me wants to punch my freshman self in the face for being such a dumbass.

I consider our earlier conversation when she mentioned following our game schedule and realize she probably follows because Ben plays.

My chubby instantly deflates when she places Poppy in my arms.

Yeah, *awkward*.

Having a kid is definitely going to cut into my sex life. Not that I've had much of one lately. I'm relieved I cut ties with Miranda when I did. Shit with her had been going downhill all semester.

What would Mira do in this situation? Would she have Gabby's patience and understanding?

I almost laugh. Probably not.

Miranda's still blowing up my phone, but at least she hasn't come around in a while, which is a relief.

I look up and find Gabby staring at me with a soft look in her eyes. This girl has been so patient with me.

It shames me to consider how she's been a really good friend to me even though I've been an asshole. Even if she's doing this out of love for Poppy, I don't know many people who would run over in their pajamas in the middle of the night to help like this. To party? For booze or drugs? For sex? Yes, yes, and yes. To help out with a kid, not on your life.

"How are you so good with babies?" I whisper over Poppy's head. "How do you know what to do?"

She fiddles with the ends of her hair. "Had a lot of practice. My aunt had two kids while I was living with her, and she got overwhelmed easily." She shrugs. "I just hate seeing little ones distressed."

Gabby is going to be an amazing mother someday.

I almost open my mouth to say it, but she points to the door. "I'd better get going. You going to be okay?"

"I'm afraid to answer that question."

We smile at each other. Her hazel eyes are so light, they're almost golden. They're mesmerizing.

She clears her throat. "Where's your phone? You can call or text if you run into trouble again."

I point to my desk, so grateful to have this woman in my corner. "You're such a lifesaver. Thank you."

But when she turns back to me, her smile is gone. She drops the phone in my hand and disappears so fast, I wonder if I said something wrong.

Frowning, I look down at my cell. The screen lights up with a million messages. Not unusual for a Friday night before a big game, but the top one is from Miranda. And it reads, *Miss you, baby. Let's fuck later. I know you wanna.*

Damn it. That's not what I want Gabby seeing.

But...

I pause.

It makes me wonder.

If it *did* upset her, then maybe she *does* care. Maybe she *is* interested after all.

And that wouldn't be a bad thing.

21

GABBY

Sienna groans with delight as she bites into her second empanada. "These are so damn good, girl."

"Thank you." Even though I don't bake as much for Rise 'N Grind because I've been so busy, I still try to whip up some goodies at home when I get a chance.

I just found out that Fanny wants to pay me a license for my recipes since so many people still ask for my *pan dulce*. That way she can also offer them at her new Austin bakery as well.

Once I've plied Sienna and Ramona with baked goods, I break out the forms.

Sienna signs the NDA with a huff and crosses her arms. "Does this mean you'll tell us what's going on now? I swear you're like living with the FBI."

She glances at Ramona, who is sporting her typical bored expression even though she signed as well.

"I couldn't say anything earlier." I pick up Poppy from her car seat, cradle her in my arms, and offer her a bottle. "But this is Rider's daughter, and I'm helping out a bit."

"What? How?"

"Really?" I raise an eyebrow. "Do we need a birds-and-bees

explanation? I thought you said you spent the last weekend boning a football player?"

She snorts. "I'll be surprised if he can run down the field today after all that sex. But seriously. When did this happen?"

I give my roommates the abbreviated version, meaning I skip the part about not knowing who the father was initially and the paternity tests *and* not knowing who the mother is. Just that she's not in the picture and he needs help.

Sienna's eyes narrow. "I thought you hated Rider."

"Hate's such a strong word." God, I sound like a fraud. "I'd say we don't always see eye to eye."

After a long moment of silence, she laughs. "He must be paying you a fortune to babysit."

I cringe but quickly school my face.

Unfortunately, Sienna notices. "So he's *not* paying you a fortune?" she asks slowly.

"He's paying me... something." What he can. I'll admit the fact that he insisted surprised me. "But I'd describe this as more of a favor for..." A friend? A guy I used to crush on super hard? A favorite but shameful Friday night fantasy? "A neighbor."

"Huh."

I turn to Ramona to gauge her reaction, but I'm not expecting the words out of her mouth.

"Listen, I'm moving in with my boyfriend."

I stare at her like she just sprouted an extra set of limbs. "You have a boyfriend? Since when?"

"Since last year."

Oh, my God. How have I not known this?

"Wh... why don't you ever bring him by?"

"He hates people more than I do." She shrugs and stands. "So you have two weeks to find another roommate."

What the hell? "What about the lease? You're on it."

"No, I'm not."

"*Yeah,* you are."

"No, I'm on our sophomore- and junior-year leases, but I had to go out of town the weekend you renewed it last May, and neither of us followed up."

How is that possible?

You had that hypoglycemic episode, passed out, and landed in the ER. That's how.

Needing a minute, I sit on the edge of the couch before I drop Poppy.

Ramona starts edging toward her room, and I tell her to wait. "I just want to be honest. I'm feeling a bit sideswiped right now. I thought we were friends." Maybe not good friends, but Jesus, she's about to bail on our lease. Regardless of what she says, I know she realizes that's wrong.

"I need some space." Her expression remains impassive even though I'm absurdly crushed she's ditching me. "You tend to micromanage everything."

I open my mouth, but only a squeak comes out. Damn it. "I do *not* micromanage. I *follow through* when we decide things."

"Whatever. Two weeks should be enough time to find someone new." And with that, she disappears into her room.

Sienna sidles closer. "Wow, that was pretty bitchy of her." When she sees my face, she gasps. "Aww, don't cry."

"I'm not crying." Except, damn it, I am, and that pisses me off more.

She slings her arm over my shoulders and pulls me into a hug. Poppy wiggles between us.

I pull away before we smother the baby and wipe my eyes. "I sometimes have a h... hard time when p... people leave." At least that's what a school therapist once told me. "Separation anxiety or some shit." I suppose that's why Rider cutting ties with me back then hurt so much.

Deep down, I know it's unreasonable to cry over this.

Ramona and I were never close. It's not like we hung out. But for a girl who doesn't have a lot of friends or family, she was someone consistent in my life since the beginning of sophomore year.

A few hours later, that anxiousness has me picking up the phone to call my aunt, which is likely going to add insult to injury. Except I need something. Someone familiar to ground me. A familiar voice. Someone who might love me. Even a little.

After putting Poppy down for a nap, I curl up on my bed and dial.

Except she doesn't answer. She never does.

22

RIDER

IT'S NOT A PRETTY WIN, but considering I barely slept last night, I'll take what I can get.

By the time I've answered all of the press's questions, I'm ready to pass out. I'm lucky no one has gotten wind of Poppy yet because I'm not sure how to field that. I guess I really do need to talk to Sully. Coach needs to know. I'm not prepared to have that convo today, though.

Back in the locker room, the guys are jacked despite the fact that we won by the skin of our teeth. Cal Winston, our wide receiver, struts around buck-ass naked while jeering the other team as though they can hear him through the concrete walls.

I lower my voice so that only he hears me. "Dude, they kicked our asses in the first half. Have some respect."

Sure, winning matters a whole helluva lot, but so does sportsmanship. Winston might chalk it up to locker-room talk, but every once in a while, this shit leaks out and lands someone in the hot seat. And the only thing worse than a sore loser is an arrogant winner.

He rolls his eyes. "Did you see me tonight? Two touchdowns.

That bad boy deep in the end zone was one-handed. Pretty sure you'll see me on *SportsCenter* highlights."

God help me.

Of course I saw him. I'm the one who threw those touchdowns.

Tank didn't want Winston living with us, and I'm glad I listened to him. Ben might be standoffish, but he's not a dick like Winston.

I hand him a towel to cover his junk and pat him on the back. "You kicked ass. Now take it down a notch before you get your head caught in the doorway."

He laughs and struts off, shouting, "Time to get some puss-ay, my little bitches!"

I shake my head and head to the showers.

Everyone's headed out to unwind and get laid. Despite the close game, I understand their euphoria. Being undefeated this far into the season is something to celebrate, but I'll be lucky if I don't fall flat on my face from exhaustion and drown in a puddle of drool.

I just want a bag of ice for my shoulder, three ibuprofen, my bed, and silence for the next eight to ten hours.

I'm in my Jeep, halfway home, when I realize I still have to pick up Poppy.

Fuck. I smack the steering wheel with my fist.

Guilt instantly floods me for resenting my daughter. This is not who I want to be.

Another layer of shame settles over me when I realize I have no idea where she is right now. I left the details of who would be taking care of her today with Gabby, and while I trust her, being an absentee parent sounds just as bad as a negligent one.

Get your shit together, man.

I pull over next to the curb and turn on my phone, which I

always shut off before a game. Although with Poppy in my life now, I probably shouldn't do that anymore.

It takes a minute to find the online folder with the updated babysitting schedule Gabby made for me. When it opens, the entire next week fills in with names and phone numbers. On a separate tab, I find the names listed alphabetically with people's addresses, notes on their babysitting experience and who still needs to sign NDAs. It's basically everything from that binder, but now people are scheduled and it's all at the tip of my fingers. *Christ.* Someday I'm gonna have to buy this woman a house or a luxury car to thank her.

After a call to Bree, who's supposed to be watching the baby, I find out she ended up staying with Gabby all day because Bree caught a stomach bug and didn't want to pass it on. She apologizes for not updating the form.

Gabby's been watching her since—I check the clock on my dash—eight this morning. So... twelve hours. Damn. She must be as exhausted as I am.

Deciding I need to treat this girl to something special to say thanks, I pull a U-turn so I can pick us up a pizza. The least I can do is feed her.

I call it in so I don't have to wait long. I order her favorite. Or at least what used to be her favorite.

I frown at the realization I don't know Gabby anymore. I mean, I know the basics. She's smart as hell and focused. Motivated. She still wrinkles her nose when she's confused. She still smells sweet, like orange blossoms and beautiful woman. When she's nerding out with a spreadsheet and clipboard, she's sexy as fuck.

But that's the surface. What's been going on in her life since she was my tutor?

I'd like to spend time with her and find out. If she lets me.

I pull up to my house and curse. There's nowhere to park

because the guys are having "a few friends over." Except cars are parked up and down both sides of the street along the entire block.

Reluctantly, I park behind Gabby's car in her driveway. When I reach her door, I wipe my palms on my jeans before I knock.

The door swings open, and Gabby is shushing me before I can open my mouth.

"She finally fell asleep, and I don't want to go to jail for strangling you if you wake her."

I chuckle as she ushers me in to her living room. It's small but tidy. A rose-print couch sits opposite a modest-sized flat screen. The old hardwood floor gleams, and there's not so much as a crumb on the coffee table.

"You must be really grossed out by the lack of hygiene at my house."

"I didn't want to say anything, but I shudder whenever I hear about the guys letting Poppy play on the floor over there."

I nod slowly. "That would make two of us. Maybe you could loan me a mop? I have a feeling I'm gonna need it after tonight's party."

Her nose wrinkles. "Are you planning to take her back to your place tonight? It's pretty loud over there."

Just more shit I haven't considered.

I close my eyes and let my head drop forward. "Honestly? I hadn't planned that far. If I had, I would've asked the guys to party somewhere else. God, I feel stupid."

After an awkward silence, she pats my arm. "A baby is a lot to deal with. You're... you're doing your best."

I give her a weary smile. "Thanks. I'm trying."

"Hey, look on the bright side. You won your game."

My lips tilt up higher. "We did." My eyes do a quick sweep down her body—snug t-shirt, sweatpants, fuzzy socks. Her hair is in a high ponytail. She shouldn't look so sexy while she's vegging out, but she does. Her tits strain at the thin fabric. In this light, I can almost see her nipples. "Did you happen to watch my game?"

She glances away. Nibbles her lip. Shrugs. "I might have caught some of it."

"Hmm."

The fact that a stiff breeze can turn me on right now reminds me of how long it's been since I've gotten laid.

Glancing around, I look for Poppy before I do something stupid like hit on the one person who's saving my ass right now.

"I put her down in my room." Gabby tilts her head toward the front of the house where she cracks open a door. I set the pizza on the coffee table and follow her.

A sliver of light falls on my daughter who's curled up like a little burrito in her pack-and-play.

"How do you get her to sleep in that thing?" I whisper. I'm lucky I could throw today after cradling her on my body all night.

We sneak back out into the living room. "I held her a lot today or wrapped her to my chest when I was doing homework, which is probably what you ended up doing last night, right?"

"That kid was glued to me."

"Because we both reassured her, I think she's feeling less clingy. So... good job." Gabby gives me a soft smile, and I have the strongest urge to kiss her.

I blow out a breath, desperate to put myself in a firmly platonic frame of mind. "Are you hungry? I brought your favorite."

She's quiet for a minute. "You remember my favorite pizza?"

"Don't sound so surprised. We shared a few of these back in the day." I lift the top off the pie. "Pepperoni, black olives, and mushrooms."

"I thought you didn't like mushrooms." She eyes the food and then turns to me.

"*Someone* convinced me they were good on pizza." I don't mention it became one of my favorites as well.

"I did not know I had the power to affect your world view." She laughs and grabs some paper plates before tossing slices on both and handing me mine. She trots back into the kitchen to grab us a couple of sodas and settles onto the couch where I join her.

On the TV, some National Geographic program is on. "Still love to geek out, huh?"

She pushes her glasses up and smiles again. "Some things never change."

"Where are your roommates? You have two, right?"

Her smile disappears. "One's out, and the other..." She shrugs again.

"Bree told me you guys are enjoying your Brit lit class."

Her eyes light up. "It's so good. We read *A Room with a View* last week and watched the movie, both of which I love." She lets out a sigh of contentment.

For some reason, it feels like she's finally letting her guard down. Being with her like this makes my whole body warm, like I'm standing next to the sun. It's the weirdest fucking thing I've ever experienced. I was exhausted when I got here, but being around her gives me a burst of energy.

I swallow, remembering how close we were back then. "Pretty sure you're the only reason I passed freshman composition."

When her eyes meet mine, I know that was the wrong thing to say for some reason.

"Let's not stroll down memory lane, okay? It's not fun for me." She sets down her food. "Look, I'll help you with Poppy as much as I can, but I don't think I can do this."

This. In other words, whatever we're doing right now.

Hell, I don't even know what I'm doing right now except I can't stand the idea of not being friends with this woman any longer.

She starts to get up.

"Gabby, wait. Please."

When she turns to me, she has wariness written all over her face. I hate that I put that reservation there.

It's time to make things right.

In fact, it's long overdue.

23

RIDER

THE WORDS TUMBLE out of me. "I'm sorry I was such an asshole. Truly, from the bottom of my heart, please know if I could go back and do things differently, I would. I was overwhelmed by football and school and my parents."

"I thought you said your mother wasn't in the picture anymore. But..." She pauses. "I remember you saying they fought a lot and that you felt caught in the middle."

The fact that she recalls my family's shit from three years ago twists something in my gut. She's the only person I've shared any of that with besides Coach. Tank knows some of it from overhearing a few phone calls, but I'm not a fan of airing out my family's dirty laundry.

I rub my hands on my thighs, hating that I let that night unravel me. No one knows this story, but I need her to understand what happened. "Not sure if you remember, but I went home that weekend." That weekend when everything got fucked up. Me. My family. My relationship with Gabby. The only thing that didn't implode was football because I poured every last ounce of what was left of myself into the game. "My parents were always pretty volatile, but that night shit detonated, and my mother left my father for another man." I stare at my hands. "I heard the argument, watched her pack her bags and take off with that guy. Haven't seen her since."

Gabby doesn't say anything, but her eyes are wide and compassionate, so I continue. "My father has always been desperately in love with my mom. Worshiped the ground she walked on, so to say he was devastated is putting it mildly. I woke up the next morning and found him nearly drowning in his vomit after he got shitfaced the night before."

"Oh, Rider. I'm so sorry." She grabs my hand, and I thread my fingers through hers. It's automatic. I don't consider how intimate this is. Just that I need her right now, and she doesn't hesitate to let me.

"It's weird to finally talk about it, but football was always what got me through shit when I was growing up. My dad's been a functioning alcoholic most of my life, but when I was little, he nearly killed someone driving home drunk."

I don't know why I'm unloading so much of my family baggage, but I can't seem to stop myself. Gabby's soulful hazel eyes seem to unlock parts of my life I try to never think about.

"My father got off on some technicality. He spent a little time in jail, but not enough. I felt like the whole town held it against me, so I worked my ass off to be the opposite of Hank Kingston. He hated sports, so I went out for everything I could and lettered in three sports, even if that meant having the crappiest gear because I was so broke. He couldn't hold down a job, so I've made it my mission to take care of myself and him financially. Some days he can barely get out of bed and tie his own damn shoes. I haven't missed a workout in two years, not since I got the flu sophomore year."

After a minute, she asks softly, "Why are you telling me all of this?"

I turn to face her. "When I said what happened freshman

year wasn't about you, I meant it. I kinda slid into a downward spiral. Yeah, football was going great, but that was because I just shut down and shut out everything that wasn't part of the game. And I'm so sorry to say that you were a part of that." I clear my throat, hating what I'm about to admit. I can't believe we're talking about this after all this time, but I have to get it out there. "I just... It freaked me out. You freaked me out."

I'm not sure what I expect her reaction to be, but she laughs gently. "Really? How did I freak you out? Did I wave too many number two pencils in your face?"

I chuckle and squeeze her hand. "I really liked you." My laughter quiets. "I *really* liked you, but after watching what my father went through, I... I thought we were too serious."

"How were we that serious? Don't get me wrong. It felt serious to me, but it's all relative, right? I didn't date that much while you did. So how did you get weirded out when you and I never really... got that intimate?"

My lips tug up. "Not for lack of fantasizing on my part."

Her cheeks flush, and she bites her lower lip. "You fantasized about me?"

"Definitely."

The playful look on her face falls away, and she untangles our hands. "You mean while you were out sleeping with other girls?"

I wince. "I admit I was a dog to ghost you like that, but I like to think I've grown up since then."

Her eyebrow pops up. "You're trying to tell me you're not a fuckboy any longer? Because I hear a lot of stories about what goes on at your house whether I want to or not, and none of them are complimentary. You should've seen the shit I walked into on Halloween night in your living room."

I can only guess. "And do you know where I was at that moment? What I was doing?"

She wrinkles her nose. "Please don't tell m—"

"I was wearing noise-cancelling headphones, asleep in my bed. By myself." I want to tell her I haven't gotten laid much this semester, but that sounds gross, even in my head.

Leaning away, she crosses her arms over her chest and rolls her eyes. "What about that girl Miranda? I saw the text she sent you last night. It popped up on your screen when I handed you your phone. Don't tell me you're not fuckbuddies or whatever."

I almost smile because, holy hell, is she jealous?

Something tells me the only way to convince her that I'm not the player she thinks I am is brutal honesty. "We *were* something like that. But we're not anymore. I tried to break it off a few weeks ago, but she's not getting the hint. And for the record, I've been very direct in my conversations with her, in telling her what I want."

Her eyes meet mine. "What exactly *do* you want, Rider?"

My throat feels tight. I take a breath. For some crazy reason, I feel like I'm trying to throw for a touchdown. "Just... I need us to be friends again. I miss you, Gabby, and I regret how I treated you. And with everything with Poppy, I'm being reminded of how amazing you are." I shrug. "I miss our friendship. Don't you?"

My heart feels like it's gonna beat out of my chest with that confession.

"And that's all you want?" she asks warily. "Friendship?"

Yes. *No.* Fuck, I don't know.

"That's all I have time for right now."

Do I miss our friendship? Absolutely. Do I want to fuck her until I can't walk anymore? Definitely. Can I handle anything beyond sex right now while I juggle all the other shit in my life? Probably not. So yeah, I guess I'd better keep my damn hands to myself.

"And you're not going to ghost me again?" she asks. The

vulnerability in her voice kills me, and I reach for her hand again. "Because it sucked to open up to you about being in foster care only for you to disappear on me."

I close my eyes. *Christ. No wonder she thinks I'm a douchebag.*

"I promise I won't disappear again. You're officially stuck with me now."

She tries not to smile, but her lips reluctantly tilt up.

I give her my best puppy-dog face. "Does this mean I'm forgiven for being an epic asshole?"

She studies me for a moment, and I wonder what she sees. Does she see trailer-park trash? The kid of an alcoholic? A meathead jock? A guy who's just barely hanging on some days?

But her eyes turn playful. "I feel like I should make you work for it."

The relief that floods me is overwhelming. "I'm willing to put in the hours."

We stare at each other as we laugh, and even though I won my game today, this somehow feels better.

24

GABBY

My eyes crack open against the early-morning sun, and I come face to face with beautiful, big green eyes.

"Hey, girlie."

Poppy smiles and coos at me and holds up her arms to me so that I'll lift her out of her playpen.

After a quick diaper change, I hoist her onto my hip and we head into the living room, where I find Ramona and Sienna staring at Rider, who's sleeping soundly on the couch.

Ramona shoots daggers at me, but I shrug. "What? You're moving."

Twenty-four hours ago, I never would've considered letting an overnight guest crash on our couch without running it past her, but then she leveled me with a breach of contract.

Okay. Maybe it's not a breach of contract. More like a breach of friendship.

Whatever the case, it still stings the morning after, and I'm in no mood to deal with her attitude.

My attention shifts to Sienna. "I already know you don't care."

"Oh, my God, I totally don't!" she whisper-squeals.

"He didn't realize his roommates were throwing a party, and he obviously couldn't take Poppy back there until..." My voice falls away so I don't say what I'm thinking. *Until they're done fornicating in his living room.*

I almost laugh. That voice in my head sounds like June Miller, the foster parent who made me say a rosary every night before bed. Really, that wouldn't have been a big deal if she hadn't made me kneel on her concrete floor to do it.

"Ladies." Rider's masculine voice has all three of us turning to him. He stretches his arms over his head, a deep groan rumbling his chest. It's a sex sound that makes my nipples take notice, as do the abs that go on display when his t-shirt rides up.

Heat burns my face, and I turn away before I do something crazy like lick those enticing muscles arrowing down into his jeans.

I'm already feeling vulnerable around him. Especially after our talk last night. Seeing him like this, first thing in the morning with that sleepy look in his eyes, makes me want to crawl into his lap and do naughty things.

Poppy giggles and claps.

I'm holding his baby. Right.

"Wanna see your daddy? Hmm?" I kiss her on the forehead and lean over Rider, who sits up to take his daughter.

"Hey, cutie pie." He peppers her with kisses and she laughs. "I have to tell you guys that having a kid is so fu—freaking surreal." As he snuggles her to his chest, his face turns up to me. "How'd she sleep?"

"Great. She only woke up twice. I gave her a bottle and patted her butt, and she knocked out again."

"Sorry. You could've woken me to do that."

It never crossed my mind. I was already right there. "We should probably work on weaning her from night feeds, but the first week in a new household might not be the best time.

Perhaps once she gets settled in, you'll need to figure that out. But you'll probably want to work some purées into her routine too. That will fill her tummy so she needs less at night."

"Purées? Like, mashed-up food?" he asks. I almost laugh at how confused he looks, but I nod. "I'll... yeah. That sounds good."

Ramona stomps back to her room and slams the door, which makes Sienna chuckle.

Rider frowns. "I hope I'm not causing any problems for you by staying here."

Sienna jumps in to assure him he's not. "The grumpus is moving out soon anyway, so it's really not a big deal." She turns to me. "And you totally don't micromanage."

I look at my ceiling, wishing she hadn't mentioned that *right now*.

"Gabby's the most amazing woman I've ever met," Rider says. "She can micromanage me anytime."

My eyes snap to his, and he winks.

"I... I... Who wants breakfast?" I glance down and realize I'm only wearing a flimsy tank and sleep shorts. I pull my thin robe closed and tie it before I dart into the kitchen. I call out, "Sienna, this is Rider. Rider, my roommate Sienna."

"I'm such a big fan!"

I tune out the rest of their conversation as I prepare a bottle for Poppy and grab a cup of coffee so I can think straight. When I return to the living room, Sienna is still going. "But too bad about that interception. At least you guys won."

"Jeez, Sienna. Way to welcome a guy." I hand him the bottle. "He was about to get sacked and lose, what, six yards? At least that's the average loss on sacks." I shrug. "On the bright side, they got the ball back a few possessions later and took it in for a touchdown. It all worked out."

I look back and forth between them. Sienna looks confused, and Rider? He's sporting a Cheshire-like grin.

I roll my eyes. "Fine. I watched your game. Are you happy?"

"More than you know."

"It was for Poppy's sake. I figured she'd like to watch her father play."

"Uh-huh."

"So you don't hate football?" Sienna asks.

"Yeah, tell us, Gabby." Rider smirks at me.

I roll my eyes. "I hate arrogant football *players*."

He just stares at me like he can see through my flimsy robe. Goosebumps break out on my arms.

Sienna backs away and waves her hand. "The sexual tension between you two is, like, whoa."

"There's no sexual tension." I take a sip of my coffee. "Because we're just friends. Right, Rider? You said it yourself."

He coughs. Nods slowly. "Sure. Just friends."

Poppy, who is cradled in his arms, drinking her bottle, reaches up and grabs his face. He smiles down at her, and Sienna sighs.

I feel ya, girl.

"Poppy loves my whiskers."

Pretty sure all women everywhere love his whiskers, but I keep this to myself. His morning scruff makes him nearly irresistible.

"Have you given her a bath yet?" I ask, needing a cold shower myself.

He lets out a weary sigh. "No, and I haven't a clue how to go about it."

I chuckle. "It's your lucky day."

25

RIDER

Just friends?

What was I thinking?

One look at Gabby, and I wish like hell I wasn't holding my daughter.

My mouth waters. And not because she just fed me a homemade *buñuelo* that literally melted in my mouth.

I lick the cinnamon sugar off my lips as I watch her move around the kitchen.

Gabby pushes her glasses up her nose and explains the bath supplies she's set next to the sink, which she scrubbed clean a few minutes ago. Her hair is tied up in a messy knot on top of her head, and she's sporting a t-shirt and cutoffs, and I swear it's the sexiest thing I've ever seen her in.

"Rider, are you listening to me?"

"Yeah, sorry."

"The most important thing to remember is to get all of the essentials ready and within arm's reach before you get started. Because you can't take your attention off her for a second." She takes Poppy out of my arms and undresses her. "In fact, I would never let anyone else give her a bath. Drowning is the number one cause of fatalities in children younger than four."

That sends a chill down my spine.

"What?" She stares at me in that way that makes me wonder if she can see into my brain.

"We have a pool and a hot tub. Neither have a fence or any kind of child barrier."

Gabby frowns. "She won't be running around for a little while, but it can't hurt to have a conversation with anyone who babysits at your house. Maybe explain that they shouldn't take her in the backyard?"

"I can do that."

"We could also get some baby gates so you can partition off certain areas just for her."

"Smart, yeah. That's a good idea."

We smile at each other, and I wonder, not for the first time, if I had a head injury freshman year that went undetected. Why else would I *willingly* push this girl out of my life? I've spent time with a lot of women, but Gabby is the only one who's ever made me feel like this. Like being around her made me more. Somehow better. More capable.

Something slams behind us, and we turn to find her roommate, the one who looks like Wednesday Addams, stacking boxes by the front door. As far as roommates go, Sienna and Ramona couldn't be more opposite if they tried. Sienna took off a little while ago, leaving us with the girl who glowers at me.

I whisper to Gabby, "I feel like she hates me."

Gabby lowers her voice. "She does."

"Why?"

Ramona gives us the evil eye and stomps back to her bedroom.

"Football players bullied her in high school, so she thinks you're all assholes."

That sucks. Bullies are the worst.

The next time she comes out, I call out to her. "Hey, Ramona. I have a couple of extra tickets to our next home game. If you'd like them. You know, to thank you for letting me crash on your couch."

She glares at me for a good ten seconds before she says, "Yeah, you can shove those right up your ass," and disappears down the hall.

"Tough crowd," I murmur and turn to Gabby, who's giving me a sympathetic smile.

"That was really thoughtful of you." Her eyes are soft, and when she tangles her pinky in mine, I feel like I did something right just now despite the verbal beatdown by her roommate.

A warm stream of liquid hits my arm, and we turn to see Poppy giggle.

"Oh, God." Gabby laughs and covers my daughter's crotch with a diaper. "Sorry about that. Hey, it's not a party until the baby pees on you."

I laugh and grab a few paper towels to dry off.

After showing me how to check the water temperature with my elbow, Gabby sits Poppy in the shallow water. My daughter squeals and laughs and splashes. It's a relief to see she enjoys it.

Gabby makes this look easy, and a huge knot of tension unwinds in my chest knowing that she's across the street if I have an emergency. Because let's face it, I'm fucking clueless when it comes to kids.

The fact that I'm so attracted to her will have to take the back burner. I have zero margin for error here. She's right. Poppy has to take precedence over everything else. And that means eat, breathe, and sleep football when I'm not with my kid so I can make it to the draft. I have to lock down this ship and focus on getting to the finish line. For my sake and Poppy's.

By the time we're done bathing her, there's water everywhere. On the floor, the counter, all over our clothes. We're both drenched. Really, the only one who is dry now is the kid, who's dressed in a onesie, trying to eat her foot, as we towel off her hair.

I get a nice eyeful of Gabby in a wet t-shirt that definitely belongs in my spank-bank hall of fame. Her round, high breasts with those tight nipples damn near mesmerize me, and I have to turn away to shift the growing appreciation in my jeans.

Fortunately, needing to take care of a kid results in instant deflation.

We're just shooting the shit when I ask, "How's the tutoring going? I never see you at the circulation desk anymore." That's where all of the tutors wait for their appointments.

Her rosy lips twist. She opens her mouth to speak but shuts it again as a flush travels up her neck.

"What? Did something happen?"

She sighs. "Remember when I got sick in May?"

I'm glad she brought that up. I've wanted to ask how she's been feeling. It was scary as hell watching her pass out. One minute she was fine, busy ignoring me while she stalked to her car. I watched her fumble with her keys for a minute, wipe her brow, and when I blinked, she was on the ground. "Of course. Is everything okay now?"

Nodding, she props the baby on her hip. "I'm fine, more or less, but I had to miss work. I called in each day, like you're supposed to do, but the girl who took the messages never passed them on to my boss, and I got fired."

"God, that sucks. 'Cause you're a great tutor." I'm not just blowing smoke up her ass. She genuinely cares about the students she works with and breaks things down so they understand. I never felt like she talked down to me. Not once. Even though it was obvious she's a little brainiac and I'm somewhat lacking in that area.

"Thanks. I appreciate that." She smiles shyly, and my eyes dip down to her mouth that I'm suddenly dying to kiss. When she clears her throat, a pink flush works its way up her neck. "I think I owe you an apology as well."

My eyebrows lift. "For what?"

Her face goes crimson. "For slamming the door on you last May. It was… it was nice of you to bring me flowers. I wish I had been more gracious."

I chuckle at this beautiful woman who is making it hard for me to keep my distance. "I'm just glad you're okay. If you could slam a door, you were obviously feeling better. That's all that mattered to me. You're doing better now, right?"

She nods, and our eyes lock. For a moment I wonder how different things would be if I'd worked through my shit with her by my side. If I hadn't run. She'd be mine right now. The thought sends a pulse of heat through me.

The doorbell rings, and it shakes me from my Gabby-induced stupor.

"Can you hold her?" Gabby hands Poppy to me.

Right. I have a child. That means I can't lose focus.

I bounce my kid and wander into the living room and remind myself there's a reason things didn't work out between me and Gabby in the past. We're in different places. We'll likely always be in different places.

"What are you doing here?" Gabby's annoyed voice makes me look up.

That douche Jason is hovering in the doorway. He has two coffees in his hands. Everything in me bristles. Especially when he eyeballs her tits.

Is it wrong that I hope she slams the door in his face too?

"I wanted to make things up to you for last weekend. It all went sideways, and I feel bad. You wouldn't answer any of my texts and then you blocked me. I just wanted to talk and explain."

She must realize he's skeezing on her wet t-shirt because she crosses her arms. "We barely know each other, Jason, but what I do know is that we're not really compatible." Her words are direct, but her voice is gentle, even though that dick doesn't deserve her compassion.

"How can you say that?"

"If we had anything special, you wouldn't have hooked up with another girl ten minutes after dropping me off."

What a fucker.

She starts to close the door, and he throws out his arm to hold it open. "Gabby, baby, it wasn't like that!"

She's not your fucking baby, asshole. And if he takes one more step toward her, I'm laying him out.

"Jason, I don't care what it was like. It's not a big deal that you were with someone else, and that's telling too. Go hook up. Be my guest. Just please leave me out of the picture."

"But we never had *the talk*. You know, where we agree to be official and monogamous or whatever."

"Honestly? I think when you find someone you really want to be with, you don't need to have 'the talk.' If you find the right woman, it would kill you to hook up with anyone else." She shrugs. "Maybe I want someone who is certain about me and doesn't need to wait for that kind of conversation to commit to me. Because in his heart, he knows what he wants and goes for it."

God, she's beautiful. I love this woman's spirit.

Suddenly, he spies me in the background.

"What the fuck? Are you dating Kingston now?" He glances at me. "No offense, man. Great game yesterday, by the way. Killer second half."

Christ. This guy.

Gabby shakes her head. "Who I'm dating is really none of your business, but he and I are neighbors."

He must see something in my eyes because his narrow. "How can you be with him and not me? He probably fucked a different girl every night last week."

Excuse me, dickhead. I fucked my hand every night last week, thank you very much.

"Rider's sex life is none of my business—or yours."

Is it wrong that I want it to be her business?

He hisses, "Do you have any idea what goes on at his house? What goes down at those parties? Did you know they call the first-floor bathroom the 'blow job bathroom'? He'll never be faithful to you."

"Really, dude?" He just got his ass banned from football parties.

I bounce Poppy on my lap so I'm not tempted to cross the room. I'm a lot of things, but I'm not a cheater. After my mother did my dad so dirty, I'd never be able to look at myself in the mirror if I ever pulled that kind of shit.

"Rider is free to bed whoever he pleases, as we are not dating. Now please get off my porch."

Free to bed whoever he pleases.

That does not sit right with me. The idea of sleeping with random girls has zero appeal. It hasn't for a while, if I'm being honest. Even having my usual fuckbuddy situation doesn't feel right these days.

I mull over what she said, about not needing a conversation to commit to someone, not if you want them badly enough.

And I'm starting to wonder if Gabby meets that criteria, whether she means to or not.

Except I'm not in a position to pursue her. No matter how badly I want her.

26

RIDER

I rap on the door, and Sully calls out for me to enter.

"You wanted to see me, Coach?" I love Sully like a father, but paternal relationship or not, no one wants to get called into his office.

"Have a seat."

I drop into one of the plastic chairs in front of his desk. At this point in his career, he could get nicer chairs for his office, but he's so old school, I'm not sure he's ever considered it.

His rheumy eyes study me for a second, and I make an effort to not squirm. "How you doing? Saturday was rough, but you pulled out a win. Wanna talk about it?"

He does this sometimes after an emotional game, has these heart-to-hearts, but usually in the locker room. I must be really putting out some fucked-up vibes for him to do this right now. In the last three years, I've had rough games—losses even—that have only gotten me a pat on the back and a "hang in there, kid."

I run my hand through my hair and push it out of my eyes. "I couldn't find my rhythm in the first half. I know I let you down."

"Nonsense. You got yourself back up again at halftime like any good leader does, regrouped, rallied your guys, and pulled out a win. I'm wondering if you wanna talk about what's going on in your head. What's been bothering you all week."

I nod slowly. There's a reason we all view Sully like some kind of guru. He has this way of looking into you and pinpointing what's wrong. It's why so many of his old players stay in touch with him. Because he really cares, and I swear he can see shit other people can't.

Swallowing, I rub my palms along my thighs. Time to bite the bullet.

"Got some news last week that's been messing with my head." And my pregame routine. Sleep. Homework. Sex life. Social life. The works.

But I think of that toothless grin Poppy gave me this morning before I left her with Bree, and my heart melts a little. That kid wrapped me around her pinky faster than Cal Winston's release off the line.

She slept clinging to me like she was afraid to let go, which is better than crying. But still. I can't get her down at bedtime the way Gabby does, and I can only ask the woman for help so many times a day. I know this is my problem and mine alone.

His chair creaks as he leans back and steeples his fingers over his stomach. "Tell me about it. Let's work through this. I want you clear-headed for our away game this weekend."

Son of a bitch. I need to get someone to watch her while I'm gone.

He taps a finger on his desk. "This about a girl? Nine times out of ten, when I have to call one of you in here, it's about a girl." He chuckles.

Immediately, Gabby comes to mind, and I almost agree with him.

Except, *no,* I remind myself.

Wait. I guess he's right in a way.

Fuck, I can't even think straight anymore.

"Yes, this is about a girl." I pause. Take a breath and try not to let my balls crawl up. I'm worried I'm letting him and the team down. I haven't spoken to my own father in weeks—he hasn't called me since I almost emptied my bank account to pay his rent and buy him groceries. But Sully is here worrying about me. I owe him the truth. "It's about my daughter."

His eyebrows lift. "Come again?"

"She's about six months old."

Silence fills the room.

He taps that finger again. "I'm guessing from the look on your face, you just found out."

I nod. See, Sully always knows things.

"That's..." He's quiet for another long minute. Damn, I rendered the man speechless, which is tough to do. I prepare myself for the lecture that's sure to come.

He clears his throat. "I guess congratulations are in order." It's my turn to be surprised. "Son, there are few things in a man's life as special as having a child."

And he goes on to give me the pep talk I didn't know I needed.

When he walks me out twenty minutes later, he pats me on the shoulder. "Is the baby mama around to help?" His lips pull up on one side. "I hear the kids use that term."

"No, sir. She's not, but, uh, I have a friend who's been helping."

"A friend, huh?" His bushy eyebrows quirk up. "A girl?"

I nod slowly.

He looks like he wants to say more but doesn't. Weird. Coach never holds back.

But he knows my family situation well enough not to ask if my parents can lend a hand. A snowball has a better chance in hell than my father staying sober long enough to babysit.

Instead, Sully pats me on the shoulder again. Despite the

motivational chat he just gave me, he looks kinda sad. Resigned, even. A knot of dread forms in my gut.

He releases a deep sigh and gives me a small smile. "Good. Well, guess you know this means you'd better get to bed on time each night. No dillydallying or you'll never get enough rest. I remember when my Beth Ann used to wake up at all hours. It was hell." He chuckles. "I don't envy you, but you're young. Healthy. You can do this. Just love up on that little girl and stay focused on her and school, and you'll be all right."

It's not until I'm in my car, driving home, that I realize he didn't mention staying focused on football.

But he must have meant to stay focused on the game too. Right?

My coach lives for football. He must know that I do as well, no matter my new situation.

27

GABBY

When I open the front door, I'm surprised to see so many people on my front porch. I'm expecting Rider and Poppy, but not my brother, Tank, Olly, and Trevor—a wall of football muscles—standing behind them. And they're all loaded down with baby supplies.

"Hey, guys. That's *a lot* of stuff."

Tank points to Rider. "Daddy here thought Poppy needed everything."

"Does Bree know you call me Daddy?" Rider asks.

We all laugh, and I take Poppy out of Rider's arms since she's reaching for me.

"Ga-ga."

I stare at her. "Did you just try to say Gabby?"

She claps. "Ga-ga."

"Aww, Poppy. I love you." I hug her close, or as close as I can get with her puffy winter jacket on. It's in the high fifties, not quite Abominable Snowbaby weather, but I love that Rider thought to keep her warm.

"Poppy Seed!" Tank cries. "How could you say Gabby first?

We were working so hard on this last night. You were gonna say Uncle Tanky first, remember?"

Amused, I watch the guys plunk down her stroller, pack-and-play, baby carrier, a car seat, and multiple diaper bags. They're wearing their lettermen jackets and looking mighty handsome.

"You guys clean up so well!" I take Poppy's hand, and we wave. "Say bye-bye to your uncles."

Trevor kisses the top of her head, and she lets out the cutest giggle. Olly pretends to gobble her tummy, and she shrieks in delight. Tank tries to eat her foot, and she's laughing so hard, her face turns red. And Ben, demonstrative man that he is, gives her a head nod. "Be good, kid."

Sienna wanders in and tells everyone to have a good game.

Rider stands like a sentinel inside the doorway as the rest of the guys file out. Tank yells, "If we win, you know we're gonna have to do this *exact* routine before every away game, right? Can't mess with good juju."

Sienna closes the door and gives me a look. "Your brother is really hot."

"I thought you were dating someone."

"Doesn't make me blind." She waves her hand. "We're not dating, though. It's probably just sex."

The idea of hookups has zero appeal to me. I'm not sure I could keep my emotions out of it, but if Sienna is happy with the arrangement, that's all that matters.

I glance at Rider, who doesn't seem like he's following the conversation.

He frowns at me. "You sure you're going to be okay?" He motions to the mountain of baby supplies in the corner. "I brought everything I could think of, everything I thought you might need while we're away." Pausing, he pulls out his phone, and I use this momentary distraction to study him.

Maybe it's because he's headed to a game, but there's a seriousness about him that's electrifying. His stubbled jaw is tense, his eyes fierce, but when he glances at his daughter, they glow with affection.

I'll admit it. Rider Kingston is the sexiest daddy porn I've ever seen.

How am I supposed to deal with this? I can handle an arrogant jock, but I have no defenses for the brooding single dad standing before me.

He continues, unaware of my internal struggle. "Let me give you the number to the hotel we're staying at. And maybe Coach's phone number. Obviously, only call him if there's an emergency and you can't reach me. I'll leave my phone on, but you never know. Do you think you need a key to my place? I don't want—"

"Rider." I put my hand on his arm. "We'll be fine. Go win your game. We'll be cheering you on. Right, Poppy? Can you say, 'Go, Daddy?'"

I bounce her on my hip and smile. Rider's so earnest about his daughter, I could kiss him.

Before, he was just a player, carefree and living in the fast lane.

In the last week, it's like a switch flipped in him, some protective father gene got activated, and he's been laser-focused on Poppy. Not to mention school and football. Honestly, he's a machine, but I'm happy for him and his daughter.

But he's been so busy, I barely see him.

Since we cleared the air last Saturday night, I thought we'd hang out again like we used to. I was hoping we'd be able to spend time together like we did last weekend, order pizza and catch up some more, but that's not happening. Between his classes, practices, shuttling Poppy between babysitters, and homework, I'm surprised he has time to sleep.

I should be glad for that.

He said it himself. We're just friends.

If I'm disappointed, it's only because my expectations got the best of me. Once again.

Cars start pulling out of his driveway.

"Guess I should go." He kisses Poppy on her forehead, and she makes a sound of contentment. She kisses him back but ends up slobbering all over his cheek until he laughs. "Be a good girl, okay? Don't give Gabs trouble at naptime."

He's standing so close, I get a good whiff of his shampoo or body wash. Whatever it is, it smells masculine and clean, and I'd like to rub my face against his chest.

I don't, obviously.

"Kick Oklahoma's ass." I look up at him, and when our eyes connect, electricity runs through my limbs. My heart thumps hard in my chest.

"Call me if you need anything," he says.

It isn't until he speaks that I realize I'm staring at his lips.

"We'll be fine. Go."

Before I scale you like Mount Everest.

Stepping away, I take a breath, and then another. When I shut the door behind him, I collapse back against it while Poppy clings to me.

I look up to find Sienna staring at me.

"Holy shit. I almost got pregnant watching you two just now. I'll be right back. Gonna go take my birth control."

She's convinced Rider and I are going to end up naked together. As tempting as that sounds, I'm not sure I could handle one of Rider's drive-bys. If we have sex, I'll get attached and get my heart broken all over again.

If Rider was overwhelmed when he became the starting quarterback, there's no way he has time for a girlfriend—or even wants one—now that he has a daughter. I'm going to spare myself this time around and take him at his word.

It's possible he did me a favor by breaking things off when he did. If we'd slept together and then gone our separate ways, I would've been devastated, more than I already was.

Because this sexy single dad version of Rider Kingston has heartbreak written all over him, and I have no plans to become his next victim.

28

GABBY

WITH A GROAN, I stretch on my belly until I can reach that last splat of apple sauce under the kitchen table. I'm on my hands and knees, about to get up, when another spoonful lands by me.

"Sienna, we're supposed to get the food *in* her mouth. I swear most of it's on the floor. Remind me again why I thought this was a good idea."

"You said having a fuller tummy might help her sleep better tonight. Or it'll give her the shits. It's a toss-up."

Ugh, please let her sleep well tonight.

"I think Rider overestimated how much she'll eat this weekend." I showcase the pyramid of organic baby food jars on the counter with a sweep of my arm.

"He's too stinking cute is what he is." She gives me a wink, and I roll my eyes. Sienna is clearly on Team Rider. After wiping the table one more time, she looks down at Poppy, who's strapped in her car seat since we don't have a high chair yet. "Speaking of cute, all the guys in their letterman jackets? Swoooon! Am I right, Poppy, or am I right?"

Reacting to the excitement in Sienna's voice, Poppy claps her hands, spattering apple sauce all over the place again. *Jesus, take the wheel.*

Although we wrapped a towel around her, Poppy is covered, and I mean *covered* in baby food.

Sienna bumps me with her elbow. "You should send him a pic of her like this."

"Good idea." I wash my hands and grab my phone. "Poppers, hey! Smile for me! We're gonna send a photo to Daddy, and he'll be so happy to see you." Sienna and I hop around the kitchen like fools, trying to make the baby grin.

An hour later, she's clean, changed, and sound asleep. Sienna and I collapse on the couch in a heap of exhaustion. I was going to try making custard-filled *churros*, but I'm too wiped out.

She groans. "How am I this tired? It's only seven. We're supposed to wear her out, not the other way around."

Yawning, I reach for my cup of coffee. "No clue, but I need to find the energy to do this assignment tonight." At least it's a topic I'll enjoy—how Lucy Honeychurch's environment influenced her to fall in love with George Emerson in *A Room with a View*.

"You have superpowers. If anyone can get it done, you can."

"Thanks." I smile at my roommate.

"Here." She hands me this little brown bottle. "It's for concentration."

I read the ingredients. Coconut oil. Peppermint. Clementine. Basil. A few other extracts.

"They're essential oils. Rub it on your palms and then breathe deeply into your hands like this." She demonstrates what she means.

I give it a try. "Smells good. Thanks."

"My mom got tired of me having the jitters from caffeine, so she got me hooked on essential oils."

"What a good idea." I mean, I'm still keeping the coffee—let's not get crazy—but how kind of Sienna to share this with me.

I never in a million years would've guessed we'd become friends like this. I'm not sure I thought we had anything in common when she first moved in. I know I was quick to judge her as ditzy and too new age-y, but the more we hang out, the more I realize how fun and interesting she is. Even the stuff she's into is pretty cool. I may not go for all of it, but that doesn't mean I should dismiss her outright because our interests are different. Sometimes I have to remind myself to stay in my own lane.

This last week, she's been around more. I think she felt bad for me when Ramona leveled me with the news that she's moving. After Rider left last Sunday, Sienna and I vegged out with a glass of wine and I told her a little about the weirdness with my brother. It made me realize I haven't had many friends in my life, female or otherwise. And I'd like to change that.

Her phone lights up with a text, and she dives for it, her eyes bright with excitement.

"Are you going to tell me who he is yet?"

"If this turns into something serious."

I mull that over. "I thought you said it was just sex."

"It is." She sighs. "I'll admit a teeny part of me would like for it to be more, but this guy has hookup-only expectations. Have you ever had casual sex?"

"No. I mean, my last boyfriend—well, my only serious boyfriend—wasn't that serious. We were monogamous and intimate and everything, but I knew he was probably leaving after graduation, so what was the point in getting in too deep?"

"See, you think you can't do casual sex, but that's what you did with your ex. Deep down, you recognized there was no future, so you had fun for now. A committed relationship for people who catch the L-word is great, but what's wrong with a little companionship in the meanwhile?"

Huh. I never thought of it in those terms. *Companionship.* I could use that right now.

"I went into it expecting more," I admit, "wanting the depth, but it didn't work out the way I thought it would."

"Who doesn't want *the depth*?" She lifts one eyebrow dramatically, and I snort. "Hey, can I ask you a personal question?"

I want to point out that this whole conversation is personal, but I get the feeling Sienna can talk about sex without giving it a second thought.

When I agree, she pulls up something on her phone. "Have you ever had a G-spot orgasm? I'm wondering if this vibrator is worth the cost." She shows me the image of a hot pink sex toy called the Curvinator.

Squinting, I tilt my head. "Are you sure that isn't a medieval torture device?"

"Don't get freaked out by that curve. It's like when a guy does that two-finger thing. At least, that's what I'm assuming."

Um.

She must see my confusion because she holds up two fingers and does this come-hither, two-finger stroke that makes me blush. I know lots of girls bond over sex talk, at least every magazine in the checkout aisle of the grocery store seems to suggest that, but I've never been close enough to anyone to have these kinds of conversations.

"Please tell me your ex did that to you. Right up against your G-spot. Maybe while he did oral? Oh, my God. That's the best." Her eyes roll back in her head as she talks about it, and I'm definitely intrigued.

"I... we..." I cough. "We didn't do much oral."

Sean wasn't into it, either giving or receiving, though I tried a few times out of curiosity, but he said he preferred the main event. I tried not to take it personally, but whenever I hear women talking about guys going crazy for a blow job, it makes me wonder if I was doing something wrong, and he was too nice to point it out.

"That's a travesty." Her eyebrows pull together. "Please tell me he gave you orgasms."

After a pause where I have to think about it, I nod. "Yeah. A couple."

"You don't sound sure." Her phone lights up with a text, and it must be her football guy because she does this little squirmy dance in her seat. "Can we pick this up again later? I was thinking I should show him how good I am at sexting."

I laugh, loving how confident she is. "Sure. Go."

She disappears into her room, and I grab my phone and pull up the toy she was talking about. After a few minutes of debate, I decide that maybe it's time I start taking more responsibility for my orgasms. At the very least, I'd like to know what she was talking about.

I click "buy," and I wonder if a vibrator qualifies as a form of companionship.

29

RIDER

Tank dumps all of his shit on the floor of our hotel room and swan-dives onto his bed, then promptly passes out.

We fly for any distance over five hundred miles, but Oklahoma is close enough that we loaded up the bus and drove, and after being in that damn thing for almost seven hours, my muscles are tight as hell.

Worse? I can't visualize the game like I usually do. I have this anxious energy I can't seem to shake, and my head won't clear.

Hoping a shower will help with my restlessness, I head to the bathroom, blast the hot water, and strip off my clothes.

Standing under the water, I think about Poppy and wonder if she's having a good night. I worry all of this back-and-forth with so many people babysitting is gonna fuck up her little psyche somehow. As soon as I get drafted, I'm getting that kid the best nanny money can afford.

If my idea of the perfect nanny happens to look like my neighbor, well, I don't think anyone can blame me.

My thoughts drift to Gabby as they have all day.

To Gabby holding Poppy this morning before we took off.

To her smile last weekend when I brought her that pizza.

To her in that wet t-shirt when we gave the baby a bath.

Instantly, I'm sporting an erection that swells when I give in to that fantasy. The one where Poppy is asleep in the other room, and it's just me and Gabby and her damp clothes.

I rest my arm against the shower wall while the hot water rushes over me, and I take myself in hand.

In my fantasy, I'd peel off her little shorts. Rub her slowly through her panties. Suck on her pretty pink nipples through her shirt. Wait until she's gasping and begging for more to dip my fingers into her underwear and smear that wetness across her tight bud until she shudders in my arms.

While she's still trembling, I'd strip off the rest of her clothes and bend her over so I could get a good look at her tight ass. Maybe drop to my knees so I could bite it. Then lick her until she screams and comes again, this time all over my face.

With a groan, I erupt all over my stomach.

Leaning against the tile, I catch my breath. Water sprays over me and washes away the evidence of what I've just done, but a hint of guilt remains. Because what I want and what I can have are two different things.

I want Gabby so fucking bad, but I won't let myself go there.

It's why I tried my damnedest not to rely on her too much this week.

I wanted to call. I wanted to ask if she'd have dinner with me and hang out while I did stuff with Poppy or while I studied. But I don't trust myself not to screw shit up again.

Especially after I talked to Coach last week. He said I needed to focus, and I'm trying. So damn hard.

With Gabby, there are too many ways things can go wrong, and she's one of the most important people in my daughter's life right now.

Sure, I have several people babysitting for me, but Gabby is the only one I trust to watch her while I'm out of town. Not only is she great with the baby, but Poppy adores her. There's a calmness that descends over her when Gabby holds her that no one else can achieve.

And I promised Gabby—just friends. Not friends with benefits. Not a few hookups. Not a fuck fest until we both pass out. *Friends.*

I've never hated a word so much in my entire life.

Like an echo from a dream, I hear it in my head—*letting her go was a mistake.*

But it's not like I can go back in time. Even if I wish I could.

After I towel off and throw on some sweats, I grab my phone and crawl into bed. Swiping the screen, I delete three messages from Miranda. I've said everything I have to say to her. She knows we're over, so there's no point in dragging out our shit.

When I pull up the photos Gabby sent me today of Poppy covered in apple sauce, grinning like a little monster, my heart instantly melts.

I smile at her messy face and run my finger over her button nose.

But it's the one with Gabby laughing in the background I pause on the longest. Her hair is pulled up into a sleek ponytail, and there's nothing more I'd like to do than untie it. Run my hands through it. Watch it fall against her pillows as I lay her down.

I haven't replied to the message yet.

Not responding to Gabby as quickly as I'd like to falls under my self-denial category. Despite jacking off to thoughts of her in the shower just now, there's been a lot of self-denial this week. I have a laundry list of don'ts.

Don't text too often.

Don't call unless there's an emergency.

Don't hang out more than you need to.

Don't hug her.

Don't kiss her.

And definitely don't fuck her.

Assuming she'd let me.

I groan when my cock responds to the idea.

"Would you just call her already?" Tank rolls over in his bed, wrapping the comforter around him.

"Call who?"

"Who do you fucking think? Gabby."

I still. "How do you know I want to call her?"

He punches his pillow, turns his head toward me, and spears me with a look. "You've been wanting to call her since you left her place this morning, and don't even pretend otherwise. And I'm gonna make it real easy for you too." He reaches over the side of the bed, grabs his headphones, plugs them into his phone, swipes it a few times, until music blares out of those small speakers. He pops them in his ears. "I can't hear a thing," he yells. "Now fucking call her so you can think straight tomorrow."

Tomorrow. Because we have a game.

Fuck. When have I ever forgotten about a game the night before?

Never, that's when.

I press my palms into my eyes.

Okay. *Calling her now falls under prepping for a game because if I'm this fucked up in the morning, we all lose.*

She answers on the second ring. "Rider. Hey."

She doesn't sound as excited to talk to me as I thought she would.

Because you've been jerking her around like an asshole. Again.

I'm screwing this up, and I haven't even touched her.

I've got to do better. I can be her friend and not lose my mind, for fuck's sake.

"Hey." I clear my throat. "How did things go today?"

"Fine. Sienna and I played with Poppy all afternoon, and she knocked out around seven." While she answers my question, her voice is reserved. She doesn't expand on her day, which she usually does when it involves my daughter.

"Sorry I didn't get back to you sooner today. Those pics you sent me were adorable. I'm gonna have to print them out." I scratch my head. "Do people still make baby books? I saw some woman talking about those on a blog."

"That's a great idea. I'm sure Poppy will appreciate that someday."

We're quiet for a second, and I hate the hesitation in her voice.

Fuck it. Maybe asking will scratch the itch I've had all week.

"Whatcha doing on Sunday? Wanna hang out?"

She doesn't say anything at first, and I wonder if she heard me. I'm about to repeat the words when she responds.

"Do you need me to watch the baby?" she asks softly. "I think I can get you some time to do homework or whatever errands you need after—"

"No, it's not to watch Poppy. It's just to, you know, hang out. Maybe order some lunch or watch a movie. I have to get some homework done Sunday night too, but Bree said she'd watch Poppy for a few hours, and I could use some adult conversation that's not about football or diaper rashes. We could even nerd it up and watch some National Geographics if you'd like."

She laughs, and the sound fills me with warmth. Or something. Whatever it is, it feels amazing.

This is what I've needed.

I smile like a dumbass. "I'll let you pick what we watch."

"That's quite enticing, Mr. Kingston. What if I pick the chickiest chick flick I can find?" Her voice curls around me, sultry and soft, and the anxiousness I've felt all day melts away.

Chuckling, I stretch out on the bed. "Then maybe you'll feel sorry for subjecting me to it, and let me pick the food we order."

"Sounds perfect."

It sounds like a date.

No, not a date. Definitely not that. It *can't* be that. More like some hang time with my beautiful, off-limits babysitter and friend.

And who says I can't hang out with a friend?

30

RIDER

Eyes stinging from sweat, I glance at the scoreboard even though I know we're tied at thirty.

I can't even blame this on screwups. We've been pretty tight this afternoon, but Oklahoma's defense has been a beast, plain and simple.

With two minutes left in the fourth, it's balls-to-the-fucking-wall time.

We burn through our downs and barely make any headway, but I can't let it go to overtime. After driving all day yesterday and sleeping in crappy beds, I know I'm not the only one dealing with fatigue. We stand a helluva better chance of ending this now than in overtime.

The defense is all over my receivers, and even though there's nothing I'd love more than to gun it into the end zone, I know that's probably not going to be an option. We need twenty yards for a first down to put us in field goal range.

Maybe it's time to make a house call.

My fingers itch to take hold of the ball. I huff out a breath and call the play, conditioning and practice and endless visualizing taking over.

When the ball snaps on the fourth down with fifteen seconds on the clock, I drop back and check my options, but I already know what I'm gonna see. And that mammoth-sized Sooner headed my way will nail my ass if I don't move.

I juke the defender, make like I'm gonna pass to psych out the second guy zeroed in on me, tuck the ball under my arm, and hightail it through a narrow opening.

Out of my peripheral vision, that red uniform blazes toward me like a neon warning sign. He dives for my legs, but I leap over his outstretched arms. I stumble but somehow manage to regain my footing as my O-line plows a path for me.

And then I run.

Fifty yards.

Thirty.

A body flies into my path, but I jerk to a stop, spin around him and keep going.

Twenty.

Ten.

End zone.

Game.

My teammates hoist me into the air, and I'm riding the best high, the kind that makes me think anything is possible. Like winning a championship and being drafted and making a name for myself in the NFL are all within reach.

The moment my feet touch the ground, my thoughts turn to Poppy and sweet, beautiful Gabby.

And I wish they were here in the stands.

31

GABBY

LIKE A KID SCARED to get caught with her hand in the cookie jar, I check to make sure Sienna's in her room before I switch the TV back to ESPN. My roommate will make a bigger deal of this than it is if she catches me watching the recap again.

But my God, that was a freaking amazing game.

I nearly gnawed off all my nails this afternoon. Sienna and I cheered our little hearts out. We even dressed Poppy in Bronco colors.

We sent Rider a photo of Poppy touching the TV when they did a close-up of him. I held her right up to the screen while Sienna snapped pics.

I pull up his response on my phone, happier than I should be that he texted shortly after his win.

Rider: Glad my girl could watch! I think she's my lucky charm. ;)

I'm ashamed to say, for a hot second I thought he was calling *me* his girl and calling *me* his lucky charm. I was ridiculously pleased.

And then I remembered, no, dummy, he meant his *actual* little girl.

I'll admit it. I've finally gone to the dark side, but how can I take care of Rider's baby and not cheer for the man?

Rider's absurdly handsome face fills the screen. He's wearing a fiercely serious expression, glaring like a Roman soldier going off to war. All he needs is a sword and shield. It's no wonder women lose their minds at his games. They come decked out in bikini tops, even in cold weather, and hold up obnoxious signs about riding him.

When I think about all of his options—this guy truly could have any girl on campus—I wonder if I'm making more of what's between us than there is. If I'm setting myself up to crash and burn.

Just like freshman year.

Am I totally misreading him?

I munch on the *churros* I made before the game while I debate if I'm being foolish.

"I knew it!" Sienna pops out of the hallway like a ninja, and I scream and leap halfway off the couch like a Halloween cat.

"What the hell?" With my hand on my chest, I try to calm my racing heart. Thank God I finished swallowing that last bite or I would have choked.

She shushes me, because the baby is asleep in my bedroom, but holy shit, this girl just shaved off an entire year of my life.

"I knew you were watching replays of Rider's game!" She howls with laughter.

"And this indiscretion demanded that you terrify me? Really?"

Thank the Lord, Poppy sleeps through our ruckus.

When we finally calm down, I give up the pretense and watch the game recap in full view of my roommate like an adult.

Once it's over, Sienna reaches for the remote and clicks the mute button and glances at me with one eyebrow high on her forehead.

I sigh. "I guess... I guess I like him."

A look of mock surprise crosses her face. "Shut up! I had no clue!"

"Smartass." I grab the mostly empty bucket of popcorn off the coffee table and toss a few pieces at her. "That's hard for me to admit because he really burned me freshman year."

She eats the popcorn that lands in her lap, and the humor fades from her eyes. "When school started back in August, I got a good look at those incoming students, and I swear a few seemed like they came straight out of middle school, but you can't find any of those little minnows in the senior class. Wanna know why?"

"Tell me, oh wise one." For all of her laid-back California vibe, I'm learning that Sienna has a really grounded outlook on life.

"Because people change *a lot* in those three or four years. And while I'm betting Rider didn't look like one of those babies when he was a freshman, it doesn't mean he hasn't undergone some massive growth spurts on the inside too."

"But what's that saying? 'Fool me once, shame on you. Fool me twice, shame on me.'"

"I totally get that, but who can you trust if you look at everything through that paradigm? Not just lovers or boyfriends, how do you have any friends if you're always afraid to take a chance?"

For a second, it's hard to breathe.

"I... yeah." I shake my head. "It's hard for me to make friends, I guess." My lips twist as I think about Ramona, and I wonder if things would be different with her if I had let her in more. She moved out this morning, a week earlier than that timeline she gave me. "Remember I told you how my brother and I didn't grow up together? Our parents died when we were kids, and I moved around a lot after."

That's putting it mildly. My social worker told me I was unusual in that I had to switch foster parents so often, but I eventually learned not to try so hard when I arrived at a new house because I knew I wouldn't stay long. Even now as an adult, I don't always know how to let down my guard.

Sienna's eyes fill with sympathy. "I'm not trying to be critical. I'd just hate for you to miss out on this thing with Rider because you're scared of getting hurt. Could he hurt you? Absolutely. But you guys have off-the-charts chemistry, man. I feel like you two will combust if you don't get together."

I almost laugh. "It feels that way, honestly."

"Has he at least apologized for whatever happened between you guys freshman year?"

"Yes. He's apologized." I fiddle with the button on my shirt. "Twice."

"So that's a good start, right?"

I nod.

"'Course, it's probably weird he had a baby with another woman." *Then there's that.* "Has he said anything about who she is?" Sienna overheard Noxious talking about the mysterious baby mama the other day at the football house.

"No, and I've chickened out and haven't asked."

"I don't blame you. Talk about awkward." When I don't add anything, she asks, "How's he been since the last apology? I'm guessing it's going well since you freaked over his game with me."

"No, I freaked over his game because I can't help myself, but he was a little distant this last week. After he apologized last weekend, I saw him a few times when he picked up Poppy, but we didn't really talk."

No one has the power to make me crazy like Rider. Okay, my

brother makes me nuts too sometimes, but in terms of men I'm not related to, only Rider makes me question my sanity. *And check my phone all day for his texts.*

Sienna must sense I have to get this out because she lets me rant. "I sent him those pics we took yesterday with the apple sauce, and it took him *five hours* to get back to me. And I literally hate myself for counting that time."

I smother my face with the small couch pillow, and she chuckles.

"He was on a bus with a million other guys. Maybe his phone died? Or he took a nap? Or he was doing whatever football players do to mentally prepare?"

Hugging the pillow to my chest, I slouch back on the couch. "All valid suggestions, but after not talking much last week, I thought maybe he was trying to send a message. That we are *just* friends. He said as much last weekend." I roll my eyes and reluctantly admit the rest because I'm not sure how to interpret it. "Full disclosure, he eventually called last night and asked if we could hang out tomorrow. But is it a friendly thing or a date? At this point, I have no idea."

"Just keep an open mind about everything just in case it's a date." She gives me a fierce hug, and I find it hard to not smile in the face of her optimism.

"How are things going with your guy? Do you think it'll turn into more?"

A huge smile brightens her face. "He said he wants more. He just needs to keep things kinda chill, though, until the season ends so he can focus on football. Which I totally get."

"That's awesome! Well, I hope I get to meet your mystery man soon."

"Me too!"

It gives me the warm fuzzies to be having this girl chat with my roommate. Ramona and I never talked like this, and I wasn't close to my roommate freshman year. It makes me wonder how much I've been missing out on by not trying harder to have girlfriends.

"Gabs, do we really need to get a third roommate this semester? I like how things are right now."

I smile at Sienna. "I know what you mean. It would be great if I didn't need to do that financially."

She purses her lips. "What if I could pitch in extra for the third room? Just for this semester. I like doing yoga in there. It gets great morning light, and I can really clear my chakras. I mean, what if getting a third roommate blocks me?" She points to her chest. "In here?"

I don't get the chakra thing at all, but if that room makes her happy enough to pay extra rent, I'm all for it. "If you don't mind forking over the cash, I can definitely get behind you having your own yoga room."

"Yay!" She claps and does this little wiggle dance in her seat, and I laugh.

We get out our homework and work side by side. I proof my essay about *A Room with a View*, but as always, my thoughts circle back to Rider and our conversation last night.

Of course I tried to play it cool. How else do you act with someone you've crushed on for so long? Because I'm starting to realize I never got over him in the first place. Combine that with all of the tender moments I'm seeing between him and Poppy, and my defenses feel as solid as a house of cards.

It's also possible I'm blowing this out of proportion once again, and the man really just wants to hang out as friends.

When the knock on the front door comes a few minutes later, I'm still not sure which way I want this to go.

32

RIDER

It's almost eleven when I finally make it back to Gabby's. While I'm sore from the game and the long drive back to Charming, I took a nap on the bus and am wide awake as I stand on her porch.

I can't stop thinking about the game and how fucking cool it was to win like that. I wish I could celebrate with the guys.

Some of our neighbors stand out on their front lawns and cheer as my roommates pull into our driveway across the street. Within minutes, our house lights up, music blares, and friends and fans stream through the front door.

I couldn't bring myself to make my roommates hang somewhere else because of Poppy. The guys won't drink too much at this point in the season. They just wanna blow off some steam. Olly said Poppy and I could crash at his brother's place since he's staying with his girlfriend. I can't exactly bring her back to the house if the guys want to celebrate.

It's weird to not be at the center of things tonight. To be calling it a night because I have to pick up my daughter. I miss my gremlin, though. I hope she had a good day. I'm sure Gabby would've called if she'd had any emergencies.

Still. It would be fun to be able to relax for one night after busting my ass all week.

This stuff with Poppy has me thinking about my own parents. I kept checking my phone on the drive back, but my father never called or texted. I shouldn't expect him to care at this point. If he hasn't by now, he never will. I already know my mother is a lost cause. I wonder when I'll stop giving a shit.

All the guys called their parents and girlfriends on the bus ride home. Some families even drove to Oklahoma to cheer us on, for fuck's sake.

I probably wouldn't know what to do with myself if I had that kind of support.

When Gabby answers the door, she gives me a wide smile. Suddenly, all the shit that's been weighing me down on the drive home fades into the background when I look at this girl.

"Oh, my God. What a game! I'm so happy for you!"

I don't know how it happens, if I reach for her or if she reaches for me, but once she's in my arms, I hug her tightly and close my eyes. She feels so good pressed against me like this. I tuck my face into her neck and breathe in her orange blossom scent. "Guess this means you watched, huh?"

"You know I did. How could I not?"

Feeling better all of a sudden, I spin her around on her front porch as she laughs. When I set her down on the ground, I keep my hands on her small waist and she keeps hers on my shoulders.

"You've been all over ESPN today. I DVR'd it for you." Her voice lowers to a whisper like she's saying something sacred when she tells me, "They're even talking about you being in contention for the Heisman."

I play it off because I don't want to think about all the things that could go wrong. Sometimes I feel like if I take one wrong step, my whole world is gonna crash down on me.

"The press is just blowing smoke up my ass right now. There's still a long road ahead."

"Rider." She gives me that stern teacher look that makes my dick twitch. "You have ten freaking wins. You're undefeated. You've played tough teams all year. Let yourself feel good about this and celebrate."

As uncomfortable as talk of the Heisman makes me, this fierce woman in my arms makes me smile.

She glances over my shoulder, and her brows pull together. I know what she sees. The party that's about to go down. "Did you, uh, want to hang out with your roommates?" Stepping out of my hold, she pulls her sweater over herself and crosses her arms. "It's okay if you do. I can… I can watch Poppy tonight. Sienna's here. She'll keep me company."

I consider it for all of two seconds. As much as I'd love to hang with the guys right now, I realize how much I wanna spend time with Gabby. This is the person I want to celebrate with.

Her roommate's head pops out of the door. I almost laugh at her eager expression.

"Rider! Hey! Hi! Listen, kids, if you wanna go across the street and have a few beers or whatever, I can watch Poppycakes for you. I'll take the baby monitor into my room while you're gone. Just be back in the morning because I have brunch plans."

"What happened to your guy?" Gabby asks. "I thought you two were going to grab a late dinner or something?"

Sienna shrugs, but she looks disappointed. "Can't make it. He says he has to hang out with his family."

"Are you dating one of my teammates?" Because I guarantee you, none of them are "hanging with their families" right now.

She shrugs again, but she obviously wants to say yes, and I debate whether to tell her the truth. I've never seen her with any of my roommates, so that makes me feel marginally better. I'd hate to have that kind of drama in my house.

Before I can say anything, she waves us off. "Go celebrate. Both of you." She gives Gabby a look. "Have a beer for me. Enjoy your senior year." Flinging her arms in the air, she yells, "Be wild and free!"

I laugh. This girl is crazy, but fun. I'm glad Gabby has such a cool roommate. Sienna is a thousand times nicer than Wednesday Addams.

And Sienna raises some good points. I have my whole life to be serious. What's one night to relax a little? I know she'll take good care of the baby.

Turning to Gabby, I grab her hand. Sure, I'd like to go to the party, but if she's not in the mood, I'd be happy to hang out with her here. The party suddenly doesn't have any appeal if she's not going with me. "What do you say? Shall we hit up the football house? I promise to bring you home at a decent hour."

Gabby smiles shyly, and my heart pounds. I haven't seen this particular smile from her since she was a freshman and we would study together. I fucking love it. "Think I could meet you there in twenty? I'd like to change. Pretty sure I have baby food in my hair."

"Whatever you want." I motion behind her. "Would you mind if I check on Poppy real quick?"

Her eyes warm. "Of course. Come in."

When I peek into her bedroom, I find my nugget curled up and sleeping like a little angel.

I love this kid. The realization hits me so fucking hard, I can barely breathe.

She came out of nowhere and kicks my ass in so many ways, but Gabby was right. Everything—all of the sacrifice and sleepless hours and exhaustion—will be worth it in the end. Poppy has wormed her way into my heart, and I wouldn't have it any other way.

Ignoring the tightness in my throat, I reach down and gently rub her back. Her perfect bow lips do this motion, like she's sucking on a bottle. It's adorable.

"I really like that machine," I whisper to Gabby.

She ordered a sound machine that fills the room with ocean waves and the cry of gulls. I'm guessing that's why Poppy didn't wake up to the noise we made on the porch a minute ago.

When I turn, Gabby's so close, I can't help myself. I tug her into my arms and kiss her forehead. "Want me to come back and get you in fifteen?"

She blinks up at me, and I wonder if she knows how much I want her. "I'll meet you there."

I can't fucking wait.

33

GABBY

After complaining about these parties for the last two-plus years, it's strange to be heading to one. Were it not for Sienna, who plied me with a stiff drink, several coats of mascara, and red lipstick the shade of a fire hydrant, I'm not sure I would've gotten the courage to leave the house.

With my heart beating far too fast for something that's supposed to be fun, I cross the street and trot over to Rider's.

But Sienna's right. Being afraid is no way to live.

I'm a take-charge girl in a lot of areas of my life. Work. School. Taking care of Poppy. Why not take a chance tonight and see how that feels?

Can I go after what I really want, even if it is a six-foot-four quarterback with sterling-silver eyes?

My pulse rate skyrockets when I think of the possibilities, when I consider not letting fear pen me in like it has so many times in the past.

Not bothering to knock, because they'll never hear it over the music, I let myself in.

A wall of heat hits me from people crowding into the living room. The lights are dim, but not so dark that I can't see. The furniture has been pushed to the side, and people dance to a pulsing beat.

In the far corner, I spot Rider, surrounded by several of the guys and a boatload of girls. The cynic in me waits for him to turn to one of those women and flirt—I've seen more than my fair share of Rider flirting with other girls over the years—but he seems oblivious to the attention.

My stomach flips as his eyes skim the crowd, landing on me almost immediately.

He smiles, and I start walking toward him, unable to resist his pull.

Breaking from the group, he joins me in the middle of the dance floor and leans down, his lips brushing my ear and sending goosebumps down my arms. "You look hot as fuck."

Ignoring the dirty looks from a few of the girls staring at us, I laugh. Is this Party Rider who compliments all women or is this something just for me? I don't know, but I'm willing to take it at face value because the compliment feels good.

I'm pleased with the outfit Sienna encouraged me to wear. It's an off-the-shoulder red sweater that's fitted but not too scandalous, which I paired with a slim black skirt and wedge sandals. Since I was only running across the street, I didn't wear a jacket.

As a freshman, I would've wanted to blend into the walls, but I'm thinking there has to be something to what Sienna said about the degree of growth people experience in college, because being a wallflower is the last thing I want right now.

"Wanna drink?"

When I nod, he laces his fingers through mine and tugs me behind him as he makes his way to the kitchen, where he grabs me a beer. I almost laugh at the setup. Three kegs, a mountain of Solo cups, and a dozen pizza boxes.

"The meal of champions?" I joke as I down a beer. It's not my favorite thing to drink, but maybe it'll help curb these butterflies.

He gives me a crooked grin, the one that makes his dimples pop and my ovaries throb. "I'm almost ashamed to say that I'm not even sure how all this shit gets here. Someone always orders. But we have plenty of food. Are you hungry?"

I let my eyes boldly pass over him. Rider's hair is messy, like he's been running his hands through it, and a golden scruff lines his rugged jaw. My pulse quickens as I think about how that would feel abrading my neck and chest and thighs.

I want to tell him I'm starving. Ravenous.

Maybe it's the alcohol or that chat I had with Sienna, but I'm more than ready to go after what I want. We're not freshmen anymore. I'm not some naive little girl, and I have no illusions about what this is.

He's wearing an old, dark gray t-shirt that stretches across his broad chest and strains at his biceps, tapering at his slender waist. His faded jeans mold to his muscular thighs.

He's sex on a stick.

And I'm ready for a serving.

Am I hungry? I cock an eyebrow at him. "Depends. What's on the menu?"

His gray eyes smolder as he stares at me. He takes my hand, pulls me against him, bites my ear gently and whispers, "Then let's get an appetizer," before he leads me back to the living room where music washes over us as we melt into the crowd.

At first I'm confused. Did I not just blatantly hit on the man? Admittedly, I've never done that before, but I thought my message was pretty straightforward.

But then he stops in the middle of the room and wraps me in his arms.

Oh. He wants to dance. Speaking of missing clues…

Like I'm a middle schooler at her first dance, my heart melts. Rider wants to dance. With me.

Don't catch all the feelings, Gabriela. Just enjoy tonight.

My pulse ratchets up as I hold up a finger, chug the rest of my beer, and toss the empty cup into the large bin in the corner.

I step up to him. His hands grip my waist. I stare at the wall of man in front of me.

He laughs, his voice deep and sultry. "Are you going to touch me or are you waiting for an invitation?"

For some reason, that makes me respond like a smartass. "Do I need an invitation?"

He shakes his head. "Not at all. You can touch me anytime you want."

Gah!

I place my hands on his shoulders, and our bodies align as we move to the sexy beat.

I have to crane my neck to look up as he looks straight down and slays me with that smile.

"You're too tall for me," I lament, my lips tugging up.

He lowers his mouth until it almost whispers over mine. "I'd say you're the perfect height."

We move to the music while I cop a feel of those incredible shoulders. He's a perfectly sculpted mountain. All muscle and sinew and strength.

Rider was tall as a freshman, but he's put on at least twenty pounds of pure muscle since then and grown a few inches. The boy I kissed when I was eighteen is nowhere in sight. The person in front of me is one hundred percent man.

His eyes darken with every shift of my hips to this sultry beat.

This close, I can smell his sexy cologne and the clean scent of his skin.

At first, there's a little space between us, but when someone bumps into me from behind and pushes me into Rider, he keeps me there, his hands tightening on my back.

My breath catches. We're hip to hip, chest to chest, with my breasts pushed up against him. Like this I can feel his length, proud and thick and long, up against my stomach. I almost choke on air at the size of him.

Every slide of his body against mine is electric.

I rest my face against him and breathe him in and try to calm the frenzied beat of my heart.

But then I hear it. His heart. Pounding almost in time with mine.

We go on like this. One song. Then another. Until that pulse has snaked down between my thighs where it taps out a staccato beat.

A few minutes later, Tank's voice calls out over the sound system, "Hey, Bronco-Nators! How 'bout that win today?"

Everyone starts cheering.

"Where's the man? You know who I'm talking about! The man, the king, the legend! Rider Kingston, get yo' ass over here!"

People start chanting, "All hail the king!"

It's a little ridiculous, this crazy adulation, but I'm so happy he's getting the recognition he deserves for busting his tail.

Rider laughs as he pulls me to the other side of the room where his roommates have set up a DJ area. I don't see my brother, but this place is packed.

When the guys spot Rider, they hoot and holler, and people start screaming. He wraps one arm around my shoulders and pumps up the other one, and the crowd goes crazy.

Tank has obviously had a few drinks, and when he spots me, he yells into the mic, "G-Force!" He waves me forward. "People, our house never woulda survived the last few weeks without the one and only Gabby Duran! Gab-by! Gab-by!"

It's so unexpected, I laugh, but then Olly, Knox, Trevor, and

Bree join in, and suddenly the whole room is screaming my name.

Next thing I know, Rider's lifted me into the air, and I'm hanging halfway over his shoulder as he spins me around. His roommates keep cheering, and I've officially entered a parallel universe where I party at the Stallion Station.

Knox hands me a drink, and I hold up my red Solo cup in the air and yell, "Go, Broncos!"

The guys pick up the chant until the whole house is vibrating with this rally cry. After I chug the beer, I'm high-fiving Rider's roommates as I cling to him with my other arm. Bree pulls out her phone, and I mug for her pic.

For a minute, it's almost like I'm at their game, celebrating their incredible win with them. I've never felt anything like this before.

Laughing, I slide down Rider. I'm still pressed to his hard body when I look up.

He thrusts a possessive hand into my hair, and three years of pent-up lust and longing rush over me as his mouth crashes into mine.

34

GABBY

A FEW MINUTES LATER, we stumble into his bedroom. He kicks the door shut behind us and shoves me up against it. With a hand fisted in my hair and another on my rear, he kisses me like we're on the eve of the apocalypse.

Keeping time with the pounding of my heart, the floor vibrates with the beat from the music downstairs.

I strain against him, trying to get closer. Needing to be closer. Wanting to feel him move through me.`

This is what was missing in my other relationship. This unquenchable fire that feels like Rider and I could burn down the whole house with the electricity sparking between us.

And tonight, I want to burn.

Our tongues twist and stroke like this is a duel. Like we might die if we stopped.

Except that's exactly what he does.

Suddenly, he pulls his body back, but he rests his head against my shoulder as he pants, "Do we need to talk first?"

It takes a second for my mind to make sense of what he's saying.

I frown. *God, no.* "No talking."

Do I need him to spell out what this means? How this is likely a one-and-done or friends with benefits or some other equally horrifying situation? I'll pass.

I know what I'm getting. Pigs would have to part the skies for this man to commit to something significant.

I'm not looking for significant at the moment.

I took it slow with Sean. Had a million dates. Waited until we were committed to have sex. And *never once* did I feel this alive.

Never once did I feel like I might come apart at the seams if we didn't rip off each other's clothes.

I have zero expectations except for what Rider might make me feel right this moment. Do I want something special with him? Of course. But will I look back on this night with regret if I don't seize this moment?

I always do the responsible thing. *Always*. Would it be so bad to take a chance right now? To live a little?

I've wanted this far too long to backtrack now.

It's my turn to tighten my hand in Rider's hair. I bring his face to mine, and our lips touch as I answer. "Wear a condom. That enough conversation for you?"

His eyes, dark in the low light of his bedroom, turn molten. "Oh, fuck."

Then I'm in the air.

He hikes me up his big body, and my legs wrap around his waist. I barely notice the ripping sound of my skirt as it gets stretched beyond what it can handle.

We're frenzied as clothes come off—his shirt, then mine—in between kisses.

He stalks across the room with me in his arms until we fall into his bed. I laugh, I can't help it. I can admit this is crazy, but I don't care. I don't want to miss what might be my one chance to feel something sublime.

We roll around and laugh, out of breath. He's in his jeans,

and I'm in a black demi bra that gives me all kinds of crazy cleavage and a skirt that's ripped almost all the way up my thigh.

He straddles my leg and grabs my other one, lifting it. His eyes are trained on mine as he unstraps my sandal, pausing to graze his lips over my bare ankle.

"You're a fucking vision. I've always wondered what you'd look like with your hair splayed out on my pillow."

My hair is everywhere, a mess, I'm sure.

Then I consider what he just said. *He's thought about me in his bed.*

I want to ask how far back that fantasy goes, if he wanted me like I wanted him three years ago, but I cut off that thought before I blurt it out.

Instead, I reach out and run my finger over his full bottom lip. "What else does this fantasy include?"

His light eyes are black, totally dilated as he nips my finger. "I must have a shitty imagination, because it did not do you justice." He unstraps my other sandal before he kisses up my calf, pausing to nibble on my knee.

My breath catches as I watch him.

His whole body is taut with muscles upon muscles, not bulky but cut and finely hewn from training. His broad chest tapers to that sexy-as-hell V, and a thin trail of dark hair dips down into his jeans where he's sporting a massive erection.

"Want to unzip my skirt?" I wonder if he knows how wet I am for him.

He shakes his head, a wry smile tilting his lips. "I must have a teacher kink I never knew about, but I think you should keep the skirt on."

I adjust my glasses that have somehow managed to stay on my face tonight and give him a stern look. "Why, Mr. Kingston, have you been a bad boy? I might have to ride you. I mean, punish you."

His gray eyes darken, his hands tightening on my thighs.

I don't know who I am right now. I was never into roleplay or anything too adventurous with Sean, but tonight I want to rock Rider's world.

One slow inch after another, I slide my skirt up, higher and higher, until he gets an unobstructed view of that thin strip of black lace between my thighs.

A deep groan rumbles in his chest. "You're killing me, Gabby."

"Delayed gratification is good for the soul." I lean up on one arm while I run my other hand through his hair. Down his chest. Over his abs. Until I hook a finger into the waistband of his jeans where I pop the button. "You're busting out of those anyway." I chuckle.

Without a word, he gets off the bed and unzips his jeans. His almost naked form, save for a pair of dark boxer briefs, comes into view.

His rugged beauty is breathtaking. In a parallel universe, he'd be a Greek god or some other immortal, his body chiseled to perfection.

He crawls over me and settles between my legs. We both groan at the contact, the pressure so intense, goosebumps break out on my skin.

He rubs his nose against the cup of my bra where I'm practically spilling over and murmurs, "Speaking of busting out…"

Our eyes lock as he sucks me through the lace. One nipple, then the other. All the while grinding our hips together.

Writhing beneath him, I run my hands over his arms and shoulders, let my fingers trail over his back.

Anything could happen tomorrow. I'm not holding my breath that he'll have some major revelation and decide he wants to do this for the long haul, so if this is the only time we'll be together, I want to remember every detail. The way his hot breath heats my skin. How his eyes sear into me as he bites my breast. How being with him makes me feel like I'm floating even though he's weighing me down with his big body.

He reaches behind me with one hand and unsnaps my bra. It gets tossed to the floor with the rest of our clothes, and I swear the look he gives me could incinerate this whole house.

"Fuck, Gabriela. You're so beautiful. You shatter my fantasies."

I lean up and graze his lips with mine. "You're better than mine too."

Hunched over me, those steel arms braced against the bed, he asks, "So you've thought about this too?"

Only a million times. *Since the moment I first laid eyes on you in the library freshman year.*

I brush the hair out of his eyes. "Maybe once or twice."

He huffs out a laugh, but then he's on me, and there's no more laughter.

Bringing my breasts together, he molds and shapes me, licks and bites me, and then makes his way down my body.

A breath shudders out of me. I can't imagine what I look like with my skirt bunched around my waist and my legs splayed across the bed, but based on the growl that rumbles in his chest, he approves.

The first slide of tongue over my panties sends sharp shivers of pleasure through me, but then he shifts the fabric and his hot tongue glides over my slick skin.

We both groan.

One thick finger pushes into me, and that pulse grows.

"I'm so close." I grip his hair, half out of my mind.

His hand tightens on my thigh as he holds me open and slips in a second finger as he licks me slowly, like I'm some decadent dessert.

One lick.

Two.
Three.
"Oh, God."
My legs quake. My back arches. My skirt rips.
Somewhere in the universe stars collide.
And I come.
So hard.

35

RIDER

GABRIELA COMES ON MY MOUTH, and it's the sexiest thing I've ever experienced. As she trembles in my arms, I work her over with soft licks to her pretty pink pussy that tastes like heaven.

I can't help the smirk on my face when she collapses beneath me like she can't hold up her knees for one more second.

When I hunch over her on all fours, she cracks open one eye. "You look pretty pleased with yourself."

Her sex voice sends a bolt of lust through me.

"You have to admit you came pretty hard." So I'm smug. Sue me. I slide off her panties. "I might need to keep these."

"You're disgusting." There's no heat in her voice. I might even go as far as to say she sounds intrigued.

Licking her off my fingers, I mumble, "You have no idea." I blatantly stare at her beautiful wet core, my cock somehow getting harder. Not gonna lie, I almost came humping my bed a few minutes ago as I went down on her.

I pull down my boxer briefs and watch her eyes heat at the sight of my cock. With a firm grip, I run my hand from root to tip where I spread the moisture, glad as hell I didn't come in my pants.

"When I thought about your pussy—and I've thought of it often over the years—it was never like this." Without losing eye contact, I graze my thumb over her swollen pink bud.

"Like what?"

Her breathy voice makes me wanna fuck her into next week. "Bare. Smooth. Glistening. So fucking hot."

Really, my imagination did this woman a disservice. I let myself take her in. Her little lithe frame with all the right curves. That sexy fucking hair all over my pillow. Those gorgeous full tits. Her hot, tight pussy that makes me wanna pop off like a rocket.

Combined with her prim skirt half-torn apart and bunched around her waist and those black-rimmed glasses, she's the ultimate fantasy.

I reach for my bedside table before I do something stupid like drag my bare cock over her folds. Holding up the foil, I ask, "This okay?" I don't wanna assume she still wants to go all the way. I might die if she doesn't, but I still need to ask.

She nods, her eyes glued to my palm working myself over. She pushes my arm out of the way and palms me. When her hand doesn't quite reach all the way around, her eyes widen. I got some girth. And, okay, some length too.

I lean down and kiss her. "We'll go slow. I promise to make you feel good."

Her lips tilt up. "I don't need slow."

Fuck me.

She licks my bottom lip as she tugs me just the way I like it, firm strokes with a flick of her wrist at the end. "Do you taste yourself on me?" I ask.

Her brows pull together, and uncertainty flashes in her eyes. "Yeah. That's... that's kinda weird."

Her words give me pause.

Have the men she's dated never gone down on her? That's a

crime against womanhood. This beautiful creature was born to be worshiped.

"I love how you taste. Next time, I'm gonna have you sit on my face." I wink at her and do my best to not laugh at her horrified expression. No, this girl definitely hasn't been pleasured enough by the men in her life.

Not that I want to think of her with other dudes.

She could've been all yours, dumbass, if you hadn't broken things off.

I battle away that depressing thought.

Using my teeth, I tear open the condom. Once I'm locked and loaded, I kneel between her legs and watch as I push into her, stretching her wide. She's so wet and tight, I have to clench my jaw to hold back.

She makes the sexiest sound, a little grunt that almost sends me over the edge as she tightens around me.

"Jesus, Gabby. I don't have words for how good you feel."

Her nails dig into my thighs as I sink deeper. I'm about to ask if she's okay, if we need to slow down, when she gives me a breathy, "Yes!" She tightens around me as a shudder runs through her, and it snaps something in me.

I fall forward and brace myself against the bed as I pump in and out of her until the frame bangs against the wall. She grabs a fistful of my hair and drags my mouth to hers where I devour her. Our bodies smack together. Sweat slicks our skin. We pant and groan as we maul each other.

We roll over, tangled in the sheets as we push pillows and bedding out of the way. Something crashes in the corner, but unless the ground opens up and swallows us, there's no way I'm stopping.

She rises up over me like a goddess, her long hair a tangle behind her, her perfect breasts bouncing as she rides me, and she's so beautiful and fierce it takes my breath away.

I grab her hips and help her pump me. Harder. Faster. But I can't finish without her coming too.

Snaking one hand between us, I run my thumb over her swollen skin until she trembles. Her eyes widen, and she tosses her head back and quakes around me with a scream.

My release barrels into me, and I crush her to me as I come.

For an earth-shattering minute, everything in my life makes sense. Because being with this woman feels so right.

When blood starts pumping to my brain again, I stroke my hand down her back, and she snuggles closer.

Dread seeps into me as I wait for the claustrophobia that always overpowers me after sex. Where the walls seem to close in. Where I have to kick her out of my bed so I can breathe again. It's why I never have overnight guests.

I swallow as I scramble to figure out what I'll say. Already, I hate myself because I know it'll hurt her feelings. We should've had that talk before. I should've explained what would happen. That I always need space.

I wait.

And wait.

But the feeling never comes.

Instead, I get the craziest urge to wrap myself around this woman. To sleep, of all things.

I tangle my hands into her hair, and she gives me a sleepy, sated smile that fucking wrecks me. Needing her close, I graze my lips over hers.

"I'll be right back."

After taking care of the condom in the bathroom, I find her snuggled in my comforter, sound asleep.

Taking care not to wake her, I slide in behind her and pull her to me, my chest to her back, but she turns in my arms and splays out half on top of me and falls asleep.

Her warmth, the way she fits against me, how her hair falls over us—it's one of the best things I've ever felt.

And right here, right now, I somehow know nothing will ever be the same again.

36

GABBY

A HUGE, calloused hand rests on my right breast. Warm breath heats my shoulder. And one oversized quarterback hugs me from behind.

That's not the only thing hugging me from behind.

I squint into the sunlight streaming through the window, hating how my head pounds. How much did I drink last night? Just a few beers. And a shot or two. Ugh, never again. I never knew I was such a lightweight.

Blinking, I try to make out the small square of torn foil next to my face.

A condom wrapper.

Holy shit, I had sex with Rider. Twice.

You'd think the large naked man plastered to me would be the clue.

Or the giant erection pressing against my ass.

Squinting again, I spot my glasses on the nightstand next to his alarm clock. It's still early, which is good because we promised Sienna we'd be home to watch Poppy in time for her to go to brunch.

As great as last night was, I'm guessing Rider is going to be weird about me still being in his bed.

I assume awkward morning-after conversations are always better dressed. With that thought in mind, I attempt to scoot out of bed. Except that arm tightens and scoops me right back to him.

I chuckle and try to make a joke, but my voice is hoarse from screaming.

Girl, good thing the music was pounding last night or the whole neighborhood would know you were getting plowed.

I can safely say I've never screamed during sex before last night. There's now a line in the sand of my life—before sex with Rider Kingston and after.

I clear my throat. "If you try to drill me again with that weapon, I won't be able to walk for a week."

We woke up sometime in the middle of the night for a second round that somehow ended up being as vigorous as the first.

He laughs, the warm, raspy sound sending tingles down my body. "Sorry. Are you sore?"

I roll over to face him, and gah! He's got this sleepy, sexy look in his eyes that makes me melt, but I know how guys get the morning after, so I refrain from pouncing on him for some morning snuggles. Sean was not a snuggler. I can't imagine that Rider wants me in his space right now.

His eyes pass over me, and his smile grows. "Come here."

Or maybe he does.

"No sex," I warn. My lady parts need a rest.

"No sex."

Not needing another invitation, I toss an arm and leg over him and rest my head on his chest.

"Mmm. You're so warm." I wiggle closer, and I can feel his lips on my forehead pull into another smile. Seriously, naked snuggling with Rider is the best thing ever. I'm almost tempted to reward him with more sex. I'm so content, I blurt out the truth. "I'm waiting for you to be a dick and kick me out of your bed."

"I'm not gonna be a dick." He sounds mildly offended. "I like having you in my bed."

God, his hotness factor just increased tenfold.

The sound of his gravelly morning voice is a potent aphrodisiac, and my nipples are hard little points, which I subtly rub against him for the friction. "You sound surprised that you like having me here."

"You keep rubbing against me like that, and you'll get a surprise." He reaches under the covers, flexes his hips, and smacks me with his morning wood.

Laughing, I sit up and attempt to tickle him, but he moves so fast, I'm on my back before I blink. Except wrestling on a queen-size bed with a massive man is a bad idea because now I'm hanging off the bed.

He chuckles. "This is an interesting predicament you're in, Miss Duran." He blatantly stares at my boobs, which are giving him a high salute as I arch off the bed.

"Let me up, fool."

Leaning down, he slowly licks one nipple before he takes it into his mouth, and I groan and run my hand through his hair.

"If I can't walk tomorrow, it's your fault."

His eyebrow arches. "Does this mean we can—"

A knock on the door has us both turning our heads toward the sound as it opens.

And Tank and my brother stroll in.

"Dude, can Ben borrow your..." Tank stops with his mouth open as I scramble to cover my chest, and Rider yanks me back on to the bed. "Sorry, man. You never have anyone..."

Ben does a double-take. "What the hell, Kingston! Are you fucking my sister?"

"Get out, Ben!" I make sure my body is covered before I realize I've hogged all the blankets and Rider is stark naked with only a hand to cover himself. Which, for the record, isn't enough.

My brother winces like he's in pain. "You told me nothing was going on between you two. You said you guys were friends. That she was only helping you with the baby."

"Goddamn it. Get the fuck out." Giving up the pretense of modesty, Rider hops off the bed and tugs on a pair of track pants.

Tank is laughing because he thinks everything is funny. A minute later, the rest of the cavalcade charges in. The guys all stand in the doorway, but no one seems terribly surprised to see me except my brother, who looks ready to explode.

Tank claps his hands together. "I'm glad our boy finally got his priorities on straight." He grabs Ben by his shoulders. "Ben, dude. Boundaries."

"Thank you!" I tuck the sheet tighter around me. "Now can everyone please get the fuck out so I can get dressed?"

The guys all freeze, and Tank does a double-take. "Whoa. Never heard our girl curse like that." He gives Ben a look. "She's pissed. Let's go. We're ruining their morning-after glow."

Ben makes a gagging sound, and the rest of the guys laugh.

Except for Rider.

Rider is not laughing.

When the door finally shuts, I collapse onto the bed and hang my head.

Oh, my God, how mortifying.

37

GABBY

"Hey."

I don't budge.

Rider scoops me up and sets me on his lap before he wraps his arms around me. "It's going to be okay."

For some reason, this small show of affection when we're probably nothing more than friends hits me hard, and my throat tightens. "Don't be nice to me right now, or I'll cry."

He rubs my back and I sink into him. "Would it help if I were an asshole?" He kisses my forehead, and my eyes sting.

"Yes." I sniffle.

His shoulders shake with laughter, but after a moment, he stills. "I'm sorry about all that. I should've locked my door last night, but I guess I got carried away."

He got carried away with me. That makes me feel marginally better.

I don't want to talk about my brother while I'm wrapped in a sheet, about to do the walk of shame through the football house, but I'm too upset to reel it in.

"We used to be so close when we were kids. When I was

little, I used to call Ben my twin. And now... now he wants nothing to do with me."

Rider's hand makes a slow trail up and down my back. "Hmm."

"What?" I sniffle again and angrily wipe my eyes.

"I'm not sure he'd want to beat my ass if he wanted nothing to do with you. Ben is not an emotional guy. He locks up that shit tight. Except when it comes to you. I've never seen him that pissed." Rider's hand makes another trek down my back and pauses to pull me closer. I lay my head on his shoulder. "I know you guys went through a lot when you were young. Maybe he needs to talk to someone about that."

I nod and swallow back the sob that wants to break out of me. Right now, I'd do anything, *anything*, to be able to cry to my mother. To ask her how to bridge the distance with Ben. The fact that he just saw me in the most compromising position only adds another layer to my humiliation.

Rider seems to know I need a minute to get my composure. Once Niagara Falls is kept at bay, I sit up and hesitantly look at the man whose lap I'm sitting on.

Because now I'm facing that other awkward issue. Pretty sure you're not supposed to have some big emotional breakdown after a hookup or whatever this is. "Well, I'd, uh, better get going."

Before he can say anything, I leap off his lap and trip around his room, gathering my clothes, which are strewn all over the floor. He calls my name, but I ignore him, too embarrassed to look at him. By the time I shut the bathroom door behind me, I want to crawl into a hole and stay there.

What was I thinking hooking up with Rider? He lives *across the street* from me. I'm going to have to see him all the time. With other women.

I swipe at my eyes again, hating myself for feeling anything. I never cried with Sean. Not once. He never made me feel anything too intense. Being with him was pleasant. Like a warm bath or a box of chocolates or a cup of tea on a cold day.

Rider's a hurricane. A cataclysm. A precipice upon which girls willingly toss themselves over the edge for one night with him.

Which is exactly what I did, and now I have to face the consequences.

I get dressed as fast as I can.

Finally, I look in the mirror. Raccoon eyes stare back at me. My hair would make a fine nest for a flock of geese.

With my skirt in near tatters, I dare say I look like Katy Perry in that music video when she's trying to survive a jungle. Well, minus the flawless makeup and anthemic self-empowerment tune blasting in the background.

After wiping under my puffy eyes with some toilet paper and dampening my hair so it doesn't look like I got ravaged by Edward Scissorhands, I take a deep breath, straighten my glasses, and prepare to open the door to Rider's bedroom. *We had sex. This isn't a big deal. He does this all the time. You can lose it at home if you need to. Not here.*

He's still sitting at the edge of his bed, but now he's wearing jeans and a long-sleeved, dark Henley. His elbows rest on his knees, his hands templed under his chin.

His eyes turn up to me, and I straighten under his perusal.

"You ready to go?"

I nod slowly, even more confused when he gets up to walk me out.

Really, I just thought I'd make a run for it.

We take the back stairs that open up into the kitchen. Where all of his roommates meander about. Including my brother.

Knox, who everyone correctly calls Noxious, lets out a low whistle. "Someone had fun last night." He eyeballs my skirt, which has a slit halfway up my thigh. "You two really went there, huh?"

"Don't look at her that way. And shut the fuck up." Rider places his palm on the small of my back.

Tank pushes Knox out of the way. "Ignore him. He hasn't been properly house-trained. He still pees on the furniture." He holds out a to-go cup to me and gives me a wide smile. "Coffee with extra cream, light sugar. Just the way you like it."

"Thanks, buddy." I grab it, grateful for a break in the horrid tension. And really, how thoughtful is Tank to know how I take my coffee?

My brother crosses his arms, pointedly looking away from us. It's the last straw.

I glance at Rider's other roommates. "Look, guys, we're all still friends, right? What I do in *my* personal life shouldn't change anything."

Trevor winks at me. "You'll always be golden in my book."

One by one, the rest of the guys agree that we're cool. Except my brother, who stares out the window.

"Really, Ben? How am I supposed to know you give a shit about me? At all. Much less care who I date?" My temples pound from drinking too much last night and from the fact I might need to punch my brother in the throat.

He scoffs and faces Rider, gritting out, "*Date*? Is that really what you think is going on here?"

I narrow my eyes at him. "Consider that a euphemism, okay? For your sake, not mine. What Rider and I do is *none* of your business. He's my friend and has done nothing to gain your ire."

Knox takes a big bite out of a bagel and talks around a mouthful of food as he slings an arm around Ben's stiff shoulders. "Your sister uses some big words. Do we know what 'ire' means?"

Ben shrugs him off as Tank smirks. "It's three letters. Figure it out with context clues."

As I start to make my way toward the front door, my brother steps in front of me and says, "I know it doesn't look like it at the moment, but I'm only looking out for you."

"By humiliating me in front of your roommates?" I hiss.

Rider is back at my side, and he and Ben give each other the death stare.

Ben points an accusing finger at his roommate. "So this means when Miranda or some other chick comes around in the next few hours or days or weeks, you're turning them away, right? Because my sister should know what she's in for if she throws her hat in your ring. That she's just one of many."

"I hate you so much right now." I push my way around him and race out the front door, ignoring Rider when he calls out my name.

38

RIDER

After nearly coming to blows with Ben, I bolt across the street, but that conversation took a good half-hour. I'm grateful I managed to calm his cranky ass without either of us getting our faces rearranged, but I'm still pissed he said what he did in front of Gabby.

That hole in the wall shouldn't be too hard to patch up. For the record, Ben took that swing. Not me. Though I really fucking wanted to, I figured Gabby wouldn't be too pleased if I planted my fist in her younger brother's jaw. Forget the fact that I need to be able to take to the field with him tomorrow. As a general rule of thumb, I try not to beat up my teammates.

Although he'll be pushing the limit if he ever says shit like that again to her.

Sienna answers the door before I'm done knocking. "Hey," she says hesitantly while she bounces my daughter on her hip. From her expression, she obviously knows something just went down, but first things first.

I scoop up Poppy and hug her to me. "How's my girl, huh?" I blow kisses into her neck, and she squeals. After loving up on the kid, I turn to Sienna. "Sorry I'm so late. This morning, uh, was crazy."

"It's barely nine. You're fine."

"How was her night?"

She catches me up on all the cute things Poppy did this morning when she woke up at ass-crack.

I reach into my back pocket and hand her an envelope of cash. "I'm sure I owe you more."

I've started paying everyone something and keeping track so I can make up the difference when I have more money. Pretty sure my roommates won't let me starve, but I can't deny how humbling this is. Being this financially desperate reminds me of being a kid again, which I fucking can't stand.

She tries to hand it back, but after I insist, she nods.

We stare at each other a second while I try to figure out what the hell I need to say when she chuckles. "Guess you wanna talk to Gabby?"

"Yes, please."

She motions behind her. "I think she's in the shower."

Likely trying to avoid me. Can't say I blame her. "I'll wait."

Sienna's expression tells me that's the right thing to say.

Poppy and I sit on the couch, and Sienna waves bye and disappears down the hall. I lean back and balance Poppy on my stomach, where she tries to stand. When she wobbles, I widen my eyes and go, "Whoa, baby! Daddy's gonna catch ya." The kid loses it, giggling until she can barely breathe.

After several minutes of this, she eventually gets tuckered out and rests her head on my chest. I pat her little butt. I have a shit ton of homework to do, but I'm determined to spend some quality time with my daughter today first. It's not her fault my schedule is insane. I promise myself I'm gonna make it up to her when the season is over.

"Da. Da. Da. Dahhhh. Dee."

I pause. "Did you just say Daddy?"

She lifts her head and gives me a slobbery grin and repeats the word that cracks my black heart wide open. Not prepared for how hearing that term would hit me, I close my eyes and give my wiggle worm a hug. "Love you, Poppy."

When I open my eyes, Gabby is standing a few feet away in a robe. She gives me a soft smile. Her hair is wet, her face free of makeup. But it's obvious she's been crying, and that fucking wrecks me.

"Come here." I pat the seat next to me. Surprisingly, she doesn't put up a fuss, but she settles a good foot away from me.

"Aww, you can do better than that." Leaning toward her, I sling an arm around her shoulders and drag her to me. The move gets me a laugh, and eventually she slides closer and drops her head to my chest, where she coos at Poppy.

My daughter makes grabby hands for Gabby, who takes her into her arms.

They obviously adore each other.

Briefly, I wonder if this could be my life. When I'm not playing football and there are no cameras or press or fans, if I could come home to this. Quiet evenings with my daughter and Gabby.

Except the thought makes me want to break out into a cold sweat.

Before I can freak out, I remind myself of the advice Tank shared with me before I came over. To take one step at a time. To not lose my shit thinking about 'down the road.'

"You're not asking the girl to marry you," he warned. "She'd probably laugh in your face anyway. Just let her know she's different."

He didn't need to explain what different meant.

The intimacy and connection I've always had with this

woman only exploded when we had sex. I've never felt anything like I do with Gabby.

It scares the hell out of me.

But freshman year taught me one thing. If I ignore this or run from it, I'm only gonna regret it. Things with Gabby are too special to ignore.

I clear my throat. "Poppy was wondering if you'd like to join us for breakfast."

"Poppy?" Gabby sits up and smirks.

"Yes, Poppy." My daughter makes grabby hands for me now, and I take her back. "She mentioned it just before you walked in here. She said, 'I really like Gabby. Let's invite her out for some French toast and coffee.'" I pat my daughter's behind with one hand, hoping to keep her chill while Gabby and I talk. Fortunately, she seems content to lie on my chest and chew on her fist.

My beautiful neighbor gives me the biggest smile I've seen from her in a while. But then her lips turn down and she looks away. "I figured you'd be running for the hills this morning. You guys are known for hit-and-runs."

Ouch.

She shakes her head. "And then my brother goes all Neanderthal on you when he's not exactly the paragon of committed relationships."

She's not wrong about her brother, but who am I to criticize how he lives his life?

"Ben's just looking out for you, and I don't blame him. If I had a sister, I'd be making damn sure whatever guy she was with treated her right."

When she doesn't say anything, I lift her chin to make her look at me. "I'm not running."

Stormy hazel eyes stare into mine. They're red-rimmed and wary, and I hate that she doesn't trust me.

"I'm not running. And that's what I told Ben." And likely why we didn't have an all-out brawl at the house, but she doesn't need to know that.

After a minute, her head tilts toward my hand, and I stroke her soft skin.

"You promise you won't run?" she asks slowly.

I nod, leaning closer where I graze my lips over hers. "I promise."

"And Ben's not going to try to kill you in your sleep?"

A half-laugh, half-groan escapes me. "Hopefully not. I think he'll be cool." Well, not cool exactly, but probably not murderous.

I think I've answered all of her doubts, but when I try to kiss her again, she leans back. "And there won't be others?"

Because I'm a dumbass, it takes me a second to understand what she's asking.

Other women.

That's an easy question to answer considering she's dominated my thoughts all semester. *You haven't stopped thinking about her since freshman year. You were just too chickenshit to do anything about it.*

"No one else."

That gets me a small smile, and I swoop in and kiss her before she can come to her senses. I have zero experience with serious relationships, but if this is what she wants, if I'm what she wants, then I'm game.

I tangle my hand in her damp hair.

"I'll be honest about a few things, though." I pull back to wrangle my daughter, who has decided to crawl up my head. "For the next few weeks, I need to keep football as my focus. How I play for the rest of the season will determine the rest of my life and Poppy's. I can't fuck that up. So I need to keep the non-football parts as drama free as possible. Seeing how I also have a kid, that's probably asking a lot, but I need to try. If you're on board with that, then I'd like to see where this goes." I give her my best smile and bring Poppy's face right next to mine. Hopefully she can't turn us away. My kid's mug is pretty cute. "What do you say? Ya want a two-for-one? We're kind of a package deal."

Gabby glances between us and rolls her eyes at my shameless use of my daughter, who I must admit is my best weapon. "You play dirty."

You have no idea how dirty I like it.

But then she nods.

"Yeah?" My heart races in my chest.

"Yeah."

"Wanna seal it with a kiss?" I'd be up for sealing this with more than a kiss, but Poppy's on deck, so I'm gonna have to settle for some PG action.

Gabby swoops in with a little peck on the lips, and when I frown, she smirks. "You're going to have to wait for the good stuff." She wags her eyebrows at me, and I huff out a laugh.

As we get ready to go out to breakfast, I wonder if it gets better than what we did last night.

I can't wait to find out.

39

GABBY

As we walk through downtown Charming toward the diner, I shove my hands into the pockets of my hoodie and study Rider out of my peripheral vision.

He's carrying Poppy in a front-facing body sling. She's clapping and kicking and utterly excited to be on this outing. The two of them are quite a sight, and everyone we pass, women especially, takes their time perusing this sexy male specimen.

I turn away, chiding myself for wanting to look.

Technically, I should be able to stare at Rider unabashedly, especially after our conversation this morning and what we did to each other last night, but I'm a little leery of letting on exactly how much I like him.

He can reassure me with words, but I still consider him a flight risk. Maybe less than he was freshman year, but I need more time to see if he means what he says. Being with Rider is like circling the sun, wondering how close I can get before I get burned.

Not wanting to derail what could be a great thing in my life, I consider how much he's changed. After all, he's fantastic with Poppy. Despite his hectic schedule, he always seems to be on top of her needs. I've never seen her sitting around in a dirty diaper. If she's upset, he immediately picks her up to try to comfort her. He's always trying to get her to laugh or smile or talk to him. That gives me confidence he's not the man child I knew and I'm not just setting myself up for heartbreak.

"You're kinda quiet over there." Before I can say anything, he slings an arm over my shoulders, pulling me to him, and I sigh, relishing how nice it is to be close to him.

"Just admiring how sexy you look with Poppy."

I swear his emerging smile sparkles. "You think I'm sexy, huh?"

"Shut up. You know you are."

He leans down and kisses me. Right there on Main Street. And then, with a devilish look in his eyes, he whispers, "You seem to be walking okay today."

I snort out an unladylike laugh. "No thanks to you."

Chuckling, he kisses my forehead, and inside I swoon hard like an eighteenth-century débutante. What is it about forehead kisses that make me so weak-kneed?

I'm about to lean up for another kiss when Poppy grabs a fistful of my hair and tries to chew it.

"You need a little love too, Poppycakes?" I blow a kiss on her chubby cheeks, and she giggles. While I untangle my hair, I give Rider a dopey smile. Ugh, fine. I'll admit it—I'm so happy I can't stand it. Despite what happened with Ben this morning, having Rider be so stalwart and steady is turning me on like a big weirdo.

We resume our walk down the street, and my level of contentment goes into overdrive when Rider tosses that arm over my shoulders again. Of course, I reciprocate by placing mine behind his back.

For the next sixty seconds, I'm in domestic bliss.

Because that's how long it takes us to get to the Road Runner

Cafe and open the door where everyone stops eating to stare at us.

"What's going on?" I whisper to him.

"Not sure." He frowns.

But then someone shouts, "Go, Broncos!" and people cheer and high-five Rider as we walk by on our way to a booth in the back. "Hell of a game yesterday, man!"

Right. The game. Duh.

I feel like a big dummy for forgetting that. Pride surges in me, even though I had nothing to do with his performance. Still, I know how hard he's been working.

Rider takes the praise in stride with a few fist-bumps and easy smiles, but he urges me along with his hand on the small of my back.

Until we reach the group of cheerleaders. They yell his name and shout questions, and he pauses to chat. I'm sure he knows all of them.

Hopefully not that well.

"And who is this little lady?" A beautiful blonde talks to Poppy, who loves the attention and babbles her greetings.

"This is..." Rider coughs. "This is my daughter."

They stare, mouths open.

Oh.

Oh.

I should pat myself on the back for the NDAs. But I'm surprised this bombshell hasn't been screamed across campus, despite those forms I made everyone sign with the threat of impending death if they gossiped.

However, I'm guessing this isn't how Rider wanted to unveil his daughter to the town of Charming.

The girls check me out and give me dirty looks as though I somehow trapped this guy into having a baby.

Of course, Zoe Evans, my former co-worker and backstabber

extraordinaire, is in the middle of the group, whispering to her friends. For the life of me, I have no idea what I did to make this girl my enemy.

You picked a fine day to dress comfortably in sweats with minimum makeup, Gabriela.

I want to yell I'm not the mother, that I didn't *do* anything to Rider, but I get momentarily distracted by thoughts of all the things I *did* do to him last night.

I force myself out of the fantasy and glance around at everyone staring at us. If Rider wanted to keep Poppy a secret, for privacy or to minimize the drama, coming here today was a bad idea.

40

GABBY

"Do you want to get some food to go?" I whisper as we pull away from the table. Internally, I cringe. Did he not just make a big declaration about needing his life to be drama-free?

"No, it's okay," he says stiffly as we take the back booth, which is set apart a little from the rest of the dining room.

I help him get Poppy out of the carrier, and since he looks like he needs a minute, I set her on my lap and get out her apple sauce.

The waitress takes our order but doesn't say anything about Poppy, thankfully. Of course, since she's sitting in my lap, maybe that takes the focus off of Rider.

"You haven't taken her out in public yet, have you?" I rip the foil off the container of apple sauce with my teeth so I don't lose my grip on the baby.

He sighs and runs his hands through his hair. "No, and I hadn't thought past how nice it would be to get her out of the house for a little while. Get some fresh air. Maybe take her to the park. Try to make up for the fact that she's gone from one babysitter to the next all week."

I give him a sympathetic smile. "You're doing the best you

can. It won't always be like this. And look"—I bounce her in my lap and she giggles—"she's perfectly happy and doing great."

"You make it sound so simple."

"Isn't it? The plan, I mean. Love her, feed her, change her, get her to bed at a reasonable hour. Survive the season. Then you can reprioritize a little. Spend more time with her."

He stares out the window. With the sun in his face, I notice the circles under his eyes.

Hmm. Maybe we shouldn't have gone to the party last night.

A pained sigh leaves him. "This is nothing. Wait until the press gets wind of my situation."

Worry snakes its way into my heart. "I hadn't thought of that." Which reminds me... My heart pounds as I open my mouth and pause. *Don't chicken out, Gabriela. Be an adult and ask!* "I hate bringing this up right now, but have you had any luck tracking down her mother?"

It's not the question I want to ask, the one I'm screaming in my head. *Who is the mother?*

His cheeks turn ruddy as he shakes his head. "Not sure what I'd say to her if I did."

For some reason, his embarrassment eases some of my own anxiety.

I reach across the table and take his hand. "I'm not trying to embarrass you by bringing her up, but do you know how you'll answer those questions the media will raise about her?" Because if he's not ready to talk to a few people at the diner about Poppy, much less her mother, then he's probably not ready to take on the press.

"Not a fucking clue." He groans, his eyes anguished as he stares at his daughter, who plays with a menu. "But this means I definitely have to tell my father."

"Tell him...?"

"About Poppy. Before he hears about it on ESPN or from some nosy-ass neighbor."

He hasn't told his father yet? Holy crap.

"Don't say it." He pulls his hand away. "Normal people talk to their parents when they're in trouble, but we're not a normal family. I can't deal with his judgment when the man can barely take care of himself. Hell, on some days he didn't even feed me when I was a kid."

Oh, my heart.

He'd probably hate if Poppy and I jumped up out of the booth so we could hug him.

Casting my eyes down, I bite my lower lip so it doesn't quiver, but kids are my weakness, and thinking about him suffering as a child nearly does me in.

"Hey," he says, his voice gentle.

I swallow.

"Gabby." When I finally look up, the soft expression on his face makes me want to crawl into his lap. It's his turn to reach over the table and grab my hand. "I'm okay. Just like you, I got through it. You don't need to feel bad about my situation. I know I'm lucky in a lot of ways to have so many opportunities now."

"You're not lucky. You're talented. I know we weren't friends for much of college, but that doesn't mean I was blind. I saw you in the library studying all the time. And now that I understand your grueling practice and game schedule better, I realize how hard you've worked."

He threads his fingers through mine and clears his throat. "Thanks for having my back. Tank wasn't kidding last night when he said we wouldn't have survived the season without you. You've been such a good friend to me when I haven't given you many reasons to be."

I look down, certain I'm blushing.

I should tell him I had my reasons. That while, yes, I would do anything for Poppy because this baby stole my heart the moment I pulled her out of that basket, I've been fighting a crush on him for years despite my better judgment. But I don't say anything.

He squeezes my hand before he releases it. "This is gonna sound strange, but I never talk about my family to anyone. Besides my coach, you're the only other person I've told. It's always been easy to talk to you. I mean, when you aren't slamming doors in my face."

I laugh. "Oh, my God. Shut up."

He chuckles, and we smile at each other. "Seriously. You're a good listener. Maybe it's because you've gone through so much yourself. You said your aunt took you in?" I nod slowly. "Do you stay with her over breaks?"

My smile fades. "No." I shift Poppy in my lap, grateful that she's busy playing with ketchup packets.

"Are you guys not close anymore?"

"She, uh, she got a new boyfriend my senior year of high school, this guy Bobby, and he's not my biggest fan."

Rider's eyebrows furrow. "Why's that?"

"Because I told my aunt Carmen that he hit on me."

"He fucking did what?"

I let out a breath I didn't realize I was holding. I'm sure Rider doesn't even know what he said just now, but without a moment of hesitation, he assumed Bobby was at fault, which is more than I can say for my aunt.

"Bobby came home drunk one night and made a pass at me. My aunt was working. I told her what happened the next day, but she took his side. Said I must have imagined it." I shrug. "When I left for college, Carmen said it was probably best if I didn't stay with her anymore. Bobby had told her that *I* made *him* uncomfortable. I've only visited a couple of times since then

—when I was sure Bobby was at work—so I could see my little cousins."

"What a cocksucker."

The fact that Rider believes me when no one else did means more than I can say. I rub Poppy's back, embarrassed to look at Rider.

"So where do you go for winter and summer break?" he asks.

"I stay around here."

I just need a reason to stay after graduation, and I'm hoping Archer gives me that anchor. Otherwise I'm not sure where I'll go.

He clears his throat. "I swear this isn't how I wanted to spend our morning, being so serious and stressed out."

I smile, even though I'm feeling shy and vulnerable. "It's okay. I like getting to know you."

"I want to get to know you too. For real this time." The smile he gives me is dazzling and makes the butterflies in my stomach take flight.

When the food comes, Rider scoots out of the booth and comes over to take the baby. "So you can eat without my gremlin trying to devour your hair." He gives me a wink.

My smile grows as I dive into my waffles while I watch Daddy Kingston feed his daughter.

"Come on, munchkin. Let's try to get more food *in* you than *on* you this time."

I pause with my fork halfway to my mouth, entranced. His t-shirt fits snug across his wide shoulders. Those big biceps flex as he holds Poppy in one arm while maneuvering that tiny spoon in the other.

Oh, yeah. This is better than porn.

A few minutes later, the waitress brings over a highchair, and we get Poppy settled in and finish eating.

When we're done, he motions toward my plate. "Are you doing better with your hypoglycemia?"

I pause. We've never discussed the details of what happened last May, but he must have overheard me talking to the paramedics that day. "Is that why you always try to feed me? First the pizza and now waffles."

He gives me a sheepish smile. "I don't know. Maybe. Is that wrong?"

"No, it's sweet. But I'm doing better. I haven't had any episodes since the night we found Poppy. That was the last time I felt dizzy. I went too long without eating. It was an accident, really."

"What happened?"

"A bad date."

"That dick Jason didn't feed you?"

I laugh at Rider's intensity. "Jason's idea of dinner was nachos from that gas station, which I passed on. That's how I ended up light-headed later. But unless you're planning on taking me on a bad date, we should be good."

Rider gives me a wolfish grin. "I plan on doing a lot of things with you. Bad dates aren't one of them."

My lady parts stand up and cheer, and I feel my face heat. "I've been meaning to ask why you didn't like him."

"Aside from him taking you out?"

I fight a smile. "Yes. Aside from that."

"I had a friend he cheated on last year, so I knew he was bad news."

Nodding slowly, I bite back the question I really want to ask, but he gives me a look.

"What?"

If we're doing this for real, I guess I have a right to know. "Have you ever cheated on anyone?"

He doesn't hesitate. "No, never. You have to be in a relationship to cheat."

"So... you've just had casual... situations in the past?"

"Pretty much. Yeah." Pausing, he looks me over, his eyes warm. "Which is night and day from what we're doing, in case you're worried." He seems at a loss for words for a minute. "I don't know how to explain it, but you're different. Maybe it's because I consider you a friend too."

My mother always said she fell in love with her best friend. My heart gives a little kick at the thought.

He leans forward, and I feel his hand on my thigh under the table. "I'm glad we're doing this, Gabby. I like hanging out with you." Those lips tilt up, and he whispers, "That's not the only thing I enjoy doing with you."

My imagination runs rampant when I consider what I'd like to do to him. And, fine, it's not a declaration of love, but for a guy who only does casual, he's surprisingly forthcoming.

I don't know how I deluded myself into thinking I could only spend one night with him.

Rider and I agreed to keep things low-key during the season, but no one said anything about feelings.

And I already have too many to count.

41

RIDER

When the professor drops the essay on my desk, I groan at the grade. Even when I try my hardest, I'm lucky if I get a C, and trying to type an essay while I bounce a fussy Poppy on my knee is almost impossible.

I really need to learn to type with more than two fingers.

The girl next to me, Waverly, grabs my elbow. "I can proof your next essay if you want." She bats her extra-long lashes at me.

Suddenly uncomfortable, I glance down at the hand that's still resting on my arm. "I'm good, but thanks."

I'm not a pro at serious relationships, so I'm unclear whether it's okay to allow random touches like this. Like, can I hug friends who are girls?

I guess that's what Gabby and I are doing, right? A "serious" relationship. I hadn't meant to dive into a full-fledged anything with anyone, especially right now when I have so much going on, but it felt wrong to have sex with Gabby and not commit.

Swear to God, having Poppy sheds a new light on *everything*. What if one day some tool has sex with my daughter only to dick her around afterward? That little shit would be dead, compliments of my two bare hands wrapped around his scrawny neck.

So if I expect assholes to treat my kid with respect, damn, I gotta up my game. And that means I can't just sow my wild oats. I need to settle down and not freak the fuck out over it. Even without Ben breathing down my neck, I know this was the right step to take.

Gabby is a wonderful girl, and I love hanging with her. She's a good friend. We have insane chemistry. And I've gotten around enough to know that what we have is special. That seems like a great place to start. Like Tank said, I don't need all the answers from the get-go.

Besides, when I think about other guys asking out Gabby? *Fuck. That.* I damn well want her all to myself.

Huh. That's new.

I rub my hand across my chin. I'm not used to feeling possessive about a woman, but that's definitely going on right now.

As class lets out, Waverly squeezes my arm again. "Want to grab some coffee? We could go over the next assignment and get a jump-start on the essay."

If her eyelashes flutter any faster, she's gonna take flight. I look down at her hand with a frown.

Since I don't have the headspace to figure it all out right now, I'd better play this safe. Had her offer not come with the batting lashes, I might consider it platonic, but it probably isn't.

"Sorry. Gotta run. But thanks." I stand quickly so her hand falls away and make my way out of class before anyone else can stop me.

I'm meeting up with Bree outside the food court, so she can hand off Poppy before her class. Just as I'm heading over, though, I come face to face with Miranda, who gives me a wide smile.

"Rider! Hey!" Thankfully, she doesn't throw herself at me

like she did that day I picked her up from Archer. She grabs my arm, but quickly releases me.

Okay. That wasn't terrible. She seems better with our boundaries now.

"What's up, Mira?"

"What's up?" She pouts, jutting out her lower lip. "Why didn't you tell me about Poppy? I would've been happy to help."

It's only been two days since I made the mistake of taking my daughter to the diner, but news travels fast. I keep waiting for the other shoe to drop and the press to get wind of Poppy. I'm not ready for that drama. On the bright side, since the secret is out, drop-offs like this one are easier since I can pick her up on campus from some of the friends who babysit.

"You want to help?" I don't mean to sound incredulous, but when I think of maternal instincts, Miranda doesn't come to mind. I shouldn't judge. I have no idea if she likes kids or wants them because, frankly, we never discussed it.

"Of course! You mean so much to me." She shoots me one of her bright smiles, and I begin to relax. When Mira and I are getting along, she really is a sweetheart. I don't know why I thought she wasn't taking our breakup well. "Listen, things got weird between us for a bit, but we've known each other too long to not get past that, right?"

"Yeah. Right." I know some of my friends don't like her, but Miranda's always been pretty cool to me, and I'm relieved there's no bad blood between us.

If there's one thing I can't stand, it's arguing. I heard my parents scream at each other through my entire childhood. When people disagree, they need to talk it out, not yell in each other's faces.

"So as *friends*, I want you to know I'm here if you need anything." She pauses, and her eyes grow wistful. "We're friends, right?"

This seems like a gray area. Is it okay to be friends with an ex? Because even though Miranda and I were only casual, it was long-term enough. *I am the one who told her we should go back to being friends when I picked her up that day at Archer.*

Am I being an asshole if I blow her off? Am I jerking Miranda around the way I did Gabby freshman year if I don't want to be friends? Fuck, I don't know, but it feels like a giant dick move if I tell her we're not.

"Friends. Yeah. Of course." I give her a patient smile. "I gotta run right now."

"Good luck with the rest of the season. You know I'll be cheering for you."

"Thanks, Mira." I give her a hug before I realize I probably shouldn't, but this feels like the end of whatever we had, and I want to leave off on a good note.

Miranda and I go our separate ways. A minute later when I spot Bree, she's shooting me dirty looks.

"What could I have done to earn that scowl?" I ignore her glare and scoop Poppy out of her stroller.

"That girl is evil. Please tell me you're not getting back together with her."

"I'm so relieved I get the honor of you preapproving the women I date, but no, that's history."

"Aww, are we finally using the word 'date'?" Wide-eyed, she claps. "Does this have anything to do with your cute little neighbor?"

"Please. You're really gonna pretend you don't know what's going on?"

She laughs. "Okay, I know a few things." Like we're the oldest of chums, she hooks her arm in mine. "And you should know this—you hurt my girl, and I will dislocate your ribs."

After I untwine my arm from hers, I give her an awkward back pat since I'm still holding Poppy. "Glad you're on her side.

She needs good friends." Then, because I'm an ass, I give her a noogie. "Now stay out of my love life."

Annnd that's a mistake.

"Now we're using the word 'love'? Holy shit, Rider, what's happened to you?"

Pretty sure her name is Gabriela Duran, and if I'm being *really* honest, that girl kinda rocks my world.

Not that I'm gonna lay this on Bree.

And not that it's love.

But it's... something.

"None of your beeswax. Now get to class before I wrangle you to babysit more."

When it's just me and Poppy, I figure I'll grab a quick lunch, play with the kid for a while, before I get her to the afternoon babysitter so she can take a nap and I can go to practice.

Except the minute I sit down in the cafeteria, I'm swarmed by people. Mostly women. Okay, only women.

And they're all baby-talking to Poppy and doing that thing where they touch my arm or chest, and since I have my daughter in my lap, I can't move away from them.

That's when I see her.

Gabby walks slowly toward me, her face stoic. She glances at the women surrounding me, and her shoulders go stiff.

Although it's been a few days since we had breakfast, we text often, but this is the first time we've seen each other.

I take stock of how this looks. If the roles were reversed, I would not be thrilled to see her surrounded by men.

Because I don't want to give her a reason to doubt my intentions, I jump up, dislodging everyone around me, and stalk toward her with Poppy on my hip.

"Hey," I say. Gabby doesn't have a chance to respond before I tangle my hand in her hair and pull her mouth to mine. Thankfully, she opens right up and sighs when I kiss her long and deep.

I'm not into PDA, but I think I can live with this.

Until Poppy smacks our faces with sticky hands.

I chuckle and end it with a few quick pecks. Lowering my voice, I whisper, "Can you make everyone leave me alone? I swear I came here for a quiet meal and some time with Poppy."

She glances around, her eyes full of humor when she lays her palm on my chest.

See, now *this* hand I welcome.

"Guess the fans want some time with their football hero."

I roll my eyes, and she laughs. "Smartass."

We make it back to my table, which is now blissfully empty, and I situate the baby in her stroller.

Gabby rearranges her glasses. "At some point you're going to have to stop cursing or Poppy is going to get in trouble for dropping f-bombs in preschool."

"Shit, you're right."

Shaking her head, she kisses my cheek. "You're lucky you're cute."

I give her my best Colgate-worthy grin. "I am, aren't I?"

Placing her whole hand on my face, she playfully shoves me away, but I grab her around the waist and pull her to me. When we're nose to nose, she's out of breath, her chest heaving against mine.

"Wanna come over and study later?" I swore I was going to limit the time I spent with her this week so I didn't get distracted, but damn, I really want to see her tonight. She has her job at Archer this afternoon, and I have practice, but running into her like this is only making me miss her more.

She gives me a gorgeous smile. "It's a date."

For once, that statement doesn't make me want to run in the other direction.

42

GABBY

My heels click across the tile floor as I make my way to Mrs. Nolan's freshman classroom. I'm still smiling from running into Rider and Poppy at the student union.

And those kisses.

God, I love his kisses.

When I poke my head in, Mrs. Nolan is already waiting by the door. "Thank you so much! My sub should be here in a few minutes, so you shouldn't have to wait too long."

Her son is sick, and she has to pick him up from his elementary school. Since I'm not credentialed yet, I can't sub, but I can sit with her class until one shows up.

"It's not a problem. I'm happy to help." A real classroom? *Yes, please!* I'd rather hang out with students than photocopy another worksheet. "What are they working on?"

"*Romeo & Juliet* packets."

I may have photocopied those for her. "It's one of my favorite plays. We'll be fine."

She gives me a grateful smile and turns to the class. "Guys, please be on your best behavior for Miss Duran. I'll see you tomorrow."

They're all sitting straight with pleasant expressions.

Until the door closes when every student seems to sag back in relief.

And then they all start talking at once.

Not to me. To each other.

I roll my eyes, put two fingers in my mouth, and blow, the resulting whistle making them all freeze.

"I'm so glad to have your attention now." I give them a chipper smile. Just because I don't plan to let them get away with murder doesn't mean I have to be a jerk about it. "Who wants to explain where we are in the play?"

A few groan, but for the most part, they refocus. One girl raises her hand, and I call on her.

"We just read the part where Tybalt kills Mercutio, and then Romeo kills Tybalt and has to leave town or face death."

I clutch my heart. "Isn't that part the saddest!"

The girls nod.

The boys look bored, so I continue. "Romeo just married Juliet that morning, right? But they haven't spent their wedding night together yet when he gets banished." I'm totally not going to touch on what consummating their marriage means. Although I'm sure most of them have Netflix and know more than enough, Mrs. Nolan can have that discussion. But I can help them grasp the significance. "Guys, just think. It's like asking the most popular girl at school to prom and she accepts, but the night of the dance—after you get your tux, buy her corsage, and pay for the tickets—you get expelled for fighting."

"That would suck!"

"My parents would freak if I got expelled!"

I chuckle to myself at their horrified faces. "Who wants to tell me the significance of Mercutio's name? Have you discussed this already?"

Everyone shakes their head. "Great. So do you know what 'mercurial' means?"

Half an hour later, when the sub finally arrives and says I can go, the kids groan and ask if I can stay.

It's one of the best moments of my life.

43

GABBY

"And then we started discussing the significance of stars and fate in the play," I say with a wave of my hands. "You know that quote, right after Mercutio's Queen Mab speech, where Romeo says, 'I fear, too early, for my mind misgives some consequence yet hanging in the stars shall bitterly begin his fearful date...'"

My voice fades as I take in Rider's expression. He and I are studying in his living room with the baby monitor so we can hear Poppy if she wakes up.

I sink into his couch, my face aflame. "I'm going overboard here, aren't I?"

He chuckles. "You're adorable. Wish I could quote Shakespeare like that."

"Sorry. I tend to nerd out sometimes. It was just exciting to really connect with students like that. I can't wait to have my own classroom."

He grabs my hand and gives me a little yank until I fall into him. "You'll be an amazing teacher someday." He kisses me. "If I had teachers like you when I was in high school, maybe I would've cared more, tried harder. English isn't a strength of mine, but from everything you just said, I'm pretty sure if I'd had your class when I was a freshman, I could've made sense of that play."

"Aww, that's a really sweet thing to say."

"Of course, if you were my teacher, there's also a strong possibility I'd be a walking, talking erection."

"Rider!" I attempt to give him a whack on the shoulder, but he grabs my wrist. Next thing I know, our textbooks have hit the floor, and I'm straddling him.

"See what I mean?" He thrusts his hips up and his massive boner attempts to bust through his zipper.

My eyes go wide. "What if Ben finds us like this?" I hiss.

Rider told me he hasn't seen much of my brother since Sunday, which works for me. I'm still upset with how Ben flipped out. At the same time, I don't want to be at the center of any more drama.

"Ben's a grown-ass man who has done worse in this house."

"Ew."

He laughs obnoxiously and tugs me down to him.

Part of me wants to resist Rider, resist this pull, but the other part, the girl who's crushed on him since she first laid eyes on him during their tutor session, wants to give in.

Guess who wins?

Surrendering, I run my hands through his hair. Breathe in his sexy masculine scent. Trail my lips over his. "We're supposed to study tonight."

He pulls me closer. "I am studying. My favorite subject. Anatomy."

I shake my head, but relent and give him a kiss, but before he can reciprocate, I hop off him. "Nope. No funny business. Homework first. You said you need to stay focused, so finish that assignment first."

He quirks an eyebrow at me. "You really do sound like a

teacher. Next thing I know, you'll be lecturing me for my shenanigans."

I giggle. "Nobody says 'shenanigans' anymore. Although it really is a great word." He's quiet for a while, and when I'm done penciling notes into my planner, I find him frowning.

"What's your teacher schedule like again?"

"You mean at Archer?"

"No, don't you have to do a student teacher thing first?"

"That's next semester. I got a placement at a middle school, but like I mentioned before, I'm hoping Archer will hire me full time in the fall. I'm going to talk to Mrs. Nolan the next time I see her and ask if she'll give me a letter of recommendation. As much as I hate all the busy work they've given me, I'm in love with their modular system. Those kids are so lucky. They basically have a collegiate schedule and use the extra time to study or get help from teachers or talk to counselors."

I barely pause for a breath. "No wonder my mother wanted us to go to school there. Because of that temp job, now I know they have a teacher retiring next year, and I can be ready to apply. Rider, my mom would be so happy to know I got a teaching job there. If I can finagle it somehow."

His eyes travel over me, his expression growing somber. "You will. I can't imagine anyone more perfect for the job."

It means so much to me that he thinks so, but when I smile, he looks away.

I'm about to ask if something's wrong when Olly and Trevor stomp down the stairs, pausing to shove each other through the doorway of the living room. Rider shushes them. "If you wake the baby, I'm gonna be pissed."

"Oh, shit. Right." Olly shoves Trevor for good measure with a chuckle. "It's his fault. He doubts my ability to make a mean turkey."

"You can cook?" Olly seems more academic than most of the

guys on the team, so maybe I shouldn't be surprised his talents extend to the kitchen.

He holds his hand over his chest. "You wound me, Gabs. Of course I can cook. Are you coming over for Thanksgiving?"

The holidays are always tough for me. Ben usually goes home to visit our uncle while I stay around campus.

I look to Rider, who nods. "If you're gonna be in town, you should definitely swing by. None of us can go too far because we have a game that Saturday. So glad we have a bye weekend first."

"You guys could definitely use a break." I squeeze his arm and turn back to his roommates. "What can I bring? I'm not great at main dishes, but I can do sweet breads. Do you like empanadas? I can make a batch."

Trevor nods comically. "I'm obsessed with the ones they sell at Rise 'N Grind. Have you tried those?"

Pride puffs my chest. "Those are mine. I mean, sometimes someone else bakes them, but they're my mom's recipe."

With how crazy my schedule's been, I forgot to tell Rider I finalized that deal with my boss. I explain how once I realized how busy I was going to be this fall, I told Fanny I couldn't come in as much to bake on the weekends, so she pays me a license fee for exclusive use of my recipes, which are mostly my mom's with a few tweaks I've made over the years.

Mom would be thrilled to know those recipes are funding so much of my life right now. I even paid off that ridiculous EMT bill and set a little aside in savings.

The look of admiration in Rider's eyes fills me with warmth. "That's awesome, Gabs. You're amazing." He kisses me on the forehead, and my face flushes.

"Aww, boo," Olly chides as he makes kissing sounds. "Our little Riding Hood is growing up."

"Shut the fuck up." Rider jumps up and pretends to punch

him, but Olly tackles him, and next thing I know, all the boys are wrestling and play-fighting.

"Don't hurt Rider!" I whisper-yell, so I don't wake Poppy. "You need him to throw balls and... things."

Olly pauses. "But I can get hurt. Don't you love me too?"

Trevor tries to sit on Olly's head but he turns to me. "You love me too, right, Gabs?"

"I love all of you idiots. Now stop messing around before you get hurt or wake the baby."

Rider shoves Olly into the floor as he pops up. "Yeah, but I'm her favorite."

I roll my eyes but laugh as he flops next to me and treats me to a kiss and quick boob grab.

Chuckling, I shove him off me. "Study first. Play later."

Once it's just Rider and me again and we can return to our homework, not two minutes go by before there's a loud bang upstairs. And then another. And another.

"What *is* that?"

He cringes. "I have an idea. Does the sound machine have a higher setting? I doubt Poppy can sleep through—"

"Waaaaaah!" Her sad wail blares through the monitor on the coffee table.

"Motherfucker. I'm gonna kill him."

"Who?"

"One of my dipshit roommates."

And? I give him a look because I'm still confused.

"Um, he's fucking some girl through his wall."

Oh. Heat sears my face. "Sometimes I'm so clueless."

His eyes soften and he hooks an arm around my shoulders to kiss me. "You're perfect. Never change."

With a groan, he heads up to his bedroom to comfort his daughter. His sexy voice comes through the monitor.

"Hey, baby, it's okay. Daddy's here. No need to cry."

I swoon on the couch while I listen to their conversation.

He's such a pro at this point, he doesn't need my help anymore. I knew he'd be a great dad. He just needed a little confidence in himself.

After a few minutes, she eventually calms down, but then someone slams the front door and she gets upset again.

I'm ready to give the offender my meanest glare, but it's my brother, who barely pauses when he sees me.

"Ben, you can't slam the door. Poppy's trying to sleep."

"Shit. Sorry." As he heads to the stairs, it's obvious he has no intention of talking to me.

"Ben. Wait."

He lets out a sigh and turns around.

"Are you going to avoid me forever? Can we please grab lunch this week?" I'm so tired of this crap. We're adults. I wish he'd start acting like one.

His jaw tightens, but he nods. "Coffee?"

"Yeah, that would be great." I open my mouth to ask what day works for him, but he disappears up the stairs.

I can't even blame his reticence on him finding me in Rider's bed last weekend. He was like this *before* that incident.

A few minutes later, Rider comes down with a tired baby on his shoulder. "I thought I'd hold her until she knocks out. Can we turn down the lights?"

"Of course."

"It's usually not this loud around here," he says. I scoff, and he chuckles. "Really. The guys are usually great. I think it's the bye weekend that has everyone excited."

Judging by the frequency of those bangs upstairs, football's not the only reason.

When he sits next to me, I rub Poppy's back. "Do you want to come over? She can sleep in my room while we study." His eyes meet mine, and they're so intense I almost lose my breath. "You, uh, you guys can stay over if you want."

He clears his throat. "I can sleep on the couch."

"Or..."

"Or?"

"You could stay, you know, in my room." In my bed. With me.

Those beautiful lips lift, and I wonder if he's thinking what I am.

44

RIDER

The bright light of the TV shines on the other side of Gabby, giving her a silvery, angelic glow. We're sitting on her couch, but I'm slouched deep into the cushions, watching her. She tilts her head, glances back at me shyly, tucks a long strand of hair behind her ear, and resumes her reading.

"Get to work." I can hear the smile on her lips.

"Fine, but finish your dinner." Now that I know she needs to take care of her health better, the least I can do is feed her.

She rolls her eyes, but a smile is playing on her lips as she finishes the hoagie she forgot about.

I should finish my presentation, but I can't concentrate on anything but her. If someone had told me a few months ago Gabby and I would be dating and that she wouldn't hate me anymore, I wouldn't have believed it.

A sense of relief fills my chest. Not making amends with Gabby, not having this, would've been an epic mistake on my part. I almost missed out on one of the best things in my life. Yes, football has to be my goal. Yes, my daughter has to be my main priority. But as for what I do for myself? I'm realizing it's this woman. Next to Poppy, she's the highlight of my day.

What about the draft? a little voice in my head warns. *What happens when you're a thousand miles away at an NFL training camp or on a pro team and she's here in South Texas teaching at her dream school? What then?*

I shake my head. *One step at a time,* I remind myself.

That's a problem, though. I feel like I'm jamming all of the difficult parts of my life into a closet, waiting for the right time to deal with them, but what happens if it bursts open? What happens if it gets too full because I can only focus on basic things right now while we finish up the season?

"You're looking awfully serious over there." Her voice is gentle. Concerned.

"A lot on my mind." I pause, debating whether I can do this. I open my mouth before I change my mind. "Can I ask a favor? It's a big one."

She sets her empty plate on the coffee table. "Of course. What's up?"

My heart hammers. Because no one from Charming knows much about my life before college. But this is Gabby. For some reason, I think she'll understand.

"I need to talk to my father this week. I wanted to take Poppy to meet him, but I could use some backup."

Her eyes widen. "You want me to come with you?"

"Would you mind? A warning first. He's an ass, not to mention an alcoholic, so don't expect a warm welcome. For either of us."

She nods. "I remember you telling me he was difficult. Just tell me what you need."

"It's, uh…" I don't know how to say the rest. It's embarrassing as hell. "We've got a run-down double-wide and a yard full of weeds. I'm pretty sure there's a hole in the ceiling too in the back room. But if he's gonna lose his shit, I don't want Poppy around that. Like you've taught me, stress isn't good for a baby. So if you could help me with her while I talk to him, that would be great. Just prepare for him to be a dick."

She reaches over and grabs my hand. "Don't worry about me. However awkward it might be, it's not going to bother me. I was in foster care, remember? The fact that you still have a father is a mark in the win column."

Fuck, sometimes I forget how much she's been through. I tangle my hand in her hair and bring her close to kiss her.

"I'm not joking when I say you're amazing." She is. Nothing gets her down. Nothing fazes her. I rub my nose against hers. "You know that, right?"

I hope we can work out all of our logistical issues after we graduate because the more I get to know her, the more I want her with me for the long haul.

She glances down, her face turning pink. Even her modesty is attractive.

I push my textbook off my lap and replace it with my gorgeous girlfriend. Surprised, she gasps and then lets out a strangled laugh as I get her to straddle me.

"Shh. Don't wake the baby." Wanting to make the most of this position, I squeeze her round ass.

That gets me a smirk. "Oh, so now you're the authoritarian?"

"Damn, you turn me on with those big words."

She laughs, and it's a beautiful sight. The sparkle in her bright eyes. Her wide smile. The joy in her voice. I want to bottle up this moment and carry it with me to every away game.

And because I can't get enough of it, I tickle her. She shrieks and bats me away, and attempts to tickle me, but come on. I have a foot of height on her. Two seconds later, she's underneath me, panting and looking so fucking sexy, I'm instantly hard as a goal post.

I whisper, "Let's see how much you can take."

"Wha... what?" The heat in her eyes nearly undoes me.

I'm sure she's thinking about what I have pressed between her thighs, but nope. I have more game than that.

"Just trust me." With a smirk I lift both of her arms over her head and drag a finger slowly, so slowly, down her palm, over her wrist and elbow, but as I get lower, she giggles and tries to yank her arms down. "Nope. See what you did?" I give her my most stern expression. "Now we have to start all over again."

"Okay. I can do this." She cracks up, and the delight in her eyes is a thing to behold. "Go ahead."

This time, even though she giggles and wiggles beneath me, I get all the way down to her perky breasts that are beckoning me with beautiful tight nipples. I drag my thumb over one, then the other, while we both watch, and I swear the heat of her sears me through our jeans.

Replacing my finger with my mouth, I suck her through her white t-shirt. By the time I'm done with the second one, she's moaning in my arms. I'm about to snake my hand into her panties when she presses a palm to my chest.

"Sienna will probably be home soon."

Hmm. "Let's go to your room."

"What about Poppy?"

Shit. She's right. But then I get the best idea. "How about we make use of the floor on the other side of your bed?"

Poppy's sleeping in her pack-and-play by her desk, but there's some space by the window on the opposite side of the room, and the sound machine is pretty loud.

It's her turn to drag her finger down my chest. "We'd have to be *really* quiet."

Oh, fuck. I'm so down for this. Please, God, let my kid sleep well tonight.

Gabby takes my hand and leads me in, closing the door so quietly, I don't even hear it click. With a sexy smile, she sets her glasses down on the bedside table before she grabs her comforter, spreads it on the ground, and tosses down a few pillows. Then I whip off my clothes and then paw hers off too. Shirts, jeans, socks. Off. Until Gabby's wearing some sheer nude bra and underwear combo that short-circuits my brain.

"You're so sexy." I can see everything through that material, but at the same time, it has an almost virginal quality to it. I collapse back on the floor and reach into my boxer briefs to fist myself.

She leans over me, her hair cascading around us, and whispers into my ear. "Are you really going to put on a show and not let me watch?"

Her eyes are wide, her pupils blown out. My sexy little angel is turned on. I pull her on top of me and point out how she needs to reciprocate.

"Wanna show me how you use your new toy?" I let the words settle in and enjoy the flush that runs up her neck, which I can see thanks to the streetlight streaming in through a space in the curtains.

She looks around and finally spots what I noticed the second we came in here earlier to put my daughter to bed.

Gabby has a hot pink vibrator sitting on her desk. With one hand, she covers her eyes.

"Baby, don't be embarrassed. We're gonna have so much fun with that." I've never used sex toys before, but I'm more than ready to try. I smack her on the ass. "Go get it."

She's frozen on top of me, her pulse fluttering in her neck.

Damn, I don't wanna push her into something she doesn't want to do.

"Hey, it's okay. Forget it." I thread my fingers into her hair and tug her down for a kiss. "Just wanna be with you. I don't care what we do."

It's true. For once, I'm not just trying to bust a nut. I love stealing moments alone with her.

She tucks her head into my neck, and I roll us onto our sides and stroke her back. I keep my thigh tucked between her legs. "Sorry. I didn't mean to embarrass you."

"Ugh, if I tell you this, you can't laugh, okay?"

"I promise." And yeah, I'm intrigued. So. Fucking. Intrigued.

Keeping her face against my shoulder, she whispers, "I bought it so I could..."

"Get off?" I chuckle at the little mortified sound she makes in my ear.

"Right. But I swear it doesn't work. I mean, it turns on. It vibrates, and it feels good, but I can't get there."

Troubleshooting sexual conundrums with Gabby has major potential to become my new favorite hobby.

"Want me to help with this?" I nuzzle her neck and nip her. "What if I used it on you? Think that might help?" She lets out a gasp, and her thighs squeeze me. "You tell me to stop, I stop." I run one hand down her back until I reach her ass, which I palm and mold before I slip a finger between her legs and rub against her damp underwear.

She swallows but doesn't say anything.

"It's okay to be turned on by this. You're so wet right now. I really want you to sit on my face, but since maybe you want to take things slow, we could start with a toy, huh?"

That gets me a chuckle.

I roll over until I hover over her and then slowly grind down on her until we both moan.

"Shh," she reminds me.

And then she pushes me away and gets up.

I'm confused, thinking maybe she's calling this off, but then she comes back with her vibrator, and my cock jerks in my boxer briefs.

She places it in my hand. Reaches behind her back and releases her bra. Her beautiful breasts bounce loose, and I'd love to push my face between them.

Using the sexiest little wiggle I've ever seen that makes everything bounce enticingly, she shimmies off her underwear until she's standing naked in front of me.

"Fuck, Gabriela. You're stunning." Screw the sex toys, I just want to feel her body and be close to her. But my sweet girl is obviously hung up on this vibrator thing, and we can't have that.

I pat the blanket next to me and she daintily sits next to me and pushes her hair in front of her. She reminds me of that famous painting of the woman on the horse. Lady Godiva? I don't know. But she has this otherworldly beauty, and I feel like the luckiest guy on the planet that she's mine.

"Lie back. Do you have any lube?"

She reclines next to me. "No, am I supposed to use that?"

I gently move her thighs apart, kneel between them and glance down. She's so wet, she's glistening. This conversation might've embarrassed her, but she's definitely turned on. Fuck, she's so hot like this.

"I don't think you have to use it, but it might help in the future. If you're by yourself." I give her a wink, and she bites her bottom lip. "If at any point something doesn't feel good or you want to stop, let me know. You're in charge."

She nods, and the trust in her eyes does me in.

The moment the silicone touches her delicate skin, she shivers, and goosebumps break out all over her skin. I take my time working it in. I never realized how erotic this would be, and I reach down to squeeze my dick and calm down.

When I flip it on, her toes curl into the comforter, and she lets out a little shriek.

Our eyes meet, and I stifle a laugh as I shush her.

"Sorry," she pants. "It's just... it didn't feel like this when I used it."

I'm pretty fucking spellbound myself as I watch her writhe on the floor. Tits high and beaded. Smooth skin glistening with sweat. Her back arched as I wind her up. All the while I move her vibe in and out of her slick little pussy.

Not to be outdone by technology, I lean in to take a long, slow lick between her legs that has her whole body tightening. Her hand winds in my hair as her lean thighs squeeze my head.

She comes on a gasp. I bring her down with gentle licks and set her new toy next to us.

A huge, satisfied grin spreads on her face as I settle next to her.

"Okay," she whispers. "I get it now."

I chuckle and pull her to me and run my hands up and down her back.

Pretty sure that shade of pink is gonna give me a raging boner from this day forward.

After a beat, she nuzzles into me and nibbles on my ear. "Can I try something?"

"Use me any way you want." I'm not sure any girl has ever gotten me this ramped up before.

She rolls me onto my back. Straddling my waist, she leans down to kiss my neck. "I'd like to reciprocate."

As she slides down my body, I get a very clear idea of what she wants to do, and I. Am. On. Board.

When she pulls down my boxer briefs, my erection springs forward, happy to greet her. Ecstatic when she grips me. Fucking elated when she leans down and swipes her tongue over me.

I tuck a pillow under my head so I don't miss a thing. Her

long hair tickles my thighs, and I pull it all up into my fist so I can watch.

First she just swirls her tongue around, teasing me. It's so fucking hot, watching her open wide for me when she finally sucks me into her mouth. She works me over until sweat breaks out on my body.

Tightening my grip on her hair, I wonder how rough she likes it and give her a jerk. She smiles, opens wider and swallows me down.

"*My God.* So good, baby." I clench my eyes shut so I don't come. I'm so close, but I don't wanna do this without her. "Gabriela," I growl, pulling her up my body.

In record time, I'm gloved up and ready. I roll her under me, pull her thigh over my hip and sink into the most incredible heat I've ever experienced.

Pleasure sizzles up the back of my spine, and my balls tighten, so I pause. We're both out of breath. Her beautiful breasts heave, and I nibble and bite them with my greedy mouth until I'm sure I won't blow too quickly.

When I thrust all the way in, the sexy sound she makes in my ear makes me shiver. We kiss, our bodies suddenly frantic to reach the finish line. Her nails dig into my ass, and I decide there's nothing better on the fucking planet than making this woman come. And I need a good vantage point when she does.

Kneeling again, I lift her hips and resume, but slowly so I can watch my wet cock tunnel in and out of her. The sight sends me right to the edge.

Needing her to come, I rub a gentle circle around her swollen nub. In seconds she's convulsing around me. Squeezing. Pulsing. So tight. So damn good.

Her mouth opens in a silent scream as she arches back.

And I finally relent, pulling her close so I can feel her whole body against me as I come with her.

I'm blissed out in a sex haze when she curls up next to me like a kitten.

As I kiss her forehead, I realize I need to figure out how to make both of our dreams come true *and* stay together.

Because there's no way I want to leave her after the draft.

45

GABBY

I WAKE to a muscular arm wrapped around my waist, Rider's chest pressed to my back, and his thick thigh wedged between my legs. It feels so good to be held like this, I let out a happy sigh.

We eventually made it off the floor last night. I blush when I think about everything he did to me. This man makes me want to combust. The way he looked at me while our bodies came together is something I'll never forget.

And he obviously liked my blow job, I think with a satisfied smile.

I know—I swore I'd never give him one, but I'm used to Sean who never offered to go there. Rider's enthusiasm for oral demands reciprocation.

Plus, *holy crap*, the things he made me feel with that toy and his mouth. Letting loose with him, not being so cautious, is the freest I've ever felt. Deep down, I wonder if I'm his Lucy Honeychurch, and he's my George Emerson.

God, please let this have a happy ending.

"What're you smiling about?" his raspy voice whispers in my ear.

"Oh, you know. The weather."

"I heard something about thick clouds." He thrusts his erection against me, and I giggle. "Might wanna wear a raincoat today. Could get wet."

His giant hand cups my breasts, and I arch back.

Just in time for Poppy to wake up. "Da! Bababa! Da!"

He groans, and I laugh and reach back to run my fingers through his hair. "On the bright side, she slept through the night."

"Actually, she woke up once," he says, still squeezing my boobs.

"Really? Sorry, I didn't hear her."

He kisses my neck. "It's okay. She's my responsibility anyway. Just because you're lovely enough to let us crash here doesn't mean you get night duty. She went down again pretty quickly, though."

With a groan, he untangles himself from me and hops out of bed. He's wearing jeans, which he must've slipped on when Poppy woke earlier. I reach for my robe.

"Morning, my little gremlin. How's my girl?" He lifts Poppy up, and the look of love in his eyes makes my heart flutter. She grabs his face and grins, totally enchanted with her father.

Girl, I know the feeling.

Sienna gives me a sly look when we reach the kitchen. "Coffee's on." She's decked out in yoga pants, ready to do sun salutations. I'm not sure I could touch my toes without puking this early in the morning, but more power to her.

Rider puts the baby in the second-hand highchair we bought last week and heads for the bathroom.

When it's just Sienna and Poppy, I whisper, "Were we loud last night?"

She shakes her head as I take a sip of my coffee. "You just look thoroughly fucked."

I choke, and coffee dribbles out my mouth.

Laughing, she pats my back. "Sorry. It's true. You just look, uh, really satisfied."

After wiping my chin, I smile. "You would not be mistaken."

She high-fives me, and we giggle like big dummies.

Wanting to get off the subject of my sex life, I pat down my rats' nest and ask how it's going with her guy. I know I wasn't a good friend to Ramona. I could've asked her more questions and gotten her to open up, but never tried that hard. She seemed closed off and I left it at that.

Sienna sighs. "We're in a holding pattern. He still wants sex, no drama, and all of his focus on football. He says the right things, though. Says we're exclusive. I just wish we could hang out more than when we're naked, you know?"

I nod, hating this for her. Sienna is such a great girl, so bubbly and optimistic. Not to mention beautiful. Would it kill this guy to take her to dinner?

I try to stay positive. "He's probably stressed out with the playoffs and finals around the corner."

"Yeah, probably."

Rider joins us, and Sienna takes off for her yoga class. After we get Poppy fed and dressed for the day, I join him at the front door.

"I'll pick you up this evening so we can see my dad."

I nod, butterflies punching holes in my belly at the thought of meeting his father. Meeting a parent under any conditions has to be significant, right?

Rider bounces Poppy in his arms. "I'm pretty sure he's gonna lose his shit when he hears about this one, but fuck, it's his granddaughter. Shouldn't she make him happy?"

"Yes, dear." I lean up to kiss him, and he laughs.

"Look at us."

"I know." We're the picture of domestication, but I don't say it. I'm a little freaked out by it myself. But like we're play-acting, I flutter my lashes. "Have a good day at work, darling. Don't forget our meeting with the PTA."

He gives me another smooch. "Yes, my lovely smartass. Have a good day."

I watch him cross the street before I close the door with a sigh. I'm glad I have some time to mentally prepare myself for tonight. I have a feeling I'm going to need it.

46

RIDER

Mortimer isn't that far from Charming, but it might as well be in another country from how different it feels. As we pass the small downtown area, I try to look at this from Gabby's perspective. All I see are faded awnings, cracked sidewalks, and a gas station sign hanging from one hinge, about to fly away in the wind.

It only gets worse as we make our way to the trailer park where the dirty yellow parking lot lights illuminate the perimeter. Half of the homes are empty now and those that remain sit at odd angles, like they're too tired to stand any longer.

Jesus, what was I thinking, bringing Gabby here? So she can see what losers we are? So she can realize, once and for all, that football is the only thing going for me?

I turn off the ignition and take a deep breath.

"Hey." Her soft hand covers mine. "I'm here for whatever you need. Telling your dad about Poppy is a big deal."

That's what I'm afraid of.

I don't say anything. What's there to say?

Slamming my door shut, I reach in the back seat to unstrap Poppy. It's late in the evening. I should be getting her ready for bed, but this is the only time I have in my schedule. And since I couldn't bring myself to do it over the phone, here we are.

As I make my way up what should be a walkway but is so overrun with weeds, you can't tell, I hoist Poppy higher and reach back to take Gabby's hand. "Careful on these stairs."

Once we're safely on the stoop, I knock.

"Go away, fucker!" my father bellows from the living room. "I told you I'd pay rent next week."

Charming. Not the town.

"Dad, it's me." I called him earlier to tell him I'd be by, but there's no telling he remembers. If he did and laid off the booze, this convo will go down easier.

I try the front door. It's unlocked.

My old man is sitting in his ancient recliner in his underwear and a stained t-shirt. A half-dozen beers litter the coffee table.

I clench my jaw. "I brought a friend. Maybe you should get dressed."

He doesn't bother to look away from his TV. "I'm fine." Tipping back his can of shitty beer, he gulps it back. "So ya finally getting 'round to see me, huh? Who died?" He scratches his balls.

Fuck, this is humiliating.

"I have some news that I didn't want to give you over the phone." I clear my throat. "Thought you'd want to meet your granddaughter in person."

He blinks. Then frowns. A full sixty seconds later, he turns toward us.

His bloodshot eyes flit from me and Poppy to Gabby and back again. "All you had to do is play football. Just one thing, and you can't even do that right," he mutters in between belches. With his chin, he motions to Gabby. "This the girl you knocked up?"

Christ.

"No, this is... uh..." Do I call her my girlfriend and make this worse? Goddamn it, why didn't I figure out what to say before we got here?

Gabby steps forward and introduces herself. "Hi, Mr. Kingston. I'm Rider's neighbor, and I babysit for Poppy sometimes."

He squints at her, then me. "Poppy, huh? Couldn't have come up with a better name?"

I wince, ashamed my father could sink so low as to ridicule a baby. Once again, Gabby saves me from having to speak. I'm not sure I can right at this moment.

"She's a really good girl." Gabby takes the baby from my arms and kisses her forehead. "Say hi to your grandpa, Poppy."

He barely glances at her before he returns to the TV. "How do you know it's yours? Any dumb bitch can say you knocked her up."

"I did a paternity test," I say through clenched teeth.

"Why did I pay all that money for you to play sports when you were just gonna blow it before the draft?" Spit flies from his mouth as he slurs the words.

"When have you ever paid for anything in my life? If it weren't for free meals at school, I would've starved. My friends' parents felt sorry for me and gave me hand-me-downs. Coaches paid for my shit with their own money because Hank Kingston couldn't get his head out of his ass and think about someone other than himself for two minutes."

"You sound just like her." Her. *My mother.* He always goes there.

I open my mouth to argue, but he cuts me off. "And don't you defend her. Who stuck around after she left? Me! *Never* trust a woman, Rider. I've said it a million times, and I'll say it again. The pretty ones will fuck you over." Turning to Gabby, who's standing so still I'm not sure she's breathing, he yells, "Even this one with her pretty little voice, and pretty little face, and pretty little manners! I see how she looks at you. You're telling me you're not fucking her too?"

Shame like I've never experienced before explodes in my chest.

I can't believe I asked Gabby to come with me today. That I brought my daughter to meet this asshole. That I was dumb enough to think my father would fucking care he has a granddaughter.

He sneers at Gabby. "Let me guess. You're helping him outta the kindness of your heart." A maniacal laugh bubbles up out of him. "But you're probably just waiting for his big payday like every other slut."

Fisting his disgusting t-shirt, I wrench him out of his chair. "Don't fucking talk to her like that. This woman has kept my ass out of trouble all semester. What have you ever done but suck my bank account dry?"

Poppy starts to cry, and I shove my father back into his chair before I beat the shit out of him.

"We'll go wait in the car," Gabby whispers, her cheeks red, her eyes bright with unshed tears.

God, what a fucking epic mistake this is. "It's okay. We're leaving."

We never should've come in the first place.

47

GABBY

My hands tremble as I lock Poppy into her car seat. She's still sniffling, but as soon as I cover her with a blanket and get her comfortable, she calms down.

It's overcast and misty as we pull away from the trailer park. Rider's silent for most of the drive, but when we pull into our neighborhood, he sighs. "I'm sorry I dragged you with me today. I'm sorry he was such an ass to you. I don't know what I was thinking. Just… I wanted him to learn about Poppy from me."

"Of course." I grab his hand, but he pulls away and runs it through his hair. It stings, but I get it. He's upset and doesn't want to be touched.

Or call you his girlfriend.

That's not entirely fair, I realize. Maybe it would be different if he was introducing me to friends, but his father obviously requires special handling.

Despite Rider's warning that his father was a minefield, nothing prepared me for what actually happened.

"I should've gotten her out of there sooner. It all happened so fast." I'd felt frozen, shocked by his father's vehemence.

"You did your best. Thank you for coming with me." Rider's

voice lacks emotion, like he's just going through the motions. I can't blame him for being shellshocked. Tonight was intense.

When he pulls up to my house, it's obvious he has no intention of staying. I can see why he'd want some space to cool down, but I hope that's all this is.

I unlock my door and turn to him. "Are we okay?"

He doesn't say anything for a heartbeat, and in that span of time, I fill in the gaps. *This is too much, too intense. I need to focus on football.*

"Yeah. I'm sorry." His brow furrows. "Arguments with my father take a lot out of me, but I'll catch you later this weekend."

Tomorrow's Friday. *He's not blowing you off.* "Sounds good."

As I step out the rain starts to come down hard, and I run inside where I peek through the blinds and watch Rider cover Poppy with his jacket before he marches her into his house.

We don't talk much over the next few days. An occasional text here and there and a quick tradeoff of Poppy when I babysit once, but all of our easygoing conversation seems to have come to a screeching halt when I met Hank Kingston.

All of the guys are desperate to use their bye weekend to get caught up on schoolwork, so I try not to let it bother me. It's not as if Rider is being rude. He's just preoccupied. I'm somewhat mollified when he suggests grabbing lunch this week.

I'm doing a shift at the Rise 'N Grind when a few of the football players enter. My heart races until I realize Rider's not with them. Olly, Ben, and Knox order coffee and bagels.

For once, I don't try to engage Ben. I know he said we'd meet up, but since he raced away without giving me a date or time, I figured that was his way of backing out. So I'm surprised to find him waiting for me at the end of the counter after the other guys leave.

"Is something wrong? Did I mess up your order?" I finish

foaming milk for a latte and hand it off to another customer before I turn back to my brother.

He shifts uncomfortably. "Thought you wanted to meet up. You mentioned coffee."

I... Wait. "Really?"

"Do you get a break soon? I have half an hour."

Holding up one finger, I trot to the back where I ask Fanny if I can take a break. When she gives me the go-ahead, I pour myself a cappuccino, grab a scone, and lead Ben to a small two-top table in the back.

At first, he just stares out the window while I nibble on the snack, which I only grabbed so I'd have something to do with my hands.

Maybe I should kick this off. We'll start easy. "How have you been?"

"Uh." Silence. "It's been a rough semester."

"What's going on? Just taking some hard classes?"

"I wish."

More silence.

"Is this about me and Rider? I feel terrible about you seeing all that. I'm sorry—"

"This is *not* about Rider, but"—he shivers—"do me a favor and never mention that morning again. Am I excited you guys are seeing each other? No, but I'm not that big of a douchebag that I'd try to tell you who you can date."

All righty, then.

I swear I never do anything that makes my brother happy, but if this isn't about Rider, then what's his deal?

A solid two minutes go by during which he says nothing. I glance at my phone, frustrated that I have to get back to work soon.

I sigh. "Ben, I can't help if I don't know what's going on," I say gently.

"That's just it. I don't want your help."

Ouch.

My eyes sting, and I stare down at my feet and blink.

He groans. "I'm sorry. I don't mean to be a dick. I... Uh... *Fuck*. This is hard for me."

"We used to be really close, Benny. It hurts that you can't stand to be near me. We lost Daddy, and then Mommy, but I thought I'd always have you." Hating the quiver in my voice, I wipe under my eyes.

When I finally look back at him, his head has dropped forward. "It's not you, Gabriela. You're amazing, and everyone knows it. My whole house, in fact. I'm the one who's fucked up."

"Don't say that. Aren't you here on a football scholarship? People hold up signs at games with your name on it, not mine."

He closes his eyes with a grimace. When he opens them, he looks haunted. "I want you to listen to me right now." I nod, eager to hear whatever he's willing to share with me. "*You* are not the problem. You have *never* been the problem." Clenching his teeth, he shakes his head. "I can't be around you. I get..."

His voice trails off, and I lean forward. "What, Ben? What is it?"

"I get nightmares." Those pained eyes look up, begging me to understand. "I get panic attacks and have nightmares when I'm around you. I have dreams that you die, and it freaks me the fuck out."

I freeze, stunned.

He swallows, a sheen of sweat on his forehead. "It started in middle school. That one time I saw you over the holidays. I went home that night and dreamed you had a car accident like Mom, and I woke up screaming. The next day, I flipped out at school. The more I'm around you, the worse it gets. Obviously, I don't lose my shit like that anymore, but the panic attacks can suck."

I bite my lower lip so it doesn't quiver, but the last thing I want to do is have some kind of meltdown right now. I had one foster mother who was really nice, and she took me to visit my brother because I told her that was the only thing I wanted for Christmas.

As heartbreaking as it is to hear this, everything makes sense now. How Ben never wants to hang out. His gruff demeanor with me. The way he sometimes looks past me when we're talking.

I take a deep breath and do my best to get my act together. "Thank you for sharing this with me," I whisper. "I never want to be the reason that you're upset or hurting. You know that, right? I love you and want the best for you, and if that means I can't be around you..." My eyes sting again. Damn it. "I want you to know I understand, and it's okay. You shouldn't have to force yourself to do anything you don't want to or can't handle."

"That sounds terrible. That I have to force myself to be around you." He blows out a breath. "For the record, I like seeing you, but I can't handle everything else that comes after."

It helps a little to hear that. "You're staying in town for Thanksgiving, right?"

"Yeah. It's too distracting to go home before a big game. Not enough time."

I twist my napkin. "I'm not sure if you know this, but the guys invited me over for Thanksgiving, but if it's going to be a problem, I don't have to come."

He holds out a hand. "Don't change your plans on my account. I have someplace to go anyway."

"Are you sure? Because I'm the one intruding on your space, not the other way around. It sucks we can't spend it together, but I get it." It breaks my heart, but I understand. I'd be flipping out too if I was having nightmares my brother died in a car crash. Besides, what's another holiday by myself? I'm used to it at this point.

"I'm sure. Anyway, Rider will kick my ass if I upset you."

I roll my eyes. "I'm sure you're overestimating his reaction."

As we both stand up, he reaches over the table and pops the last bite of my scone in his mouth. "Pretty sure I'm not. The guys like to give him shit about how the big bad quarterback has fallen for the babysitter." He chuckles as he makes his way to the front of the cafe.

I like hearing my brother laugh, but then I process what he just said and wish I was as certain about Rider's feelings for me as my brother seems to be.

48

RIDER

When the final whistle of the day blows at practice, I'm so tired, I'm pretty sure I could fall asleep standing up. Thank God we're off tomorrow for Thanksgiving.

"Stay out of trouble, boys! Idle hands are the devil's workshop," Sully teases as we head to the locker room. He pats my back as I walk by. "Extra ice on that shoulder, son."

"You got it, Coach."

For some reason, Poppy had to be held half the night and my throwing arm was numb when I woke up. I'm still working out the kinks.

After a hot shower, I wrap a towel around my waist and collapse on the bench.

Some of the guys are talking about their plans this week.

Winston air-humps his locker. "She's so flexible, I bet she can sit on my face, do some kind of back bend thingy, *and* suck my dick at the same time." His buddy Derek gives him a high-five.

Those two tend to have the nicest girlfriends for some reason. I don't get it, because behind their backs, they cheat, and mess around, and talk like douchebags.

"Think she has a friend? Maybe we could tag-team this weekend. Or you could share," Derek suggests.

Winston shakes his head. "I'm saving all her holes for myself."

Now that I have a daughter, I can barely listen to this bullshit. And I'm too tired to keep how I feel under wraps. "You kiss your mother with that mouth?"

He chuckles, but it lacks humor. "*Yours* didn't have any complaints. In fact—"

Tank yells, "Shut up, Winston. Yo mama so nasty, she brings her own crabs to Red Lobster."

Everyone laughs, and I shake my head. "We really should respect women more," I mumble. If I ever have sons, they're never gonna say this kind of shit.

On my way to Gabby's, I mentally calculate how Poppy and I can survive on what I have in the bank for the next few weeks. I have one more thing I can try to sell to make that money stretch, but it's gonna be tight.

Since that day at my father's house, Gabby and I have avoided talking about what happened. Granted, we haven't really hung out since. That's my fault, but school has been kicking my ass, and I've barely had a moment to breathe.

The upshot is having time to get over my humiliation. But I can't put off seeing Gabby any longer. Not that I want to. I miss her like crazy. I just hope she doesn't think I'm a fucking loser. First, I can't tell her, *for sure*, who my baby mama is, and then my father insults her to her face while he scratches his nut sack. Not to mention the pennies on the dollar I'm paying her to babysit. *The Kingstons have so much class.*

Which is why I'm pulling up to Whiskey Row before I head home. I overheard Gabby tell Sienna that she loves the po' boy sandwich at the Yellow Rose, so I thought I'd treat her. Yeah, I know this isn't the wisest use of my money, but am I really supposed to wait until May to do something nice for her? Fuck that.

Since so many students have taken off for Thanksgiving, the Rose isn't too busy. Ethel, who's probably old enough to be my grandmother, takes my order, pops her gum, and gives me a wink. "Take a seat, sugar. I'll get that ready for ya."

"Thank you, ma'am." I park my ass on a bench by the door and scroll through my phone.

"Look who's here!" One guy almost falls off his barstool when he sees me.

I take a deep breath, ready to sign whatever he wants. The closer we get to the playoffs, the more often this happens.

But when the man gets closer, I realize it's that dick Jason. His eyes are bloodshot, and I can smell the whiskey on his breath. His two friends saunter up behind him.

"This asshole banned me from the football parties. Can you believe that? I used to root for you, fucker." When he sways, his buddy puts a steadying hand on his shoulder. "Did y'all hear how he got stuck with that baby?"

I stiffen. It's one thing to talk trash to me. It's another to bring up my kid.

"He knocked up some slut." Jason chuckles and then stage-whispers, "'Course, it could've been one of his roommates. They're too fucking stupid to know for sure."

Do not beat the shit outta him. I repeat the words in my head twice more for good measure. The last thing I need is to break my throwing hand on this dumbass.

I knew Jason was there that night, but by the time I got downstairs, everyone had gotten kicked out. Still, if the truth about Halloween got out, it would be a PR nightmare. It's why we went through the trouble of having everyone we could sign those NDAs.

Ethel calls my name, and I stand. Jason's eyes widen when he realizes how much bigger than him I am.

I lean in close. "I wouldn't go spreading baseless rumors if I were you. Because one night you might come across a few of my friends, and I guarantee they won't have the patience to walk away from you the way I am tonight. Especially if you mess with someone they love, and they all love my daughter. No one wants you at our parties anyway."

"Fuck you, asshole. Jus wait an' see. You're gonna regret this." His words slur together.

I repeat Coach's advice—this moment isn't worth losing everything I've worked so hard for. *Keep it together.*

Jaw tight, fist clenched, I grab my order as Jason's friend whines, "Man, why'd you go and piss him off? I wanted an autograph."

Good luck with that, asshole.

My jaw aches from grinding my teeth by the time I make it to Gabby's. When she opens the door, her whole face lights up.

Seeing her somehow erases the shitty week I've had, that bullshit with Jason, and the fact that my father is an epic dick, none of which I want to discuss tonight.

It's so good to see her that I pin her against the wall and kiss her until Sienna starts chanting, "Take it off!"

I laugh awkwardly. "Sorry. Didn't see you there."

"Don't mind me. I was enjoying the show."

Gabby and I look at each other and crack up. I kiss her again for good measure and lean down to get the bag of food I dropped when I momentarily lost my mind and tried to maul this woman.

"Thought you might be hungry."

"I'm starving." We unload the food in the kitchen, and fortunately, everything was wrapped well, so it didn't suffer when I accidentally dropped it. "Po' boys are my favorite. How did you know?"

For a second, I wonder if she means me. Because I'm broke AF.

"I pay attention." I give her a wink and enjoy the pink that brightens her cheeks.

It's late, unfortunately, so I know my gremlin is asleep. After I check on her, I return to the kitchen where the girls are talking quietly.

Sienna tugs on her coat. "Don't wait up for me, kids."

"Don't you want to join us?" Gabby asks. "We can share my sandwich. I can't eat it all."

"Thanks, but I have a date! Be good and wear condoms! Toodaloo!" Then the little tornado whirls out of the house.

Gabby and I stare at the front door.

"That girl does not have a filter, does she?"

"No, but that's part of her charm." Gabby's face flushes again, probably from the suggestion that we are gonna have sex.

For the record, I did not buy her dinner so we could get naked, but I wouldn't turn down any offers.

She gives me a shy smile, and I lean back against her counter and stand her between my legs. She runs her hands under my jacket as I run my nose up her neck and breathe her in.

"Missed you this week."

"Really?" Her big hazel eyes turn up to me, and I rub her nose with mine.

"Yes, really. I'm sorry I haven't been around much." I shake my head. "And I'm sorry shit's been weird since we saw my dad."

Her arms wrap around my neck and she kisses me. "I don't care about any of that." Her hips press into mine, and my body responds. "You look stressed, though."

I grab her ass and prop her up on the counter. "Less stressed now that I'm with you."

Hank Kingston's double-wide is a million miles away, and I realize Gabby's opinion of me hasn't changed despite what happened.

It feels amazing.

She feels amazing.

Things are too good between us to ruin it with talk of what happened earlier tonight.

Gabby wraps her legs around me, and I take a slow lick of her bottom lip. "You know what they say helps with stress?" I ask as I press my growing erection into her.

She rolls her eyes, a playful smile on her lips. "No, what do *they say* helps with stress?"

"Backgammon." A beat goes by, and we both laugh. "Honestly, I have no clue how to play backgammon, but it sounded funny."

"You dork." She grips my hair and pulls me into a kiss.

This time, we don't stop until she's moaning my name and trembling in my arms.

49

GABBY

Tank lets out the loudest burp I've ever heard, and we all groan.

"That's nasty, bro. You're gonna make me lose my appetite." Olly shovels one more bite of stuffing into his mouth and groans in delight. "Amazing stuffing, ladies. You can stuff my turkey any day."

"Watch your mouth. My woman will not be going anywhere near your turkey," Tank barks as he leans over to kiss Bree.

We all snicker.

Rider sets down his plate with barely a crumb left behind. "That was the best pumpkin empanada I've ever had."

"I call dibs on the last one in the kitchen!" Knox jumps up to get it, shoving Olly out of the way, and I smile. It's amazing to be appreciated like this.

Bree, Sienna, and I put together a pretty decent dinner if I do say so myself. The guys didn't want anyone spending all day in the kitchen, so some of it was premade, but we whipped together a few homemade favorites too and had a blast hanging out.

Even though I still haven't heard from my aunt and likely

won't, today is the best Thanksgiving I've had in a while. Ben even texted me before he took off to hang out with some friends.

I look around at our group. The guys all treat me like a little sister, and Bree, Sienna and I have bonded since we're all involved with members of the football team. Sienna has been tight-lipped about who she's dating, but I know she's embarrassed he won't spend time with her publicly. Hopefully once the season is over, he'll make her the priority she deserves to be.

I lean back into Rider, who has one arm draped behind my back and the other wrapped around Poppy.

"Sucks we have to get on a plane tomorrow." Knox groans as he collapses back into the other sofa.

Rider lowers his voice. "You sure it's not a problem to watch the munchkin?"

"Not at all." I kiss him. "It's just one night. We'll be fine." He hates leaving Poppy for away games.

He smiles and pulls me into a hug.

I turn back to the group. And find that everyone is staring at us. "What?"

Trevor laughs. "Y'all are pretty cute. All kissy-kissy and whatnot."

"It's true." Olly nods. "I'll admit I'm pretty shocked by the domesticated vibe you two give off."

I make a face and sit up to grab my iced tea off the coffee table. "It's not like Rider's never had a girlfriend before." What I mean to say is that it's not like he's never hung out with girls before, but whatever. Potato, *potahto*. I'm too tired to correct myself, so I laugh awkwardly.

"Rider's not big into girlfriends." Olly tosses a napkin at Rider, who bats it away almost angrily. I try to make eye contact, but he's so focused on Poppy, it makes me wonder if he's avoiding looking at me.

Did I say something wrong? Is he upset because I called myself his girlfriend? I mean, aren't we dating? I don't typically get naked in my kitchen for a man I'm not *dating.*

Or does he really not consider the women he's been with in the past girlfriends? He said he's never had a serious relationship, but Miranda certainly gave off a territorial girlfriend vibe, and I saw them together plenty over the years.

I don't know the answers, and it's not like I can ask these questions right now.

He didn't call you his girlfriend with his father and now this, a little voice reminds me.

Suddenly uncomfortable, I scoot forward to grab my drink off the coffee table and let out a breath when the conversation continues around me. I obviously can't get to the bottom of this with the whole house here.

Tank claps. "Before everyone goes their separate ways, I need to remind you about Sunday."

"What's on Sunday?" I ask.

"It's the captain's birthday. We're getting him a tattoo to celebrate."

I turn to Rider. "Really? It's your birthday?"

Tank interrupts and points a giant finger at me. "I like this woman. She doesn't Google your whole life like your other fangirls."

Ah, yes. The masses of fangirls.

Bree smacks his gut. "That's enough, boo."

"I meant to invite you, actually," Rider whispers in my ear. "I'm getting a tattoo for Poppy and wanted your help. We're headed to Austin on Sunday. Wanna join us?"

Aww, he wants me to come?

I'm instantly relieved.

The fact that he'd invite me to do a bro-thing like this with the rest of the guys means a lot to me. "I'd love to."

He kisses me.

It's sweet. Tender.

I run my hand through his hair and kiss him back. Someone throws another napkin at us, and Poppy smacks our faces and giggles.

Maybe he isn't upset with me for using the g-word after all. He told me he's taking us seriously.

Maybe I need to cut him some slack, enjoy what little time we spend together and stop second-guessing everything.

50

GABBY

THE KNOCK on the door makes my heart race. I'm not expecting the guys back from their game for another hour, but when I open the door, Rider grins at me.

"Hey, Mr. Heisman Contender." He killed it today. Sienna and I cheered the team on as we watched the game with Poppy.

A quick glance over his shoulder tells me the rest of Charming knows the boys are back because their driveway is filling up with cars.

"Hey, babe." As he stalks in, he picks me up for a kiss. I breathe in the scents of cold Texas air and the leather from his varsity jacket before he spins me around.

When he sets me down, I laugh. It feels so good to see him this happy. "Missed you," I say quietly.

He nuzzles my jaw. Drops soft kisses along my neck. Runs his hands up and down my back. "Mmm. Missed you too, baby."

Closing my eyes, I rest my forehead on his chest, absurdly pleased. When I've heard other people use that endearment, I've rolled my eyes, but having Rider use it? Well, that's a whole different story.

I can't help the huge smile that tugs on my lips.

"What?" His grin matches mine.

I shrug, reluctant to explain how giddy I am because of one little word. "Just happy to see you, that's all." I push up on my toes and kiss him again before I pull him inside, grateful that we have the house to ourselves since Sienna is out for the night.

"Did you see the press conference after the game?" he asks as he slips off his jacket.

The media finally broke the story about Poppy. "I can't believe they only asked a few questions."

"Coach got wind of it and the staff prepped me." He looks like a weight has been taken off him.

"You must be so relieved to have it out there and done."

He grabs his chest. "I didn't even know I was freaking out about it until the press conference was over and I could breathe again."

When they asked if it was true that Rider had a daughter, he very politely said he did but wouldn't be discussing any details so he could maintain his and his family's privacy. And then the press went right back to asking him about the game and being in contention for the Heisman.

"They used a photo of you walking around with Poppy in that Bjorn carrier, but you couldn't see her face, just that pink beanie."

"That's fine. It could've been worse, right?"

"God, yes." I was terrified the press would rake him over the coals for this, but that was when I thought they'd learn about how his whole household had to take paternity tests. One player having a baby apparently isn't a big deal. They just noted how an elite college athlete has a lot to juggle. They're not lying. Rider has been going nonstop since Poppy landed in his life. "You handled it like a champ."

"Thank you again for going with me to talk to Hank. My

father would've lost his shit if he'd learned about her from *SportsCenter*."

To think what actually happened was Hank being calm. No wonder Rider is sensitive about his dad.

Changing the subject, I fill him in on Poppy and how she now says 'nana' for banana and, praise Jesus, how she slept through the night. He tiptoes into my room to check on her and then collapses next to me on the couch.

"Were you planning on going back to your party?"

He tosses an arm behind my head and toys with my hair. "Just wanted to hang out with you, if that's okay."

Wow, Rider is turning down a football party after an epic win?

And when I say epic, I'm not exaggerating. I could hear my neighbors cheering. Down the street.

I sit up and press my hand to his forehead. His head tilts as he watches me, confused. "Just checking to see if you have a fever."

"Shut up. Get over here." He scoots me onto his lap and kisses my neck. "Don't tell anyone, but I'm over parties. Wanna watch a movie or something?"

Or something, I think, as he runs a big palm up my hip.

But the tender look in his eyes tells me this isn't just a booty call.

"Have you eaten yet? We could get a pizza."

We call in our order, and then I hand him two ice packs.

Surprise registers in his eyes. "How did you know I needed to ice down again?"

"I saw that late hit in the third. You okay?"

He rubs a hand over his face. "Yeah. It just knocked the wind out of me for a bit. Need to ice my left lats, though."

"I figured you'd need to ice something."

We watch some sci-fi thriller, and I thoroughly enjoy being

wrapped up in Rider as we snuggle on the couch, but we're not even twenty minutes in before he's fast asleep.

When the movie's over, I turn in his arms and stare at him unabashedly.

He looks so young when he's relaxed. His hair is getting long and hangs in his eyes, disheveled from the long day. Stubble lines his rugged jaw.

His arms tighten around me, and his deep, gravelly voice sends chills down my arms. "Are you watching me sleep like a little creeper?"

I laugh. "Maybe."

He makes a deep sound of contentment and pulls me closer. "I hate away games," he whispers. "I hate leaving you and Poppy."

I drag my finger over his eyebrow. Over his cheekbone. Over the bridge of his nose. "It was just two days."

"Two days too long." He gives me a long, somber look. "You know it'll be worse after I get drafted, right?"

I still. This is the first time he's mentioned anything down the road. Since the idea of relationships seem to spook him, I've been cautious not to make any long-term plans.

"You take it one day at a time. One game. One practice." I pause, my heart suddenly racing. "We, uh, can FaceTime." With how crazy our schedules have been, I'm surprised I haven't considered it sooner. "You can see Poppy whenever you want."

"And you? Can I see you too?"

A blush heats my cheeks. "I'm all yours. You can see me whenever you want."

Those aren't the words I really want to say, but I'm not sure he's ready to go there yet.

But it's probably all over my face—I'm in love with Rider Kingston.

And if I'm being honest with myself, I have been for a while.

His forehead touches mine. "I'm sorry we haven't been able to spend more time together. Do normal things. Go on dates." He speaks against my lips. "I promise I'm gonna make it up to you. You mean so much to me, Gabby."

Euphoria fills my heart.

I curl my hand into his hair to pull him to me for a kiss.

We don't say anything as our clothes come off and he slips on a condom. With just the flickering light of the TV behind us, we come together. Side by side, he lifts my thigh over his. Shifting between my legs, he rubs himself against me until I'm trembling.

"Gabriela." He says my name like a prayer when he finally pushes into me.

I'm used to our combustible chemistry. To breathless rounds where we tear our clothes off each other to have sex.

But I'm not prepared for the intimacy of this moment and the way he watches me as he thrusts into me.

I clench my eyes shut and drop my forehead to his chest, afraid to get any closer. I want to tell him how much I love him. That I'm scared he'll leave after the draft. That I don't want to lose him to his career.

He gently cups my chin and lifts my lips to his. "Don't hide."

My eyes tilt up to his, and the connection between us is almost overwhelming.

"Touch yourself," he whispers.

Staring into his eyes, I slip my hand between us.

Losing myself in this moment is easier than admitting I'm struggling with too many feelings.

Him watching me is heady, and it makes me bold. As he moves between my thighs, I circle my hand around his base and squeeze.

"Fuck," he grunts, swelling inside me. "Baby, you're gonna make me come."

He kisses me, fierce and possessive. I'm so close, but then he licks a finger and drags it down my backside.

"I've never..." I pant when he pushes it against me.

"Does it feel good?" He watches me as he gently nudges in to the knuckle. In and out, he matches the rhythm of his hips.

It feels wrong. So wrong. *And amazing.*

"Oh, God." I toss my head back as I come so hard I can't breathe.

My release sets him off, and we moan and shudder together.

He holds me while we pant and come down off that high.

"Love..." He pauses.

My breath catches in my chest.

But then he clears his throat. "Love being here with you."

A twinge of disappointment nips at me, but I tell myself to enjoy what we have. It's not like I've been brave enough to say those words. *If* the L-word was what he contemplated just now. "There's nowhere else I'd rather be."

After we've cleaned up, I lead him into my bedroom where he holds me until Poppy wakes up in the morning.

Even though I'm afraid of all the things that can go wrong, I hope and pray we can get it right this time.

51
GABBY

"Thanks for squeezing us in." Rider tosses his arm around my shoulders as he talks to Brady, who owns Saints & Sinners, a swanky tattoo parlor in Austin. He glances around at the framed photos on the exposed brick walls. "This place is cool."

"Thanks, man." Brady is maybe in his mid-thirties with tats up and down his arms. He has striking green eyes and an edgy biker vibe.

When I catch him studying me, I look away, embarrassed.

"Sorry I'm staring," he says with a chuckle. "You remind me of my sister-in-law." He tilts his head, his eyes narrowing. "My wife too a little."

Aww. "No problem."

Rider squeezes me just a bit closer, and I bite my lip to keep from smiling. Is he jealous?

"Your girl getting a tattoo too or just you today?" Brady asks.

I turn to Rider, and he lifts his eyebrows. "What do ya say, Gabs? Wanna get inked too?"

"Ha. No, thanks."

His lips tug up before he kisses me. "Chicken."

"Pretty much, yeah."

Rider explains what he wants, and Brady nods and starts sketching. When Brady heads back to his station and tells Rider to follow, I'm wondering if I should join Tank, Knox, Olly, and Trevor on the couch, but Rider tugs me along.

"Aren't you gonna hold my hand?"

I snort. "Sure. And I'll give you a lollypop afterward."

He stops so fast I run into him and whispers in my ear, "We don't need lollypops. I got something you can suck."

Looking around to make sure no one heard, I elbow him. "Don't be a perv. You know we only discuss sucking after hours."

He barks out a laugh and pulls me into a hug as we amble to Brady's station.

"You guys are cute. How long have you been dating?" Brady asks as he gets out his supplies.

I look to Rider, unsure how he wants to answer this. Plus, there's that tiny issue of him never calling me his girlfriend, but this weekend has been so great, I don't want to cast doubt on what we're building.

"Technically, just this fall, but we've been circling each other for a few years now. She finally wore me down." He has a teasing twinkle in his eyes.

"You liar." I laugh and playfully smack him. "I did no such thing."

He wraps a thick arm around my neck and kisses me again. "Fine. I finally got my head outta my ass and begged her to go out with me. Better?"

"Much. Thank you." I flush, pleased as a peach that he doesn't seem to have a problem admitting that we're an item.

Everything around us stills as we stare at each other. I shiver, remembering how he touched me last night.

"Thanks for coming today," he says quietly before he drops a featherlight kiss on my lips. "It means a lot to me."

"Happy birthday, Rider."

"Thanks, darlin'."

I beam back a smile, combusting on the inside with messy feelings and hopes for the future. He made me swear not to get him anything for his birthday. He said he just wanted to spend the day together. He doesn't play fair. How am I supposed to *not* fall for him?

Brady clears his throat, and Rider and I turn our attention to the matter at hand. Tank bounds up to us and leans in to Brady. "Are they eye-fucking each other again?"

"Pretty much, yeah."

"We could see it all the way on the other side of the store."

"Oh, my God, Tank." I point to where the others are waiting. "Go away. If you're good, we'll get tacos later."

"Tacos, you say?" He rubs his hands together and strolls back to the guys.

That was embarrassing. I make a point to be less obvious about my feelings. I plop down into a chair, grab a magazine and start flipping, leaving Brady and Rider to discuss the details of the tattoo.

I love that his roommates are getting him this thoughtful gift. I'm a little ashamed I deemed them all meatheads before I really knew them. Sure, they can be rambunctious, but they have really big hearts.

I check in with Bree to make sure Poppy went down for her nap, and then Rider calls me over after Brady transfers the art onto his skin.

"It's going to be beautiful." Brady has sketched an incredible abstract that will wrap around Rider's biceps.

"Not sure beautiful is what I'm going for, babe."

"It's a field of poppies for your daughter. How is that not beautiful?"

He grunts, and I hold in a laugh.

And I'm right. The final piece, once it's filled in with reds and pinks and blues in this amazing brushstroke style, takes my breath away.

After Brady finishes up, I lean up to whisper in Rider's ear. "Your tattoo is sexy as hell."

He lifts an eyebrow. "Really? How sexy?" He flexes his big gun, and I shake my head.

"Show-off."

But then his expression turns serious. "When I find out Poppy's birthday, I'd like to add it right here." He points to his arm where two flowers diverge.

For some reason, that really hits me hard, how he doesn't know his daughter's birthday. And from the look in his eyes, it upsets him too.

"We'll figure it out," I whisper.

I don't want to bring her up because we've had such a good day, but I can't help wonder about the woman who left that adorable baby in the middle of a raging party. Does she miss Poppy? Does she even think about her?

I'm distracted when two women come up to Brady's station. One kisses him and then turns to me.

When I get a good look at her face, I freeze.

She looks *so* familiar.

Her eyes widen.

And we both start talking at the same time.

"Oh, my God."

"Do I know you?"

I open my mouth, not sure what to say.

Brady smiles. "Gabby, this is my wife Kat and her sister Tori."

Tori moves next to her sister and stares at me for a long minute before her lips twist. "Do your pinky fingers form a V?"

"I'm sorry. What?"

"Like this." She places her hands in front of her and turns

them so her palms face her. Then she brings them together so her pinkies form a V.

Um. "I have no idea." So I try it. And lo and behold, they do.

How did this girl know my pinkies were crooked when I've never realized it?

Tori snaps her fingers. "You're a Duran, aren't you?"

My eyes bug out. "How did you know that?"

"Because we are too. Or we were before we got married." She waves a finger between her and her sister. "Not to each other, obviously. You know what I mean."

Turns out we're cousins.

I stand there a little dumbfounded because I didn't know I had cousins in the Austin area. Most are down near Corpus Christi.

The three of us have the golden Duran eyes.

Twenty minutes later, we're still huddled, trying to figure out our family. Kat places a hand on my shoulder. "We heard about your dad, but your mom died too? I'm so sorry. How did we not know that?"

"My father was estranged from the family," I explain, trying to make sense of it myself. "So we weren't really close to anyone when my mom passed a few years later."

"You have a brother too, right?"

"Yes. Ben. He's also a student at Lone Star State."

We chat a few more minutes and exchange numbers. As we stroll to the front, Tori hooks her arm through mine and motions toward Rider. "So you're dating him, huh?" When I nod, she giggles in my ear, "Girl, I want all the details!"

I'm so excited to meet female relatives who *act* like family, I could cry.

It hits me how much my life has changed this semester.

I have Rider and Poppy, who are the best part of my day. Sienna is the sweetest roommate ever and one of my best friends. I'm almost done with college and maintaining my grades, and I'm dying to student-teach next semester. My temp job at Archer will hopefully translate into a full-time teaching position in the fall. Ben and I aren't totally at odds, and now that I understand where he's coming from, I'm hopeful we can build a bridge.

And I've also connected with Kat and Tori, who want me to stay with them over winter break!

It's almost too good to be true.

52

RIDER

I watch Gabby's ass sway as she strolls up the walkway to her house. She turns around to wave just before she ducks into her house.

I return the wave, still smiling like an asshole after she shuts the door.

I rub the tight spot in my chest, the ache that only seems to appear when I drop off Gabby.

Holy. Shit.

How did this happen?

I have a whole truckload of feelings for this woman that I have no idea what to do with.

Do I tell her how I feel?

Do I even *know* what I fucking feel?

That I can't breathe without her? That she makes the fucking rainbows shine on rainy days? That I can't find peace until she walks into the room?

"Hey, dickhole," Knox barks from the back seat. "You planning to sit here all day and daydream about your girlfriend's luscious ass?"

I've had such a great day, nothing could derail my mood. I

shove the crazy feelings in a box because there's no way I can deal with that shit at the moment, and I rattle off the good things in my life:

An undefeated season as we head into our last game.

The sweetest daughter on the planet.

A gorgeous girlfriend who's definitely way, *way* above my pay grade.

One of the best O-lines in the country.

But Knox will try to get away with murder if I let him. Biting back a smile, I hold up my middle finger, throw my old Jeep into drive, and caution, "You'd best not stare at her ass."

The guys chuckle, and Knox reaches over to smack my arm. "Gabby's like a hot little sister."

Cringing, I turn to Tank, who's sitting in the front seat. His expression matches my own. "I don't think you're supposed to consider little sisters 'hot.'"

Tank tilts his head back to razz Knox. "That's weird, bro. I mean, maybe it's like that in *your* family."

The taunting continues until I park in our driveway behind Trevor's truck. Tank pulls Knox in a chokehold and drags him up the walkway of the house.

Where we come to a stop.

An older woman with a sleek gray bob glares at us from our porch like we're pissing on her favorite pair of slippers.

I step forward. "Can I help you, ma'am?"

"I'd like to speak to Rider Kingston. Is that you?"

Something about this woman sends a jolt of anxiety through me. Maybe it's her steely gaze or the rigidness of her shoulders, but whatever it is, it's unnerving.

Tank clears his throat. "Can I ask what this is in reference to? You see, we get a lot of female fans offering their wares, looking to meet Mr. Kingston. I serve as a buffer to filter the riffraff."

Offering their wares? Riffraff?

"Ignore him." I shake my head. "He's been reading his girlfriend's Regency romance novels again."

"They're damn good, son."

"I'm Rider," I say hesitantly. "How can I help you?"

Those rheumy eyes take me in, starting at the top of my head and ending with my scuffed-up boots. Internally, I bristle at her judgment, which is as clear as our team's neon scoreboard. It's the way everyone in my hometown looks at me. Like I'm shit on the bottom of their shoes.

"You can bring me my great-granddaughter, Poppy." She sniffs. "I'm prepared to fight for custody."

That's when my whole world tips over and comes crashing down.

53

RIDER

THIS IS NOT GOING WELL.

Mrs. Hildebrand perches at the very edge of our couch. She's about two minutes from clutching her pearls.

Surprisingly silent and motionless, Tank and Olly sit next to me. I figured it couldn't hurt to have a couple of people on my side in case this woman starts making threats again. Tank messaged Bree, so she and Poppy are on the way over.

"You mean to tell me my granddaughter dropped off the baby in the middle of a frat party?" Mrs. Hildebrand screeches.

And now she's clutching her pearls.

"We're a football team, ma'am, not a fraternity," I note as calmly as possible. Given that she came in here guns blazing with talk of trying to get custody of *my* daughter, I'd say I'm doing pretty damn well. I suppose all of that time in front of the media and doing interviews is keeping me from losing my shit. "She dropped Poppy off *at the end* of the party. It was pretty late. I was already asleep, and my roommates got me up when they found her."

Mrs. Hildebrand shakes her head in disbelief. "I never should've left her alone."

"Who? Your granddaughter?" When she reluctantly nods, I continue. "Can I ask where she went?" I swallow back the tacos that are doing their best to spew up my gullet. "Her name is Cricket, correct?"

Please, God, let her name be Cricket, or I'm about to look like the dumbest motherfucker who ever existed. Just the other day, Olly told me he remembered a few details from that weekend, and he seemed to think the woman who brought the brownies was named Cricket.

It's either Cricket or Cicada, and I'm praying it's not Cicada.

After a hard eye roll, Mrs. Hildebrand sighs. "That's what her friends call her. She thought 'Margot' was too highbrow."

Margot. I let out a breath. Finally, I have a name. "So... Margot... *Hildebrand*?"

Her head cocks to the side. "Do you really know nothing about my granddaughter, young man?"

Well.

I know that Cricket makes one hell of a drug-laced brownie that could knock out an elephant, but I'm thinking Grandma here doesn't want to know that.

I open my mouth before I close it again.

Come on, Rider, think. Say something.

"Cricket," I say slowly, "took excellent care of Poppy."

There.

That gets me another eye roll. "*I* took excellent care of Poppy."

I rub the back of my neck, hating life. "Listen, can we start over again? I got Poppy on Halloween, and I've been doing my God's honest best to take care of her. She's happy and healthy and really fucking smart. She calls me 'dada' and says 'nana' for banana. She tells me 'mo' when she wants more. Before that night, I swear I had no idea I had a daughter, much less that Cricket had gotten pregnant, or I would've been there for her."

I'm not sure where that declaration comes from, but after a moment where I search myself, I know it's true. I would've gotten my shit together and helped Cricket even though I don't know her from Adam. But I apparently got that woman pregnant, and this baby and even Cricket, to a certain extent, are my responsibility.

Which leads me back to that awkward question Mrs. Hildebrand never answered. "Can I ask where Cricket went? Her note said something about calling me when she got there." Not that she had my number, but I don't note this detail. "She didn't mention *where* she was going, and I've had no way to contact her."

I'm a little ashamed to admit I haven't been more actively looking for Cricket. I was mostly pissed she dropped off Poppy the way she did. Embarrassed I didn't know jack shit about who my baby mama is. It never occurred to me that something could be wrong. That this woman might be in trouble or in some kind of danger.

"I... you see..." Mrs. Hildebrand twists her hands in her lap. "Margot is a free spirit. While she was pregnant, she managed to stay on a good path. I took her to her therapist every week and acupuncture and I got her a spiritualist who taught her how to meditate so she could be healthy for her pregnancy. And she did it. She was the most sober I've ever seen her. She was excited for Poppy." She smiles, but it fades quickly. "Afterward, though, she returned to her old ways."

"Partying?" I ask gently.

Reluctantly, she bobs her head once. "Her friends wanted her to join them for the fall harvest at the Green Triangle in California. No"—she pauses, pursing her lips—"not the Green Triangle. The..."

Tank snaps his fingers. "The Emerald Triangle."

"Yes, that's it."

I turn to my roommate. "What's the Emerald Triangle?"

The excitement in his eyes disappears, and he folds his lips. "It's, uh." He cringes. "It's like the largest cannabis-growing region in the country."

Pot's legal in California. What's the big deal? "Okay, but why the face?"

He grimaces. "The reason I know about the Emerald Triangle in the first place is because of this Netflix show called..." He pauses. Scratches his head. Looks at Olly who shrugs. Then whispers, "*Murder Mountain.* According to the documentary, more people go missing there than any other area in California."

"Fucking hell."

Olly holds up his hands. "But that doesn't mean Cricket went missing. Right?"

We all turn to Mrs. Hildebrand, who has tears streaming down her face. I shoot Tank a dirty look.

"What? Did you want me to lie?" he whisper-yells at me.

I reach for the box of tissues that Gabby put on our coffee table last week because Poppy kept drooling on our textbooks.

Mrs. H takes it gratefully and daintily dabs it at the corner of her eyes. "Apologies."

Once she looks composed, I ask, "When was the last time you heard from Cricket?"

Her eyes fill with tears. "Two weeks ago."

Tank claps his hands. "That's nothing. I've gone a month before calling my mama. She was *pissed*. But still. Not a reason to call the popo."

I hand the woman another tissue. "But you've tried calling her? Or her friends?"

Before she answers, the front door swings open, and Bree, Gabby, and Poppy come strolling in.

Fuck, has it only been an hour since I dropped Gabby off

across the street? Christ, I feel like I haven't seen her in a year. How did this day go sideways?

I open my mouth to make introductions, but Gabby sees Mrs. Hildebrand and yells, "Adele! How are you?" and scurries over to her to give her a hug.

"What the hell is happening right now?" Tank asks without moving his lips.

I want to ask the same question.

54

RIDER

Gabby stands in the middle of the living room. "Why are y'all staring at me?"

I wave back and forth between her and Mrs. Hildebrand. "You two know each other?"

"Yeah," she says slowly. "She used to get coffee at the Rise 'N Grind." Turning to *Adele*, she asks, "What's going on? I haven't seen you in ages. How have you been? And what in the world are you doing here? Not that I'm not happy to see you, because of course I am. Are the guys helping you with something?"

But Mrs. H doesn't hear a thing. She's staring at Poppy, who waves her hands and kicks her legs in excitement.

I clear my throat. "This is Poppy's grandmother. I mean, her great-grandmother."

"No shit?" Gabby collapses into the chair behind her, looking as stunned as I felt a little while ago.

Mrs. H takes Poppy from Bree and cracks the smallest of smiles when the gremlin tries to cover her in slobbery kisses. After a few minutes, Mrs. H's scowl returns and she leans in to sniff her.

She just sniffed my kid. I almost laugh.

"You've kept her clean. She's gained weight, so that's positive. And you're right, she is a happy baby. No worse for wear, I suppose."

Don't lay on the compliments too hard there, lady.

Bree whispers to Olly, who's closest to her, "Does this mean we know who the mother is now?"

Fuck. Heat crawls up my neck.

Hoping that Mrs. H doesn't hear that comment, I wait a good long minute before I turn her way, but nope. She's staring back, nostrils flaring all over again. "Don't tell me you don't remember my Margot."

Tank holds out his hands. "*Remember* is such a specific word. I'm not sure our boy here…"

She quiets him with her laser-beam glare. "Are you telling me you don't remember what happened that weekend? Were you that high or drunk or whatever you all do here, that you don't remember… *having relations*?" She almost chokes on that last part.

Did I think having my father freak out in front of Gabby was the most embarrassing moment of my life just last week? Today definitely ranks a close second place.

What the hell do I say?

"Mrs. Hildebrand, I'm not sure what to tell you." I swallow, gearing up for her to ream me out.

Olly leans over to furiously whisper to Gabby. When he's done, she takes Poppy into her arms and gently pats Mrs. H's arm.

"Adele, this might be difficult for you to hear, but from what I've understood about the weekend in question, Margot brought some… homemade edibles… with her. And perhaps she didn't realize how strong they were. I don't know if they were hash brownies or if they contained any other drugs—"

The Varsity Dad Dilemma | 291

"Sweet Jesus." Mrs. H presses her hand to her cheek.

"Now I'm not absolving Rider from any responsibility. However, I don't believe anyone understood how intense those brownies would be. Because Rider is not the only one who can attest to their potency. Olly here"—she motions to him—"he can also tell you. As a result, the guys barely remember that weekend, much less who was there. And your granddaughter left a very vague letter when she dropped off Poppy, so they had no way of knowing who she was or they would've tried to contact her."

Yeah, all of that.

I let out a breath, once again so fucking grateful for Gabby. The second I have more than a few bucks left to my name, I'm buying this woman a million roses and taking her to a spa weekend or whatever girls like to pamper themselves.

Mrs. H seems overcome, and we're all quiet while she collects herself. Eventually, she turns to me. "If you don't remember Margot, then how do you know this baby is yours?"

I open my mouth to explain, but dread knots in my stomach as I wonder what she'll do if she doesn't like my answer. Will she try to take Poppy from me?

"Adele," Gabby says quietly, "all of the roommates took paternity tests. Just to be positive. You can rest assured that Rider is the father, and he's done a damn good job of taking care of Poppy if you ask me."

Mrs. Hildebrand's frown smooths out slightly, but then she spears me with another razor-sharp gaze. "Young man, if I get any indication that you're not caring for Poppy properly, I will take you to court for custody. Do you hear me?"

The tone of her voice is like déjà vu. It's how most of my teachers in Mortimer talked to me. As the son of Hank Kingston, the resident derelict and town drunk, I triggered everyone's suspicion through my very existence.

Through clenched teeth, I say, "No offense, ma'am, but I'm not the one who abandoned my baby in the middle of a football party full of strangers and took off to harvest pot on the other side of the country. If you have a bone to pick with someone about neglecting Poppy, I believe your anger is misplaced."

Her knuckles tighten in her lap. I daresay the old bird wants to kick my ass. That's fine. I'm not too fond of her at the moment either.

And what the fuck was Cricket thinking? Anything could've happened to Poppy that night. We're lucky as hell Gabby found her.

Gabby scoots to the edge of her seat. "Adele, I'm curious why you waited all this time to approach Rider."

Boom. Good fucking question.

I cross my arms over my chest as she hums and haws and finally admits she wasn't sure which one of us was Poppy's father.

"Cricket never gave me many details. You see, it wasn't until I saw you on the news the other day and they showed a photo of you carrying Poppy with that little pink hat I crocheted that I put the pieces of the puzzle together."

That fucking press conference.

She sniffs again. "When can I see my great-granddaughter again?"

At least she's asking.

I nod and take a breath to calm down. Trying to consider this from her perspective, I go with the most flexible response I can manage. "Whenever you want. I have a crazy week because the last game of the season is coming up and finals are around the corner, but if you don't mind squeezing in a visit during my lunch break or study time, we're always happy to have you."

Judging by Gabby's wide smile, that was the correct

response. She pats Mrs. H's hand. "Let's swap numbers so you two can reach each other."

And then, thank Christ, that woman finally leaves.

55

GABBY

POPPY SITS ON MY LAP, and we watch Rider pace from one end of his living room to the other and back again.

We're alone now. The house is quiet, eerily so considering several of his roommates are home, but everyone seems to know today rocked Rider.

After a few more minutes, I can't stand the silence any longer. "Are you okay?"

He jabs his hands into his hair, his eyes wide. "No, I'm far from being okay right now."

"Well, just stay calm. Adele looked appeased by you offering to let her see Poppy anytime she wanted. That was really nice of you, by the way."

"Did I have a choice?"

The veins in his neck are all sticking up and pulsing like he's run a marathon. That can't be good.

"Of course you did. You could've been a dick and told her she'd have to go to court to get any time with the baby."

"Like I have the money to fight her in court right now. And that's what scares the shit out of me. What if she decides my punk ass shouldn't have Poppy? Will she try to take her from me?"

The desperate look in his eyes tears at my heart. "I don't think she will. Adele's bark is bigger than her bite. Deep down, she's a big softie."

He doesn't look convinced, but at least he stops pacing.

"Come here." I pat the seat next to me.

When he doesn't budge from the middle of the room, I adjust my glasses and use my teacher voice. "Come. Here. *Now*." My voice quiets. "Please."

He frowns but trudges toward me, landing in a heap on the couch like a big baby.

"See, was that so hard?" I whisper as I scoot up to him with Poppy. "You just need therapeutic snuggles."

"Therapeutic snuggles, huh?" He tosses an arm around us, and I rest my head on his shoulder. His daughter wiggles over to him, and he wraps his other arm around her.

"They're the best kind," I say sleepily. "Free of charge. Readily given." *Clothed or naked,* I want to add, but hold back since Poppy is in our little trio. I close my eyes, exhausted but feeling safe. For some reason, being in Rider's arms makes everything better.

But as I think about what happened this afternoon, I wonder if there's any truth to Adele's threat to sue for custody. Worse, what's going to happen when Cricket returns? Will she try to take Poppy back?

56

GABBY

On the fifth ring, someone finally picks up.

"Larissa? Is that you? It's Gabby."

"Gabby!" my cousin yells. I haven't heard her squeaky little voice in so long that my eyes instantly fill with tears. "I've missed you! Why haven't you come to visit?"

Because your mom doesn't want me to create "drama." Because her boyfriend is an ass.

I take a big breath as I wipe under my eyes. "College is so busy, honey. You know I would be there every chance I could if it were up to me. How have you been? How's your sister? Did you get the birthday gifts I sent over the summer?"

"Yes! Thank you! I loved the jewelry kit. I made you a bracelet, but Mom says she doesn't have your address."

"I can give it to you."

I'm not sure I'll ever get over Aunt Carmen's rejection, but I can't stay mad at her. She saved me from foster care.

She might've only taken me in for the free babysitting I did daily, but it doesn't change the fact that staying with her was the safest I'd been since my mom died. I was so happy to have a home, I didn't mind taking care of a baby and a three-year-old.

Larissa and I catch up for a few minutes, but then voices fill the background for a minute before Carmen's voice fills my ear.

"Gabby. How nice to hear from you." The words are right, but I can hear the false cheer. Larissa must be standing right there.

"Hi, *Tía*. How are you?"

She's quiet for a minute before she obviously goes to the other room because a door shuts and her voice instantly changes.

"What's up? Do you need something?"

I don't ask if she's still with Bobby. The fact that she's so curt tells me everything I need to know. "No, I just—I wanted to tell the girls hi and see if I could drop off some Christmas presents for them over winter break."

Her voice lowers to a whisper. "I don't think that's a good idea. They get really upset after you leave."

I get really upset after I leave, but that's because she rarely lets me visit.

But I would hate being the reason Larissa and her sister Letty cry.

When I get off the phone, my hands are shaking. I could hear Larissa begging her mom to let her talk to me again, but Carmen said I had to go.

My teary gaze pauses on Poppy's blanket, and I freeze.

As great as this last weekend went, as much as I care for Rider, last night's standoff with Adele proves how fast things can change.

I already know Rider's schedule will let up a little after the season, but he'll still have NFL recruiting and agents to deal with as he preps for the draft, and I'll be student-teaching in the spring, which is supposed to be super stressful.

What if Rider and I can't survive the pressures we both face this year?

What if he and I go our separate ways after we graduate?

Not only will you lose Rider, but Poppy too.

Fear grips me as I'm reminded of my mom. One day she was singing off-key and making Benny and me waffles, and the next she was gone.

Life never offers any promises.

Neither do quarterbacks, a cynical voice in my head warns.

The sandwich settles like a rock in the pit of my stomach.

Ever since that phone call with my aunt this morning, my anxiety is through the roof. I can't help feeling like something bad is going to happen.

My thoughts circle back to Rider. I tried to keep things positive with him last night, saying everything would be okay with Adele, but that's because I wanted him to calm down. While it worked and chilled him out, I realize I'm waiting for the other shoe to drop. Waiting for Adele to call and say Cricket's back and wants Poppy.

And possibly Rider too.

I'm almost ashamed to admit it's a concern. Poppy's welfare should be my sole focus. And yet Rider and I *just* started seeing each other. Hello? He hasn't even officially called me his girlfriend.

I bite my bottom lip and wonder if I'm overreacting.

I've survived so much by keeping a low profile and being cautious. By not taking stupid chances.

And Rider's always been the exception to my rules.

Now I'm in so deep, if something happens now and we break up, I'll be devastated. What happened freshman year will pale in comparison.

As implausible as it might seem—that Rider would want to get with Poppy's mother—people do that all the time. Date or even marry for the sake of a child.

I would know. It's why my parents married. Because my mother got pregnant with me.

Rider won't ditch you like that. He might not use the word 'girlfriend', but he's treated you like one.

I tell myself he's just gun-shy. After all, there's no rule that requires him to stamp a label on our relationship.

We have time to figure everything out.

We do.

When Sienna texts me that she'll be out tonight with her guy, I can't help but compare my situation to hers.

They're not the same, Gabriela. You and Rider do things in public together all the time. He's not like Sienna's mystery man.

But I'm bothered enough to want to share my concerns with him. If it weren't days before his last regular season game, I would bring it up. It's not like me to hold back. Except I want to respect his need to keep things drama-free between us. If I put myself in his shoes, being a sudden single parent would be more than enough to max out what I could handle.

After this weekend, he has almost a month before the playoffs. I'll wait until next week to bring up my concerns. Really, what's a few more days?

Crumpling the wax paper from my sandwich in one hand, I look around the student union as it gets busier. Rider said he might stop by here this afternoon, after he talked to his professor. He's obviously running late, and I need to get to class.

As I throw away my trash, a familiar female voice calls out, "And who do we have here?"

I turn and find Miranda arm-in-arm with Zoe.

"You two are friends." Of course they're friends. Zoe made

my life miserable professionally, and Miranda nearly ruined my love life. It figures the universe tag-teamed these two.

Miranda's fake eyelashes flutter as she feigns a smile. "We were roommates freshman year."

I'm guessing that's why Zoe hates me, although I've never done anything to Miranda either except get dumped, which gave her the opening she wanted with Rider.

What did he see in Miranda beyond looks?

She's beautiful, dummy. Did he need a reason beyond her being runway-gorgeous?

"Cool. Well, I have to go." With a blank expression on my face, I swing my bag onto my shoulder, hoping to get out of here as quickly as possible, but as I start to pass them, Zoe holds her arm out in front of me. In her hand, her phone is cued up to a video.

"Go ahead." Her feline sneer is a warning. "Press play."

I won't like whatever I'm about to see, that much is certain. *Walk away, Gabriela. Don't give in to this game she's playing.*

"I have to get to class."

She holds up her other hand. "I just want you to know what you're getting yourself into and why you shouldn't get attached to Rider."

Miranda, with the ultimate guileless expression, shrugs. "It's true, Gabby. Rider and I have something special, and I don't want you to get hurt."

Um. Sure. You're just looking out for me.

"Sorry, I need to—"

Ignoring me, Zoe presses play.

The footage is shaky and within seconds I recognize Rider's front lawn. It's a party. Everyone's in bathing suits.

Someone walks by carrying furniture. He's so out of place, it's almost funny. And I realize it's Rider.

That's the party they had in late August. When I interviewed Sienna.

He's shirtless and glowing in the bright sun like a god. Smiling and too handsome for words.

For a brief moment, I think, *He's mine.* This beautiful man who's turned out to be an incredible father, he comes home to *me* at night.

But then the ultimate record scratch halts that line of thought when Miranda, who's wearing the smallest bikini known to man, leaps into his arms.

Even though I know this happened months ago, even though I tell myself I shouldn't let this bother me, I'm not prepared for how much it hurts to see him laugh and grab her ass and casually toss her over his shoulder.

Or watch her slide down his body and seal their mouths together.

My heart is in my throat as they paw at each other. His hands are in her hair and on her rear.

They look like they're two seconds from fucking on his front lawn.

Onlookers freaking cheer them on.

Bile pushes up the back of my throat, and Zoe finally shuts it off. Her sickly-sweet voice purrs, "Since you've been busy playing Suzy Homemaker, I thought you might need a reminder of what Rider is really like." Zoe lowers her voice as she waves the phone in my face. "Just ask Mira—she and Rider fucked all night long after this party."

My eyes dart to Miranda, whose expression of pity makes me want to punch her in the throat.

Zoe hooks her arm in her friend's. "She and Rider have been an item on and off for *years*. Whose bed do you think he was in right after he dumped your ass freshman year? Miranda's.

Listen, he's going to get tired of you like he did then, so don't get too comfortable in her territory. She and Rider are only taking a little breather. It's what they do. Ask him."

And then the two saunter away as though they didn't just torpedo my heart.

57

RIDER

I park my ass down in a front-row seat while I wait to talk with the professor. After a quick glance to the clock, I pull out my phone to text Gabby that I won't be able to meet her for lunch, but when I turn it on, a dozen messages fill the screen so fast, I know something's wrong.

My first thought is Poppy, and my stomach knots itself as I scroll through the messages, but no one mentions her. The grim tone in every single text doesn't make me feel any better, though.

Get yo ass to Coach's office. He's pissed. —Tank
Bro, shit's goin' down. Get to practice. —Olly
911, motherfucker. —Noxious
Dude. WTF RU? —B-Rod

I know it's bad when Ben messages me. He's been mostly radio silent since Gabby and I got together. He's polite, but keeps shit as brief as possible. After our last game this weekend, I'll make more of an effort to dig into that, but since he might also want to kick my ass, I've decided a respectful distance for now works for the team. No sense in dredging up drama.

But judging by the messages flooding my phone, drama has found me anyway.

Was in class. Headed there now. What's going on? —Rider

I'll have to catch my professor tomorrow. Ten minutes later, I pull up to the sports center and grab my phone, even more worried that none of my roommates responded to my text.

When I reach the weight room, I see why. Knox and Olly are in Coach's office, and my other roommates are stationed outside like they're waiting to see the principal.

Winston pauses mid-deadlift to bark, "You're in such deep shit. Weren't you the fool telling me *I* needed to respect women? Kettle black, meet the pot."

"It's 'the pot calling the kettle black,' dumbass," Trevor yells from the hallway. "And you don't know what the fuck you're talking about."

I don't get a chance to ask what the hell is going on because Coach sticks his head out of the office and bellows, "Kingston. In here. Now!"

Oh, fuck me.

In four years, Coach has never spoken to me like that.

When I reach the hallway, Tank juts out his lower lip and whispers, "Coach took our phones."

They say when you're about to die, your life flashes before your eyes. Judging by the expression on Coach's face, he might be gearing up to strangle us.

A million things go through my mind as I enter his office.

This can't be about Knox's marijuana garden. I watched him till that shit last summer.

Olly stopped writing essays for players last year. I made him swear he wouldn't start up again.

I told the guys to stop doing beer slip-and-slides across the yard months ago.

This could *be about the parties.* But with one or two exceptions, my roommates have kept their drink max to two beers.

I cringe. *I've swapped tickets for babysitting.* Each player gets four tickets per home game. Did I violate the terms of my athletic scholarship by doing that? Or, fuck, am I now ineligible because I violated conference rules?

There's one goddamn game left of the regular season. What the fuck did I do? How did I screw up so close to the playoffs?

"Close the door." Sully's voice is ice.

After I shut it, I sit next to Olly and Knox, who look like they're about to shit their pants. I know the feeling.

Coach grits out, "What did I say at the beginning of the season? Anyone remember?"

Olly clears his throat. "You said—"

"That was a rhetorical question. I don't need you to open your traps."

"Yes, sir. Sorry, sir."

After a long pause, Coach sighs. "I asked y'all to stay out of trouble. To be men of honor. To maybe not give me a stroke before I retire."

My heart is beating so hard, I can hear it in my ears. Feel it in my throat.

He shakes his head. "Imagine my surprise this morning when I got a phone call from that fancy sports channel asking if there was any truth to this."

One leathered finger pushes a piece of paper across his desk.

It's an article from a sports gossip site, *Locker-Room Talk*.

Top-ranked football team embroiled in paternity scandal.

. . .

Poppy. I clench my hand, wishing I could strangle the fucker who dug this up. I skim the article, hoping I don't spew that energy bar I ate during class.

Last week we heard the Lone Star Broncos sired a baby Bronc. The all-star quarterback recently admitted he's the proud father of a six-month-old baby girl, but what he didn't tell us is that when she literally got dropped off on his doorstep, none of the athletes in the house knew who fathered her and everyone had to take paternity tests. Considering how hard they party down in the heart of Texas, it's no wonder they can't keep track of their conquests at the "Stallion Station."

Fuck. My. Life.

The blog entry is accompanied by photos. Mostly of crowds dancing, but there's one of me holding Gabby over my shoulder the one time she actually came to a party. Thank God no one is named.

"Coach, I can explain."

He taps his desk. "You'd sure as hell better. My phone's been blowing up for the last hour. Your roommates gave me their versions. I'd like to hear yours."

Christ. Please let our stories match up.

I lay it out for him, every detail—from the moment Olly woke me that night, to the girls setting up babysitters for us, and Gabby swabbing everyone for paternity tests.

"So you see, Sully, I came to you almost as soon as I knew I was the father. That day when I asked for your advice." Fuck, I'm sweating. I wipe my forehead. "Yes, I left out the paternity issues we had, but I was embarrassed. We all were. And we decided if Poppy did, in fact, belong to one of us, we didn't want to get children's services involved. I have a friend who was a foster kid, and we didn't want Poppy to go through anything traumatic like she did. So that's why we handled things the way we did." I glare at that piece of paper. I'm surprised it doesn't burst into flames from the strength of my outrage. "And of course we didn't want to embarrass you before you retired."

He rubs his temple. "And what do you know about your baby's mama? You... do know... who the mother is, right?"

I could kiss that little spitfire Adele for coming over yesterday, even if she wanted to ream my ass out.

"Yes. I know who she is." *Finally*. I cough. There's no fucking way I want to admit to this last detail, but I have a feeling if I don't and Coach finds out another way, it'll be worse. "I'll be honest—I did not know who she was at first." I rush to explain that summer party and her special brownies.

Staring down, he mulls this over for a long while. "You kinda got roofied there." He rubs the crinkled spot between his eyebrows.

Huh. I'd never thought of it like that before. "I don't think it was malicious." At least, I hope it wasn't. "It was definitely poor decision-making on my part."

I'd say it was the worst decision of my life, but that thought gives me pause. Because how can I regret Poppy? I can barely keep my head screwed onto my shoulders with how crazy everything's been since she came into my life, but I love my little gremlin. So while I'm not proud of how that weekend went down, I'll never say I regret her.

"Where is she now, the mama?"

"She drove out to California to harvest pot. Decided to drop off our daughter first." Weird as hell to say 'our' daughter, but sometimes it's easy to forget I'm only half the equation.

His eyebrows lift. "I don't think I've ever heard that one before."

"Me neither, sir. But you can confirm this with her grandmother."

He blows out a breath and waves a finger between my two roommates. "Frick and Frack. Wait in the hallway. Tell the others they can get their phones."

When it's just me and Sully, he heaves a tired sigh. "You're being a pain in my ass right now. You're lucky you're a damn good quarterback."

I want to smile, but he's not in a joking mood. "Thank you, sir. I'm sorry for the trouble." Palming my entire face, I scrub it. "I know it might not seem like it, but I really was trying to stay out of trouble this season, and I've been working my butt off trying to take care of my daughter and stay on top of my classes."

"That's good, son." Folding his hands on his desk, he shakes his head. "I wish you had told me the whole story the first time you came to see me so I could prepare myself in case this story got out, but I understand why you didn't, and I want you to know I believe you."

That makes my throat tighten. No one in my hometown ever believed me or believed in me. This man always has, from the very beginning. The older I get, the more I realize that trust is everything in this world.

He shuffles through a stack of messages. "Now, I wish I could say you are out of the woods, but I still need to talk to the provost, who's also been flooded by media requests."

Dread seeps through my veins. "Am I in trouble with the school? For, like, conduct violations or with my eligibility?"

"Can't say just yet. It's possible. I'll know more on Thursday when the board of conduct meets." My stomach threatens to drop outta my ass. And then he levels me with a stake to the heart. "We're tentatively starting Meyers on Saturday."

Meyers. My backup who's barely played this season. Against Texas, our biggest rivals who are undefeated.

"Are you serious?" What the ever-loving fuck?

"I'm sorry, but if you aren't allowed to play, I need a backup plan. We'll see how things play out in the media this week. See if we can spin this the right way. I want you to meet with our public relations expert. In the meanwhile, I'm hoping for the best and planning for the worst." His lips tighten, his eyes full of regret. "I think you should do the same."

I nod and agree, but the truth is, I'm worried my career just got tanked by one night and a stupid decision to eat some girl's brownies.

How am I supposed to support my daughter as a washed-up football player with mediocre grades?

He keeps talking, but the only thing I hear is my lifelong dream might be over.

58

GABBY

"This is bullshit!" Tank roars from his side of the couch. Bree pats his back and gives me a worried look.

Rider paces from one end of the living room to the other and back again while everyone complains.

Even though that conversation I had with Miranda and Zoe this afternoon is eating at me, I do my best to focus on the current crisis.

The guys called a household meeting after practice. The practice Rider was not allowed to attend. But he came home and hit their weight room, which also has a treadmill, and got in a workout in case he's allowed to play this weekend.

Based on the private conversation he had with Sully, there's a whole range of potential consequences, several of which result in getting kicked off the team. He's understandably devastated.

Poppy's upstairs in bed, and I have the monitor in my lap while everyone commiserates over the crushing news.

"Meyers is scared of his shadow. He'll never pull this off if you can't start." Knox groans.

Rider points at him. "Don't say that shit this week. If I can't play, he's our best bet. You better build him up. That kid has some good instincts. He just needs confidence, people to believe in him."

"He's not you."

"But he could be. Look, I didn't fall into this position freshman year with the skills I have now. Sully might have kicked my ass day in and day out, but he filled me with positive thoughts. Made me think I could do it."

Tank leans forward to grab his can of soda. "Coach is the O-line whisperer, man. It's true. You know he loves the offense. We're his boys."

"Regardless of how you feel about Meyers, you need to keep the negativity on lockdown. Give him what you give me, and he might surprise you."

The room goes quiet. Until my brother, of all people, speaks up.

"It feels disloyal to you." He shifts uncomfortably. "You and I have had our differences"—he gives me a quick glance from across the room—"but you kick ass on the field. You make it fun. I don't know—maybe you channel all that stuff Coach tells you and you funnel it into us, but our time here wouldn't be the same with a different man at the helm. You're the heart of our team. Just want you to know I have your back. We all do."

Rider cracks a smile, the first one I've seen all night, and Tank sniffles and holds up a fist. "That's beautiful, man. I feel that." He pounds his chest. "I feel it right here, brother. Right here."

After he clears his throat, Rider nods. "I appreciate that. More than you know. I don't think I need to say this, but y'all have my permission or whatever to support Meyers. You're not being disloyal. I know you've got my back, and I'll never forget it."

When the meeting's over, Rider sinks on the recliner. "I'm so tired, my eyes hurt."

When he showed me that blog, I almost had a heart attack when I saw that photo of me hiked over his shoulder, waving a red Solo cup like a moron. Fortunately, I'm not named, and it's a little blurry. I almost feel guilty, like I'm getting out of this with a pass while Rider's in so much trouble. He's reassured me he can handle it, but I can tell the stress is getting to him.

One thing keeps bothering me, though. How in the world did a blog based in Los Angeles get dirt on a player in Charming, Texas? Especially the kind of dirt that was mostly locked down by NDAs? And out of all the photos online of Rider—at games, at parties, around town—how did the *Locker-Room Talk* get an image that hadn't been published on any of the popular Broncos fan sites? Because the first thing I did was reverse-search that photo, and it didn't land anywhere local until *after* that blog post.

Bree took pics, but she showed them to me, and they're from a different angle. Not that she'd ever stoop so low as to leak something to make us look bad. I think back to that party, trying to remember who else was there besides players, but unfortunately, the whole of my attention was on Rider that night.

As the guys commiserate, I consider whether I should tell him what happened with Miranda and Zoe this afternoon, but Rider looks too upset to broach the subject. The thought that he might not play the biggest game of the season, that he might actually get kicked off the team when he's so close to achieving his lifelong dream, is devastating and trumps the hissy fit I want to have about his ex.

I scoot closer to him and rub his knee. "What can I do? Want me to grab you some dinner?"

"No. Thanks, though. I'm gonna guzzle an energy drink and hit the books. Might as well use the extra time I have this week to try to pass my classes."

I frown. "Are you struggling with something? I thought you

said you've been turning everything in on time." He needs to keep his grades above a C to maintain his eligibility.

"When am I not struggling, Gabby? When has a good grade ever come easily? Never, that's when. Even when my shit's on time, it's never good enough. I'm not smart like you are." The edge to his voice catches me off guard.

"I... I'm not trying to give you a hard time," I say gently. I know he's sensitive about how difficult school is for him sometimes. "And don't be ridiculous—of course you're smart. I'm just saying I can help if you want. Do you need anything proofed? I can look over your assignments and explain—"

"That's just it. You can't always swoop in and do my shit for me."

I still, a mix of anger and hurt colliding in my chest. My eyes sting, and I blink quickly. "I'm not the enemy, Rider. I'm on your side."

Groaning, he rakes his hands through his hair. "I'm sorry. I'm freaking out. I don't mean to take this out on you. You've been great." He gives me a weak smile, one I don't really believe.

This is what he does when he gets stressed. I'm starting to see the pattern. How he pulls away.

After a fight with her husband, I once overheard my foster mom talking to her friend about a book she had called *Men are from Mars, Women are from Venus*. According to this book, when men get stressed or worried or freaked out, they retreat into a cave. Women prefer to talk and figure things out, but men isolate themselves.

Since I was ten, I had no idea what "hiding out in a cave" meant, but now I understand. Rider is in his cave. He's protecting himself. He did it freshman year, and a bit right after we reconnected this fall.

A knot tightens my throat as I think about how well that turned out the last time.

I place the baby monitor on the coffee table and sling my bag over my shoulder. "You obviously don't want any company, and I get it." Even though he's apologized, I still feel the bruise where he stung my pride. I can't bring myself to reach for him to hug or kiss goodbye. He doesn't reach for me either. "Everything will be okay. You'll see."

He nods, wordless.

So I leave.

59

GABBY

WITH MY PALM, I smooth down my hair before I knock on the door to Mr. Barstow's office. When he yells to come in, I enter.

"Thanks for seeing me, Mr. Barstow." I printed out my résumé so I could have it on file when that opening becomes available. I sit in one of the cushy leather chairs in front of his desk. "I've heard the English department has someone retiring at the end of the year, and I was hoping to interview for that this spring." At his incredulous expression, I stutter. "Or... or this summer. Whenever you conduct interviews."

His eyebrows crinkle together. "What are you talking about? That's not why I asked you to come to my office."

"You... Wait. What?"

He waves a pudgy finger toward his door. "I sent someone to fetch you."

"Oh. Um. What did you need?" This is embarrassing.

Keep it together, Gabriela. So he called you in here for another reason. That doesn't mean you can't discuss that position.

As he grabs a container of TUMS, he shakes his head. "We won't be requiring your assistance anymore. I need you to gather your things, and I'll escort you to your car."

I open my mouth, but nothing comes out except an annoying squeak. "I'm sorry, sir. What?"

"I can see you don't understand. Let me be more clear. You're fired."

I almost laugh because this has to be a mistake. I'm early for my shifts. I do what I'm told and never complain even when the staff is rude or demeaning. And I always do a great job because I never cut corners. What in the world could I have done to upset him?

Unless he doesn't like me because of Miranda.

I swallow. "Yes, sir. I heard you, but I'm confused. Why am I being fired? This is my last week on staff since I was told Archer wouldn't need any temps during finals. Do you mean my temp position has ended early because of staffing needs?"

"No, you're fired. You do know what fired means, correct?"

To my great shame, my eyes fill with tears. I cough and blink and stammer. "Yes, sir, I understand what being fired means. I just don't understand why you would fire me. Especially so close to the end of my contract."

He sighs like talking to me is the greatest inconvenience of his life as he leans away to grab a file off his credenza. After he slaps it on his desk, he pulls out a stack of papers.

"Do you remember signing your contract?" he asks sarcastically.

I grab the stack with trembling hands. "Of course."

"And do you recall the clause pertaining to moral turpitude?"

"Yes, sir," I whisper.

"Then can you explain why photos of you partying with the football team are all over the internet?" He grabs another folder and flings it across his desk, and several sheets of paper slide out and float to the floor.

As I pick them up, it's as if that other shoe drops.

Yesterday, I felt guilty that I'd gotten off somehow after the guys got in trouble.

Now it's my turn.

The first photo is of me hanging over Rider's back at that party. Along with several others I've never seen before. Of me and Rider dancing chest to chest, with his giant hands practically covering my ass. Of him looking down at me so we're nose to nose.

Think, Gabriela. Defend yourself. You didn't do anything wrong. Not really. This might not look great, but it's not as though you murdered someone.

"With all due respect, Mr. Barstow, I'm twenty-one. It's not illegal for me to have a few drinks at my boyfriend's house after a football game."

"The clause states that you will not do anything that might reasonably be considered immoral, deceptive, scandalous or obscene *or* that will incur, tarnish, damage or otherwise harm the good reputation of Archer."

"And you think I've tarnished Archer's reputation? Simply by being at that party?"

"Those athletes are in the middle of a horrific scandal, especially for a community our size in the heartland of Texas. Your photo got flashed on television not ten minutes ago. Everyone, and I mean *everyone*, will get a good eyeful of these images in the next few days. You pose too great a liability to keep you on staff as a result."

Oh, God.

I scramble to think of something. "But my name hasn't been attached to these photos or this alleged scandal. I live across the street from those guys. They're all my friends, and while I realize those photos don't look great, they're good men. Rider is a wonderful father. He mows the lawn of his elderly neighbors, for heaven's sake. This whole thing is getting blown out of proportion."

"Regardless, this is not the kind of... situation... we want connected to our prestigious institution. What am I supposed to say when a parent sees this and recognizes you?"

"That I was simply enjoying an evening out with my boyfriend, and those images are taken out of context." God, were all of those photos on television or did he get these new images from Miranda?

He squints. "You keep using that word. *Boyfriend.* But from the press conference I just heard, Rider Kingston is single."

I shake my head. Mr. Barstow must be confused. "We've been dating almost since Halloween."

"Really? Then someone should inform him."

The haughtiness and disbelief in Mr. Barstow's voice snaps the last shred of my composure. "Is this because your daughter used to go out with Rider? Because if you're concerned about your image, just yesterday she showed me a video from this summer of her hanging all over him in her barely-there bikini." One in which her ass cheeks played a starring role.

His jaw tightens. "*She* is not my employee. *You* are. Or you were." He stalks to his door, and as he opens it, he hammers the final nail in the coffin. "And don't waste my time applying for that job in the fall."

The words are unspoken, but I feel them just as intensely as if he'd yelled them in my face—he'll never consider me for a position now.

60

GABBY

EVERYTHING MOVES in slow motion as I exit the building. Kids talk and laugh, and I feel like I'm underwater and being pulled deeper. I want to rage and scream and cry, but nothing I do right now will make a difference.

Just like when Zoe got me fired from my tutoring job.

My nostrils flare. Did that bitch have something to do with this too? Or was Miranda working behind the scenes then, and I had no clue? But why would she give a damn about me back in May? She didn't even know who I was.

But if I had to guess how Mr. Barstow got so many pics of me acting like an idiot at a football party, images that aren't even available anywhere online, I'd bet everything in my bank account Miranda had a hand in it.

When I reach my car, I turn and stare at the sweeping, cathedral-style campus one last time as an overwhelming sense of helplessness wraps around me.

After my mom died and I went into foster care, I kept telling everyone I had family. I knew I had relatives somewhere who might take me. But no one listened. No one cared. One foster mother eventually had some pity on me and explained that while, yes, there was more family, they only wanted to adopt Ben.

So even though I ended up with my aunt, I knew better than to trust it was permanent.

That's why I've always kept to myself. That's why it was hard to open up to roommates and boyfriends. Until Rider and Sienna came crashing into my life, I've been an island.

I keep it together until I reach the outskirts of Charming, where I pull into a fast food joint and park beneath the shade of a giant oak tree.

That's when the tears start. They're mostly from a place of anger and regret. Regret that I got carried away that night with Rider. Anger because that asshole fired me after I worked so hard at such a thankless position.

But when I think about how I busted my tail all semester just to get humiliated like this, a sob breaks out of me when I realize my dream of working for that school is over.

It makes me miss my mom so much. I wish I could curl into her lap and have her tell me everything will be all right.

For a brief moment, I consider calling my brother, but then dismiss it. It'll hurt more if he's reluctant to talk to me, and I can't handle anything else today.

My thoughts turn to Rider.

He'll understand. He'll want to be there for me. After everything we've gone through together this fall, he'll get it.

I dig my phone out of my purse and dial, but it goes straight into voice mail. I frown. He usually picks up in the evening.

I hang up. Maybe he'll come over later tonight, and we can talk then.

When I'm down to sniffles, I wipe my face and finally pay attention to my surroundings. The sun has almost set, so the burger joint glows brightly in the waning light.

Which is why I notice the couple in the window.

My pulse quickens to a frenzied beat.

It's Miranda Barstow.

She looks perfect as always. Hair perfectly highlighted. Makeup done. Dressed in some designer outfit, no doubt. Even from my car, I can tell how put-together she is.

But it's the sight of the man seated with her that tightens my throat.

Rider.

Is this why he ignored my call? Because he's with her?

My brain scrambles to make sense of this while blood pounds in my ears.

Maybe it's the stress of the last few hours or the craziness of the scandal this week or the fact that I just bawled my eyes out for the first time in years, but my mind instantly goes down a dark hole, one where all of the worst-case scenarios barrel toward me.

Has he... has he been seeing her behind my back? Is that why she threw down yesterday?

Immediately, I chastise myself for being so pessimistic, for not trusting Rider. Until this moment, he's been nothing but reliable.

But my heart hammers as I realize I can't reconcile what I'm seeing with what I know about this man.

Their conversation looks serious. Until she reaches across the table and grabs his hand.

I wait for him to shrug her off, but he doesn't.

Instead, he smiles.

Stunned, I watch them talk for a few more minutes. All the while holding hands. As they walk to her car, she slips her arm through his. Again, he doesn't object.

They're so chummy, he even drives her car.

Like a boyfriend would.

And it makes me wonder if everything I know about Rider is a lie.

61

GABBY

SEETHING, I wait for my phone to ring.

The longer it's silent, the dumber I feel. It's an inverse reaction, an algebra equation I can't seem to solve.

Or maybe I don't want the answer.

I finally watched the press conference Barstow mentioned, the one in which Rider Kingston told the press he's single and "solely focused on playing football and taking care of his daughter."

It wouldn't have bothered me yesterday. Okay, it would've bothered me a little, but a part of me understands why he'd say that. We've only been dating about a month. I can understand why he'd not make any announcements yet.

But after seeing him with Miranda, it bothers me more than I care to admit.

"If you pace anymore, you're gonna wear a hole through the floor." Sienna pops a grape in her mouth. I told her everything when I got home. What happened with Miranda and Zoe yesterday at the student union, my meeting with Miranda's father today, and what I saw from the parking lot of that burger joint. "Have you called him?"

"Yes."

"And you left a message?"

I roll my eyes. "No, but he knows I called."

"But you didn't leave a message or text?"

"I take issue with how rational you're sounding right now. Please go away." I grab my phone and punch at the screen. When I'm done I show my roommate the message, since she hasn't budged from the couch.

"'Call me.' All caps. Hmm."

"Simple and straightforward. And if he's really smart, he'll get the subtext—that I'm planning to murder him in his sleep if he's been screwing Miranda all this time."

She pauses with a grape midway to her mouth. "You're a little scary right now."

"I got fired today. I have every right to be a bitch and rage."

With one hand, she holds up a beer. "That you do, girlfriend. I'm not denying you've had a shitty day. But you might want to tuck away the sharpened knives until you talk to Rider first and see what he says. There might be a perfectly good explanation for what you saw."

"There you go, being logical again. Why are you doing this to me?" I'm joking but I'm not.

All of the reasons I'm upset with Rider collide with what happened with Miranda's father today, and I'm almost dizzy with anger.

I put a steadying hand on the wall and close my eyes until the spinning stops.

"Are you okay?" Her voice comes to me through a vacuum.

"Yeah. Just... I'm fine." I open my eyes and wipe my clammy forehead with my palm.

"You could always go over there."

She's right. I should take charge. I mean, why am I waiting

for this guy to call me? He lives thirty feet away. Why should I torture myself like some helpless Disney princess waiting for some dumbass to climb through her window and rescue her?

I'm going to get the answers I need.

And if Rider's been cheating on me, he can fuck right off.

"You're brilliant." After I slip on my shoes, I yank open the door. I'm halfway across the street when I see Miranda's bright car parked next door.

Oh, God. She's here.

Her shiny Lexus wasn't there when I got home a little while ago.

My eye twitches wildly, like it's trying to outpace my heart.

The front door of the football house opens and I stop on the lawn and watch Miranda pause in the entryway. She sees me and gives me a snakelike smile before turning to talk to Rider, who's now almost right next to her.

He doesn't see me.

They're so close, their bodies almost touch. And when she slings her arms around his neck, my heart is in my throat as I watch his wrap around her. His head tilts down and he must say something in her ear because she giggles, and she fucking slides her hand into his hair.

I cross my arms and wait for them to separate.

I'm so incensed, I'm surprised my head doesn't blow off my body.

When he sees me, he stiffens. That's a guilty response if I ever saw one.

Miranda grins at me. "Hey, Gabby."

"Fuck you," I say. Her mouth opens in a gasp. "Don't stand there and pretend you didn't know I was here the whole time you groped him in the doorway."

"Gabby." Rider coughs. "It's not like that."

"Really? Then enlighten me."

Miranda scoffs, her voice a baby-soft coo, as she places her hand on his chest. "You don't owe her an explanation, Rider."

"Miranda," I growl. "If you value your face, you will remove it from my sight before I pluck out both of your beady little eyes. You got me?"

She looks to Rider, who remains stoic and silent. "I'll call you later with what we talked about." And then she trots her annoying ass to her luxury vehicle and drives away.

"Was that really necessary?" Rider asks quietly.

"You tell me. Why are you hanging out with her? Don't you see she's manipulating you?"

His brows furrow. "Why do you think she's manipulating me?"

Can he really not see it? How she's all giggles and flutters? Is he blatantly lying to me or willingly deceived?

A wave of dizziness hits me. I take a deep breath, somehow able to brush it back, but my train of thought is trashed.

I struggle to find the words. Struggle to piece it together.

I need to tell him I got fired, that I think Miranda and possibly Zoe got me fired, but that's not what comes out of my mouth. "Don't you think it's odd that suddenly there are all these photos of you everywhere? Of me too. Putting both of us in the worst possible light?" Barstow had so many from that party, photos I haven't seen anywhere else, but I'm flustered and tongue-tied and groggy. I don't know how all of these pieces fit together, but I keep rambling. "It all somehow dovetails perfectly with this paternity issue that no one has gossiped about until now?"

As I say those words, my hazy theory that Miranda is somehow behind some, if not all, of what happened this week, grows stronger.

Rider scoffs. "What are you saying? That Miranda would deliberately try to wreck my career? That doesn't make any sense. She loves the team, has always supported us. And she's been nothing but kind since we parted ways."

I bet she has.

His jaw tightens. "If anyone is behind the paternity scandal, it's likely that tool Jason."

It takes me a second to process that. "Wha—why would Jason have anything to do with this?" That dizzying sensation wraps around me again, and my knees almost buckle, but I manage to catch my balance.

He glares at me. "Why are you defending him?"

Outrage energizes me, and I stand taller. "I'm not defending him. I just don't understand what he gains by disparaging you."

"Are you kidding? He's pissed because I banned him from our football parties."

Jesus. I rub my pounding temple. "Rider, I know you think everyone is dying to attend your fucking parties, but they're not, okay?"

His nostrils flare, and I know I've struck a nerve. I don't meant to curse, to cast such vitriol, but the emotions whipping around inside me are volcanic.

"Why are you defending her?" I take a pained breath. "Are you… are you sleeping with her?"

He stills, his jaw tight. "Why would you think that?"

Not an answer. *Or a denial.*

The reasons rush at me, the hurt bubbling up in my chest. "During your press conference, you said you were single. I come over and you're both clinging to each other in the doorway, and Miranda's raking her fingers through your hair and giggling in your ear. When I called you earlier, you didn't pick up. Because you were busy having dinner with her."

I'm out of breath, the hurt coiling tighter as I recount all the ways he's chosen her over me this week. Maybe longer. *Maybe*

Zoe was right and he did cut ties with me freshman year so he could be with Miranda.

The more I think about it, the more tormented I feel.

He got borderline upset with me yesterday when I offered to help him with his homework. He was edgy and didn't want to hang out. But he had enough time today to hang out with Miranda and grab a bite to eat.

The grooves in his forehead deepen. "How did you know I had dinner with her?"

At least he's not denying it.

"Because I watched you from the parking lot."

Eyes narrowing, he crosses his arms. "Were you fucking following me?"

"Yes, Rider," I say sarcastically. "I have nothing better to do with my time than to follow you around town."

"Because it *sounds* like you were following me."

"Well, it *looks* like you're cheating on me." I wave my arms as my voice rises. "By the way, it must be nice to just hop in a car as expensive as hers and drive it around town. Do you drive all of your exes' cars? Is my car the only one you haven't driven yet?" I'm losing it, my control slipping with every screeching word out of my mouth. I'm out of breath and dizzy and sweating. I want to cry and rage that he seems to be choosing Miranda over me *again*.

When he doesn't respond, I yell, "Say something!"

I feel like I'm standing over a sinkhole and watching the ground around me erode into the darkness.

His eyes glint with anger. "If that's what you really think of me."

My throat tightens, and I nod slowly. "So that's it, then. You're not going to explain?" What I mean to say is, *You don't care enough to explain? You're just going to walk away like you always do.*

He talks through clenched teeth. "You already have it all

figured out, don't you? You have all the answers. Does it even matter what I say at this point?"

Hot tears roll down my face. "You disappoint me, Rider."

He laughs. It's an ugly, dark sound that twists something inside of me. "Don't you know by now? I disappoint everyone."

Then he stalks into his house and slams the door.

62

RIDER

The moment the door slams, I know I've made a mistake. A big one. But I'm too pissed to do anything about it.

I feel like I've been taking hits from a battering ram all week. From Mrs. Hildebrand on Sunday and Sully reaming me out, to teammates who are pissed and even professors who stopped me to tell me how disappointed they are in me, it's been a giant headfuck.

It's like being back in my hometown where everyone glares at me with suspicion.

Like I never escaped.

Like the last four years never existed and I'm that loser Hank Kingston's good-for-nothing son, all over again.

The last thing I expected was to have Gabby on my front lawn accusing me of something so laughable.

I'll never get back together with Miranda. I told her as much. And I'd certainly never mess around behind Gabby's back.

But Miranda called me yesterday and offered her support. Said her father wants to offer his attorney if I need legal representation, that her family would be happy to pay for it. Apparently, her parents are huge boosters, and her dad wants the team to go all the way this season. He's afraid Meyers can't hack it.

Which makes sense because I'm not sure Meyers is ready to do the job against a team like UT either. Maybe against a different school, but not against the number two team in the country. Hell, UT might kick my ass, and I've had four years to prepare for this game.

Miranda swore she just wanted to help. And I quote, "From one friend to another in a time of need."

I don't have the money to pay for an attorney. Hell, I can barely pay for babysitters and diapers right now.

And as Miranda pointed out, I might need an attorney. One who has my best interest at heart and not the school's. Especially since so many photos have come out this week of me partying with random women over the years. Not that anything happened with most of them. I swear they were edited to look more damning, but there's no way I can prove that.

I'm not sure what to make of Gabby accusing Miranda of having some kind of involvement in this scandal. I rack my brain and think back to all the times Miranda showed up to my games, to our parties, but nothing suspicious comes to mind. She even seemed cool that I've moved on and fine with our platonic status.

I scramble to figure out what might have made Gabby so angry above and beyond the scandal, which she's had a front-row seat to the entire time.

Did I say I was single during that press conference? Yes. As per the school's public relations expert who told me to keep the narrative simple. That I would only be dragging Gabby into the cesspool if I named her as my girlfriend. That I did not want the negativity and nastiness that people would level at her.

I think back to my interactions with Miranda today. To anything Gabby might have seen.

Did Miranda grab my hand in the restaurant? Yes. But it was accompanied by a, "Rider, don't go thinking I'm making the moves on you. I just want you to know I'm here for you. No judgment."

Did she grab my arm while we were walking to the car? Yes, because she said she was light-headed from her migraine medication, which is why she asked me to drive. And since I stood there like a dumbass when Gabby passed out last May, I figured I'd better be safe than sorry.

Did Miranda hug me when she left? Yes. Did I feel weird about it? No. I wasn't feeling her up. Did it give her the wrong impression? Doubtful. She knows we're never hooking up again.

Did she put her hand in my hair? Yes. She said there was a leaf in it.

So fucking sue me.

I'm not sleeping with her.

More than anything, though? I'm stunned by how fucking hurt I am that Gabby accused me of it. That she's so ready to condemn me without giving me the benefit of the doubt.

After the shitty week I've had, it's crushing.

I'm a fuckup. I get it. Message received. Loud and clear.

63

RIDER

"Hey, asshole," Tank says. "Stop slamming the cabinets. The hinges are gonna fall off."

I grumble an apology while I stand in my underwear in the kitchen and make my daughter's formula. With a flip of my wrist, I turn up the monitor, so I can keep an ear out for the baby.

"Another bad night? Did you try those cool cloths?"

"Yeah. Her fever is down, but now she's congested and cranky."

Since my luck is what it is, the gremlin got sick this week. Poppy had a hard time sleeping on Monday night, but I assumed she'd sensed my anxiety over possibly losing my spot on the football team. So I rocked her and held her and paced my bedroom to help her relax. Then last night, she had a fever. Fortunately, it broke quickly, but I'm so tired I'm seeing double.

"I'm surprised Gabby's not here. You know she'd help."

I'm not prepared for how much it aches to hear her name.

I sink down onto a chair and let out an aggravated groan.

Last night was not my proudest moment. I handled that situation with Gabby all wrong and let my pride get the best of me. I was exhausted and stressed out and pissed that my last week of the regular season has been marred by bullshit. Instead of talking about my pass completions and touchdowns, the media is digging up stupid crap.

And then I woke up this morning after those restful twenty minutes of sleep and saw that Gabby had removed herself from the online babysitting schedule. She very conscientiously replaced herself with other people, but it still stings.

"I doubt Gabby will be coming over here any time soon. For any reason." I had to eat some serious crow the first time to get her to consider being friends again. I can't imagine what this will take.

"Why's that?" Ben asks quietly as he enters the kitchen with Knox and Olly.

Fuck. Nothing this week is going my way. Might as well tell her brother the truth. I'm tired of people thinking I'm keeping secrets. "She thinks I'm cheating on her."

He laughs. Like, a big-ass belly laugh. "Why would she think that? Even I know you're crazy for her. And trust me, I had my doubts at first."

I *am* crazy for her. Crazy *about* her. Constantly thinking about her. Wanting to be around her. Insane in the membrane. Even after I swore I wouldn't let myself get attached to anyone before I locked down my future with the NFL.

And she fucking thinks I'm cheating on her.

That anger rises up in me again, and I wanna punch a hole in the wall right next to the one Ben made a month ago.

"You should ask her. She yelled at me across the lawn. Told off Miranda. Actually, she said she would pluck out Miranda's eyes if she didn't leave." My woman's wrath is breathtaking. I almost covered my balls.

She's not your woman anymore, dumbass. Because you screwed up. Royally.

Ben laughs again, the dick. "That there is your first problem. Miranda totally wants to fuck you. Everyone knows it."

I frown. "No, she doesn't. She swore up and down she was cool being friends." Tank gives Ben a look. "What?"

Tank scoffs. "And you believed her? Even I can see her little psycho heart-eyes from a mile away. You're lucky there's no bunny to boil."

"Why the hell are we talking 'bout rabbits?"

"Aww, son, you're such a young 'un."

"You and I are the same age, asshole."

"But I'm an old soul with a vast knowledge of 80s movies." He shrugs. "My momma loves Glenn Close. Ever seen *Fatal Attraction*? Bunnies were boiled, my brother. It wasn't pretty."

That gives me pause.

Can Miranda be snarky and short-tempered? Definitely. But the guys seem to think she's bunny-boiling crazy.

I freeze as I consider the accusations Gabby made about her last night.

I'm almost afraid to ask the question, but I trust Tank's judgment. He might be outrageous sometimes, but he's usually right about people.

A sinking sensation of dread washes over me as I realize I should've trusted Gabby's judgment too. She's never steered me wrong before.

Needing to piece this together, I say the words. "So do you think Miranda is unhinged enough to, say, leak the scandal in the first place?"

Everyone's quiet, until Tank nods. "Definitely."

"But why would she do that? What does she stand to gain from this?"

Tank smirks. "Did you or did you not hang out with her this week after not having seen her in over a month?"

"Because she offered to help me get a lawyer."

"Conveniently offering to fix a problem she caused in the first place? And maybe sinking her talons into you at the same time." He shrugs. "Maybe this scandal got outta hand. Maybe it started small, a way to weasel her way back into your life."

Knox nods as he chugs some juice. "Something to stress you out so you'd seek carnal comforts."

"Carnal comforts. Really?" I make a face. Jesus, do these guys think I'm a complete animal? "Don't Mrs. Hildebrand or even that dick Jason have motives too?" Since my roommates were all here on Sunday to see shit go down with Adele, I explain the run-in I had with Jason the other night.

We debate this for a while, until I realize it doesn't matter anymore. The news is out. My shame is being played out on national news for the whole damn world to see. Nothing is going to change my situation until the meeting with the provost.

But I'm finding the cinderblock on my chest has to do with Gabby, not football or the scandal.

"Shit got ugly with Gabby last night," I finally admit. "She obviously sees what y'all do in Miranda and I didn't handle her suspicions well, mostly because I felt attacked. Like I was some dirtbag she didn't trust."

Tank winces. "You did kinda ditch Gabby freshman year for Miranda, right?"

What the fuck?

He holds up his hands before I can respond. "Don't get upset. Gabby and Bree talk, okay?"

Hell. He heard this from Bree?

He makes a face. "I always wondered this myself, so don't get mad at the girls."

Christ. Really?

Olly pours some coffee. "No offense here—I love Gabby—but shouldn't we focus on your hearing tomorrow? You know, the one being held in less than twenty-four hours?"

"It's not a hearing exactly. Coach said I can present my side of things to the board of conduct to see whether or not I've violated any school rules, which will determine if I can play this weekend."

Olly joins us at the table. "One fire at a time, and the most pressing issue is your meeting. Then we should focus on football. Again, I love Gabby. Adore her, really. And if you weren't dating her, I'd totally make a play for that girl." *Seriously?* He smirks at my reaction. "But I'm guessing she'll still be there once you deal with the rest. And if you can't get your head on straight, even if they let you play, we're all fucked."

He's right. He's so damn right. My head is a mess. Assuming I can play this weekend—and that's a big assumption—I'm screwing the whole team *and* Sully if I can't concentrate.

Tank holds out both his arms. "*Or*, one might say a happy daddy is a focused daddy."

"There you go again, calling me Daddy."

The guys laugh. Even I crack a smile.

"Just saying, if you get things straight with Gabby, it's easier to align everything else. Trust me. My woman would agree."

Knox snorts. "That's 'cause Bree wears your balls like hood ornaments on the dash of her car. Of course she's gonna agree."

"Says the guy who never gets laid."

"Children!" I tilt back my chair and grab the box of donuts I picked up last night after my blowup with Gabby. "Here. Have some carbs, and then you can help me strategize. I need to get my woman to forgive me for being an ass."

Tank chomps on his donut and points at me. "I'm gonna refer you back to 80s rom-coms and the grand gesture."

I have no idea what he's talking about, but if it'll help me make things right with Gabby, I'm all ears.

By the time we're done talking, I'm relieved to have a plan. It feels good to know the guys are on my side.

But then my father calls later in the day, and just like that, that brief feeling of optimism evaporates.

64

GABBY

"Thank you." I sniffle as I take the box of tissues from my counselor. Her wrinkled brow smooths when she gives me a concerned smile.

"This might surprise you, but you're not the first student to cry in my office."

"That makes me feel better." Or it could be the half-hour I just spent purging my story to Ms. Vasquez.

She taps her pen on the desk. "The good news is what happened at Archer likely won't affect your student-teacher placement. We have longstanding relationships with these public schools, and since you're an excellent student and Hillcrest Middle School has already accepted you, I doubt they'll have a problem. Especially since your name isn't associated with those blurry, dark photos."

"That is good news. Thank you."

"It helps that you came to me first to explain the situation." She tilts her head. "How is Rider taking everything? I understand he has a code of conduct review tomorrow. He must be incredibly anxious as well with so much riding on that meeting."

My stomach drops.

Since I got fired, I've been solely focused on my situation. I was so hurt Rider didn't even try to explain why he was hanging out with Miranda, I didn't stop to consider how his whole future is in jeopardy and that stress could be a factor in his actions too.

Not that I'd ever forgive him if he did, in fact, sleep with Miranda.

But now that I've had some time to cool off, I don't actually believe he hooked up with Miranda. Although I do feel like I'm playing second fiddle this week, which I don't understand since I'm the one who's been helping him with Poppy this semester. Miranda hasn't helped with Poppy, not once, yet she's the one he's hanging out with?

Ugh, I hate how desperate and clingy that sounds in my head.

I rub my temple as I think back to last night and cringe. Yelling at Rider on his front lawn is not how I wanted to handle everything.

I'll admit perhaps my accusations were unfair.

Not that this excuses my behavior, but I did have dangerously low blood sugar, which might have contributed to my reaction. I realized this when I got home and nearly passed out. Thankfully, Sienna grabbed my arm before I brained myself on the kitchen counter.

Even though I'm still upset about what Rider said to me, on my way home, I make a phone call, one that I hope will bolster his case.

Because while I'm hurt by what's happened between us, I know he's worked his tail off this semester to step into the role of father. Rider adores Poppy. He might not have been thrilled with the situation at the beginning, but it's obvious he loves her.

I'm standing in front of my bungalow, staring at Rider's house when I realize what a basket case I was last night. I didn't even give Rider the whole story. I was running on emotion and light-headed and upset, and instead of detailing how I know Miranda is a snake, I freaked out.

I groan and run my hands through my hair.

He has no idea Miranda and Zoe approached me on Monday. He has no idea Miranda's father fired me yesterday with those photos, only one of which was circulated with that blog article. How can Rider side with me when he doesn't have the big picture?

Before I can talk myself out of it, I cross the street and knock on the door.

Tank opens it a minute later and scoops me into a hug so fast, it knocks the wind out of me. "Girl, it's good to see you."

After he sets me down and I can breathe again, I chuckle. "I saw you Monday night. It's only Wednesday afternoon."

"Yeah, but it's been a long-ass week."

That it has.

Motioning behind him, he says, "Rider's in his room." He makes a face. "He's been talking to his dad for a while."

Oh, Lord. That can't be good.

When he sees my reaction, he chuckles. "But that's why I'm sending you up there. Besides, I have to get to practice."

I'm about to ask if Rider is going to be late for practice when I remember he can't attend until after tomorrow's hearing.

My heart softens. I don't want to be mad at him right now. Not with so much riding on what happens at that meeting. Even if we end up going our separate ways, I don't want a repeat of freshman year where we just stopped being in each other's lives. Isn't that what adults do? They put aside their differences to talk?

As I head up the stairs to his room, I decide I can do that. I can be mature and focus on tomorrow. Maybe ask if he needs help with Poppy and be a friend. I'll save any ranting until after his meeting. If I were in his shoes, that's what I would want.

His door is open a crack, and I can see him pacing while he talks to his father.

"I'm doing my best, Dad!"

Even from here, I can hear Hank yelling, but I can't make out any words.

"In case you haven't gotten the memo, it's not easy to take care of a baby, go to classes, do my homework, *and* play football. I've barely fucking slept this semester."

Rider lets out a groan at Hank's response. "Don't fucking talk about her."

I still, my heart suddenly erratic in my chest. Is he talking about me or Miranda?

I shouldn't stand in the hallway eavesdropping. Nothing good can come from me overhearing a private conversation.

As I turn to go, his next words cut me to the core.

"When has a relationship with a woman meant anything to me?"

Oh, God. He can't be talking about me. About us. Is he?

His voice is glacial, flaying me open as he goes. "I've said it once, I've said it a thousand times—I'm just blowing off steam. Just fucking around. All the women I'm with know the deal. It's never serious! No one is gonna be hanging on to me when I get drafted. Is that what you want to hear? You've always said love is a lie. A con."

My blood pounds in my ears.

It's never serious.

Blowing off steam.

All the women.

Love is a lie?

What the hell?

For the third time in two days, I try to choke back the tears, but the torrent makes its way down my face.

I can't confront that asshole while I'm crying!

Devastated, I back away from his door. Fly down the stairs. Out of the house. Across the street.

Once I'm locked in my room, I collapse on my bed and let out a sob.

At least now I know how he truly feels.

I give in to the heartbreak and hopelessness and the despair. I feel it all the way into the cracks of my soul.

Because I'm not just losing Rider. I'm also losing Poppy.

For a flash, I'm eight years old, in the back of a social worker's dusty car, driving away from my mom's ramshackle house all over again. Losing my brother. Losing my beautiful mother. Losing everyone who meant anything to me.

I shake my head. *I can't do this again. I won't.*

And I decide right here, right now—this is the last time I shed a tear over that man.

Fuck Rider Kingston.

65

RIDER

I LOOSEN my tie and try not to cringe when Poppy fists it in her sticky palm.

When I woke up this morning and realized I didn't have a babysitter scheduled, it sank in just how much I've taken Gabby's help for granted.

I'm such an asshole.

The shame grows with every passing moment, but I promise myself that the moment I get out of today's meeting, I'm hauling it to her place to beg her forgiveness. I've never begged a woman for anything, but I'll do it for Gabby.

The more time that passes since our argument on Tuesday, the more I realize she had every right to be pissed. If I'd seen her hanging out with an ex the way she saw me with Miranda, I'd be ready to toss tables too. *I never should've listened to Olly and waited to talk to Gabby.*

Tank smacks me on the back as he sits next to me and gives me that look, the one he gives me when it's do-or-die time, which is typically when I'm facing three-hundred-pound linebackers, not a room full of academics. But Coach warned me these people have the power to end my football career today.

It's a humbling realization.

I'm seated at a long conference table across from eight administrators, which includes the provost of the school and the athletic director.

I hope I don't regret turning down Miranda's offer to help me with an attorney, but I thought long and hard about what Gabby said the other night. Combined with my roommates' impressions that Miranda was after more than what she's been suggesting, I didn't want to owe her anything.

Whether Miranda's somehow responsible for the situation I'm in right now, I'm not sure I have any way of finding out. Except I trust Gabby. As pissed as she is at me right now, she has a good head on her shoulders, something I lack at times, as my current situation reflects. But between her instincts on Miranda and my roommates, I think it's best to distance myself from Mira right now.

The door behind me creaks open, and I turn to find the rest of my teammates entering. Everyone's wearing a suit and tie.

The provost, Dr. Isaacson, jumps up. "Gentlemen, we cannot fit the entire football team in the conference room."

Olly steps forward. "We're here to support our captain. We'll be quiet." And then they all line up behind me.

Dr. Isaacson glares at Coach, who shifts in his seat before he turns to the team. "Boys, I know Rider's grateful you're here, but some of today's discussion will be private, so I need you to wait downstairs."

Tank gives me a sympathetic look as he fist-bumps me. Half the team grabs my shoulder. Even Meyers, my replacement, leans down to wish me luck.

It kinda chokes me up, to be honest.

Once the guys are gone, the door opens again, and heels click across the Spanish tile, and for a brief moment, I think it's Gabby.

It hits me. I love that woman. So fucking much. And I'm the biggest idiot on the planet for not begging for her forgiveness the other night.

Yes, I've been freaked out about football and what's going to happen with my career. Yes, I've been sleep-deprived and worried sick, but above all that noise, the truth levels me: if I get the game back, but she walks out of my life, it'll wreck me.

I swallow. Hard. How the hell am I gonna make it right between us again?

I've been a mess all week. When my dad called to bitch me out yesterday, I lost it. At first, I hoped he'd called to support me, to say something fucking fatherly for once. To offer some advice. But no, he just wanted to rub my face in the scandal and call me a dumbass for getting serious with Gabby.

I snapped, yelled shit I knew he wanted to hear just to get him off the phone, but it rattled me. How could someone who supposedly loved me believe the worst about me?

Of course, if Gabby really thinks you're fucking someone else behind her back, maybe you are the dumbass your father claims you are for falling for her when you should have your eyes on the prize and your heart on the game. Not on your neighbor who may want to rip your balls from your body.

As stern, unsympathetic faces stare at me from across the table, I shake my head. Now is obviously not the time to be obsessing over Gabby.

I cradle Poppy in my arms, and she sniffles. Grabbing the wad of tissue from my coat pocket, I wipe her little face and hand her a bottle from the diaper bag. She takes it eagerly. Thank God she has her appetite back.

When Mrs. Hildebrand stands next to Coach, I do a double-take.

Oh, fuck.

Why the hell is she here? Is she going to detail all of the ways

I'm a sub-par parent? Maybe start making the case about why she should get custody?

I wipe my sweaty palms on my slacks and try to look stoic instead of scared shitless.

"Adele, dear. What are you doing here?" Dr. Isaacson asks.

If I thought I was fucked before, it's nothing like the out-of-body experience I have when I realize Poppy's great-grandmother and Dr. Isaacson know each other. My mouth goes so dry, I cough.

"Hello, James. It's lovely to see you. I apologize for showing up unannounced, but I think I can put this little situation behind us quickly."

When he offers her a seat, torment twists my gut as I realize my whole damn career lies in Adele's hands.

Everyone looks at me, and I shrug. What the hell am I supposed to say? I scramble to think back to last weekend when we met for the first time. Was I a total asshole to her? Gabby was the only one who could calm her down.

I look around for a trash can in case I puke.

Because this goes down in one of two ways—she either saves my ass or puts the final nail in my coffin.

It's a toss-up.

I half-thought she was behind the blog article so she could get custody of Poppy. The coffee I had this morning threatens to come up, and I swallow hard.

Mrs. Hildebrand eyes me for the longest minute of my life before she turns to the provost. "James, do you remember my granddaughter Margot? God love her, but she tends to land herself in trouble. As you can see." She holds her hand out toward me where I rock Poppy in my lap.

Dr. Isaacson suddenly looks very uncomfortable. "Are you… are you saying that Margot is this child's… mother?"

"Yes. Now, I realize the optics of what happened are somewhat unsavory. However, I have personally investigated what occurred. When Margot could not care for her child, she dropped off the baby at Mr. Kingston's house. Unfortunately, her note... seems to have gotten smudged or became illegible, so the boys were not certain to whom it was written, which is how the paternity question arose."

That's one way to describe it, but I keep my mouth shut. She gives me another long look where my balls shrivel a little because I have no fucking clue what she's about to say.

And then, to my surprise, her lips tilt up.

"I have found Mr. Kingston to be a wonderful parent. You know how much these boys have to juggle with football and classes, but he is also caring for my darling great-granddaughter."

A swift wind could knock me over right now.

She pulls out a leather briefcase and hands him several spreadsheets. "You'll find that he had babysitting covered with people who signed nondisclosure agreements. You can even see how he tried to squeeze in time with his daughter during his lunch breaks. And I have it on good authority that he's an attentive father, caring and loving."

It hits me so fucking hard. I feel it in my gut—Gabby did this. She made sure Adele came armed with evidence to support me. How else did she get all of those spreadsheets?

Adele chuckles. "When I first heard a football player was the father, I was prepared to rake this young man over the coals and get custody of Poppy if needed. But as you can see, I fully support Rider." After a long pause, she taps the desk. "Of course, I'll provide additional funding to the library renovations. For your time and trouble."

The man sitting next to Dr. Isaacson, who has been taking notes the entire time, leans forward and asks, "Could your granddaughter possibly attest to these events?"

Dr. Isaacson glares at him, but Adele pipes up before he can say anything.

"Carl, I'm going to pretend that you're not questioning my word. Margot would be perfectly happy to meet with you, but she's in an Austin rehabilitation facility at the moment. However, she can provide an affidavit if needed."

I'm relieved to hear Cricket is back from California and safe.

Adele's eyes harden. "I trust everything I've shared today is confidential, because if I hear gossip spread about Margot, I will revoke my funding."

Isaacson stands quickly and comes around the table. "Of course, Adele. Of course. I completely understand, and we're happy to make accommodations in this situation."

Adele gathers her things. "I hope this also means Rider will be reinstated to the team. That he'll be able to play this weekend and his eligibility will not be threatened. Because I will not be able to sleep at night if the father of my great-grandbaby is somehow harmed professionally due to this little misunderstanding."

"Absolutely." He glances at me before he begins kissing her ass again. "It'll be like nothing ever happened."

The little firecracker winks at me as I let out a relieved breath.

Christ almighty.

I have to talk to Gabby. That woman has saved my ass. Again.

But that's gonna have to wait because Coach pats me on the back and whispers, "No time to celebrate. Get your butt to practice. We have to prep for the game this weekend."

Sweeter words have never been spoken.

Except...

"Coach." I cough. "I don't have a babysitter."

He rubs the gray bristles on his chin. "Do you have that sling thing? If the coaches can take turns wearing her in that contraption, I think we can handle it. Don't worry. We'll keep her off the field so she doesn't get beaned by a ball or anything."

Adele comes up to us and gives Sully a big smile. "I can lend a hand if you would like. To make sure everyone has the ropes."

He nods slowly, his eyes brightening. "That'd be mighty helpful."

She turns to me and lifts an eyebrow. "It looks like you have a ball game to train for, young man. Best get to it."

I smile for the first time all week. "Yes, ma'am."

66

RIDER

After practice, I trot my happy ass over to Gabby's. I'm dying to talk to her and share my good news. Thank her for everything. Ask her out on a real date where we're not juggling the baby and pacifiers.

I've got my baby, I've got a great woman, and I'm gonna win the fucking game on Saturday.

When no one answers after I knock, I check my phone again.

Gabby hasn't returned my calls yet, but she works at Archer's on Thursdays, so it's not a big deal. She often stays late to help with after-school programs.

I head back home and try to focus on the essay I need to write. It's tough to concentrate, though, when I keep checking my phone every two minutes to see if she's read my texts or called me back and I somehow missed it. *She hasn't.*

Yes, I've turned into a fucking teenage girl.

After another hour goes by with no word from her, unease settles over me. For the first time, it occurs to me that Gabby might not have forgiven me.

I figured since she sent Adele, she must've realized I blew my cool and didn't mean the dumb shit I shouted the other night.

"Ba na na gaga!" Poppy tosses her toy right out of her playpen.

"Whoa, baby. That was quite the pitch." I lift her out and set her on my lap. "We might need to get you signed up early for softball, huh?" Is that a sexist thing to think? "Hell, kid, if you wanna go for MLB, I'm down for that too. With this arm, which I'm pretty sure you got from your daddy, I bet you could give them a run for their money."

She jams her fist in her mouth, pausing to shout, "Na na na!"

"Want a banana?"

"Nana!"

She missed her nap since she came to practice, ended up falling asleep later in the day, so now it's past her bedtime, and she's wide awake. The coaches were great with her, and it was cute seeing them all love up on my baby, but now I have to pay the price for her schedule getting thrown off whack.

I prop her on my hip and make my way down to the kitchen where Tank, Bree, Trevor, and Olly are studying.

"I need sustenance!" Tank shouts. "I cannot work under these conditions."

"Eat your apple slices and carrots and stop complaining." Bree rolls her eyes at him as she gathers her purse, pausing to shoot me a dirty look.

I mash up some banana for Poppy before I address the hostility in the room. "Got something to say there, Breanna?"

"I have a lot of shit to say to you, but I'm pretty sure you don't want to hear it. Namely, how could you back that social climber Miranda and not Gabby? How could you—"

"It wasn't like that. And I've been calling Gabby all day, but she hasn't returned my messages."

"What a tragedy."

Irritation straightens my spine. "I've left apologies on her phone. She hasn't called back."

"My guess is she doesn't believe you. Wonder why."

Tank cringes and tries to bury himself in his textbook.

I look back and forth between Tank and his girlfriend. "What aren't you telling me?"

"Go ahead." Bree nudges Tank. "Tell him what Gabby *overheard* him say yesterday."

"What are you talking about?" I didn't even see Gabby yesterday.

"Woman, you're gonna be the death of me." When he turns to me, the seriousness in Tank's eyes catches me off guard. "Don't be pissed."

Olly holds up his hand. "Didn't we just say we should focus on the game this week? Our biggest game of the year, against the only other undefeated team in the league, is the day after tomorrow. Maybe we don't wanna go down this road right now."

Fuck. He makes a good point, but not clearing the air with Gabby is gonna give me an ulcer. "My head is all over the place right now anyway. I need to make things right with Gabby."

This is the situation I've spent my football career trying to avoid. Getting so wrapped up in a woman that she takes the focus away from the game.

But I'll never forgive myself if I lose Gabby over this. And judging by Bree's demeanor, my window to make things right with Gabby is shrinking by the minute.

Tank sighs. "Gabby came over yesterday. While you were on the phone." He pauses for a second. "With your dad."

I think back to that conversation. The horrible things I yelled to get him off my back. I was so pissed.

My father was drunk. He'd seen the coverage. Nothing rational was going to talk him off that ledge. He was so sure Gabby was trying to lure me into another baby mama situation. It was ridiculous.

All I remember is telling him how I've never been in a

serious relationship. That they've all been for fun. To blow off steam.

Lies. All lies.

Because Gabby is the real deal. She has me wrapped around her little finger almost as tightly as my daughter does.

My stomach knots, that sinking dread spreading through my limbs.

Christ. I said love was a lie. That I've never been serious about anyone.

"She never knocked. I never saw her, but..."

"She must've heard," Tank mumbles.

"It's worse than that," Bree adds as she grabs her car keys. Then she levels me with a cannon blast. "You got her fired from Archer. Well, you and Miranda."

67

GABBY

Ever notice that simple, everyday things feel like drudgery when you're depressed?

My feet feel like millstones as I drag myself around the grocery store. I don't need much since I'm taking off for winter break soon, but cooking is cheaper than buying takeout.

When I turn the corner, I accidentally bump into someone's cart. "Sorry about that," I mumble.

The woman turns, and I find myself face to face with Ramona. *Ugh. Just what I need today.* Another reminder of how terrible I am at relationships of *any* kind.

I look down as I attempt to push my cart around hers.

"Hey. Wait."

I pause, shocked she wants to chat.

"Look, I'm just going to lay it out, okay? I'm sorry I was a dick when I moved out. My boyfriend says I'm a lot to handle." She snorts. "And now that I live with a man child, I wanted to tell you that you were a really good roommate and friend. Even if I didn't make it very easy."

I'm a little choked up by her confession, but right now, I'm pretty sure almost anything could make me cry. "Thanks. That means a lot to me." I blink, relieved the waterworks don't break free.

"You okay? Do you, like, need to talk about it?" Her fearful expression makes me laugh.

"I think I'll be okay. But thanks for asking."

She rolls her eyes. "If you wanted to get coffee sometime, I'd be down for that."

I stifle a smile. "How about after the holidays?"

"Yes, after that." She shivers. "You know how much I hate the holidays."

I'm not looking forward to them anymore either, although I'm grateful that I won't have to spend them alone in Charming again.

I resume my shopping, but not five minutes later, someone else calls my name.

I turn, surprised to see my brother. Why is it when you're miserable and feel like death you run into everyone?

"What's up, Ben?" I grab a box of Pop-Tarts and toss them into my cart. I don't wait for him as I trudge up the aisle. He probably doesn't want to talk anyway. He never does.

He jogs to catch up to me. "Uh, I was wondering if you were coming to the game this weekend?"

I haven't been to any games this fall. The thought depresses me. I should've enjoyed one during the five minutes I was dating Rider. But all of those tickets sold out at the beginning of the season, and I hated him then.

Why did I open myself up to getting hurt by him all over again? Pure idiocy. And I'm supposed to be a smart girl!

"I'm going out of town. So no." I pause in front of the frozen section and eyeball the ice cream. A breakup definitely calls for ice cream. I could basically eat my weight in Ben and Jerry's right now.

"Really? So you'll be back on Monday?"

I frown. Since when does he care? My inner voice has gone full-on bitch mode since things went south with Rider. I should have some compassion toward my brother. I know what he struggles with, but I don't have the energy to deal. "I'm done with classes and turning in my final projects tomorrow, and I don't have any finals, so there's no need to return until January."

"But finals don't start until next week."

I swear talking to Ben is like having a discussion with a brick wall sometimes. "I don't have any finals."

"Are you staying with Aunt Carmen?"

"I haven't stayed with her in years." Again, this is stuff I've told him. "I'm going to Kat and Tori's for winter break. They invited me."

"Our cousins."

Someone give this man an award for actually remembering something I told him. "They have farms about an hour away. I'm taking off tomorrow."

"Before our game?" he asks, incredulous.

"Yeah," I say slowly and spell it out for him since he's not connecting the dots. "As I'm not dating a football player, and since I don't have tickets, I'm not going to the game."

Besides, I don't think I can handle seeing hordes of women fawn over Rider. It'll hurt too much. Never mind what will likely go down at the party across the street after they win.

Oh, God. What if they lose? It's been such a crazy week for the team. Rider must be going out of his mind.

No, Gabriela. Stop sticking your nose where it isn't wanted.

Once again, I'm tempted to check my phone and listen to Rider's messages, but what's the point? I already know how he *truly* feels.

When I think about Tuesday night when I saw him with Miranda, what really hurts is how I felt he chose her instead of me. And if there is any truth to what Zoe said, he cut ties with me freshman year for Miranda too.

As a foster kid, I've had a lifetime of being passed over. Of being second best. Of not being good enough. Why would I willingly sign up to get hurt again?

I'll talk to him eventually. Maybe when I get back from winter break. But for now, I need to regroup and find some balance.

My brother jams his hands in his jean pockets. He asks in a hushed voice, "Don't you wanna see me play? It's the biggest game of the season. You know UT is undefeated, right?"

What? Turning back to the ice cream, I try to control my breathing so I stay calm. "Ben, you've never invited me to *anything*, so I had no idea you'd want me to come. Especially after everything you shared with me a few weeks ago."

He shrugs. Shuffles his feet. Clears his throat. "Well, I'd like for you to attend this game. I already gave two tickets to Sienna for you guys to come."

I stare at him, shocked. "That was really considerate. Thank you." I push the cart around the corner.

"Does that mean you'll come?"

"That means I appreciate the effort you made. It was thoughtful. But I'm not sure I can handle going to a game right now." To my horror, my voice quivers. I cough. "I'll record it, though. I'm sure you'll do great. I'll watch it when it doesn't feel like my heart is being ripped out of my body."

I don't mean to be so honest, but I'm too hurt to care.

"Rider feels really bad about everything," he says abruptly. "He's grateful you sent the kid's grandmother."

"Great-grandmother."

"Yeah. I don't know if you heard, but she was awesome." He runs a hand over his head. "We're all grateful."

"It was the decent thing to do. You guys deserve a chance to play at a hundred percent. Adele's a wonderful person, so I knew she'd stand behind Rider if she knew the truth."

Ben grabs my shoulder, and I turn to him. "He really cares about you. Rider wasn't yanking your chain or anything."

I don't want to give Ben a reason to hate his teammate, especially when they have a huge game ahead of them and need to work together. Rider isn't his problem.

"Listen, I've had a horrible week." I blink until the heat in my eyes subsides. "I'm sorry I can't go tomorrow, but I'll be rooting for you. I'll always root for you."

His brow crinkles. "But you're coming back, right? Second semester?"

"Of course. And listen, you're not going to have to worry about me being in your business anymore because I'm looking to swap sublets with someone who lives on the other side of campus next semester. It's closer to the school where I'll be student-teaching."

That way I can avoid Rider and Miranda.

Because she was probably right—if history proves correct, he always goes back to her. What's to stop him now?

I clench my jaw against the wave of sadness that washes over me.

Once, when I was a kid, my foster mom drove past a house that had been devastated by a tornado. A great oak draped across the lawn like a crime victim, its roots mangled and jutting out from an enormous hole that gaped from one edge of the yard to the other.

Right now, this awful twist in my chest feels like that hole.

In my case, that tornado has a name and a face, one I hope I don't have to see anytime soon.

Ben doesn't appear excited about the news of my move, but

I'm tired, and I still have to go home and pack and clean and put a few finishing touches on one of my assignments.

"I'll catch up with you in the new year. Good luck at your game." I force myself to smile and continue down the aisle.

I put one foot in front of the other. Because that's all I can manage at the moment.

68

RIDER

Sienna's voice is cautious. "But what if she won't come?"

Holding the phone to my ear, I cross the room to stare out my front window where I look down on Gabby's house. "I'm begging you. She won't call me back. She doesn't read my texts. I've gone over there three times and can't seem to track her down."

"She's been coming in late."

"I feel like a stalker from how often I stare at your house. I swear I'm going insane."

Gabby told her brother she was fucking moving. Because of the dumb shit that came out of my mouth.

That seems kinda extreme, so she's either really pissed or terribly hurt. Neither of which bode well for me. And fuck, I never meant to hurt her. I adore that girl.

The clock is running out—I can feel it—and if I don't make a play soon, something big, Gabby's gonna walk out of my life forever.

I'm never the guy who gets crushed by a woman. I've never let myself get that close to anyone.

Until now.

Sienna laughs. "I hate to say this because you sound suitably tortured, but you sorta deserve it."

"Thanks, dude. Appreciate the vote of confidence."

"I'm just worried that if Ben couldn't talk her into coming to the game, why do you think I'll have better luck?"

"Because you're craftier than Ben." Although I'm grateful, I'm shocked the guy offered to help, but he and his sister don't have the best relationship. "I know you'll think of something."

"Short of doing something crazy, I'm not sure anything I say will persuade her." The humor in her voice fades. "She's been pretty upset this week. I've heard her crying at night, and she's not one to be emotional like that. I'm usually the crier."

God, that kills me. "I swear on football and my beautiful daughter that I'm trying to make this right."

She's quiet on the other end. "Do you promise not to hurt her again if I can somehow pull off this miracle?"

"I promise I will never again give her another reason to doubt me or my intentions toward her. I love that girl, and I just need a chance to tell her."

I can't believe I'm telling her roommate before Gabby, but there it is. I love Gabriela. To the fucking moon and back. And if I don't get a chance to tell her before she writes me off, I know I'll always regret it.

Sienna sighs. "Okay. That was kinda swoony. Count me in for Operation Win Back Gabby. But if you fuck this up again, mister, I will not be assisting you in any more covert ops."

"It's a deal."

Later that night, I get a text from Sienna. *All systems go. I've got a plan. Bring your A-game tomorrow! And while you're at it, beat UT!*

69

GABBY

AGITATED, I roll over again, except I get tangled in the sheets. It's almost three a.m., and I don't think I've slept more than ten minutes.

With a groan, I yank off the bedding and trudge to the kitchen for a glass of water. When I'm back in my room, I find myself in front of my window.

I think back to Halloween and all the cars on the street and the sounds of revelry spilling out of the football house. To how angry I was to stomp over there in my slippers and robe.

It would be amusing if I didn't miss Rider so much.

Would everything be different right now if I had stayed home that night? Would Rider and I have ever reconnected? Would they have kept Poppy after they found her? Or would she have gone into social services?

At least she has a family that wants her. Adele and Rider would go toe to toe for a chance to raise that baby. She's a lucky girl.

I grab a throw blanket and wrap it around my shoulders.

For the first time in a while, I feel so alone. Now that the possibility of a job at Archer has been removed, I have no idea what to do after graduation. Or where to go.

Aunt Carmen doesn't want me to move back home. Ben's busy here at school. I don't have a lot of options.

Deep down, I think I was using Archer as an anchor. To have a place I was wanted. Needed. With the promise of that job, I didn't have to worry about where I would go after May.

Now I feel like I could disappear into the floorboards, and it wouldn't make a difference to anyone.

Some little part of me hopes I'll have such a great time with Kat and Tori they'll ask me to come back after graduation, but that's irrational. They're just being nice to have invited me for the holidays. Besides, their ranches are in the middle of nowhere. How would I find a teaching job there?

I stare at the football house.

What's the harm in one peek? It's not like Rider will know. It's three in the morning. He's sound asleep.

I peel back the curtain farther and lean over until I can see his window.

The light is on, and the sight of it makes my heart pound.

Is something wrong with Poppy? Is he nervous about tomorrow's game? Is he worried about school?

Am I being an idiot for not giving him another chance? *If he even wants that.*

I could put myself out of this misery and listen to his messages.

Is that being weak? I don't know anymore. I thought I needed space to make sense of everything that happened this week.

The thought of listening to his voice sends such a bittersweet pang through me, I have to reach out and brace myself against the wall.

What harm could there be in *listening* to messages?

I swallow and stumble back to bed where I reach for my phone.

Seven missed calls. Five texts. Three messages.

Rider doesn't usually leave me voice mails.

The texts are all from him on Thursday. They ask if I'm around, that he needs to talk to me, to text him back. That he has good news.

He must've sent them after his hearing let out.

With a trembling hand, I press play.

"Hey. It's me. Give me a call when you get a chance. We need to talk. I, uh, I need to apologize for a few things." The sound of his voice, deep and low and raspy, sends chills up and down my arms. The second one is similar.

The last message came in late last night. "Gabby, please call me back. I wanted to thank you for sending Adele. I owe you so big. Once again, you came to my rescue. I've stopped by your house…"

He's quiet for a moment, and I almost stop breathing as I wait for him to say something else.

"I was hoping to apologize in person for being an ass the other day, but I'm kinda afraid you're not gonna give me that chance, so I'm doing it in a message. I hope you'll forgive me. I'm so fucking sorry my shit got you fired. I just found out about that. I promise I'll make it up to you if you give me a chance. And I completely understand why you were suspicious of Miranda. You obviously had every right to be, and I'm a dumbass for not realizing that." His voice lowers to almost a whisper. "I have my own issues too, you know, but that's no excuse."

It's silent again, and I wonder if that's the end of the message, but then he sighs. "Please know that nothing happened with Miranda. When you and I first started talking, it was long over with her. I meant that then, and nothing's changed except you were right about one thing—I think she was manipulating me. But I would never go behind your back and betray your trust. Anyway, I hope—"

And the message cuts out because my voice mail is full.

Son of a—

My whole body shakes with adrenaline. Is it too late to call him back?

I scurry back to the window with my phone in hand.

Except his light is out.

The biggest game of his life is tomorrow. You can't call or text him at three in the morning, Gabriela.

Frustrated, I jump back into bed and pray I'll know what to do in the morning. Maybe I can call him before he leaves for the stadium.

Except when I wake up, I realize I've slept through my alarm, and it's so late, all of the cars across the street are gone.

They've gone to the game.

I stare at his house, and that sense of emptiness grows.

A little part of me wonders if it's better this way.

Rider's going to get drafted in May, and he'll leave. It's not as though he pledged his undying love to me in his messages. He's never even hinted at the L-word. He feels bad about what happened, probably guilty that I helped by sending Adele. He's just grateful. Nothing more.

And I can't forget what he told his father.

Because in all likelihood, that's how he really feels. We have great chemistry. He knows I adore his daughter, so he doesn't want to mess with a good thing. While he's here. While he's in college. For the next few months.

But that doesn't mean he loves me or ever will.

70

GABBY

I turn the key, and my engine clicks and clicks but doesn't start.

I try again. Same result.

Ten minutes later, I'm freaking out. *What the hell?* Will nothing go right in my life this week?

Angrily, I grab my small suitcase from the back seat before I storm into the house.

Sienna stares at me as she shovels cereal into her mouth. "Back so soon?"

"Unfortunately."

She lifts an eyebrow, and I groan.

"Can I ask a favor?"

"Anything!" she says around a bite of food.

I pause at her enthusiasm, but shrug off the hesitation. Sienna dances to the beat of her own drum. She's probably excited she got her chakras aligned.

"Could you possibly give me a ride to my cousin's house? I know it's a hike, but I can pay for gas, both ways, and spring for lunch."

"Yes, I can totally give you a ride."

Thank God.

"But!" She chomps another bite of granola. Swallows. Holds up one finger. "You have to come to the game with me first."

My shoulders slump. "Why? The drive is only going to take maybe two hours. Two and a half, tops."

"Traffic, dude. Traffic. The guys are undefeated. UT is undefeated. Do you know what that means? That means every Tom, Dick, and Daisy will be tailgating from here to Austin."

"You mean Harry. Tom, Dick, and *Harry*."

She waves a hand. "That's sexist. Why do the guys get to have all the fun? There's no Harry in my version of things."

I blow out a breath. "Okay. Fine." She's probably right about the traffic. "So... could you pick me up after the game?"

"Ha! As if I'd let you get out of this momentous occasion! No, my little bumblebee, I will not pick you up after. I am dragging your ass *with* me."

"No. Out of the question."

"I have two tickets and no one to go with me. Ben begged me to bring you this week. Are you really going to let me go by myself? That's so sad. Isn't our friendship worth more to you?"

My heart sinks. Is this how Ramona felt when she moved out with nary a look back? "Am I a terrible friend?"

Her eyes soften and she nibbles on her bottom lip. "No," she says. "Not a terrible friend at all. In fact, I love you to pieces. It's just..." She swallows. "I really need you to come with me, okay?"

The pleading in her voice does me in. Sienna never asks me for anything. Will it hurt to watch Rider play today? Undoubtedly. Can I turn down Sienna? No.

But then she adds, "Hear me out on this. Let's say, on the *off chance* you and Rider work things out, do you really want to miss what will undoubtedly be a huge game in his career, possibly the biggest of his college career?"

Ugh. If there's even the *teeniest, tiniest* chance he and I end up together, she's right. I'd probably hate myself for missing the game when Sienna has tickets and is offering to drive me.

My heart lurches as my stomach does a deep dive. I'm not prepared to see him again. But I'm not sure I can walk away either.

"You drive a hard bargain."

When she tackles me in a hug, I laugh. Something I didn't think I'd be able to do today.

Maybe watching the game won't be so bad.

71

GABBY

"You're kidding me." I glare at Sienna, who's trying to paint purple grease stripes under my eyes.

"Not at all. We're about to face our biggest rivals. The energy of each and every fan in there matters." She points a finger at the lines of people streaming toward the stadium. "Do you want to mess with their mojo? Of course not! We're team players. Never mind your differences with Rider. Those guys are our neighbors and our friends. Aren't they?"

Damn it. She has a good point. My beef with Rider notwithstanding, I love those big lugs.

You love Rider too, you dummy.

I huff out a groan. "Fine!"

Sienna grins wildly. "Awesome. Now be a good sport and put this on." And my roommate shoves a Broncos t-shirt at me. "Hurry up, we're gonna be late if you dawdle any longer. And I need some snacks and other provisions. I really have to pee too." She pinches her knees together and does a little dance in the parking lot.

"Have you always been this pushy and I've just never noticed?" I narrow my eyes at her as I pull the t-shirt over my black Henley. It's freezing outside, so what's another layer? No one will see it under my jacket, and if putting this on will get her to shut up, I'll do it. Besides, with tens of thousands of fans, it's not like Rider's going to notice me.

I close my eyes against the tsunami of emotion that comes whenever I think about him.

It's one game, Gabriela. You'll go, you'll cheer because you're not a big baby. You'll enjoy time with Sienna. Afterward you'll slink off with your tail between your legs and visit Kat and Tori. Then you'll have time to get your act together.

It all makes sense in my head.

I can be a good sport.

As much as I want to grumble about being dragged to the game, it's hard to ignore the infectious energy of the crowd as we make our way to our seats. But my wariness grows as we make our way down the stadium steps. Farther and farther we go.

"Where are our seats exactly?"

Sienna mumbles something I can't quite make out.

"What did you say?"

"They're in the friends and family section."

Oh, hell's bells. "You're kidding me." I stop so fast the guy behind me bumps into me and almost sends me sprawling down a flight of concrete stairs.

Sienna turns around and trots up to grab my hand and yanks me along. "I can't leave you anywhere. Come on. This is awesome."

When we reach the freaking *front row* and stop in front of the fifty-yard line, I think I might hurl. "So this is the Broncos side? The guys will sit there?" I point to the row of benches *right* in front of us.

"Yuppers. Isn't it great?" With a hard elbow to my side, she asks, "Aren't ya glad I made you get decked out?"

I glance around. Everyone, and I mean everyone, is wearing school colors and face paint.

"I... yeah... I mean..." I'm so overwhelmed, I don't have words.

She hugs me so tightly, I squeak. "Thanks for coming with me today!" Then she starts jumping up and down with me in her arms, so I'm forced to jump like a moron. "I'm psyched to see my guy play."

"How's it going?" I ask when she releases me. She hasn't brought up her mystery man lately, and I didn't want to pry.

"Awesome."

"So did my brother give you these tickets or did you get them from your dude?" I had some nosebleed seats my freshman year, but these are insane. I'm not sure Ben can swing seats like these.

She doesn't get a chance to respond because the announcer comes over the loudspeaker, and yells, "Let's hear it, Charming! Help us welcome the undefeated Lone Star State Broncos!"

Paradise City by Guns N' Roses blares through the stadium, and eighty thousand fans lose their minds as the guys charge through the smoke-filled tunnel.

I clap and scream too. Sing all the words. I can't help it.

Bree joins us, and the three of us cheer on the guys. I immediately search for Rider. He's talking to his coach and looking cool as a cucumber.

God, he's gorgeous in his football uniform. Those white pants should be outlawed, they're so sexy on him.

Some girl behind me screams, "I love you, Rider!"

And the man freaking looks my way.

I'm standing in a sea of people, but it feels like he and I are the only two people here. Everything slows down. My heart. The air around me. The earth pauses its rotation around the sun as we stare at each other.

I consider Sienna's words earlier today about these players

being my friends, and I decide I want to be here for Rider. No matter what happens between us, I want to support him. Today is one of the biggest days of his career, and after everything we've been through together, the least I can do is cheer for him against his biggest rivals.

I mouth the words, *Good luck.*

A slow smile spreads on his beautiful mouth as he winks at me.

At least, I think he directs it at me even though the screamer behind me shouts some very graphic remarks about what she'd like to do to Rider after the game and how she'd love to have his baby too.

Tank slaps him on the back, waves to us, and pulls him away.

"Holy shit," Sienna whispers. "I almost got pregnant just now. Please tell me y'all are gonna make up after this. No smudge stick in the world will cleanse your karma if we don't get some positive resolution." She elbows me again. "Preferably naked, am I right?"

"We'll see. I don't want to make any hasty decisions fueled by this circus show."

Her fingers snap in my face. "If you don't at least talk to him after all of this, I'm never going to forgive you."

I laugh and shake my head. "Okay, Miss Bossypants."

I'll admit it's hard to stay mad at him.

Bree nudges me from my other side. "Make him work for it."

I'm huddled with my friends when I see Miranda and Zoe standing a few rows away, glaring at me. Miranda's carrying a sign that says, "Rider, go deep!" with a pic of Jennifer Lawrence in *The Hunger Games* when she holds up her hand as tribute. She and Zoe are wearing shirts that say "I've Ridden a Bronco."

I roll my eyes heavenward.

Although a miniscule piece of me admits that shirt is cute.

I think back to his messages. If what Rider says is true,

Miranda doesn't pose a threat. And I owe it to both of us to hear him out and let him explain why he was hanging out with her.

By the time the game starts, I'm too focused on the field to care about her.

The game's intense. So intense, I barely breathe the first half. The Longhorns quickly pull ahead, but then Rider throws two touchdowns and we go into halftime tied.

I lose my voice sometime in the third quarter, and by the fourth, I've gnawed off all of my nails.

When we go into the last five minutes of play tied, again, I'm so choked up, I can barely breathe.

That's when I finally admit the truth: I have it bad for Rider.

72

RIDER

I'M TEMPTED.

For the first time since I spotted Gabby and Sienna in my seats, I let my eyes wander over to where she's standing with her hands folded under her chin.

If anyone were to ask me why I want to win the game, my automatic response would be for the team. For the coach who's always stood by me. For my roommates who have my back.

But the reason I *need* to win is huddled in the stands, shivering her cute little ass off, and my daughter, who's probably asleep in her great-grandmama's arms in that giant house Adele calls "a cottage."

"You okay there, Captain?" Tank asks as he steps into the huddle.

"It's all good."

You know, just gotta win the game, clinch a playoff berth, and get the girl back.

And nothing I've planned to get the girl back works if we don't win. I'm not an idiot—just because Sienna twisted Gabby's arm to get here doesn't mean she's forgiven me. I know I have my work cut out for me today.

But first things first—we're tied at forty with three minutes on the clock.

No pressure.

I take a deep breath.

"Who's ready to win this and put the Horns out of their misery?" I ask my guys. Their eyes spark with intensity as they shout in agreement.

We had a shitty return on the punt, so we're looking at seventy yards for a touchdown. We don't need a Hail Mary just yet, and I'm not ready to chance it when there's time on the clock.

When we break from the huddle, I clear my head of everything except the play I need to execute.

I smile to myself. Been dying to try this all season.

The ball snaps.

I drop into the pocket and pretend to search downfield. I fake a pass to Ben with my right hand, but the ball is in my left, which I hold out to Winston as he skirts by and hightails it downfield.

A beautiful Statue of Liberty handoff, if I do say so myself.

He runs it forty yards. Fuck yeah.

First down with thirty yards left.

Unfortunately, we get bogged down on the next play and still need twenty-five yards with a minute left.

On the next snap, UT blitzes, and those fuckers come at me full speed.

A brick wall of brown uniforms blaze my way, and I dodge the first guy, but the second one slams into my left shoulder, shoving me backwards.

God, no.

I'll kick my own ass if I get sacked right now.

Scrambling, I pray to the gods of gravity to keep me upright.

With a heartbeat to spare before I go down on my ass, my peripheral vision snags on that beautiful Bronco uniform in the end zone, and I gun it over the bodies that close over that small window.

I hit the ground hard, the wind getting knocked out of me, but I'm too busy trying to figure out if I nailed that pass to breathe.

A silence descends over the stadium. A million lifetimes condense into that split second.

Then the crowd roars as Trevor catches my pass for a touchdown, and I gasp for air.

Hell, yeah. Looks like we're winning this game.

Standing on the sidelines as we nail the extra point through the goal post, I smile as my teammates smack me on the back. The crowd is so loud, I can't hear anything except the roar of excitement.

I turn to the stands, like I have for so many games, but when my eyes snag on Gabby, I realize I have a family. Damn, I've missed her.

She and Sienna and Bree are hopping around and yelling, but like she feels me watching, Gabby turns to me and mouths, *Oh, my God! You did it!*

And for the moment that our eyes connect, there's no turmoil between us, no arguments or misunderstandings or hurt feelings. She has no idea how much it means to me that she put all of our shit aside and came today to support me.

It makes me love her even more.

The crowd starts to rush the field when the clock runs out. A mass of fans are headed right toward us. Against the traffic, I bolt toward the stands and leap up to hang off the railing.

Gabby's gorgeous smile greets me, but before she can say anything, I lean up, grab her beautiful face, and kiss her.

As soon as our lips meet, all the puzzle pieces click together.

This is what's been missing in my life. This woman right here. And now that I have Gabriela, I'm not letting go.

73

GABBY

I SMILE against his mouth as he ends a kiss I'll probably still be thinking about when I'm old and gray.

"Come on, baby." Rider motions like he wants me to freaking scale the railing.

My eyes widen. I look around. Everyone else is headed onto the field to celebrate.

Bree motions to the field. "Girl, get your ass down there."

My roommate waves me on in agreement.

I pull Sienna and Bree into a group hug. "Thank you. For everything." I wouldn't be here right now to celebrate this win with Rider if it weren't for Sienna, and Bree has listened to me whine all week.

Sienna whispers, "Go get your guy before the succubus tries to ruin our moment."

Miranda rushes up to our group and starts gushing over Rider. He motions for her to come closer since he's hanging off the railing. When she leans down, he growls, "Stay away from Gabby. If you get anywhere near her again, I'm getting a restraining order. Is that clear?"

She pales and her eyelashes start fluttering. "But Rider, I thought maybe—"

"I mean it. Back the fuck off."

Bree nudges her out of the way and mumbles something in her direction as Miranda edges away.

And then Rider reaches for me and gives me the sexiest grin. "I got you, Gabs. Trust me."

Trust me.

I blow out a breath. Can I trust Rider?

As I look down into his gray eyes brimming with emotion, everything in my heart says I can.

I say a little prayer I don't die as I swing one leg over, but he's there to catch me before I break my face.

I'm just about to plant both feet on the ground when he swings me into his arms. I laugh as he kisses me and spins me around.

"Glad you could make it."

To think I almost missed this game. Sienna was right. I never would've forgiven myself for not coming today. "I'm so proud of you! You did it."

"*We* did it. You and me. Poppy and I never would've survived without you. Without you sending Adele the other day, I wouldn't even be here today. I owe you so much, I don't know where to begin."

Those words hit me hard, and I give him a teary smile.

I would do all of those things again because I love you. I want to say it. I almost say it, but someone bumps me from behind, and I chicken out.

He rubs his nose against mine, not seeming to care that hundreds of fans are rushing the field around us, patting him on the back, vying for attention, but he only sees me. "We're doing something to honor Coach since this is his last home game, but can you stick around so we can hang out after all this? So we can talk?"

I nod, hating that we didn't clear the air sooner. I obviously need to get the whole story about what happened with his father on that phone call earlier this week, but based on how Rider's looking at me, he's just as excited to have me here as I am to see him.

Threading his fingers through mine, he tugs me along through the crowd until we reach a makeshift stage where the team is assembling. With a parting kiss, he trots up there. But when Ben sees me, he leaps off the stage and heads my way.

I'm speechless when he swoops me around in a hug.

After he sets me down, I place my palm on his damp forehead. "You okay? Did you get concussed?"

"Smartass."

"Takes one to know one."

We smile at each other. "Congrats, brother. Proud of you."

When Sienna pops up next to me, he lifts her in a hug too.

She cackles. "You're sweaty."

"You smell amazing," is his response.

My eyes widen. *What is going on?* Because I'm pretty sure she's dating some other guy on the team.

When Ben returns to the stage, I tug her hand. "You and my brother got a thing going on I don't know about?"

She blushes but shakes her head no. "I would never break girl code like that."

I have so many questions, but the presentation is starting, and I have to bite my tongue.

Bree joins us, and we watch Coach Sullivan get choked up when the players present him with a huge, engraved crystal plaque. After he says a few words that have everyone wiping their eyes, he calls over Rider. "Time to give away the game-time ball! This here is what it looks like to have the heart of a champion."

He hands Rider the mic, and the crowd freaks out. He describes how Sully helped him become the quarterback he is today. He thanks his other coaches and the O-line before he makes eye contact with me as he holds up his football. "I'd like to dedicate this to my daughter and my gorgeous girlfriend Gabby. I love you, sweetheart. Thanks for having my back. I promise I'll always have yours."

Oh, my God.

My friends shriek in excitement as tears well in my eyes, and I shout the words back to him. "I love you too, Rider!"

The wait to see him after the press conference and postgame hoopla feels like it lasts forever, but when he finally walks toward me in his suit, I leap into his arms.

And I promise myself I'm never letting go.

74

GABBY

We drive in silence, my hand cradled in his as he maneuvers through town. The sun is setting, sending long shadows across the manicured lawns. After not seeing him all week, my body is buzzing with excitement to be near him again. Adele is babysitting Poppy until tomorrow morning, and we have all evening to talk through everything.

When we pull up to his empty driveway, I frown. "Where is everyone?" We were practically the last people to leave the stadium.

He lifts my hand to his mouth where he presses a kiss. "Out."

"I figured your house would be bursting with people by now."

"Not tonight." He smiles at the confusion on my face. "I'm over parties. Kinda have my hands full with a kid, school, football, and a girlfriend."

My insides feel like a whole field of butterflies have taken flight. I don't think I'll ever get tired of hearing him call me that.

After exiting the car, he comes around to open my door. He closes my jacket and kisses my forehead before he tucks my arm into his and leads me through his house. We come out in the backyard, where my mouth drops open. I've only been out here once, and while it has some nice amenities with a pool, hot tub, and bar, I wouldn't describe it as romantic.

But it's definitely romantic now.

"Hold on a sec." He dips behind the bar, flips a few switches, and the firepit lights just as soft music croons from speakers somewhere. Even though it's December and it was cold all afternoon, it's not so bad now, but this is Texas, so this kind of crazy weather is to be expected. "The guys cleaned the hot tub for us, so if we wanna take a dip, it's all set."

"This is beautiful." White twinkle lights zigzag from one end of the deck to the other. By the jacuzzi, all kinds of desserts and champagne are laid out. From behind the bar, he pulls out a box and opens it to show me a steaming mushroom, black olive, and pepperoni pizza. My favorite. "Did you do all of this?"

"Had a little help. Bree and Tank did the decorations. Olly had friends set up the food after the game so it would be hot." A bashful smile crosses his lips. "Ben got you the tickets, and Sienna... well, she might've yanked some spark plugs outta your car."

A laugh bursts out of me. "You're kidding."

"Nope. Had to get my girl to give me another chance, and that meant calling in the troops."

He pulls me to him, and I drape my arms over his neck. "Listen, I'm sorry—"

"I wanted to apologize—"

I smile as he leans down to kiss me. "Go ahead."

He shakes his head. "I'm an idiot. Once I got some perspective, I realized you were right to question Miranda. I'm so sorry you got tangled up in her bullshit. I can't believe you got fired. I've been fucking wrecked about that."

My heart twinges, still bruised from the hits I took this week, but it helps to hear these words. "Thank you for saying that.

Obviously, Archer isn't the place for me. Barstow treated me like crap the whole time, but when he fired me he was brutal."

"I'm so sorry, babe." Shaking his head, Rider glances away. "That's what's weird. Having Miranda offer legal help in the face of all of the paternity crap and yet her dad was busy firing you. And Bree said he had pics of you that weren't published on any blogs." He pauses. "I asked Miranda about that."

"What did she say?"

"She pretended she didn't know what I was talking about, and when I called bullshit, she tried to make the moves on me."

I glare. "And? Got anything else to get off your chest? Do I need to punch you in the throat?" I'm teasing, but only a little.

A slow smile spreads on his mouth. "The only thing I need to declare is that I love you, Gabriela Duran, and would never hook up with anyone, even if we were arguing or on the outs."

My eyes fill, and I try to blink them away, but one manages to slide down my cheek. He cradles my face and wipes it gently with his thumb.

"To be clear, I was talking to her on Tuesday about her father's offer to help me with an attorney, which, for the record, I did not accept. But that's the only thing that happened. I swear it on my career. I know this has been the shittiest week ever, but even with all of the pressure I had this week—the hearing, the game, our argument, Poppy catching a cold—I would never do anything shady behind your back."

"I've missed you." My voice wobbles as it hits me how close I came to running away and tanking something so good in my life. "I was just so hurt by everything. Getting fired and then seeing you and Miranda looking like you had picked up where you left off earlier this semester."

He cringes, his eyes earnest. "Nothing at all happened between us."

I sniffle. "I get it. It probably didn't help that she confronted me the day before."

"What?"

I recap the horrid conversation before I sigh. "To be clear, it was Zoe who said everything, but Miranda stood there, giving her stamp of approval and trying to come off as being the nice one. But yeah. Basically said you ditched me freshman year because you wanted to be with her."

When I finally look up, Rider's jaw is tight, and I can see that little vein pulse in his temple. "Shit did *not* happen like that freshman year. I did *not* end things to be with her, and I definitely didn't leave any door open to get back with her this year. Baby, I've been clear with her that things are over."

I nod, offering a relieved smile. Hearing the indignation in his voice, seeing how angry he is about Miranda and her lies, knowing that he believes me—this is what I've needed to hear.

"I didn't realize she and Zoe were friends." I chew on my bottom lip while I think back to last spring. "Zoe was the girl who got me laid off from my tutoring job. When I called in sick for those few days when I was dealing with my hypoglycemia, she never passed along those messages to my boss."

He closes his eyes, and when he opens them again, they're full of regret. "Miranda was with me when I saw you pass out. She was pissed I stayed with you to wait for the ambulance. She and Zoe used to be roommates and have always been tight."

He doesn't have to voice what we're both thinking—that Miranda had Zoe get me fired from that job too.

"I'm so sorry, baby." He pulls me back into a tight hug. "Bree said several of the photos Miranda's dad had were from the same series."

"Yeah, but only one was posted on any blogs. The one where I'm hanging over your shoulder, waving a red Solo cup, but there were several more taken, like they were shot a few seconds apart.

That's what I found suspicious, that Barstow would have access to all of those when only one was available online."

"The whole thing is fucking suspicious. I'm wrecked you got wrapped up in Miranda's crazy shit."

Laying my head on his chest, I sigh. "The party—that's on me. I should've been more careful and paid better attention to my surroundings. Funny thing is, I don't regret that night. That was a big win for you and the guys, and I'm grateful I got to celebrate it with you."

He kisses the top of my head. "That night was special for me too."

My whole chest fills with warmth when I think about what happened between us after that win. How intimate we got. How much that whole experience meant to me.

I clear my throat, needing to say one more thing. But, God, this is embarrassing. Except I need to know the answer. "Can I ask why you never went that far with me freshman year?"

When his expression goes blank and it's clear he hasn't a clue what I'm talking about, I plod on, despite the burning in my face. "We only kissed. You kept things pretty tame when that was not your standard operating... practice. Was it because I was a virgin?" I accused him of this at Target, but we never talked about it. "Or because I told you I was a foster kid?"

He grabs my hand and rubs it between his, a pained look in his eyes. "Honestly? I wasn't ready for you, and I think a part of me realized it. I knew if we went there, things would get serious, fast, and I wasn't prepared for that step. In my gut, I knew you were a forever kind of girl."

A forever kind of girl? Biting my bottom lip, I nod. "But... you're ready now?"

"More than you know." He kisses my forehead. "And of course it wasn't the foster kid thing. You've seen my sad excuse for a home. I'd never judge where you came from."

I smile. Deep down, I already knew this, but since we're clearing the air, I don't want to hang on to any reservations, however miniscule. If we have any hope of making it long term, I know we have to communicate better.

He's leaning down for a kiss when my mind finally processes something he said a few minutes ago. "Wait. Poppy was sick? What happened?"

"She's fine now, but she caught a bug this week, which made everything worse because she wasn't feeling well."

"Poor baby." I feel terrible I didn't talk things out sooner. "I wish I had been there for you guys. It's just... I came over the day after our argument and... overheard something."

His eyes soften. "You heard me talking to my dad."

"Yes. How did you know?"

"I eventually put it all together because Tank said you came over as he was leaving for practice."

That horrible day comes back to me, and I cringe. "Right. So..." I shift away, but he tightens his grip on my waist.

"Don't walk away. I know what you heard, and I'm so sorry it hurt your feelings. I tried to tell him what he wanted to hear to get him off my back. Just like that damn press conference. The school's PR person told me to keep the story simple, that I probably didn't want to bring you into it unless you were ready to deal with the haters, and with where things stood between us, I wasn't sure you wanted that kind of pressure."

When I don't look at him, he lifts my chin.

"Gabby, you know I don't have a problem claiming you as mine, right? I love you, and I'm ready to tell the whole fucking world. You're the only woman who's met my crazy-ass father. You're the only woman I want in my daughter's life. You're the person I want standing next to me at the draft. Do you hear me? You."

Everything in me melts. I don't want to cling to this anger anymore. "So I'm yours, huh?"

"One hundred and ten percent. And I'm all yours too. Starting with this."

And he grabs my hand and places it on his heart.

GABBY

The steady rhythm of Rider's heart beats beneath my palm. I slide my hands up his shoulders and stare at him as shadows from the firepit play across his face.

"I love you too, Rider. I think I have for a long time."

"If I'm being honest, I never got over you freshman year," he whispers. "And I'm sorry I ran. But I'm not running anymore. I'm not that freaked-out kid any longer. I'm ready for this."

He kisses me. Deep and long and hard. Electricity shoots through me. Down my spine. Zinging lower.

And then I'm in his arms. My feet leave the ground, and I wrap them around his waist.

With a panting breath, I rip my mouth away and rub his shoulder. "Are you sore? Do you need to ice anything?" The man played four quarters of the most intense football game I've ever seen. Maybe I shouldn't be scaling him like a jungle gym.

A wolfish grin tugs at his lips. "I definitely have something that needs attention," he mutters as he grinds his enormous erection between my legs.

I chuckle and thread my fingers through his hair. "Well, we can't have that. I should probably check for swelling."

"And swelling you shall find."

Laughing, I slide down his big body and gently push him down on to the bench behind him, where I stand between his splayed legs. I glance around, but the trees in the backyard block the view from his neighbors.

"The guys promised to be out all night, and no one can see back here. The side gates are always locked."

"Does this mean you're all mine tonight?"

"Tonight. Tomorrow night. Every night."

My heart swells with love. With gratitude for this second chance that we've been granted.

Since I'm warmer now with the heat of the firepit behind me, an exterior patio heater I hadn't noticed before, and the wall of Rider's solid body in front of me, I slip off my jacket and Bronco t-shirt until I'm down to my long-sleeved Henley that buttons to the middle of my chest.

I'm not typically a strip-down-in-the-backyard kind of girl, but after a day of so many firsts, I'm feeling bold.

With a grin, I unhook my bra and tug it out through the arms of my shirt. After I pull out my ponytail and shake my hair, I glance up shyly as I pop out each button on my shirt, until it gapes open on my chest.

"You're fucking beautiful, Gabriela, inside and out. So sexy and sweet. I'm lucky to have you in my life." He reaches out, tangles his hand in my hair, and places open-mouth kisses on my lips, my neck, down to my chest, where he nudges aside my shirt and sucks one very attention-starved nipple into his mouth.

Groaning, I let my head fall back while he laves my skin, all the while palming my other breast in his giant hand.

"Let's take care of that swelling," I tease as I sink down onto my knees.

I graze his muscular thighs with my nails as I slide them

against the smooth fabric of his slacks. "You look handsome as hell in this suit, by the way." But it doesn't hide a thing when he's in this state. I outline his thick length with my finger. "This looks serious, sir."

His heated stare has me squirming even though I'm the one unclothing him. First the button, then the zipper, until I reach his boxer briefs, which are stretched to the brink. When I release him from the fabric, he springs up to greet me.

"Missed me, huh?"

"You have no idea." He laughs while he runs his hand through my hair.

I lick the drop of moisture off his wide head before I suck it. Softly at first. Teasing with licks until he gives me a pained groan.

Watching him watch me is turning me on so much, I squeeze my thighs together to ease the pressure.

When his jaw clenches, I take him to the back of my throat. Work him over with my hand. Hum in approval when he fists my hair.

I'm surprised when he gently pulls me off him.

"It's my turn." His gravelly voice sizzles through me, and I nod. He motions toward the hot tub. "Wanna take a dip?"

"I don't have a swimsuit." I laugh when I realize I'm standing there with my shirt open, and his pants are halfway down his hips. "But maybe we don't need them."

We watch each other as we strip out of our clothes. I shiver, but then he wraps my shoulders in a thick towel.

He drags the heater closer to the hot tub and spreads out another towel. Pats the edge. "Sit here."

I do as he says, curious as to what he has planned.

Studying the planes and ridges of his incredible body, I watch as he slowly descends into the water. When he stands between my legs and gently pushes me back to lie down, I figure it out.

He kisses one ankle, then the other, as he places them on his shoulders. A low sexy groan rumbles in his chest when he drags a thick finger through me. "Damn. You're so wet."

"What can I say? I'm a giver."

"I fucking love it." The sound of his voice gets muffled as he works me over. Long, slow licks that have me arching and groaning. One finger joins in, pushing deeply into me. Then two.

I don't know if it's being out in the backyard and mildly exposed, or being splayed out for him, hanging halfway into the hot tub with my legs over his shoulders, or the way he touches me, like I'm the most erotic woman he's ever been with, but I'm cresting in record time.

"Oh, God, I'm coming." My legs tremble and my whole body tightens. It feels so good, I can't keep my enthusiasm contained. A scream rips from my body.

He doesn't stop, though. Just works me through it. Slows his movements. But the steady rhythm has me panting all over again.

"Rider. Babe. I want you in me." He helps me sit up. I'm sex-drunk and woozy from coming so hard and getting right up to the edge again. When I sink into the water and into his lap, I groan from the contact. "I need you."

"I'm here. I'll always be here." His whispered words are the promises I've yearned to hear from him. He gently strokes my cheek. Kisses my temple. "Let me grab a condom." He reaches over me toward his clothes, but I stop him.

"I'm on the pill if you want to… go bare." I've been on it since I decided to start dating again this fall, but I wasn't ready to forego other protection until I was sure he was committed. "If you're worried about accidents, we don't have to. I've actually never gone without."

He turns back to me and wraps me in his arms. "You're the most responsible person I know, so no, I'm not worried. And when we're both ready for more kids, we'll definitely revisit this topic."

I smile from the depths of my soul, loving that he's talking about our future like this. Of course I want to have Rider's babies. Lots of them. Someday. A brood of brothers and sisters for our beautiful little Poppy.

"I've never gone without a condom before either," he admits, "but I like having this first with you. I want the rest of your firsts too."

"They're yours," I whisper against his lips.

Hands tight on my hips, he stares into my eyes as he works his way into me. It's intense. Sublime as he stretches me. Just on the brink of pain, but on this side of bliss as he fills me and our bodies rub against one another in the water.

"I love you, Gabby. I never want to be apart from you again."

"Never again. It's a promise."

"Let's always work it out." He grits out the words.

"Always," I pant.

Dipping one hand into the water, he rubs tight circles on my swollen clit, and I can't hang on any longer. "Rider!" I bury my face in his shoulder as I come. He pulls me down harder and erupts inside of me.

We hold each other, shivering from the aftershocks, overheated from the water and steam and intensity.

I smile against his skin. "I'm going to make you so happy."

He kisses the top of my head. "You already do, baby. More than you know."

76

RIDER

ONE MONTH LATER

A HAND PRESSES AGAINST MINE, which are thrumming anxiously on the steering wheel. I turn to look at Gabby, who gives me a reassuring smile.

She points to a billboard with a photo from our championship game, and I shake my head with a laugh. "The parade wasn't enough? The town needed a giant sign?"

"The townies love you guys, and everyone's proud. Plus, there might be two more signs."

"Are you serious?"

She nods and chuckles at my expression. "Get used to it, champ."

"It's weird to look up and see a giant photo of my face."

She grabs my chin and gives me a smooch. "Good thing this is a pretty mug."

I snort and thread my fingers through hers. Only Gabby could get me to laugh today. I was a nervous wreck this morning. "Thanks for coming with me. Adele swore Cricket wanted to meet us, but this still feels awkward as hell."

Cricket has been in rehab since she returned last month, but she couldn't see visitors until now. She got wrapped up in some heavier drugs when she went out west, but Adele got her to agree to get some help if she came home.

"Not even a Heisman or national championship can prepare a man for this kind of thing," I mutter as I stare at the facility, which looks like a fancy hotel. But just like all the other crazy moments this year, Gabby is right by my side. "What if seeing us makes her relapse?"

"She's in a place where professionals can help her if she struggles. That's why Adele agreed it was a good idea to do it now, but if things don't go well, Poppy and I can wait here."

In the back seat, my daughter hears her name and babbles back to us.

I'm so conflicted about everything, except I want to do what's right for Poppy, and getting off to a good foot now with Cricket will only help down the road. I don't want to be one of those people who argue over a kid. That wouldn't be healthy for my daughter, so I'm setting aside my reservations to try to mend this bridge.

It helps that Gabby is so supportive. After everything she went through with Miranda, I wouldn't blame her if she didn't want to meet Cricket or be involved today, but my woman is amazing. She says that Poppy comes first and agrees this is a good step.

My girlfriend sends me off with a kiss, and I head in, hoping I'm making the right decision.

"Mr. Kingston," a receptionist greets me. "We're expecting you. This way."

She escorts me down a long hallway. This could be the Four Seasons for how nicely it's decorated. Were it not for the security cameras and locked main entrance, I wouldn't know the difference.

She knocks on one of the rooms, and my heart pounds as I enter behind her. "Cricket, dear, you have a visitor." The receptionist closes the door behind me.

The waify woman who greets me is not what I expect. For one, I don't recognize her. At all. Two, she looks like a little fairy princess with long, blonde hair, but is so slender, she might disappear behind the curtains if she steps behind them. Third, she gets right to the point.

With an embarrassed smile, she introduces herself. "Hi, Rider. I'm Adele's granddaughter." She twists her hands together. "Sorry I drugged you and got knocked up."

From what Adele tells me, Cricket was just as surprised by the strength of those brownies as I was.

Blowing out a breath, I fix a smile on my face and hold out my hand. "Nice to formally meet you." After a tense minute of silence, I just admit it. "I'm sorry, but I don't really remember you."

She grimaces. "It's okay. I don't remember you either. And you're definitely not the kind of guy a girl forgets."

I shift. Run a hand through my hair. "Things obviously got out of hand. I'm so sorry if… I ever did anything you didn't want me to do." God, this is awkward.

"Please, don't apologize to me. I'm sorry my asshole dealer gave me a bag of pot laced with PCP, and I made an extra-big batch of brownies."

Well, that would explain how Knox landed in someone's garden naked.

Damn, I guess we're all lucky no one did anything extra-crazy and died that day.

She rubs her hand down her arm. "Is Poppy doing well?"

I'm still reeling from her admission. I clear my throat. "She's great. She's here with my girlfriend Gabby if you want to see her," I say hesitantly. Adele assured me she would make sure

Cricket knew I was in a committed relationship so there would be no confusion.

Her head bobs.

I have no problem accepting her apologies for what happened to me that weekend. People make mistakes. I get it. But I do have a problem with how she dropped off the baby.

"Can I ask a question?" When she agrees, I ask, "Why did you leave Poppy at my house like that? Why didn't you talk to me? I'm not an ogre. We could've discussed things like adults."

Her eyes fill with tears. "I'm so horrified to admit this, but..." She sniffles. Wipes her eyes. "I wasn't sure who the father was. I kept seeing the Broncos on TV because y'all were doing so well. I thought it was a sign, that I needed to get Poppy to her father."

She's full-on crying now. I hand her a box of tissues that's sitting on her coffee table. Sensing she needs a minute, I'm quiet.

After she blows her nose, more tears stream down her face. "Now that I'm here and have had time to process everything, I feel like the worst human on the planet. Like, how could I leave her like that? Anything could've happened to her. I just felt so overwhelmed and couldn't stand it any longer. I know I should've talked to you or one of your roommates, but I felt so ashamed."

It might take me some time to come to terms with this, but after watching my father struggle with an addiction his entire life and still not beat it, I want Cricket to know I'm on her side. Gabby and I are on her side.

"Everything worked out. I'm not crazy about how it happened, but she's one of the best things to ever happen to me." I pat her shoulder awkwardly.

I don't want to be angry at her anymore. Life's too short. She knows she made a mistake and obviously wants to make amends. Hell, I'm not sure I would've known what I would've done in her position, so I can't go throwing stones.

"Poppy's doing well. I love her so much. She's getting big." The more I talk, the calmer she grows. "You should see her with my roommates. It's like she has a house of uncles. She's never lacking for love or attention. My girlfriend..." I trail off when I think of how much Gabby has done for me. "She's amazing. She helps me so much with Poppy. Gabby loves her. Adores her, really."

"So you don't hate me?"

I take a deep breath. "You carried the most precious human for nine months. How could I hate you?"

She gives me a watery smile. "Do you think Poppy remembers me?" she whispers, her voice pained.

I nod. "Yeah, I do. Want to see her?"

When she agrees, I call Gabby on my cell. A few minutes later, she and Poppy come through the door, and my heart fills with warmth. God, I love them. I kiss Gabby and grab her hand.

"Cricket, this is my girlfriend Gabby." Now that I understand how Gabby felt before I announced we were together, I use the g-word whenever I can. I never want her to doubt me again.

And someday soon, I'm planning to level up to the w-word. *Wife.* Because Gabriela Duran is *it* for me.

My daughter stares at her birth mother and grins. She reaches out an arm to Cricket, but when Cricket tries to hold her, Poppy makes grabby hands for Gabby until the two women are standing side by side so my gremlin can hug them both.

I have no idea how we're all going to work through this, but with Gabby in my life, I know we will. For the sake of my new family.

EPILOGUE

GABBY

Huddling into Rider, I smile. We're freezing our tails off, but I don't care. This is too cool.

"Do you realize we're sitting in the same seats I had a year ago when you beat UT?" I mean, the exact same seats.

"No kidding?" His eyes are lasered to the players on the field. Pretty sure he wants to leap down there and play with them.

I tuck the Broncos blanket around us. Lowering my voice to a whisper, I add, "This game isn't as good, but I might be biased."

The Broncos are losing.

"Give the boys a chance. There's still time."

I stare at his stoic profile. He's so serious when he's watching a game.

The team is honoring him today by naming a scholarship after him during halftime. Coach Sully is here, and several of Rider's teammates came too.

Another student skids to a halt when he sees my boyfriend. "Holy shit, it's you. Man, I'm a huge fan. Like, huge!"

The last twelve months have catapulted Rider into mega-athlete-stardom, but he still tries to talk to everyone who approaches him, especially when he's on campus.

"Hey." Rider gives him an easy smile, which I know takes effort since he's trying to pay attention to the game. The team has had a tough time transitioning to a new coach, but I think they're finally coalescing under the different style of leadership.

Rider chats with the fan a few minutes and signs some autographs, but when the timer on his phone goes off, he excuses himself and turns to me. "Don't forget. Stay put or I'll never find you."

I point to the seat beneath me. "I'll be right here." After he kisses me on the forehead, he stares at me a long moment. "What?"

"Nothing. Just feeling lucky I have you. You look amazing in my jersey, by the way."

I won't lie. I've always wanted to wear his old Broncos jersey. "Well, I'm incredibly proud of you. Go get more accolades." I wave my hand toward the field. Then I whisper in his ear, "When we get to the hotel, I'm gonna take everything off *except* the jersey."

"Mm. Love the sound of that, Gabriela."

I never thought I'd get so turned on by the sound of my name.

He plants a kiss on me that gets the students around us cheering. I laugh and playfully shove him away.

Without his body heat, it's cold and my butt goes numb as I sit here, but I don't care. I'm having too much fun. His NFL games in Dallas are amazing, but there's something really special about being on Bronco turf.

I'm almost teary-eyed when I think back to standing in this spot during his UT game last year. If I hadn't given in and gone to that game, I would've missed so much—the Cotton Bowl. His championship. The Heisman. All his hard work paid off when he went number one in the draft.

My heart swells with pride and love for that man.

For a moment, I close my eyes in thanks. That Rider and I got on the right track. That we fought to make it through so much. That we're the best of friends. That we're still crazy about each other.

And tonight we can get as loud as we want since Adele is watching Poppy!

While I'm loving my first official teaching job in Dallas, I'm definitely grateful for this long weekend away with Rider and plan to make the most of it.

During halftime, the band does a number, and then the cheerleaders form a circle in the middle of the field. The president of the university walks out there with Rider, and the crowd goes crazy when he gets introduced.

My boyfriend accepts an award, says some nice things about his time here, but then he peers into the stands, pausing when he sees me.

"This is where I'm gonna need your help, Broncos. See that beautiful woman over there? Gabby, baby, can you wave?"

Holy crap. *What's he doing?*

The woman next to me elbows me. "He's talking to you, right?"

I nod slowly, speechless. Like he asked, I wave back at him, even more confused when he stalks toward me, mic in hand.

"Gabby Duran is my best friend. My ride-or-die. I love her so much, it's a little scary, if ya know what I mean."

My mouth drops open.

He talks to the crowd like there aren't tens of thousands of people in the arena. "For the last several months, I've had a really important question I've been dying to ask her. And since

Lone Star Arena is where I first told her I loved her, I figure there's no better place than our home turf to do this."

The crowd goes crazy. My heart's in my throat.

No way.

"And from what I know about women, you gotta make the grand gesture, right?"

Oh, my God.

"So that's where y'all come in."

I race down to the rail so I can see him peering up at me.

"Babe, our friends here are gonna help me out. Starting over by the tunnel." The entire section unfurls an enormous sign that says, "WILL." He points to the next that says "YOU."

"MARRY."

"ME?"

The look of love on his face does me in, and tears spring to my eyes.

But then eighty thousand people start chanting, "Say yes! Say yes! Say yes!"

I cover my mouth with one hand and hold on to the railing with the other because I need something to steady myself.

He tucks the mic into the back pocket of his jeans and looks into my eyes. "Gabriela, I love you with my whole heart and soul. You're everything I've ever wanted in a best friend and girlfriend. Make me the happiest man on the planet and be my wife."

Then he freaking scales the stands and leaps over the rails, landing in front of me with a laugh. Going down on one knee, he reaches into his pocket and holds out a black velvet box.

Before he even opens it, I grab his face with both hands. "Yes, you crazy man. I will marry you."

He grabs the mic and yells, "She said yes!" before he drops it, pulls me into his arms, and dips me for a kiss. When we part, he rubs his cold nose over mine and smiles. "I promise I'll be a good husband."

"I have no doubt about it." I pepper kisses all over his cheek. "I promise to be a good wife and mother."

"Poppy and I are so lucky to have you."

"I'm the lucky one. Love you, Rider."

I'm pretty sure I always will.

And that's how we started our own happily ever after.

BONUS SCENE
EXTENDED HEA

GABBY

"Your son is obsessed."

Aiden's little face screws up to match Rocky's on the screen as he mimics the sit-ups. Ever since my husband watched *Rocky* last week, our three-year-old begs us to turn it on so he can do the workout scene.

Rider grins. "That's my boy."

With a laugh, I shake my head and try to scoot past Rider, who's sitting on the couch, but like lightning, he swipes an arm around my waist and tugs me into his lap. But I land gently, because Rider is always careful when I'm in this state.

I trail my fingers through his thick hair. "The party yesterday was out of control."

"I know. I'm sorry." He tries to contain his smile when he kisses me but fails.

"Don't pretend like you're sorry. Or that it won't happen again. Can you imagine what the neighbors must be saying right now?"

Kiss. Kiss. Longer kiss.

"It's true. We had too many chicks."

We stare at each other a beat before we crack up.

"A petting zoo, Rider?" I snort as he rubs my growing belly.

"I can't help it. I wanna spoil her before the season starts."

I grab his beautiful face in both hands before I plant another kiss on his lips. "You're forgiven. Poppy was ecstatic. When you said I should leave the details to you, I was a bit skeptical, but you outdid yourself."

Our backyard was filled to the brim with every furry creature he could find. They were all penned in carefully and organized so the bigger animals wouldn't freak out the smaller ones. Adults supervised every child to ensure they were gentle with the animals. Most were rescues, and we used yesterday to showcase them to our neighbors and friends, many of whom adopted a furry friend or donated to the cause.

Poppy just turned seven, and she's absolutely precious to both of us. Maybe more so because she's the reason we got together in the first place.

When Rider is offseason or home between games, he's very hands-on with our children. Even when he travels, he checks in every day to video chat with me and the kids.

Our lives have been a whirlwind since we graduated, but in the best way.

We were ecstatic when Dallas drafted him. He even won himself a Super Bowl ring two years ago. And Rider's championship win his senior year garnered all the funding the Broncos needed to renovate their aging facility.

After my student-teaching stint, in which I figured out I enjoyed public school over Archer any day, I got a job at a Dallas high school. But having Poppy and then Aiden, I realized what I was missing during those college years when I was trying to figure out my life wasn't a teaching job, but having family.

Since Rider's season is so intense, I decided to homeschool

Poppy, which helped me stay involved with a field I found truly rewarding. We meet with several families that get together to teach our kids, and I'm having a blast. Poppy is doing so well, and because we're part of a larger coalition, she doesn't miss out on any sports or extra activities with other kids. Plus, the parents share the responsibilities across the different subjects so everything doesn't fall to just one person who might not have the expertise.

When I'm not prepping our class activities, I'm whipping up treats for my small baking side gig, which isn't so small these days. After I had so much luck licensing my baked goods to Rise 'N Grind, Rider encouraged me to pursue that. As a result, my mom's recipes formed the bedrock of my company Dulce, which now serves dozens of bakeries in Texas.

As I sit on his lap, engulfed in his muscular arms, I'm overwhelmed with gratitude.

"Whatcha smiling about there, sweet mama?" he whispers in my ear as he caresses my belly with a slow stroke.

"Just how lucky I am. How much I love our family." I tilt my head back to look at him. Trace a finger over his lean, stubbled jaw. "How much I love you."

"Love you too, baby." His lips descend to mine, and we're in our own little bubble for two point two seconds. Until a little voice goes, "Ew!"

We break apart to see our daughter standing there with her hands on her hips. "Y'all are always so kissy-kissy. Cody Stevenson says kissing's where babies come from. Is that how come we're getting another brother?" Poppy points to my belly. "Because of the kissing?"

No, it's because Daddy loves when Mommy gets new sex toys. I chuckle to myself and make a mental note to thank Sienna for her latest recommendation.

I feel Rider shake with silent laughter beneath me. "You're

getting another baby brother *or sister* because I love Mommy." Beneath his breath, he adds, "And I can't keep my hands off her."

Aww.

Cricket rushes in from the backyard. "Good news and bad news, my peeps. The good? We found the rogue goat. The bad? He got into Adele's garden."

Adele wanted to be near all the babies, and since we have a huge place, we invited her to move in with us last year. She's getting older, and this way we can keep an eye on her.

"Yikes. Well"—I pat Rider's chest—"guess I know what you're going to be doing next week."

He gives me a crooked grin. "Planting lots of eggplant."

I chuckle and kiss him again, and Cricket tosses a dishrag at us. "Hey, gross. I got that joke."

"What joke?" Poppy asks, looking between us.

Changing the subject, I try to scoot off Rider's lap, but laugh when he won't let me. Giving up, I ask Poppy, "Did you organize your toys?" When Poppy nods, I smile. This kid loves organizing almost as much as I do. "Let's go through your closet for anything we can give away."

Her little nose crinkles. "Why do we have to do this again? I like having lots of stuff."

"Not all kids have toys, and since you have some you don't play with anymore, I thought we could give some presents to children at this foster home I found and maybe make some new friends."

After a pause, she gives me a decisive nod. "I like that idea. Will you help me, Mommy?"

"Get started and I'll be up in ten minutes."

Before she leaves, she turns to Rider. "Daddy, can we put together the Ferris wheel puzzle tonight?"

"After dinner, squirt."

When she races off, she grabs Cricket and drags her behind her. I chuckle at the mock look of exasperation on Cricket's face.

Cricket told us early on she never had the parental gene but wanted to be in our lives in whatever capacity we were comfortable. Poppy knows Cricket is her birth mother, but considers me her mommy. That's never bothered Cricket, who likes that she's more like the nutty aunt who gets to swoop in on the weekends to spoil my kids. Since Rider and I both know what it's like to have a single parent, we figured the more people in Poppy's life who love her, the better. And since that rehab, Cricket has worked hard to stay sober.

I sink back onto Rider's lap and smile as I watch our son pretend he's a boxer. We have a few weeks before Rider has to go to training camp, so I want to soak in every minute I have with him.

"What time is Sully coming over?" I ask drowsily as Rider rubs my belly in a soothing rhythm.

"He'll be here for the barbecue."

We see Sully so much that Poppy calls him Gramps.

On a side note, "Gramps" has been making eyes at Adele for a while, but she'll never admit they're hooking up. Sometimes his car is in our driveway until morning. I can't bring myself to tease them about it. Yet.

I plant a quick kiss on Rider's handsome mug and scoot off his lap. With a groan, I attempt to straighten the family room, which looks like an F5 tornado just blew through.

"Leave it, babe. I'll clean up."

I give him a grateful smile, but I can't help straightening the photos on our fireplace that somehow got cockeyed.

Smiling, I study the photo of Adele and Sully at the Super Bowl. Both are wearing the Ride-or-Die t-shirts I made for our little crew of friends and fam. I trail my finger over our other photos. Pics of us with my cousins Tori and Kat and their families. Shots of us with Rider's old Bronco roommates, who had a big reunion last summer. Images with his new teammates.

Rider's father Hank is noticeably absent, but he refuses to visit. Once Rider got drafted, he bought Hank a house and set up a grocery delivery service to make sure he always has food. But Hank's so bitter, he refuses to make an effort. It breaks my heart that he won't try for his son. I think that just makes Rider more determined to be a better father for our own children.

I don't really see much of Aunt Carmen either, but I've stayed in touch with her girls. They know they can always reach out to us if they ever need anything.

Pausing at a photo of my brother, I glance at my husband. "Is Ben still up in the guest room?"

He and his wifey went upstairs to "take a nap." They've been visiting this week to celebrate Poppy's birthday and to help with the surprise I have planned for Rider later today.

It's been a tough road for me and my brother, but our relationship has come a long way.

Rider shakes his head. "Where's *my* nap, huh? I think Mommy needs to tuck me in."

I toss a throw pillow at him. My look says it all. *This morning wasn't enough?*

Fortunately, our son only pays attention to us when we talk about food. He's now jogging around the room with his arms raised in a victory lap, his pull-ups on the way to his knees.

"Child, get over here." I re-clothe my kid, kiss his sticky face, and give him the sniff test. "You're definitely getting a bath tonight."

"Na da baff."

"Yes, the bath, champ. Even Rocky took baths."

He pauses at that. Looks at his dad, who nods. But because Aiden has the attention span of a squirrel, he scampers off to roll around in his makeshift fort.

"I'd do anything to have that kind of energy." I sigh and sit my pregnant ass down on the couch next to Rider, who says he'll be right back and heads to the kitchen. I need to regroup so I can help Poppy go through her toys, but my God, I'm tired.

"Eat." He hands me the most beautiful thing I've seen all day. Finger foods. Sandwiches, cut into quarters. Apple slices. Cheese—so much cheese. Green and black olives. Nuts. He's a charcuterie board genius. I'm so excited, I almost cry.

I still have a hard time remembering to eat sometimes. When Rider's home, he's always making sure my blood sugar doesn't get low. When he's working, he sets timers on my phone so I don't get run down.

"When did you do this?" Grinning, I double-fist mini-sandwiches and shovel them in to my mouth.

"After I spoke to Brian." His agent.

Ugh. "I almost forgot. I'm afraid to ask."

After what happened in college, we both turned off our social media notifications. Rider is constantly in the spotlight, so people are going to talk. Most is good, but a lot can be negative or critical or just plain mean. We decided a long time ago that if we really needed to see something, his agent will let us know. We'd rather focus on our family than waste energy dealing with negativity, most of which we can't do anything about anyway.

"Miranda's getting sued for trying to blackmail the guy."

"Can't say I'm surprised."

He rubs my shoulder. "She threatened him with photos of him passed out and naked."

Sienna always tells me to leave it up to karma, that people get what they deserve. She points to Zoe Evans as a prime example. Zoe had a few million followers online, married some celebrity, and wrote a book about what it takes to make a marriage. Only for everyone to find out that she and her husband had both been cheating on each other.

And who was Zoe's husband cheating on her with? Miranda. Who was blackmailing him.

"Aren't you glad you married me instead of her?" We always wondered if Miranda had something to do with his paternity scandal hitting the media when it did. Maybe she was upset he was dating me and wanted revenge or somehow thought a scandal would break us up. I frown when I think about how close we got to letting that happen.

"Babe." He kisses my temple. "She was never an option."

"Really? You never considered marrying Miranda?"

The horrified expression on his face makes me laugh. "God, no." He looks me up and down. "You, on the other hand... Had to lock you up tight, as quickly as possible."

"To think you almost lost your chance," I say playfully as I pinch his side.

"Stop rewriting history. I always knew you were the one."

I'm still smiling as I help Poppy and Cricket figure out which toys we can donate to the foster home. By six o'clock, another flurry of activity has everyone rushing around the kitchen to prepare for the barbecue.

Rider doesn't know it yet, but I have a teeny-tiny surprise for him.

Once we're assembled outside for the barbecue, I greet our guests.

"Thanks for coming, guys," I say loudly so everyone in the backyard can hear me. "It means a lot to Rider and me that you could spend some time with us this summer before you head off to training camp."

I could've done this yesterday, but I didn't want to take away the focus from Poppy's birthday. Our girl deserved her special day.

Rider steps up to me and wraps a thick arm around my shoulder.

I clear my throat. "Honey, I have a surprise for you and the kids."

His eyebrows lift. "You got us a boat?"

I shake my head. "Boats are dangerous. No."

Everyone chuckles, and I run my hand up his chest. "This is even better, but you're definitely going to need to buckle up for the ride." I turn to the small crowd and call Poppy to our side. Adele comes closer with Aiden in tow. "I had a doctor's appointment this week that I *may* have forgotten to mention."

Rider's head jerks toward me. "What? Naughty girl." He gives my ass a little smack, and I laugh.

"I may have found out the sex of the baby. Are you ready?"

He nods excitedly. Rider lives for this kind of stuff.

I give Tank the signal, and he fires the paper cannon. Pink and blue streamers hit the sky.

At first, everyone's quiet, and Rider turns to me again. "Why are there two colors? Did they make a mistake?"

"Nope." I reach into my pocket and pull out the sonogram photos. "We're having twins! A boy *and* a girl! Congrats, stud! You're getting two-for-one."

"Holy shit. Are you serious?" Before I respond, he lifts me into the air and plants one on me.

"This is why they keep having babies," Poppy yells. "Daddy won't stop kissing her. I heard Mommy tell her friend she lives for his special kisses, whatever that means."

Rider's teammates howl, and I blush furiously.

My husband looks into my eyes and smiles. "And I never will stop kissing you. Love you, sweetheart. My little ride-or-die."

"Love you too." I rub his arm where he has his tattoos. A field of poppies for his daughter. Some jasmine, because that's my middle name. A blazing sun for Aiden, since the name was derived from the Celtic sun god and means 'fiery.' "You're going to have to start on the other arm."

"Hell yeah, I am." Leaning close, he whispers in my ear, "Don't tell the guys, but this might be better than winning the Super Bowl."

I thread my fingers through his hair. "So you're not freaked out?"

"With you by my side, pretty sure I can do anything. Having my babies, giving me a beautiful family, is about the best gift you could ever give me. Thank you, Gabriela."

I feel the same way. Rider is my home, and he always will be.

And the best part? We've only just begun.

TO MY READERS

Thank you for reading The Varsity Dad Dilemma! If you enjoyed it, I hope you'll leave a review. I try to read each one.

To receive an email the next time I release a book, be sure to be sure to **subscribe to my newsletter**, which you can do on my website, www.lexmartinwrites.com. I hope you'll stay in touch!

Did you know that The Varsity Dad Dilemma is a spinoff of The Texas Nights series? Those books kick off with **Shameless**, which is about Brady (the tattoo artist) and Kat (Gabby's cousin). Keep flipping to read the Shameless blurb.

SHAMELESS SYNOPSIS
A USA TODAY BESTSELLER

Brady...

What the hell do I know about raising a baby? Nothing. Not a goddamn thing.

Yet here I am, the sole guardian of my niece. I'd be lost if it weren't for Katherine, the beautiful girl who seems to have all the answers. Katherine, who's slowly finding her way into my cynical heart.

I keep reminding myself that I can't fall for someone when we don't have a future. But telling myself this lie and believing it are two different things.

Katherine...

When Brady shows up on a Harley, looking like an avenging angel—six feet, three inches of chiseled muscle, eyes the color of wild sage, and sun-kissed skin emblazoned with tattoos—I'm not sure if I should fall at his feet or run like hell. Because if I tell him what happened the night his family died, he might hate me.

What I don't count on are the nights we spend together trying to forget the heartache that brought us here. I promise him it won't mean anything, that I won't fall in love.

I shouldn't make promises I can't keep.

Each book in the Texas Nights series features a different couple and can be read as a standalone.

ACKNOWLEDGMENTS

Thanks for reading The Varsity Dad Dilemma! Even though it's technically a spinoff of the Texas Nights series (who recognized Brady and Kat?), the sweet, fictional town of Charming, Texas felt like a new world for me. I really enjoyed this deep dive into college life and hope you did too!

Growing up, I watched countless Notre Dame games with my dad, who enjoyed critiquing my Varsity Dad football scenes and gave them a thumbs up. (FYI, he wasn't allowed to read the rest!) In real life, my dad IS Coach Sully. He was a coach and marathon runner, who broke several city and state records in his day, and his former athletes still message me to tell me how much my father's influence meant to them. I was lucky to have him as my coach for various sports when I was younger and know he's a big reason for my optimistic outlook on life. Love ya, Pops!

A word to my Longhorns fans: I needed the Broncos to play a great Texas team, so I hope you viewed that pairing as a compliment. Hook 'em, Horns!

Since foster care was such a central element to this story, I want to note that both my close and extended family have had extensive experience adopting younger relatives. And I'm so happy to say most of those instances were positive, but it's certainly a challenging endeavor, which is why I wanted to explore those two very different situations with Gabby and her brother. It's a topic I care deeply about and hope that I approached with sensitivity.

On another personal note, I have many fond memories of trying to make sweet breads and candies with my *abuela*. I'm pretty sure I almost broke a tooth trying our *leche quemada*, but we had a blast together in the kitchen nonetheless. I'm sure she'd be delighted to know she influenced this part of my story. She loved her *dulces*!

A big thanks to my husband Matt, who's amazing. For the last six years, we've *both* worked out of the house, which means we see each other all day, every day. He's not sick of me yet, so I take that as a good sign. And if you've ever been around me on a deadline when I haven't showered and I'm hangry and my to-do list is several pages long, you'll know how much Matt must love me. I'm a lucky girl!

Thanks also to my agent, Kimberly Brower, who works tirelessly (and at all hours!) for her authors. I really appreciate her insight and wisdom and am grateful for her friendship.

Lauren Perry worked her magic once again and took some gorgeous cover photos. Najla Qamber is my go-to person for design, and she nailed this cover.

Rj Locksley (editing) and Julia Griffis (proofreading) helped me polished this book until it shined.

A big thanks to Jo and Kylie at Give Me Books for their help with promotion.

I'm so grateful to Serena McDonald for overseeing my Facebook group and ARC team. For those great beta notes. For sending me daily inspiration. For being an outstanding PA. She seriously kicks ass. Plus, she's funny AF!

Leslie McAdam always listens to my half-baked story ideas and helps me percolate those nuggets into actual books. I'm pretty co-dependent at this point. Thank you, Leslie!

I also have an amazing team of beta readers. In addition to Leslie and Serena, I want to send my thanks to Stacy Kestwick, Victoria Denault, Kristie White Bivens, Korrie Kelley, Amy Vox Libris, and Kelly Latham. Your input is invaluable.

To the many bloggers who helped promote Rider and Gabby's book, thank you for the book love!

And to my fabulous readers, you're why I get to do what I love every single day. You have my deepest gratitude. I hope I'm able to bring you a little joy with my stories.

xo,

Lex

ALSO BY LEX MARTIN

Texas Nights Series

Shameless (Kat & Brady)

Reckless (Tori & Ethan)

Breathless (Joey & Logan)

The Dearest Series:

Dearest Clementine (Clementine & Gavin)

Finding Dandelion (Dani & Jax)

Kissing Madeline (Maddie & Daren)

Cowritten with Leslie McAdam

All About the D (Josh & Evie)

Surprise, Baby! (Kendall & Drew)

ABOUT THE AUTHOR

Lex Martin is the *USA Today* bestselling author of the Texas Nights series, the Dearest series, and *All About the D*, books she hopes her readers love but her parents avoid. To stay up-to-date with her releases, subscribe to her newsletter or join her Facebook group, Lex Martin's Wildcats.

www.lexmartinwrites.com

Printed in Great Britain
by Amazon

41055279R00245